ELASTICITY

ELASTIC PRESS: 2002 - 2009

ELASTICITY

The Best of Elastic Press

Edited by Andrew Hook

NewCon Press
England

First edition, published in the UK July 2017
by NewCon Press

NCP 131 (hardback)
NCP 132 (softback)

10 9 8 7 6 5 4 3 2 1

ISBN: 978-1-910935-55-2 (hardback)
978-1-910935-56-9 (softback)

Cover art by Alexi K
Text layout by Storm Constantine
Cover layout by Andy Bigwood

CONTENTS

INTRODUCTION: AT FULL STRETCH

Andrew Hook

I expect most readers of this book will be familiar with Elastic Press, the independent publishing company I ran from 2002 until 2009. My impetus for establishing the press has been well-documented, but in brief I had been writing short fiction since 1994 and in 2002 I began looking for a publisher for a collection of mostly published stories. At that time, however, such publishers were few and far between. Certainly it was harder for a relatively unknown author to place a mixed-genre (slipstream) collection with anyone. Following the chance conversation with a friend who had produced a book comparatively cheaply as part of a media course, I began to wonder whether I could publish the collection myself. I didn't consider this to be vanity publishing as most of the stories had already appeared elsewhere, all I was doing was reprinting them in one volume.

With that idea in mind I then realised there were many other short story writers who were in the same position as myself – whilst they might have felt they had built a body of work via publication in various magazines, a collection would validate that. There was an obvious hole in the market with a readymade audience attached, and considering my passion for short stories I felt sure that publishing collections would be a great idea. I decided to start with my book, *The Virtual Menagerie*, to test-run the process, and I contacted friend and fellow Norwich author, Andrew Humphrey, to ask if he had a collection I could take as the second title. He was both interested and flattered. Following advice about publishing from Andy Cox of TTA Press ("don't"), it wasn't long before I had announced the project online and was reading my first submissions.

The remit was simple: to publish mixed genre short story collections by relatively unknown writers. It wasn't quite a sound business plan, as unknown authors, mixed genre and short stories generally are renowned as hard to sell. But that was a challenge, not an obstacle. I chose the name Elastic Press through an unwillingness to burden the company with a restrictive genre title. Whilst I might have written science fiction, fantasy, horror and – as *they* like to call it – literary fiction, I tended to prefer the all-encompassing 'slipstream' moniker and wanted the press to reflect this and have the *elasticity* to publish whatever genre I enjoyed (often within the same book).

Serendipitously, my venture into publishing came exactly at the moment that digital printing made the operation more affordable. It couldn't have been more perfectly timed. Unlike some of the other independent press publishers who were selling high-end limited edition signed hardbacks, I wanted to produce affordable, attractive paperbacks that could compete with mainstream publishing at a low price. I considered how much I would be prepared to pay for a book by an unknown author and fixed the price accordingly. I wanted my authors to be read. With digital printing minimising my outgoing costs I knew – at the very least – that I should be able to edge a profit to cover my initial outlay, and that the sales of one book would fund another.

Following *The Virtual Menagerie* Elastic Press published another thirty titles, sticking to a regular quarterly schedule. And over seven years we won six separate awards (two Best Small Press awards and three Best Anthology awards from the British Fantasy Society and one East Anglian Book Award). Then in our final year I entered *The Turing Test*, a collection of stories by Chris Beckett, for the prestigious Edge Hill Prize. The collection beat Booker-nominated authors to win, not only garnering Chris £6000 in prize-money, but facilitating a book deal and enabling him to work part-time so he could concentrate on his fiction. These awards validated everything I had done with the press and were a great recognition of the work I had put in, but by the time Chris won I had already decided to quit. The press was taking up too much time – I had a regular day job and was a single parent for most of those years – and my own writing had begun to suffer. I made the decision to quit whilst I was ahead and I knew it was the right one. My work was done.

Whilst shedding the press was a relatively easy task, it was always at the back of my mind as to whether I would revitalise it. It was also a question I was often asked. I considered it on and off over the years – including a 'best of' anthology – but never seriously. My publishing fix was satisfied by editing *New Horizons*, a British Fantasy Society publication, for some years, and then latterly through assisting my partner, Sophie Essex, with her poetry/prose magazine *Fur-Lined Ghettos* and then expanding that into Salò Press (if unknown short story writers weren't a hard enough sell, then surrealist and experimental poetry and prose…). Having discounted the possibility of an Elastic revival, I was therefore surprised and delighted when Ian Whates of NewCon Press telephoned me to enquire if I would be interested in editing this book. It was a great honour not only for Ian to acknowledge Elastic's influence on his own publishing company, but to have someone other than Elastic Press publish an Elastic Press book. I had no hesitation in accepting the task and immediately began to consider the contents.

Decisions were easily made, and I'll run through my selection in a moment, but firstly a brief note on one aspect of the process. Other than our anthologies, many of the stories in our single-author collections were already reprints. I decided early on that a *Best Of* had to be exactly that, those stories which excited me whether I had originally published them or not. For that reason, some of these pieces might be widely known and oft reprinted, but their inclusion here is an essential part of the Elastic Press canon. As it happens, of the fifteen stories you are about to read, nine were originally published for the first time by Elastic, and six previously elsewhere.

I'm opening with *Grief Inc* by Andrew Humphrey, an author whose themes of loss, disconnection, and the frailty of relationships were an integral part of the Elastic Press zeitgeist and which are brilliantly realised in this particular story. Brian Howell's Japanese-themed collection, *The Sound of White Ants*, was one of my favourite Elastic books, not only inspiring some of my own fiction but also for its – often subtly vicious – themes and quality prose. It was difficult to choose one story to represent that compelling book, but *The Tower* gives you a flavour of a collection well worth seeking out secondhand. Mike O'Driscoll was an author I had been hoping to publish, and his literary horror hinging on fractured relationships and the nature of identity, is ably demonstrated here in *Evelyn Is Not Real*. Neil Williamson's *Amber*

Rain was a story I had remembered reading in The Third Alternative before including it in his collection, *The Ephemera*, and the revelation in the final two paragraphs continues to resonate with me.

When Allen Ashley pitched a proposal to edit an anthology based on numbers I could never have foreseen that it would lead to the creation of one of my favourite stories: Jeff Gardiner's sublime *351073*. It's one of a handful of stories that has reduced me to tears. From the same anthology I've included Marion Arnott's *When We Were Five*, a strong story merging political history with personal memories and the inexorable process of vengeance. Gary Couzens was a writer I had hoped to work with right at the beginning and I was overjoyed when he submitted his collection. *Four A.M.* was a story I remembered reading when it was originally published and for me it remains a perfect example of slipstream fiction. Gary later went on to edit *Extended Play*, our third anthology to win a British Fantasy Society award.

Brief though it might be, *Shopping* by Antony Mann is a novel in microcosm. I challenge any writer not to be jealous of not only its perfection but also means its execution. As an aside, it was whilst I was editing Antony's crime collection, *Milo & I*, that I became inspired to write crime fiction. Four novels later, I have a lot to be thankful to him for. The publishing process can be a mutually symbiotic process.

Allen Ashley was an early supporter and has since become a firm friend. As well as editing two anthologies for Elastic (*Subtle Edens* and the BFS award-winning *The Elastic Book of Numbers*), we've also collaborated on short fiction with a collection, *Slow Motion Wars* published in 2016. *Somme-Nambula* is my favourite story of his and his collection, *Somnambulists*, sports my favourite Elastic Press cover.

Having originally met Nick Jackson at a local writers' group I've regularly championed his quietly concise and beautifully perceptive fiction. It was a privilege to publish his excellent *Visits To The Flea Circus* collection, with cover art from Devo's Mark Mothersbaugh, from which this title story is taken. Nick was also in our first anthology *The Alsiso Project*, where – for reasons too complicated to explain – every story was titled *Alsiso*. I've chosen Justina Robson's story to represent that anthology because I feel it perfectly encapsulates the spirit of the theme, illustrating what can be written from the starting point of just one single word.

When Allen Ashley (again!) pitched the idea for a slipstream anthology, *Subtle Edens*, I knew the circle was complete and it would become our final title. From that book Andrew Tisbert's *Jasmine* encapsulated the sense of excitement when reading a perfect submission: it set the bar for the other stories to follow. Similarly, *Televisionism* was one of two stories Maurice Suckling submitted when pitching his collection, *Photocopies From Heaven*. I loved the piece, which led to me publishing his collection (one of the most unusual Elastic books, it included a comic strip as well as various experiments with text).

An Elastic *Best Of* wouldn't be complete without something by Chris Beckett. I love his quiet, reflective, morally questioning SF, and *The Marriage Of Sea And Sky* is a firm favourite. If Chris is one of a band of quintessentially *Elastic* authors, then the most quintessential of all would be Tim Nickels. When compiling a *Best Of* to a strict word limit it might be considered inadvisable to include an almost 15,000 word piece on the grounds that perhaps another three or even four authors might have been included in this retrospective. However, without a shadow of a doubt, if I had to select only one story to truly represent the Elastic ethos then it would be *fight Music*. It's a magnificent piece of writing – curious and wonderful – originally selected by Gary Couzens for *Extended Play*, and as this anthology closer I hope it continues to resonate this last chapter in the Elastic Press legacy.

Now for a few thanks. Amongst the highlights of publishing were the friendships that I made. It wasn't until I started Elastic Press that I began to attend events and conventions and it was there that I found my *family*. And whilst I haven't met all my *Elasticians* personally, I'm indebted to all those authors whose collections I published which made Elastic Press such a unique enterprise and an enjoyable ride. In publication order: Andrew Humphrey, Gary Couzens, Marion Arnott, Antony Mann, Kay Green, Brian Howell, Allen Ashley, Steven Saville, Nick Jackson, Tim Lees, Matt Dinniman, Tim Nickels, David Swann, Neil Williamson, Mike O'Driscoll, Maurice Suckling, Mat Coward, Tony Richards, Robert Neilson, Jai Clare, Mike Dolan, Daniel Marcus, Gareth L Powell, Chris Beckett and Geoffrey Maloney. Thanks also to Marie O'Regan who typeset and Dean Harkness who designed and/or prepared the cover layouts for many of the books. Additional thanks are due to those authors published in our anthologies and for all of the

11

readers. Thanks too for Ian Whates at NewCon Press for championing my own fiction over the years as well as for proposing this anthology. *Elasticity* has created a great opportunity for me to revisit these stories and to enjoy them all over again.

Andrew Hook, June 2017

GRIEF INC

Andrew Humphrey

As usual the woman who opened the door was at the wrong end of middle age, mildly unkempt, her eyes shiny and blank with fresh loss. She was, Carter thought, a template for seventy, maybe eighty percent of his customers. He followed her through a shabby hallway into a bleak, bare living room. The house, too, was typical of most of the homes Carter visited these days; clinging to the thinnest thread of respectability, full of the stench of defeat and imminent ruin.

Carter stood by the sofa. The woman motioned for him to sit down. "I'll stand," he said.

She nodded. The collar of her cardigan was frayed and she tugged and fretted at the loose piece of wool. Carter wanted to slap her hand away. Wanted her to look him in the eye for once, to get to the point. Instead he forced a half smile and pointed at a photograph on the table next to her. "Is that your husband?"

She nodded again and looked at the bland, slightly blurred face in the picture, ran a hand across its surface.

"When did he die?"

"A week ago."

Carter waited. Usually the details would come easily now, whether he asked for them or not. But the woman did not elaborate. She seemed lost in the past somewhere. It didn't affect his work, how much, how little he knew. But there were conventions to observe. And Carter was mildly curious.

"How did he die?"

He expected one of the usual answers; maybe he was a conscript, killed on the Welsh border. Or he was shot by a sniper as he walked to work through the city centre. Or perhaps he was simply picked up by the Council and they went a little too far in the soundproofed cells beneath City Hall. She'd have a letter of apology somewhere and a small amount of compensation.

"He was ill for a long time. I nursed him for… two, three years? I don't remember exactly."

"Right," Carter said, surprised. "That must have been… hard."

She didn't bother answering that and Carter didn't really blame her. She started to pull at her collar again and said, "How much will this cost me?"

"A hundred and fifty euros."

She looked him in the eye then and didn't blink. "The Council would be cheaper."

"I doubt it. I hear they charge nearer two hundred these days."

"But I'd get a guarantee."

"True. You'd probably get a mind probe, too. Do you want them poking around in all your little secrets? They don't need much excuse to stop your benefits, pull you in for questioning."

She thought for a moment, chewing her lip, her eyes turned inward. Carter shivered. He still had his coat on but it seemed colder in this dull little room than it had outside. He pulled a Palmtop from his coat pocket. "Do you want to see some testimonials?"

"You've probably rigged them," she said wearily.

Of course he had. Web-time and live video links were virtually unobtainable these days. "Or I can just go. You can get through this the old fashioned way. I've heard it gets easier with time. A year or two and things will probably seem a whole lot brighter."

She looked at him bleakly. "Do you seriously think any of us has that long?"

"Sure. Why not?"

She shook her head and almost laughed. "How does this work, anyway?"

"Search me. It just does. I need the money up front."

She retrieved her purse from a deep pocket. She did everything slowly. Her face was the colour of weak tea, her eyes wet and accusing. Before she handed him the cash she said, "I won't… forget him, will I? This feels a little like betrayal."

"You won't forget him. You just remember the good bits better, that's all. I take the sting away. You'll be able to sleep again, without dreaming. You'll appreciate what you had."

She nodded quickly and her eyes gained a little fervour. She gave him the money and glanced at him almost coyly. "What must I do? Should I take off my clothes?"

Jesus. Why did they always think that?

"No need for that. I hug you. That's all."

"You hug me? What good will that do? I want my money back."

He sighed. They never believed it could be so easy. They always expected, even wanted, needles, pain, some degree of suffering. "Just do it," Carter said.

"And if it doesn't work?"

"Then you haven't lost anything."

"Apart from my money."

"Well, yeah, apart from that." He was across the room in two strides and he took her in his arms. She resisted but he pressed himself against her. She was so light, so insubstantial. And she smelt too, but Carter was used to that. He'd worn his own clothes for more than a week. He caught a trace of his odour occasionally and it made his eyes water.

Then she became soft, pliant, folded against him. And he felt the usual slow warmth and tasted something dark and bitter at the back of his throat. She murmured, 'My God, my God,' into his chest and he held her, stroked the top of her head, and felt something tender, something close to love. Even though he charged for this and although he didn't actually give a shit, Carter was suddenly imbued with a tainted, accidental, sense of virtue.

She broke away from him. She looked instantly younger. "My God," she said again. She grabbed the photograph and stroked it. Then she looked at Carter and her eyes were warm and bright. "Thank you."

He gave a little shrug. He didn't take a bow. "No problem," he said. At least she'd been grateful. He hated it when they wouldn't admit it. He'd see in their eyes and face that it had worked and they'd say, 'I feel no different. I want my money back.'

'Fuck you,' he'd say.

Now the woman was still thanking him. "Good," he said. "Now I've got to go."

"Stay," she said. "I have some tea. No milk, though. But still. Stay for a while."

And there it was. The usual invitation. It almost always came. Man, woman, young, old. And he almost always turned it down.

He headed for the door. "Sorry. Lots to do."

"Come again," she said, following him. "Any time." He was at the door, out of it. "You don't even know my name." He was through the gate, onto the empty street. She was calling something to him but he hummed to himself so that he couldn't hear.

Late the next morning he met Josie for coffee. The day was cold and dull. There were more troops on the streets than civilians and Carter nodded at the ones he knew.

She was late as usual. Carter grabbed their usual seat, by the window, with a view of the ruined entrance of St Andrew's Hall. It had been firebombed two years earlier and never re-built. Kieran, the coffee shop's owner and sole employee, tried to make some small talk but Carter wasn't in the mood.

Then Josie bounded in, smiling, short of breath. "What's up with your face?" she said, shrugging off her jacket and hanging it roughly on the back of her chair.

"You're late. Your coffee's cold."

Josie shrugged. She had quick, green eyes with dark smudges under them and curly, tousled hair. She looked too young, too sweet and Carter wanted to touch her face and her small, soft mouth. Which annoyed him. "Grumpy old sod," she said.

"I have an image to live down to. You look like shit. Late night?"

"Something like that. Anyway, did you hear the news? They're going to build a wall around London."

"About time," Carter said.

"To keep out the insurgents, the immigrants. Translates as anyone with a northern accent."

"Midlands too, so I hear."

She sipped her coffee, grimaced. "It *is* cold. Get us another."

"It tastes just as bad hot." Carter watched a handful of troops pick their way through the rubble outside St Andrew's Hall. They didn't seem to be looking for anything in particular. A couple of them were smoking and laughing at something out of sight. Carter thought suddenly, randomly, of the gangs of teenagers who'd loitered on street corners, bored and vaguely threatening, when he was young. "The world is getting smaller and smaller. Soon it'll be every town, every city, for itself."

"You don't sound that bothered by the prospect."

"What can you do? Anyway, Norwich as an independent state? That would be cool."

"We'd starve."

"That's what they said when the borders first started shrinking. We'll be ok. Most of us."

"Those of you with particular gifts."

"Mine is a humble gift. Which makes it perfect, of course. Now if I were a Healer or a Seer…"

Josie snorted. "If you were a Seer you'd be behind that wall in London. Locked up in a luxury hotel, every whim catered for."

Carter gestured at the streets, the rubble. "Hardly repaying the investment, are they?"

"Maybe it's not their fault. Perhaps they're being misused. Pointed at the wrong targets."

"Almost certainly. Or ridden too hard, burnt out in a week or two. I'm glad my gifts are of less strategic value."

"But ample enough to line your pockets."

Carter gave her a look of mild disapproval. He liked her flashes of anger, though. The way her eyes shone stirred something inside him. "Now, now, my dear," he said, deliberately patronising, provoking. "Isn't that biting the hand that feeds?"

"I can look after myself," she said. Her expression turned sullen and he took a quiet delight in that too, the sulky softness of her mouth.

"I don't doubt it. I'm a mercenary. I'm a cold, self-centred bastard. No argument. But I pay for your accommodation, most of your food. I keep you safe, or as safe as I can, at least. Am I right or am I wrong?"

"I pay you back."

"I can get that anywhere. Without paying for it."

Her head snapped up. "Well, fuck you then. I'll take my chances." She stood suddenly and her chair fell behind her with a clatter. One of the soldiers beyond the window, his rifle at port arms, turned his gaze lazily towards them. Carter's hand pinned Josie's thin wrist to the table.

"Sit down. I'm sorry."

"Are you? Really?"

Carter found that he was. He nodded.

Josie sat again. "You're so cynical, Carter."

He looked out at the ruined street again and laughed. "Really? That's a wonder, isn't it?"

"You don't have to be that way."

He sipped some of the weak, over-priced coffee. "Do you watch TV, Josie?"

"I try not to. Wall to wall news? I'd lose my sunny disposition."

"Not the state stuff." She was right about that. Footage from the wars in Wales and Ireland. Summary executions from the Scottish border. "There's a cable channel that plays overnight. All shows from years and years ago. Most of it crap, of course. Makes me angry, how they always moaned, never appreciated what they had. Pissed it all away. But there's this one show, a cartoon, called *The Simpsons*. I like that. It actually makes me laugh. And it's prescient."

"How?"

"This guy, Homer, he wants his relationships defined. His friend Moe, the bartender, says that he's a well-wisher, in that he wishes Homer no specific harm."

"That's not funny," Josie said. "And how's it prescient?"

"It's the definition of a friend today. Someone who wishes you no specific harm. It's the best we can hope for."

Josie looked at him for a long moment. "I feel sorry for you, Carter."

"I'll accept your pity. I'll accept anything that's offered."

"And you'd better hope that you're wrong. Business will suffer."

"How do you work that out?"

"No friends, no love, no grief."

"Interesting. More death, less grief. It's true that most of my customers are from a generation that indulged in love for its own sake."

"Indulged? Jesus."

"What else would you call it? Everything is currency now. People are what they can do for you."

"Is that all I am? Currency?"

"*Honestly?*" He saw the hurt in her eyes and sighed. "Ok. Let's turn it around. What, exactly, am I to you?"

"Beyond the obvious?"

"Which is?"

"Your money, the fact you have no discernible skin disease."

Carter smiled in spite of himself. "Ah, romance. Yes, beyond that."

"I don't honestly know."

"I know, Josie. I am nothing to you. And that's exactly how it should be. We are what we can do for each other. That's all."

"Well, that's made me feel warm all over. And you're wrong. I just don't think that way. There's got to be more to things, to people. Got to be." Carter could see in her eyes that she meant it and he felt a cold premonition, a warning sweep over him. From a few streets away the tinny clatter of small arms fire grabbed the attention of the troops still patrolling the building opposite.

He leant towards her, lowered his voice. "Just remember this; keep neutral. The Council, the rebels, they're both equally incompetent, equally corrupt. Don't commit to anything, anyone."

"Where did that come from? Do I look as though I need a lecture?"

He studied her face, searched for a trace of calculation, of deceit. Just because he couldn't find it didn't mean it wasn't there.

A little later he said, "I've got to go. Work to do. Some rich bitch out on Newmarket Road."

"Hey, moving up in the world."

"Yeah, it's odd, though."

"What?"

"This girl, she's only twenty..."

"Trying to make me jealous?"

"Right. The thing is, as far as I can see, she hasn't lost anyone. I wonder what, or who, she's grieving for."

"That does sound strange. Be careful."

"I considered cancelling. But the family has money, I can charge more and anyway, I'm curious. Probably just grieving over a pet or something."

"A pet? They've been illegal, what, two, three years?"

"So has alcohol, people still drink. When they can."

"Yeah, lucky bastards."

"Speaking of which," Carter said, "if you come to mine tonight I can offer you shares in a bottle of wine and a large bar of milk chocolate."

"Really?" Her face lit up. Carter was touched by her delight. He turned his face away, irritated.

"You'll come?" he said.

"Try and keep me away," she said.

The gunfire became more persistent. A heavy machine gun joined in, its bass rattle dominating. The door opened and a youngish man entered. He wore a donkey jacket and had dark, unruly hair. His face was pitted with old acne scars. He hesitated, taking in the identity of the coffee shop's occupants. Josie returned his gaze and Carter thought he caught the faintest hint of recognition. The man walked to the counter, ordered a coffee, then said, "They've got a couple of Scousers cornered in the Cathedral." His voice was neutral, wisely accent-less. Carter sensed he was working hard to keep it that way.

"Scousers?" Carter said. "What the hell are they doing here?"

"Dying, I should imagine," the man said.

Carter looked at him. Again something seemed wrong. The answer was too smooth, almost rehearsed.

Although he hadn't requested it the stranger was served his coffee in a takeaway container. He glanced at it, started to say something, then gauged the atmosphere in the room and took the hint.

After he'd gone Carter said, "Do you know him?"

Josie shook her head. "Why do you ask?"

Her green eyes were guileless. "No reason," Carter said.

Carter hadn't been to the outer edges of Newmarket Road for many years. The house was large, detached, set back from the road, bordered on two sides by a thick line of conifers; a chunky, barbed wire-topped wall surrounded the rest of the house.

The girl who answered the door was like a throwback to the ancient television programmes that Carter watched. She was young, pretty, her hair was long and black and glossily clean. She wore make up. Her lips were a shiny red that made Carter swallow involuntarily. She smelled clean. More than clean, actually. The musky scent of her perfume overwhelmed him. Her clothes were immaculate; crisp white blouse, long dark woollen skirt.

She extended a hand toward him. "It's Carter, isn't it? I'm Val. Thanks for coming."

Her grip was cool and firm. Carter drank her in. Then he took a breath, shook himself mentally. "No problem. You've got one minute to tell me why I'm here. Or I'm gone."

"I'm sorry?"

"There's no grief here. I can smell death a mile off. All I can smell is you, Val. Nice as that is, I'm a busy man."

Val smiled briefly. "Things aren't always as they seem."

"Actually, I've found the opposite to be true. Has anyone died here? Yes or no?"

"No."

Carter shrugged, started to turn.

"But I have lost someone. And I'll pay double your usual fee. Give me five minutes? Please?"

Carter faced her again. Her skin was pale and smooth. Carter wanted to stroke it. He thought of Josie and felt a stab of guilt that surprised and worried him.

He closed the front door.

"Five minutes, then."

The living room was large and airy and pleasantly furnished. Val bought him a mug of real coffee and a little jug of cream.

"I wonder if I can guess where your dad works?"

"It's not a secret," Val said. "Loads of people work for the Council."

"He's high up, though, isn't he?"

Val shrugged dismissively, but her tone was defensive. "Not really. And he works hard. For the good of the people. Things are getting better, he says."

"Well, that's ok, then."

"Really. The M11 should be clear soon, then the shops will be full again, you'll see."

"Heard it all before, Val. And anyway, we digress. Who have you lost?"

She sat back on the sofa, pursed her lips with calculated cuteness. "You'll think it's stupid."

"Probably. But I'm not sure that matters. Money talks, after all."

"Right." Her face went blank and all calculation fled. "I've lost my lover. That's all. She is… was… everything to me. And I can't stand it."

"I see. But that's not really…"

"Grief? I think it is. It feels just like it. She has someone else now.

She's dead to me." Carter said nothing. "I don't care how stupid I sound. I just want you to help me."

"You loved her, then?"

"Of course. What's so funny?"

"Just reminds me of a conversation I had earlier. What's her name?"

"That doesn't matter. I don't want to talk about her. I just want the pain to go away."

"Do your parents know I'm here?"

"It's just Dad. Mum left when I was a kid. And he doesn't even know that I'm a lesbian. It wouldn't... go down well."

"Given the Council's moral stance I can't say I'm surprised. You must have been discreet."

"Very. It was a nightmare. But worth it. Will you help me? I'll give you three hundred."

"It probably won't work."

"Then it's even easier money." Carter hesitated. "Come on, it's just a hug, isn't it?" She fished the money from her bag and handed it to him. "I'm a sceptic, actually. Prove me wrong."

He stuffed the cash into his jacket pocket. They both stood. He held out his arms and she slid into them. He held her tight. It wasn't a chore. "Jesus. Carter," Val said. The same words, almost the same tone that Josie used sometimes when she came. With his face in Val's hair and her warmth seeping into him, Carter felt close to orgasm himself. He composed himself before he pulled away.

"Do you want your money back?" Carter said.

Val still had her hands on his shoulders. She seemed unsteady. Her face shone and her eyes were wide open as she stared into his face. "Shit, no. Jesus Christ. I feel stones lighter. I feel... cured. How does that work, Carter?"

"I don't know. Honestly."

"I almost wish I did men." She shook herself. Carter let his breathing slow. Val's pupils were fully dilated. He found her gaze impossible to hold. "I'm curious, though. When you hold someone, when you screw; is it different?"

Carter sank back into an armchair as he thought about that. Josie's face after the first time; her bewildered delight.

"Jesus, Carter. What the hell did you do to me?" Then, "Do it again."

But days, weeks later…

"Each time we do it you take something from me. I'm becoming less, Carter."

"You like it, though?"

"It blows my fucking mind. But still. There'll be nothing left soon." Then she'd reach for him. "Why do you pay me for this?" He couldn't answer that. Didn't try.

Val was watching him closely. He thought he could see the energy fizz and crackle around her. "No different," he said.

"Really? I might just ask Josie next time I see her."

It took a second to sink in, then he was on his feet, inches from her, close enough to smell the coffee on her breath. "What the fuck does that mean?"

"Easy."

He grabbed her shoulder. "Are you doing a number on me? Remember, if I go to the Council with this dyke stuff then that's you and your dad ruined. Or worse."

She shrugged his hand away. "Jesus. Talk about over reaction. I know your girlfriend, big deal."

"Know her from where?"

"I've trusted you. I heard you were ok. A bit of a bastard, maybe. But ok."

"Why didn't you tell me you knew her? She doesn't mix with people from this side of the city. A little above her, I'm afraid. Probably why I like her. Where did you get her name from?"

"She doesn't know where I live. Or that I look like this. Doesn't know me as Val, either. I live most of my life in disguise, remember? Josie sings in a couple of the clubs that I go to. Used to go to."

"She sings?"

Val's composure was returning now. Her eyes had become normal, her features were flat, neutral, beautiful. "Well, I assumed you knew that. Very good, too. Popular. Everyone loves Josie."

"Do they?" He thought of Josie on a stage, all eyes on her. The image wouldn't hold. "Those bloody clubs. Full of radicals, free thinkers, activists."

"People with minds of their own."

"God, I hate those bastards."

"Then you hate Josie."

"What?"

"She's the original free spirit. Surely, Carter, even you must have noticed that." Carter said nothing. He kept his eyes on the carpet. "You don't know her at all, do you?"

"I've got to go," he said.

Carter drank most of the wine, Josie ate most of the chocolate. Then they went to bed. Afterwards Carter said, "How much of you is there left now, Josie?"

"What?" Her breath was short. She had a hand on her forehead as though checking for a fever.

"A while back you said that I was making you less. Reducing you, something like that."

"I'm still here. Just about."

The wine that Carter had drank earlier tasted sour at the back of his throat. "What do you do when you're not with me?"

"Careful, Carter. It might sound as though you care."

"I just wondered."

"I sit and wait for your call." Her voice was dry, without inflection.

"As I thought."

They were quiet for a while. It was cold in the bedroom and Carter pulled the bedclothes over Josie's breasts, tugged a blanket up to her chin. "Thanks, Dad," she said.

"Perhaps later you'll sing for me."

There was a small, taut silence. "Who told you?"

"A mutual friend."

She turned his face towards him. "You don't have any friends."

"Why didn't you tell me?"

"Because I knew you'd be like this. And it's none of your business."

"You've been talking about me."

"So what? Perhaps I tried to put some work your way. You've paid your dues, to the Council and the rebels. Why are you so paranoid?"

"It's what keeps me alive. I think I must be losing it, though."

"Slip through your armour, did I? You're so busy covering your back, keeping everything, everyone at arm's length, you've forgotten that you're alive."

Carter put a hand on her bare shoulder. "And why does that matter to you, Josie? I pay you well." He took the hand away and gestured at the bed. "We both enjoy… this. Why try and get close? What's your agenda?"

"My agenda?"

"Those clubs are a breeding ground for…"

"My fucking agenda?" She hurled the bedclothes onto the floor and knelt on the bed, facing him. He loved the sight of her naked, in spite of her bony hips and tiny breasts. Because of them, perhaps. "You think I'm working for someone? Trying to set you up?" She straddled him, opened her legs wide. "Do you want to check for a wire? I mean, you've been pretty thorough over the last half hour or so, but be my guest." Her eyes were wild but he didn't look away from them. Then she flipped onto her front, reached a hand behind her to part her buttocks. "Go on, Carter. Have a good look. I must have something hidden, mustn't I? Some ulterior motive. In your world, everybody has one."

Then she was crying. Carter wanted to hold her, but didn't. "I can't trust anyone. I'm sorry."

"Why not?"

"I don't know. I'm old, you're not."

"And that's it?" She was dressing now.

"It's the best I can do."

"It's crap. I left someone because of you."

Carter tried to hide his surprise. "I didn't ask you to do that."

"I thought…" Josie stopped, put a hand to her mouth. She sat on the bed, next to him.

"You thought what?"

"I thought you might take me to London. Before the wall goes up. A bigger world. We'd be safe. Maybe even happy."

"This city is all I know. London is just… more of everything. More thugs, more death, more grief."

"More business for you, then." Her smile was forced, wrong. "It's not the city. It's the being with you."

The tenderness in her voice shocked him. "I'm sorry."

"Why? No guarantees, no money back." Josie's voice was brisk now, business-like. "I always knew where I stood."

She kissed him and left.

He didn't sleep. That wasn't unusual, but this was harder than he'd thought it would be. The night passed. They always did. But they rarely seemed as long as this.

The following lunchtime Carter visited the coffee shop opposite St Andrew's Hall. The streets were quieter than ever; even the usual gaggle of troops was absent. Carter had heard that a small, futile and utterly doomed uprising had broken out on the outskirts of Taverham. Maybe the troops were there; quelling it with their usual enthusiasm.

The coffee shop was empty except for Kieran. Carter didn't seriously expect Josie to turn up but he kept checking the door anyway.

He and Kieran made guarded, neutral small talk. Then Kieran said, "She's gone, then." Carter nodded. "Pity. That's half my regular custom gone at a stroke."

"Sorry about that."

Kieran washed already clean cups under a stream of warm water and said nothing. His face seemed incapable of holding an expression. His voice too, rarely altered from its dry monotone. Carter had never known Kieran to register surprise, joy, despair. He thought that maybe he was hewn from rock. Next to him, Carter seemed flamboyant.

"Did you know that Josie sang?" Carter said.

"I know nothing," Kieran said. Something tiny flicked across his face. Carter guessed it must have been a smile. "And, of course, everything."

"Of course. What am I thinking. Expecting a straight answer."

"You always were an optimist."

"Compared to you, perhaps."

Kieran dried a white mug carefully, examined it, then lobbed it over his left shoulder. It smashed on the concrete floor. "I've got too many mugs. Far too many. Perhaps I am an optimist."

"Waiting for business to pick up?"

"Something like that."

Carter sipped some coffee, tried not to grimace. "We're roughly the same age, you and I?"

"Probably," Kieran said.

"Do you miss it?"

"Miss what?"

"The old days. Technology. Aircraft. Nuclear weapons. The threat of one big, global war instead of all these stupid, endless, civil ones."

Kieran thought for a moment. "Nah, I don't miss it. I prefer things this way, I think."

"Why, for God's sake?"

A pause. "Dunno. Must be the company." His voice was bone dry. Carter laughed, Kieran didn't. "It makes no difference, Carter." Carter was mildly shocked by the use of his name. "Whatever path we chose, we'd have fucked it up."

"That's deep," Carter said.

"Coffee and philosophy," Kieran said. "I should put my prices up."

Carter half-smirked. He thought Kieran was joking, but it was so hard to tell. "I'd better go," he said.

"Have you got a message for her, if she comes?"

"She won't come."

Kieran nodded.

"I'll be seeing you," Carter said.

"Watch your back," Kieran said.

"What?" Carter was halfway to the door, but now he turned towards to the counter.

"There's someone coming for you. Tonight. He'll kill you if you let him."

"Tonight?"

"Sorry I can't be more specific. But what time would you reckon? Just before dawn? Between three and four, say. Hardly original, but…"

"Who is it?"

"You'll find that out, won't you? But you'll recognise him."

"Who is he working for?"

"You'll find that out, too. Probably."

"How do you know this?" And at last Kieran's face did register an expression. It was pity. Carter held up a hand. "Sorry. I don't expect an answer."

"Just as well."

"And if I hadn't dropped in today?"

One of Kieran's eyebrows moved a fraction. "Then you'd probably be fucked."

Carter took a deep breath. He didn't doubt Kieran. Information was his currency. Carter felt younger, suddenly. Enervated. "Do I owe you for this?" Kieran shook his head. "Thanks," Carter said, as he turned back towards the door.

"Got to try and keep one customer," Kieran said.

The day was a washed out grey, barely cold enough to count as winter, too bleak and featureless to be anything else. There was no wind to speak of, little cloud, just the sense of things waiting, of nature in abeyance. Carter walked for a while. Past the skeletal ruins of the old library and the handful of shops clinging to life in the city centre. He didn't think much, just let a slow, cold anger build within him.

He was home before dark. He checked the inside of his flat thoroughly then retrieved his father's old revolver from the rear of the underwear drawer. He ate some soup with the gun by his right hand. Then he sat in the armchair in the living room and waited.

Carter was good at not thinking. It was a skill he'd spent most of his adult life trying to perfect. But now, when he needed it most, it deserted him. It was mostly Josie, of course, nagging at the back of his mind. But Val was there, too, and the Council, and Kieran, and the faces of all the people he'd known over the years who'd died, or disappeared, or both. The anger subsided. He let his mind wander. Either the dawn would come for him or it wouldn't. All his paranoia, all the bribes and frantic arse-covering; when it came to it, he found he wasn't that bothered how things turned out.

He nodded off for half an hour at about midnight and woke, terrified and disorientated, his tongue stuck to the roof of his mouth, his familiar room, shot through with darkness and shadow, suddenly alien to him. For a moment he expected his waking to be brief; he imagined the cold muzzle of a pistol pressed against his forehead. Then, with his wits returned and his head clear, Carter waited again.

It happened, pretty much as Kieran had anticipated, just before three-thirty. Carter heard something scrape against his front door. He stood, his mind emptying, hid himself behind the door that led from the small hallway into the living room. He listened as the lock was picked, quietly, but not quite quietly enough. He stilled his own breathing. His eyes were used to the dark and the figure that padded past him into the living room was large and male and walking in an almost comically exaggerated crouch. He waited a moment then shot the man in the back of each leg. The figure crumpled with an oddly emasculated squeal. Carter was at the man's head in an instant, his gun pressed against an eye, his knee pinning the intruder's wrist to the floor, his free hand retrieving the weapon that had spilled from the other man's grasp.

"Who are you? Who sent you? In ten seconds or I blow your head off."

"You shot me," the man said. His teeth were clenched, his voice high, incredulous.

"Well spotted," Carter said. Even in the semi-darkness the features were becoming familiar. A shock of dark, unruly hair. The pockmarks and wide set eyes. "You were in the coffee shop a couple of days ago."

"It hurts like fuck. I'm bleeding to death here. Get out of my face, man, please."

Carter stood and backed up to the light switch and turned it on, blinked down at his handiwork. "That's the carpet ruined. What's your name?"

"Tony."

"Make yourself comfortable."

Tony twisted so that his back leant against an armchair. Below the knee his legs jutted out at odd angles. The bottom half of his faded jeans were black with blood. His face, in contrast, was the colour of skimmed milk and his eyes were wide and without focus. "Just finish it, man."

"Your voice is different. An accent, or a bit of one. Who sent you?"

"What's the point?"

"People trying to kill me, it makes me curious. I'm strange like that."

"I wasn't going to kill you. Just a warning, that's all."

Their eyes met for a moment then Tony grimaced, turned his head to the side and vomited. "That's bollocks," Carter said, without heat. "I hope she paid you well."

"Not well enough, obviously." A ghost of a smile in the death-white face. "Going rate, though, for a first timer."

"Did she call herself Val? Or something else?"

"I'm nearly done, aren't I?" Tony said.

Carter looked at the soaked carpet. Tony tried to stem the flow with his hands but fresh blood pulsed through the fingers. "I think so. I must have nicked an artery."

"Nicked? You fucking shredded it, man."

"I'm sorry."

Tony laughed weakly. His eyes were less wide now and the light was going out of them. "Val. Yeah, fucking dyke."

"I thought I cured her," Carter said.

"What?"

"Nothing."

"I don't know much. Just that you were banging Josie and that pissed Val off."

"Do you know Josie?"

"Just from the clubs. Where I met Val."

"How well do you know her?"

"Just nodding terms, that's all. I saw her sing a couple of times." He closed his eyes. He suddenly looked very tired.

"Is she good?"

"Yeah, she's hot." He swallowed rapidly four, five times. "Too good for you. And Val. Too good for all of us."

Then he stopped talking. His breathing became shallow, irregular, and his head slumped to the side. By the time Carter crouched next to him and placed a hand on his chest he wasn't breathing at all.

It was almost dark by the time Carter reached Newmarket Road. In the half-light it seemed less immune to the rot and ruin that afflicted the rest of the city than it had on the day before. Or maybe he simply noticed more; the boarded up windows, a spray of bullet holes across a gable end, a trail of dried purple vomit, the corpse of a Golden Retriever at the foot of an oak tree. Sink estates bleeding into the suburbs.

He reached Val's house. He'd kept Tony's gun, ditched his own. Tony's was smaller, newer and fully loaded. He was going to kick the front door in, but he tried the handle first and it was unlocked. He pushed it open and the stench of death hit him immediately; physically and mentally. Physically, the smell was similar to one he'd left in his own flat. Cordite, blood, involuntary human functions. Mentally, the sense of fresh loss was like a punch. He reeled from it briefly, then pushed on through the hallway into the neat, ordered living room he'd visited only the day before.

Val's hair was cut brutally short. The make up had gone. Her face was pale, scrubbed far too white, her eyes were liquid, darting, searching for a foothold. She was hugging herself. She wore a sweater and combat trousers.

There was a man half-slumped in the armchair by the fireplace. Most of his face had gone. A pistol similar to the one Carter held in front of him lay on the carpet close to the man's right foot.

"Your father?" Carter said. Val nodded. "Why did you kill him?"

"What?" Her eyes swung up towards Carter's face, achieved some sort of focus. "I didn't. Well, I helped him out at the end, I suppose."

"Helped him out?"

Val shook herself and took a long, shuddering breath. "He shot himself in the mouth. Silly old fucker couldn't even get that right. Bullet went through his cheek. I had to put him out of his misery."

"Am I missing something here? Why did he want to kill himself?"

Val backed up to the leather settee, fell into it. "Carter, I thought you had your finger on the pulse. The Council is all but finished. That thing at Taverham has grown, spread. City Hall will go tomorrow, they say. They've tried to clean up the cells, destroy all the records, but... it won't be pretty."

"The rebels are winning?"

"The Council has always grossly exaggerated the extent of their forces. The rebels finally managed a shred of cohesion and found them out." She looked at her father's corpse. "He knew it was a matter of time before they came for him."

"And you?"

She gave a bitter smile. "I'm reviewing my options."

"You don't seem that surprised to see me."

"You get what you pay for, don't you? Tony was an amateur. I figured it was fifty-fifty."

"Why did you want me dead? I thought I helped you."

"That's partly why. You took something from me. When you hugged me, I mean. I thought that was what I wanted, but I was wrong. It was as though I'd never loved her. I needed the pain to keep Josie real."

"I did my job. You paid me."

"It was spite, too. And jealousy. The fact that you had her and I didn't." She gestured towards her father. "Losing him hasn't touched me. Even the ghost of the feelings I had for Josie, the ersatz grief you left me with, dwarves what I feel for him." She saw the look on Carter's face. "Hey, I never said I was a good person."

"You're lying. I can feel your loss. It's making my head throb."

Val's laugh was harsh, stunted. "You old romantic. It's self-pity you can feel. The imminent loss of myself. The stupid, random unfairness of it."

"I'm not going to kill you."

She looked at him as though he were an imbecile. "I know that. You haven't got it in you." Another nod towards her father's body. "But I'm his daughter. I'm fucked."

"You said you've lived most of your life in disguise. Why not do it again?"

She fingered her stubbled hair. "I thought of that. I've tried to straddle both worlds. But…" She shook her head slowly. "Do you have any idea how bad it's going to be, Carter?"

"Maybe not."

"If they catch me, if they find out who I am."

"I've lived in both worlds, too."

"Better than me." She dropped to the floor and scuttled across to her father's feet. She picked up the pistol.

"Val."

"What are you going to do? Shoot me?" She pressed the muzzle to her forehead. "If I fuck this up…" She closed her eyes, grimaced.

Carter turned away as she pressed the trigger.

He found Josie twenty-four hours later, on a small stage in the crypt of an abandoned church. She was finishing her set in front of a rapt audience. The song that Carter heard was sweet and trippy and incomprehensible. It moved him more than he cared to admit. Her voice, its imperfections somehow adding to its charm, raised the hairs on his arms and neck. She stood in front of a room full of strangers, dressed in a baggy purple sweater and worn leggings, emptied her heart and soul, without pretension or affectation. When she finished she clasped her hands in front of her and bowed her head slightly. Before the applause had finished he was by the side of the stage, waiting for her. When she saw him surprise registered briefly then her eyes became hooded. "You," she said.

"Talk about fiddling while Rome burns."

"What?"

"Can't you hear it? The pitched battle at City Hall. They're fighting hand to hand in the Old Market Place. Some of the Council buildings are burning. The skyline looks quite pretty from a distance."

"What do you want? The keys to your apartment? I'll get them for you."

He grabbed her arm. A young couple had come over to talk to her but they saw the look on Carter's face and moved away again. "The city is imploding. My city."

"And this is my problem, how?" She gestured at the crowded crypt. "We're all taking our chances. Maybe we'll burn. Maybe we'll get to wake up tomorrow. This is your world, Carter. I thought you'd relish it. All that extra business."

"Look, things have changed, I…" He stopped, cursed under his breath. Feelings were bad enough, trying to express them was absurd. "I've got a car. I'm going to London. Come with me if you want."

"You've got a car?" She faced him now. All hostility dropped away, astonishment replacing it.

"I've called in all my favours. Most of my money's gone as well."

"A car? And some petrol?"

"I thought petrol might come in handy. I'm leaving now. I want you to come. But I'm not going to beg."

Her smile was the widest he'd ever seen. "Beg? Shit, Carter, what are we waiting for?"

She grabbed his hand, kissed his mouth. He followed her into the cold night. He heard the low, protracted crump of a building collapsing somewhere to the east. Some gunshots, some screams. He gripped her fingers. His heart sang. He'd never felt happier.

It was an old Ford. Nothing special, but Josie stroked the rusted paint work and cooed over the plastic seats. Carter fought his impatience, remembered her age compared to his, all the things that he'd seen that she hadn't.

"We've got to go."

She curled herself into the front seat, almost purred. "I can't believe that you came for me."

He gunned the engine and headed, one last time, for the Newmarket Road. "I don't know if we'll make it, Josie. We'll have to take the back roads, the motorway is too dangerous and probably blocked anyway. And we'll have to walk the last ten miles or so, Christ knows how we'll actually get into London." She was still smiling and hugging herself. "I'm trying to warn you, Josie." He thought of something Val had said. "Our chances are fifty-fifty. At best."

"I like those odds."

"Seriously. I'll drop you somewhere, anywhere. No hard…"

She squeezed his thigh. "Onward and upward, Carter."

He shrugged and drove. Through Colney and Cringleford, then left into a narrow lane he remembered from years before. He let some old, almost forgotten instinct guide him, let the darkness and the country quiet envelop them, found that gradually his breathing approached normality for the first time in two days.

"This is why I could love you," Josie said a little later. Norfolk's flat fields still surrounded them.

"What?"

"You do things. You know stuff. You act."

"Am I supposed to be flattered?"

"The boys I know, the ones from the clubs, they're sweet and kind and totally ineffectual. Most of them will be dead within two years."

"I'm hardly immortal."

"But you're real. In the world. You make me feel safe. These things matter."

"Just currency, Josie. By any other name."

She started to deny that, then settled on a half smile and pursed lips. She'd used the word love, though. That warmed him. He wanted to reciprocate, but didn't know how. Eventually he said, "Back at the crypt I said that things have changed. You didn't ask how."

"Didn't I?"

He approached a crossroads and was pretty sure that a left would take them towards Thetford. He started to speak, then stopped.

"What?" Josie said.

"Do you care?"

"About what?"

"The past."

He watched the road intently, felt her eyes on his face. "Recent past, or years ago?"

"Any of it." He thought of Val and wondered what name Josie knew her by. Then pushed her memory aside. She was gone as utterly as his own parents and grandparents. He thought of Kieran, too, briefly and with an unexpected pang. He'd dropped in on the coffee shop on the way to meet Josie. The front window was shattered, most of the tables and chairs inside strewn across the street. There was no sign of Kieran. Carter noticed that all of Kieran's clean white mugs had been smashed against a wall. He found that sight much sadder than seemed appropriate.

"None of it matters," Josie said at last in an odd, tight little voice. Carter suddenly realised that she was close to tears. "Time starts now."

"I like that," he said. And he believed it to be true.

THE TOWER

Brian Howell

The image of Seya that Keiko remembered from the dream was simple but disorientating. She might have said haunting, except that she still retained a sense of warmth from it. He was in his office in another country, looking out of the window, many storeys above the miniaturized life below. His mouth seemed to be moving, but no sound registered. One might have expected his gaze to be askance, concentrated on some distant landmark, yet it was directed at her.

To his right was a vertical strip of a different hue to the background, very slightly out of plumb, which made it look as if he were staring out of a framed oil painting that had been knocked out of true. So tight was her focus on him that this detail might have been the frame of the window itself or the wall that was flush with the window, or even some part of the room's interior architecture.

During the morning she looked for a meaning. She looked for it as she combed her fourteen-year-old daughter Kurumi's long hair, a shining black waterfall that ended in an abrupt, perfect line below her shoulder blades. She looked for it as she started to make inroads on the seasonal changeover of clothes, which meant the storing of winterwear in special containers, an arrangement that would only end once the humid months had passed. She looked for it, too, in a desultory conversation with a salesman through the intercom, a conversation which might have yielded a code with which to decipher the meaning of her dream, for what use was such a pointless exchange on this morning of all mornings? Cruelly, too, the salesman's voice reminded her of Seya's, and for a brief instant she thought he had returned unannounced, to surprise her. He sometimes did that sort of thing.

Taking her four-year-old son Naoki the short distance to the daycare centre on her bicycle offered up few clues. Installed behind her,

Naoki recited the familiar roster of observations that defined these daily trips – *sports car, red, dangerous, you have to stop, Mummy* – as they came to the level crossing. The inevitable warning bell started to sound before they rounded the corner, which meant that she could not make it without endangering herself and Naoki. The horizontal barrier came down softly, from perfect ninety degrees to wavering zero, as if reducing the angle of possibilities in life. Definitively. *Train. Another one.*

After the crossing, pedestrians wandered from one side of the pavement to the other oblivious of the bicycle traffic behind them. Gingerly, she moved onto the road, but a stream of cars quickly appeared behind her and forced her back to the other side of the raised curb, until she came to another bottleneck of people.

She was conscious of her sombre state of mind. This was not unusual; she just got on with things. Perhaps having had Naoki was partly an urge to fill the loss of that routine as Kurumi grew up. But she had not reckoned with Seya being posted overseas for a year.

With Naoki safely deposited in the centre and mercifully no scene about saying goodbye, she folded up the back seat and swung it to the other side so that it could be used as an extra basket. The sides of the basket, from which Naoki's and countless other children's limbs on similar bicycles daily dangled as they were transported by their mothers, were now shored up against spilling shopping bags by two metal panels that had moved into place. She could not recall ever thinking before about this simple resituating of one plane to another, but this morning the process held her temporarily captive.

No, she did not normally think like this. She spent too much time alone, not totally, it was true, but certainly time without a man.

In her mind's eye she still saw Seya as he looked in her favourite photograph of him, taken just before he left to go abroad. In it he sported a pencil-thin moustache and prominent carbon-black eyebrows that looked painted on and possessed a hint of vaulted arches in their centres. His hair, which had a permanent wave, had more body than that of most men of his age, though it betrayed tinges of grey and harked back to the style of Western movie stars of ten years before. Beneath his smart single-breasted suit and white, collarless shirt, she allowed herself to reminisce with a touch of nostalgia, he was wiry and muscular from a combination of working out and regular tennis.

He had been gone only five months; the idea was to go out and visit him after six. In truth, she was slightly anxious that this trip might be jeopardised if things did not go well with Lancet Securities; she had seen news reports in the last few weeks that some irregularities had been discovered in Seya's company. But there was hardly a day when you did not hear or read of such things in Japan today. She had not discussed it with him. He would listen to her, but why worry him?

Having squeezed her bicycle into a rare wedge of space under the shelter in front of the supermarket, she shopped, circuitously, coming to things obliquely, as if skirting a commitment, as if delaying a pleasure, or a pain. Her shopping only half done, she realised she was afraid of something. For five seconds she could not move; she could not think what was wrong. She would go home, and wait.

Outside, the air seemed stiller than before, as if on the verge of becoming a vacuum. Though she had only been away fifteen minutes, she had to disengage her bicycle from a mass of others, which, insect-like, with their various metal projections – vertical, horizontal, angled – had clustered around hers like drones attending a queen, their frames jutting into hers and each other's in the aftermath of one solitary bicycle's collapse.

At the crossing on the way back she was mocked a second time by two trains passing each other, their two sets of carriages containing suits, jackets, jeans, and dresses topped with oval faces that superimposed themselves briefly the one on the other, as the eye retained the one image and carried it over to the next; for a few seconds the figures engaged in a waltz in which they seemed to pull their partners one way, only to override and cancel out that movement as they swung back round. Then they were gone.

The short trip cleared her mind a little, but once she was back home the sense of dread returned: it was still there, still hatching. Things like this only happen, she told herself, if you allow them to seep through the cracks.

She had not finished packing away their winter clothes. She estimated that she could fit everything in the four cardboard boxes that she had saved from previous years. It was not her habit to separate each family member's clothes from the others'; this was the first time the idea had occurred to her. There were slightly fewer of Seya's items to pack away, as he had taken a number of things with him. She wondered whether she might be able to fit them into one box with her own after all.

She assembled the boxes one at a time, thinking of slow-motion replays of buildings steadily reconstituting themselves or people jumping up into the air from a great height as the film was played backwards. She liked the idea of reversing or fast-forwarding action, of sliding space back on itself, or pushing it through some other dimension. If she could do that with time, things might not be so bad.

The packing went smoothly, but once she had layered Seya's clothes with her own, a shudder went through her, forcing her to redistribute his things to his own box. It was a momentary instinct that she did not consciously force herself to ignore; her action was more akin to a character in a film being unaware of a ghostly figure that only the audience can see.

When she had put the last of the boxes in the cupboard, Seya's somewhat lighter than the rest, she went into the bedroom and lay down on the futon.

Seya was in the same room as before. She was drawn into its narrow, two-dimensional space, which she remembered knowing somehow, but just as she closed in on him, the view widened and pulled back, wrenching her with it, making her dizzy.

He was in an office in a high tower whose upper reaches speared the clouds. Yet, as the top storeys of the building were revealed, she could see that the tower contained only one office on each level, like some enormous rocket, a fact emphasized by the curvilinear, art-deco contours and ogival extremity of the building.

He was looking at her again, but now she was back in the room. She had this feeling often in her dreams, the sense that she was inexplicably distant and up close at the same time.

The last thing she remembered was holding hands with him, feeling at peace, as they looked down and out over the city below.

The message she had been expecting on waking had still not come. No phone call, no sound at the door. Only time and space to fill for the rest of the afternoon. She switched on the TV to the daytime soap about the Office Ladies and all the machinations that their function as daytime soap characters must inevitably entail. Normally, she would let it infuse her mind, attach itself like nectar to a honeycomb, but today it meant nothing, less than nothing, even. For once it barely brought back the usual nostalgic memories, of how she had met Seya when she had been a secretary in the large, open-plan office they had shared. He had been the young head of the company who could not walk through the open-plan office without five or six of her colleagues tracking the slim line of his figure all the way up to his non-conforming face. Despite her attraction, she had not nourished fantasies that she would ever date him, at least not seriously, and yet, and yet, it had happened, and now they had Kurumi and Naoki. Only Seya's promotion had spoiled the idyll.

Then she did hear a sound, the abrupt recoil of the letterbox flap, followed by the report of something light dropping in, and, for confirmation, the hasty retreat of the postman on his moped, as if fleeing the scene of a crime.

She read the letter:

Dear Keiko

Are you well? Kurumi, Naoki? Keiko, this city is so wonderful. I almost feel guilty for liking it here so much, and the only thing that detracts from its perfection is your absence.

There's not so much pressure to get back to the office as at home, so in my lunch hours I walk along the river through a beautiful park. The mothers with their kids make me think of you and our own family.

It's an amazing city, as I've said. There are so many places to explore away from the main streets, and I must admit to sometimes losing myself in certain alleyways and the shops they contain. Bookshops, especially. I have so little time for such places back in Tokyo. But here we can often leave as early as five o'clock. Some of my colleagues even wondered if there was some significance in being allowed to go home so early, but I scotched any such discussion. It's bad for morale. You have to be positive.

I probably haven't told you yet about one particular building I've discovered. It's actually hard to describe. It could almost be anywhere that had high-rise buildings, I suppose. Except that it contains a room on the fortieth floor which is rather old; it puts out a rather musty, cloying smell, to be honest. At the same time, the building, the tower, as it were, is modern. From the first time I stepped into it (I had been misdirected, I seem to recall, having followed a sign for a Japanese restaurant), I was overcome with a sense of deep calm. The thing about this room, you see, is that actually, you can make it be anything you want; you can stretch its dimensions or you can contract them, so that it fits around you like the arms of a particularly

41

comfortable armchair, or like a picture frame that situates you at just the right place in some symmetrical design. It's a feeling of general wellbeing, I can assure you. And then there is the view.

The island is the heart of this beautiful city; it trails up along the coast like an enchanting, checked shawl, its streets a circuit board of equidistant nodes.

How does the room allow itself to seduce its occupant in this way, you are doubtless asking? Well, you have to learn, and I was lucky enough to be taught by a man who was there the day I first stumbled in. (You might already even call me a disciple of his.) He greeted me as if he had been waiting just for me, but there was nothing disconcerting about the experience. He knew that I was a little lonely, a little lost. Why else would I find myself walking into this room in a building that seemed to have no other purpose than to serve my curiosity?

Now I just come here whenever I feel a little run-down or low. It's a kind of meditation, I suppose.

I really must go, as people are wont to say in letters of this kind, but I shall write or talk to you soon. Give my love to the kids.

Love,
Seya

Keiko finished the letter feeling rather as she had on waking from the dreams. Shouldn't she perhaps be comforted by some of its content, at least? she had to ask herself. And yet it was in some ways as if she were an object being remotely controlled from a great distance by some force. If it was indeed Seya, then she surely had nothing to worry about, but if it were someone or something else, it would be another matter.

She was looking at the reticle of lines across the surface of the paper. She had not failed to notice the network of folds in the letter; she had just been too impatient to read its contents. Now she realised that these folds were nothing less than instructions to do exactly this, fold along the already many worn lines, origami-fashion. It did not take her long to realise that she was looking at the shape of the island Seya was on, and in its centre was, cleverly revealed, a black square. Except that it was not a black square; it was a hole through which she saw to the carpet below, and where, now, like the side of some huge ship slipping out to sea at night, seen too close-up actually to show what it was at first sight, she saw a cockroach.

Instinctively, she drew her legs up to the sofa and watched as the creature scuttled towards the skirting board, as if drawn there by the surface tension of water in a puddle. She would wait until it stepped off the carpet before she crushed it.

Later that evening, with the kids in the house and a warm thrum of domestic activity giving structure to her life again, Keiko was feeling better. She was cutting a honey-injected apple into quarters, Kurumi was peeling the potatoes for the curry, and Naoki was emptying the clear plastic boxes of toys and books – normally stacked neatly on top of each other – onto the carpet in the centre of the living room.

Now he was looking at his *Thomas The Tank Engine* book, which had Thomas proceeding to the seaside in a race against time, the excitement of the journey enhanced by a button set into each page which relayed the sound of the loveable locomotive's chukkety-chukk all the way down to its occupants' blissful coastal destination.

Keiko pictured the last page, which revealed an idyllic seaside scene where families relaxed or played with their children on the beach or in the water. She knew what Naoki would say next.

"And this is Naoki-kun, red, this is Kurumi-chan, orange, this is Mummy, yellow."

The colours referred to the figures' swimwear.

"And where's Daddy?" Kurumi asked her brother.

"Daddy? *No* Daddy!"

Keiko turned off the gas and picked up the book, desperately looking for a figure who could reasonably be identified with Seya, but she couldn't find one. She was sure she had identified just such a figure many times before. He always wore blue trunks.

"Kurumi-chan, where's Daddy here? I'm certain he's usually on this page, isn't he?"

Kurumi was silent, just staring at her.

"Kurumi? What's wrong?"

"There's no Dad. There never was a Dad."

Upon which outburst, Kurumi ran upstairs to her room.

"Kurumi!"

She left her to calm down on her own; she knew she would not stay upstairs more than half an hour.

Kurumi, long hair in braids, eventually came down, bowing profusely, saying *Sorry* over and again.

Naoki was now playing with his blocks and had built a tower, already looking quite precarious, on the rather uncertain foundations of the thick, soft carpet. One, maybe two more blocks would do it, and the whole edifice would come down.

"It's O.K. I miss him too," she said to Kurumi, "but it won't be so long."

"Mum. Can I sleep with you tonight?"

"Of course."

"Naoki too?"

"That's a great idea."

She was happy. She had been saved the embarrassment of reaching out to her own children to get her through the night. Is this what it must be like when you have a bereavement? she wondered.

There would be a dream tonight, she told herself, and it would be a struggle to come through it O.K.

The thought coincided with the mini-crash of Naoki's blocks, at which he gasped in wonderment. She offered a consoling expression which said, *What can you do?*, though she was trying to conceal the trembling in her lower lip.

Before she went to bed, she looked at the letter again, at the city and its construction. She realised that she had known this place well before Seya had gone there. She had had a poster of it on her bedroom wall as a child. She had memorised street names and prominent landmarks, which she had heard of again and again in books and films, without referring to the old map or even to any that she could have found in a book. Gradually, she felt, she had lost the ability to locate places in her head, but she had not had the curiosity to look them up. Above all, what had stood out were the various towers, which, on the poster, had been drawn to convey a three-dimensional effect, as if she were actually there. They were like giant armatures, reaching out to points in her head. She had always thought that that was neat, and now she felt a warmth inside her, a gratitude to Seya for having indirectly reunited her with this image.

But the dream did come, and she couldn't escape it. Seya was now at the top of the tower, though in the same room. He had a beautiful, contented smile on his face. It was dark, now, to be sure, but it *was* Seya, and behind him, another person: Keiko herself. Now, as if it were of no more consequence than stepping onto a bus, he was opening the window of the room in the tower. It was the swivelling type, which when opened formed a right angle with the rest of the frame. Out he stepped, into the air, into nothingness, and she, this shadow version of herself, followed him, unquestioningly.

EVELYN IS NOT REAL

Mike O'Driscoll

Ray was in movies. Or he used to be. Low budget, independent, left-field, cultish – these were the words he used to describe them to strangers. When you got to know him, when he felt you were on his side, he dismissed them as movies nobody saw.

I got to know to Ray a year after my husband Nick was killed. Nick was driving across an intersection in Daly City when a man in a blue Explorer ran a red light and ploughed into him. Ten minutes earlier, the man had robbed a drugstore in San Bruno. The night before we had spent two hours talking about our trip to Europe. It was to be our two year delayed honeymoon. We would go to all the places we had read about in books, seen in movies, or already walked through in our dreams. We would hire a car and spend four months on the road, driving wherever fancy took us. Amsterdam, Innsbruck, Sarajevo, Venice, Barcelona, Lisbon. The names tripped off our tongues like potent mysteries. We might camp out under Tyrolean skies or check into a small, family run pension where the owners would speak not a word of English and Nick and I no word of whatever tongue it happened to be. But fancy had other plans which saw Nick's life bleeding away before the fire crew could cut him free from the mangled wreck of his Toyota.

Ray had been in twenty movies or so. The 'or so' was an addendum to cover the four of five from which, he suspected, his part had been cut. Suspected because, in those cases, he had never seen the finished product. When he said he'd appeared in movies nobody saw, I hadn't thought he meant himself. Ray's proud boast was that he'd seen the work of all the greats but not worked a scene with any of them. I'd never met anyone like him, and yet, he was the only man apart from Nick who could take me outside of myself.

After Nick was killed I sort of fell apart, but only for a short while. After a week I pulled myself together and decided to get on with my life. Despite the protestations of well-meaning friends to let it out, to process the hurt, I could see no benefit in it, either to Nick or to myself. To wallow in hurt and misery? Surely the man I'd loved deserved something more. So I threw myself into my job, zeroing the space into which any hurt might be born. I managed the downtown branch of a medical recruitment agency, and in the six months following Nick's death, my commissions rose by thirty per cent. And then I sold the bungalow we had bought in Pacifica, took out a loan on a one bed apartment on Sunset about a mile from Ocean Beach, quit my job and flew to Paris.

I bought a second-hand Peugeot, a small convertible, and for three months I drove to one fabled city after another, trying to find traces of the life Nick and I had dreamed. I imagined myself chasing after some intangible essence, trying to relive an emotional transaction whose worth I'd never quite grasped. Without Nick, the places through which I moved seemed populated only by ghosts. By the time I hit Athens I felt as if the world was receding from me. In an effort to draw closer to it, I took a job in an Irish bar, began to take account of people, started to put names to faces. And then, when I felt the first stirrings of what I thought was hurt, I inoculated myself against further pain by falling, briefly, in love with the owner of the bar. He was an Athenian who, ten years before had married and been abandoned by an Irish girl after she had ran off with his best friend. We drank a lot together, told each other jokes and had sex. Our relationship was built on a mutual desire for forgetting. Yet, neither of us had the will to get all the way there and so, after five months away, I returned to San Francisco and found that all the hurt I had been running from was waiting right there for me.

We were eating shrimp with mango at *Firecrackers* on Valencia the first time Ray spoke about Evelyn. We had been to see David Lynch's new movie, a remake of Von Sternberg's *The Scarlet Empress*. Ray always wanted to eat Chinese after a movie, as if celluloid provoked an appetite that only noodles and the like could satisfy. I didn't get Lynch, nor most of the films Ray liked to watch. My tastes were what he called mainstream. It didn't matter to me who directed a movie, though I knew names like Hitchcock, Ford and Hawks. These were the guys whose movies Nick used to watch. He had turned me on to Hawks, particularly the films he'd made with Cary Grant. I watched them all the time, except for *Only Angels Have Wings*, which I couldn't bring myself to look at since his death. Not that Ray was a snob about movies. He liked Hawks too, and I think the fact that he'd acted in a few stinkers kept him grounded.

He was talking about the film we'd just seen, telling me, in between mouthfuls of shrimp and Mexican beer, how Lynch had failed to out-perverse Von Sternberg. He stopped suddenly, chopsticks held a few inches above his plate, his gaze fixed intently on my face.

"What is it?" I said.

He continued to stare at me, as if at a stranger he thought he should know.

"Ray – what's the matter?"

He seemed to see me then, for real. He scrunched his eyes and pinched the bridge of his nose. "Nothing," he said. He looked down at the last few shrimps on his plate but left them there.

"Tell me."

"Sometimes you remind me of someone I used to know."

"Should I be flattered?"

He shrugged, then laughed. "I don't know. Evelyn was, ah, somebody I worked with once."

"She was an actress?"

He nodded. "We made a film together."

"How do I remind you of her?"

"I'm not sure – maybe I glimpsed it before in you, but never clearly until now."

"Glimpsed what?"

"This is going to sound stupid, but it's a kind of serenity."

"Serenity, huh?" I sipped my wine to stop from guffawing. "You think I'm serene?"

"You have a certain stillness. Evelyn had it too."

The way he spoke about her suggested a deeper connection than professional respect. I felt something odd then, something vaguely familiar which I didn't want to feel. Ray and I had been seeing each other for four months and one of the things I liked about him was that he never quizzed me about the past nor offered to fill in the details of his own previous affairs. From the first he had seemed to realise how much I was hurting, and that it was delayed but necessary hurt, one that I could no longer run from. He didn't try to tell me it was time to move on, or that the grieving process was a healing one. He offered no homilies, just listened when I wanted to talk, and made me laugh when that was what I needed. "I never thought of myself as having 'stillness'," I said. "I can't really imagine myself that way."

"Forget it. I don't know why I brought it up."

"You and Evelyn – you were together?"

"For a while," he said, distantly.

I guessed that he didn't want to talk about it. If it had ended badly between them, I could understand the desire to escape the past. And yet, I was already intrigued and no matter what hurt it might bring, I let my curiosity get the better of me. "Tell me about her," I said.

Ray reached across the table and took my hand. "There's nothing really to tell. It was short, intense, and then it was over."

Before I could stop myself, I was asking him how long ago it had been. Ray stood up, leaned across the table and kissed me on the lips. "Forget it, Grace. You're nothing like her."

Outside, as we walked west along Jackson Street, Ray started speaking about *The Scarlet Empress* again, comparing it unfavourably to Lynch's earlier films. A young couple walked by us, engrossed in their own conversation. A cable car rattled south along Powell, a peculiar beast at odds with the stillness of the hour. Ray's voice drifted in and out of my head and as we walked I felt the presence of someone else nearby, watching us. I looked back over my shoulder but the street was empty. Ray seemed oblivious to the unnatural quiet, and to the sudden quickening of my heart. I wanted to ask Ray how I wasn't like Evelyn but the moment passed and did not come again until much later.

It felt like I had been away a lot longer than five months. The city seemed different, and not just because of the winter rain. I had sold most of the furniture from Pacifica, keeping only what I needed to occupy the emptiness of the apartment on Judah. It wasn't much and what there was I no longer recognised as belonging to me. I got a job with a medical temp agency at two thirds the salary I had been earning before I went away. Christmas came and went and I told myself I didn't mind spending it alone. Being with friends would have made it harder. I wasn't ready yet for all their best intentions, their reassurances, their talk of how well I was doing. In the new year a few people began to call, asking how I was. How had Europe been? Had I settled into my new apartment? Not a word about Nick. As if they were afraid the mention of his name would be intolerable to me. Only after I had spent time again in the company of those we had called our friends did I realise that it was themselves for whom the memory of Nick had become intolerable. By getting killed, Nick had transgressed the rules. And, as I began to understand by the silent, coded signals that passed between them, my presence was an unwanted reminder of the frailties they refused to recognise in themselves.

I met Ray for the first time in a DVD rental store on Sutter a block from my office. I was browsing through the new releases, looking for something to numb the pain for a couple of hours. Nothing grabbed me and so I graduated towards the back of the store where the older films were being offered at a 'rent two for the price of one' deal. I picked up a copy of *Bringing Up Baby* and smiled at the picture of Cary Grant and Katherine Hepburn on the cover. Nick used to do a perfect imitation of Grant as David Huxley taking delivery of the intercostal clavicle.

"A match made in heaven."

A man in a black leather sports jacket was standing at my shoulder. Before I could say anything, he gestured at the DVD I held and said, "Nobody ever died of sadness watching Grant and Hepburn."

"I can choose my own film," I cut him off and replaced the DVD on the shelf.

"It's true. I know from experience."

He had an accent, British, I thought. He had brown eyes and light brown hair that hung almost to his shoulders. "Excuse me," I said, moving away from him.

"And with the two for one deal you should take this too."

I glanced back at him. He was holding *His Girl Friday* towards me. Despite myself I smiled. "How do you know what I should watch?" I asked him.

"I was in movies," he said. "I have an instinct for these things."

"Are you serious? You're an actor?"

His smile seemed awkward somehow, even a little embarrassed.

"Not sure if I still am."

"What do you mean?"

"Haven't worked on a movie in a while. It's like, if you're dead, can you still call yourself human?"

The absurdity of the question made me laugh. "See, you haven't even watched it yet and it's already working."

"I've seen them before," I said. "All of them."

He nodded, turned away and moved off to another part of the store. Puzzled, I stared after him for a moment than returned to browsing. A minute later he came back. "Try this," he said, handing me a DVD called *My Back Yard*.

I looked at the cover and recognised a younger version of the man standing in front of me. In the picture he was standing on the porch of a ramshackle house, looking out over a weed-strewn yard. "It's you."

He shrugged. "It makes people forget their woes."

He couldn't have been more than twenty-five, twenty-six, when the film was made, I thought.

"That was fifteen years ago. Second picture I made in America."

"I never heard of it."

"Yes, well. It wasn't exactly a hit." He looked forlorn for a moment, then smiled. "But please, I think it will make you laugh."

"All right." I looked at the cast list. "Raymond Dunbar, I'll give it a try."

"It's Ray now, just Ray."

"And if it doesn't make me laugh?"

"Then you won't see me again. But if you do laugh, then I'll be waiting here this time tomorrow evening." With that he turned and left the store.

I rented the movie and *His Girl Friday*, just in case. At six the following evening he was waiting for me at the store.

I have a brother who plays in a band. They almost made it big five years back. Got some kind of recording deal, made a couple of albums, toured the West Coast. I took Nick to see them play support to Jim White downstairs at *Johnny Foley's*. My brother had grown his hair long and a thick beard covered his cherubic features. Maybe that's why he grew it. His voice though, was still as sweet as an angel's. He called me after Nick was killed, from a hotel room somewhere in Amsterdam.

The band was touring northern Europe to promote their new CD. He sounded despondent. I thought it was because he had really liked Nick and was going to miss him. But what it was he was afraid the band was going to break up. He felt things weren't working out for them the way he'd hoped. He was thinking of going back home to Kentucky. He wanted me to tell him not to lose sight.

In *My Back Yard*, Ray played a young man who returns to the family home in northern California after an absence of ten years. He finds the place abandoned and run down, full of ghosts and memories. The story takes place over the course of a twenty-four hour period, with Ray's character connecting with all kinds of people and memories from the past. It could have been depressing, but the truth was, it was funny as hell. He was pleased when I told him that, said he was glad he was able to make me forget myself for a little while. I wondered how he'd known that that was what I wanted to do but I didn't ask. I was too busy agreeing to let him take me to dinner.

Sixteen years ago Ray had left England after appearing in three highly rated TV shows and half a dozen low budget movies, a couple of which had played the city's art houses. One night, after we'd been seeing each other for a month, we caught one of these early films on cable. It was an odd, kind of surreal gangster thriller called *Lester Bows Out*, and halfway through, I realised I'd seen it before. It felt weird, I told him, seeing a movie I'd forgotten I'd seen, while lying naked next to the man who played the lead role.

His hand stroked my belly. "Some of the shit I appeared in I wish I could forget."

"That bad, huh?"

"Hey, you're supposed to defend my thespian skills."

I rolled onto my side and kissed him on the mouth. "Raymondo," I said, reaching down between his legs. "I could never fault your performance."

Earlier that evening, when he'd called into my office downtown, Ray had picked up the framed photograph of Nick I had on my desk. He stared at it intently for nearly a minute while I watched him, curious and a little apprehensive about what he would say. "Losing someone you love," he said. "It's beyond belief."

I hadn't known how to respond to that. Before I was even aware of it, my eyes were full of tears. Ray came and knelt next to my seat, put his hands on my cheeks and told me Nick was the luckiest ghost alive. I don't think I'd ever heard anything so corny, but it brought a smile to my lips and diminished a little more the lingering pain.

Ray did commercials now, mostly voiceovers, with the occasional front of camera job. I tried to encourage him to get back into serious acting but he laughed and said commercials were more honest than anything else he'd done. They told it straight, he said, no bullshit.

I began watching out for his movies on TV. Whenever one was broadcast on some obscure cable channel in the graveyard slot, I'd get him to come over and watch it with me. They weren't what you'd call mainstream. Apart from his first three American pictures, all the others were made by small independents and had either got a limited release or gone straight to video or DVD. We sat through two or three together, including one in which he starred as an ex-child actor with a doll fetish. He didn't seem interested in them. He'd make the odd comment, criticising his own performance, or that of the other actors; he'd pick holes in the script or laugh at some directorial ineptitude he hadn't spotted before. Mostly he seemed listless, irritated by the films, as if they reminded him of part of his life he would have preferred to forget.

On Saturday I was cycling in the Haight district, stopping to browse in the book and music stores. In a thrift store on Lower Haight I saw a rack of second hand DVDs and on impulse I asked the lanky kid behind the counter if they had any Ray Dunbar films in stock.

He shook his head and gestured at the shelves. "Just what's there."

I started to look through the films. "He was in *My Back Yard*, and another movie called *Joey Elegant*. You know those films?"

The kid had come out from behind the counter and was rummaging through a crate of junk by the shopfront. "What'd you say that guy's name was?"

"Raymond Dunbar."

"Gus hasn't catalogued this stuff yet. Only came in yesterday." He reached down into the crate and pulled out a slim, plastic case. "But maybe this is something."

I walked to the crate and he handed me a DVD case with a sheet of lined paper inside the sleeve. Handwritten across the front were the words 'The Last Time, with Raymond Dunbar.'

I opened the case. There was a handwritten label stuck to the disc.

"You know this movie?"

"Naw. I just seen that name on the cover this morning."

"Is it kosher?"

"Five bucks and it's yours."

I gave him the money. Outside the store I called Ray on my cellphone. "Ray, when you come over tonight, bring wine and a Chinese."

"I thought we were going out to catch a movie."

"We'll catch one in. One of yours."

I heard him groan. "Must we?"

He arrived just after eight, and once we'd eaten, I showed him the disc.

"Jesus – where'd you get that?" He seemed surprised.

"Store on Haight. It is one of yours, right?"

He took the case from me and hurried through to the living room. By the time I had followed him there, he already had the disc in the DVD player and was sitting on the edge of the sofa. He seemed excited and edgy as he waited for the film to load.

"What's up, Ray? I usually have to bribe or bully you to make you watch your own films."

He dragged his eyes from the screen. "Come and sit down," he said, eagerly. "It's the one I told you about before. The one I made with Evelyn."

I can't say I was much taken with *The Last Time*. It was too dark, too obviously indebted to Lynch in its weirdness, but at the same time it seemed oddly lifeless, as if the characters were somehow aware of their own unreality, conscious of themselves only as 'characters'. Sometimes the actors spoke dialogue that seemed unrelated to their respective storylines. The protagonist, played by Ray, was some kind of cop or detective, though I couldn't figure out exactly what he was working on. There was a blonde woman, very beautiful, a femme fatale, with whom the PI became enthralled. I figured this was Evelyn. It was never clear whether she was helping or hindering Ray's character solve the mystery that lay at the heart of the film. At the end she disappeared, at which point the plot seemed to feed back into itself, as the cop began to investigate the fate of a missing woman.

The film unsettled me. Thankfully, Ray didn't seem in the mood to discuss it. I could tell it meant something to him, more than any of the other films we'd watched together. I guessed it was because of Evelyn. While watching it, he'd made none of his usual jokes or sarcastic comments about the script or the performances. Instead, he'd remained silent, intent on the convoluted story as if searching for the key to its mystery. Maybe it had more to do with what had happened between him and Evelyn than with the storyline. I wondered how it had ended between them.

Afterwards, Ray sat staring into space, as if transfixed by a film that was still playing in his head. I watched him for a while, puzzled at the effect it had had on him. Was it not how he had remembered? Or had it dragged some painful memories to the surface? I made coffee, brought it back to the living room. I would have asked him what he was thinking but I wasn't sure I really wanted to know. Instead, I cuddled up next to him and laid my head on his chest

He put an arm round me and raised my head with his other hand. There was an intensity in his gaze that startled me, but before I could ask him what the matter was he pressed his mouth hard against mine. In the few months we had been seeing each other, Ray had always been a tender lover, but now he seemed hungry, almost ruthless as he pressed himself on me. I thought about Nick for one moment, pictured his handsome face before it morphed into the image of a broken body on a morgue slab. I shuddered and responded to Ray, clamping my mouth against his. I tore at his shirt and pushed him down on the sofa, feeling something primitive and savage come awake inside me.

Josh and Lynsey were talking movies one morning when I arrived at the office. Both had worked for Meditech for over a year. I think they were sleeping together, but I wasn't sure. I poured myself a coffee and made small talk with them. Josh seemed to be something of a movie freak so I asked him if he'd ever seen *The Last Time*.

"Who was the director?"

I shrugged. "No idea. I'm not big on directors."

"You know who wrote it?"

"No," I confessed.

"You missed the big question, Josh," Lynsey chipped in. "Who're the stars?"

"Actually," Josh said, disdainfully, "I was going to ask the year of production."

"British actor called Ray Dunbar played the lead role," I said.

Lynsey had never heard of him.

"Dunbar?" Josh frowned and tapped the edge of Lynsey's desk "Raymond Dunbar. Starred in *My Back Yard, Joey Elegant, The Daemon Next Door*. Made a couple of decent thrillers in England before taking the Hollywood buck."

"I'm impressed," I said. "What about *The Last Time?*"

"Is it one of his Brit movies?"

"No, American. Not Hollywood though. Independent, low budget."

"So, anytime in the last fifteen years?"

"More recent, say five or six years ago."

"What's it about?"

"It's kind of a weird, noir type of thing. Confusing, amateurish in parts, but compelling too." I racked my brain trying to give Josh something more specific but the storyline was hazy and all I could really remember were one or two striking images. "Near the end," I tried to explain. "There's a scene where the protagonist, a cop, opens a door in a motel room, expecting to find the woman he's looking for. He knows she's there. He's seen her go in just a couple of minutes before. He opens the door and steps inside. She's not there. The room is empty. There's no other way out."

Josh shook his head. "Sounds familiar, but there's maybe a hundred movies with similar scenes."

"You really don't know it?"

"No," he said, sounding disgusted with himself.

Ray got a contract to do a series of scotch whiskey commercials down in LA. Said he'd be away a week, maybe longer. I didn't want him to go. I guess that meant I was falling in love with him.

One morning while he was away, I was riding the BART downtown to work when I was struck by the oddest sensation. I felt sure that someone was watching me. It only lasted a moment, but it was enough to raise the hairs on the back of my neck. The next morning I felt the same thing, only stronger. There were a dozen or so people in the carriage. I stole glances at each of them, but saw nothing to indicate that any of them were watching me. All the way downtown I couldn't shake off the tension, and though it had gone by the time I reached the office, it left me feeling on edge through most of the day.

That evening as I walked south from Sutter towards Market Street Station, I kept a close watch on the faces of the people I passed, furtively scanning them for someone I recognised. I called Ray that night, wanting to tell him about it. He would have had some explanation, I knew, something about how maybe I was feeling guilty at getting over Nick and this was my subconscious getting its own back. But instead, Ray talked about the commercial, how much he was missing me and what he'd do to me when he got back. He said we should get out of the city for a weekend, maybe spend a couple of nights in Sausalito.

Next morning, after another fraught journey to work, I asked Lynsey if anyone had been trying to get hold of me. She reeled off a list of clients and the names of three people I had scheduled to interview. "Anybody sound... wrong?"

"Wrong?"

"I don't know. Like they were pissed off or something."

"Sure Grace. Every last one of them."

Lynsey's flippancy did nothing to ease my fears. Every time the phone rang I'd hesitate before taking the call, half-afraid of what I might hear. I kept an eye on my colleagues, wondering if one of them was responsible, if he or she was playing some sick joke at my expense. I was aware too, of a strange allure in letting my guard slip, in suspending myself in a kind of disbelief, as if this would somehow weaken my sense of dread.

Ray was away six days. When he got back, we hired a car, drove out to Sausalito and checked into a quaint old seafront hotel. He'd bought me a present, a blue Hermes scarf from a boutique on Rodeo Drive. He insisted I wear them out to dinner. We ate lobster and fries and got half drunk on white wine. We made love by moonlight on the beach and talked afterwards about where we went from here. He asked me if I thought we were moving too fast. I thought maybe we were but I didn't tell him that. Despite my doubts, being with him felt so right. I didn't tell him either, about what had been happening to me. The paranoia, if that's what it really was. It felt distant, as if it was something that I had heard about, but which hadn't really happened to me.

Back in the city, the sensation of being watched, of being the object of someone's close scrutiny, returned. It wasn't there all the time. Just certain moments when I'd be talking on the phone or typing something into my computer, I'd feel the weight of an unknown gaze creep over me. I'd stop what I was doing and scan the faces of my colleagues, the passers-by out in the street, trying to hide my own anxiety. Then, just as quickly, the sensation would fade and I'd feel foolish and self-conscious as I became aware that my colleagues really were looking at me, wondering what the hell Grace was so jumpy about.

Tuesday morning walking down Sutter on my way to the office, I bumped into Josh. The ride in on the BART had been uneventful. I'd felt nothing untoward. I was okay, a little edgy, but nothing I couldn't cope with. Josh fell in beside me and we started talking, the usual office gossip. Right then I felt it. Someone following me, watching my every move. I froze in the street, heart racing. I was afraid to turn round.

"Grace?" Josh cried. "What's wrong?"

I tried to say something but I couldn't. Josh took hold of my arms and tried to reassure me. "It's okay Grace. It's okay."

I forced myself to respond. Slowly, I looked back over my shoulder, terrified of what I might see. There were just people I didn't know, moving past, oblivious to my fear. And just as suddenly as it had come on me, the feeling disappeared.

I told Ray about it that night. We were at an Italian restaurant on Noriega. "I know I sound paranoid, Ray, but I think somebody really is following me."

"You think of any reason someone would do that?"

"No – but crazy people don't need reasons."

Ray grinned. "I'm sorry," he said, seeing how pissed off I was. "Look, I'm not laughing. I'm trying to understand, Grace, really I am." He did his best to reassure me, saying that if I really believed someone was following me, he'd go with me to the police tomorrow and report it. I could tell he didn't really believe me, but his concern was genuine and the last thing I wanted was for him to think I was neurotic.

We went back to his place in Ingleside. He had something to show me. He poured me a glass of chilled Pinot Grigio and disappeared into his bedroom. He came out a few moments later carrying a Neiman Marcus bag. "Close your eyes," he said.

I did as he asked, and when he told me to open them I saw a black skirt and jacket draped over the back of the sofa. I looked at Ray. "You don't have to get –"

"I wanted to. I like buying you things. I want you to look beautiful."

I shrugged, feeling a little light-headed.

"Do you like them?"

I picked up the jacket and pulled it on, then held the skirt to my waist. "Yes," I said. "It's a beautiful suit." And it was.

That night, I dreamed about Evelyn.

The next morning I felt feverish and weak. I got out of bed but didn't have the strength to get dressed. I called work and told them I was ill. Ray said I had a cold coming on and told me to go back to bed. He brought me a cup of tea and some aspirin. After swallowing the tablets and drinking half the tea, I managed to doze off.

When I woke again, it was after midday. The fever had abated somewhat but I still felt weak. Ray had gone. He'd left a note saying he'd be back around six. I put fresh coffee on to brew and took a shower. The Neiman Marcus outfit was still draped over the back of the sofa. After I'd dried myself I put it on, then went back through to the bathroom and wiped the steam from the mirrored wall. The suit looked good on me. It made me feel sexy, alluring. There was something right about it, I thought, something familiar. Maybe Ray had an instinct for clothes. The mirror began to steam over again. I moved closer to it, looking at my face. What did Ray see when he looked in my eyes, I wondered? Did some vestige of pain still linger there? Or was it the absence of grief, the emptiness inside me that attracted him? It seemed a strange notion but I couldn't shake it off. I puckered my lips and pulled the hair back tightly behind my head. What would he think if I dyed my hair blonde?

After eating a bowl of cereal my head began to ache again. I took another couple of aspirin and curled up on the sofa. I closed my eyes but the pain grew sharper when I lowered my head. I sat up and gazed round the apartment, surprised at how sparsely furnished it was. There were no pictures on the walls, no nick-nacks or books on the shelves behind the TV, none of the accumulated junk we use to make statements about ourselves. I slid off the sofa and crawled across the floor to where the widescreen stood on its metal stand. A few DVDs lay on the metal shelf between the DVD player and the TV. I recognised the covers of *My Back Yard*, Lester *Bows Out* and *Joey Elegant*. The fourth film was *The Last Time*, still in its handwritten cover. I opened the case, took out the disc and put it in the DVD player.

I sat on the floor a few feet in front of the screen. Like a child, I told myself, feeling an odd but not unpleasant sense of detachment. As the opening credits rolled I mouthed the words 'the last time', trying to recall what had happened in the film. Evelyn was more beautiful than I remembered. She had an air of profound mystery and sadness about her, as if she knew in advance that some terrible fate awaited her. The story was told in flashback, with Ray's character investigating her disappearance. As he got closer to the truth he became obsessed with Evelyn, determined to save her from her inescapable fate. I felt myself being drawn deeper into the twists and turns of the narrative, yet I still struggled to make sense of everything that was going on.

The ending was different. I was sure of it. The first time, Evelyn had vanished. It was that event, I remembered, which had triggered the circular narrative. I realised now that she had been trying to get away from the cop whose obsession had begun to destroy her. This time she was still with him at the end. The camera froze on Evelyn standing at a window. I noticed the blue scarf tied around her pale throat. Her eyes seemed haunted as she stared out from the final frame, searching for someone or something beyond the camera.

When it was over I slumped on my side, feeling empty and drained. It was an impossible love, I thought. I could never hunger for somebody that way. Such feelings would consume me. I remembered the intensity, the excitement in Ray's eyes the night we had watched the film together. Was he still in love with Evelyn? I wondered. Was that why he had showed me the film? So I would understand?

I took a taxi to Bowley Street of Lincoln, and headed north through the picnic area, and on over the dunes that bordered Baker Beach. There were dozens of nude sunbathers along the northern shore, most of them male. They didn't pay me much attention and I had no interest in them. I had wanted to get out of the apartment for a few hours, think about me and Ray, where we were going. I had only been to Baker Beach once before, with Nick, when he'd brought me to see what he said was the best view of the Golden Gate Bridge from anywhere in the city. Maybe that's why I hadn't been back since he was killed. Still hiding from the pain.

I wanted to ask Ray about Evelyn, but at the same time I didn't want to open any old wounds. I thought about the space he had given me to come to terms with losing Nick, and felt guilty for doubting him. Yet, I was sure that if I did ask, he'd be more than willing to tell me. So why my hesitation?

I got up, packed away the few things I had brought with me, and slung the backpack over my shoulder. I wandered south along the shore, till I had to clamber back over the dunes and follow the path as it rose towards the cliffs. As I climbed up higher the tension ebbed from me and I began to feel exhilarated. I could hear the sea pounding into the rocks below, and the gulls screeching as they sped over the surf. I was sweating and breathing hard as I reached the highest point. I threw my backpack on the ground and sat down. I let my eyes take in the vast sweep of the ocean, the rocky coast to the west, the mile long stretch of Baker Beach to the north, the bridge, and the Marin headland beyond. I'd never walked those cliffs before, and yet everything about them was familiar to me. I knew that a little way off to the west, the coast would fall steeply to China Beach. I could picture myself swimming there in the ice cold ocean some years ago, but when I tried to flesh out the memory it slipped from my grasp like a morning dream.

Up there on the cliffs I was alone, cut off from the world. I was no longer even sure why I was there or what it was I had hoped to find. There were gaps in my memory, empty spaces where important parts of my life had been. Get a hold of yourself, girl, I told myself. You're fretting too much. Overanalysing. Letting old fear and doubts bring you down. It was because of Ray, I knew. I was in love with him, and that scared me. Was I ready to put myself through this? To risk losing him? I wondered what or who it was that I might lose him to, but deep down, I knew.

The bad feelings began to recede, and I no longer worried about someone watching me. Ray said it was because I had moved on, come to terms with the past. He was right. Once I had acknowledged my fears, it became easier. Not having to deny the way I felt about him seemed to make everything clearer. He was so good to me, really, I couldn't have been happier. He bought me clothes and jewellery, showered me with all kinds of things. He said he wanted to make me beautiful. I wondered if I had ever been beautiful before. In a sense, Ray said, I had recreated myself. I took him at his word and dyed my hair blonde.

We were in a bar on Geary one night, when I recognised a song by my brother's band. Jim sang about the sound of a beating heart being the only proof anyone would ever need. Proof of what? I wondered, unable to hear the words clearly above the talk and laughter. "You hear that, Ray?" I asked him. "You know what that means?"

Ray smiled and squeezed my leg beneath the table. "What is it Evelyn? What's bothering you?"

"Nothing," I said. "I'm fine." Had I heard him right? Or had I just imagined him saying what I wanted to hear?

"You want to go?"

I nodded. Ray called a cab. It took us west out of the city, all the way to the ocean. A great bank of fog rolled up along the shore from the south as we stumbled down on to the beach and kicked off our shoes. The sand was cold beneath our feet. I pressed my body against Ray. He pulled me down to the ground where we tore off each other's clothes and had quick, frantic sex. It was not the first time we had done this. I asked him if he had ever brought Evelyn here. If he had ever fucked her on this stretch of beach.

He didn't say anything for a while. The fog was cold and tight about us. We pulled on our clothes and sat listening to the invisible surf. "Would it matter if I had?" he said, finally.

"I guess that depends," I said. "On what you really want from me."

"What does that mean?"

"Do you still want her? Do you still love her?"

"Evelyn is dead." The words were brittle on his tongue. "She died shortly after the film finished shooting."

"I'm sorry, Ray. I didn't know."

"How could you have?" he said, bitterly. "She was never anyone."

I put my arms around him and held him tight. I squeezed all the love I could into him and told him it was all right. I was here. Nothing else mattered.

Of course other things mattered, but what mattered most was not feeling any pain. For me that meant not losing Ray. I understood now, that hunger I had seen in his eyes when he had looked at Evelyn. I felt I had cured him of her, that the feelings that remained were all for me.

Ray moved into my apartment. Next Spring we would buy a place outside the city. Somewhere north of the bay. He made the future seem real, brought snatches of it alive in the here and now. We were always making plans, for tomorrow, next week, or next year. We'd get married. We'd move out of the city. I'd quit my job and we'd have babies together. All of this would happen, he said. Soon.

I kept my job, waiting for the day. After a while I noticed that Ray was always home before me. He began to look tired and dishevelled. He no longer shaved every day, the way he used to do. There were some days I was sure he never left the apartment. I'd managed to track down most of his films on DVD. I felt he needed them to remind him that he had once been someone. But he rarely looked at any of them, apart from that one pirated copy of *The Last Time*. I never had been able to find an original. He kept asking me to watch it with him but I couldn't. I was afraid it would have changed again.

I came home one evening and found the place in darkness. I turned on the lights and saw timber boards nailed over the window frames. Ray was lying on the floor, drunk.

"Goddamit Ray" I said, stunned. "What have you done? What's happening to you?"

He mumbled something indecipherable.

"Say it Ray, tell me what this is."

His eyes flickered open and he looked up at me. "Evelyn? Where you been?"

"No Ray," I said, infuriated. "It's not fucking Evelyn. It's Grace."

"Grace?" He looked confused. He crawled to an armchair and I helped him up onto it. He grabbed my arm and pulled me close. "Tell me," he whispered.

"Tell you what?"

"Tell me it isn't true."

"No Ray. It is true. She's dead. You told me yourself, remember. She's gone." I tried to pull myself free but he held on to my wrist.

"Lying bitch."

"Listen to me, Ray, you're not yourself."

"No, Evelyn," he said, grinning drunkenly. "You're wrong."

I couldn't stand it anymore. I lashed out as hard as I could, catching him in the mouth. He fell back in the chair, unconscious. I stood over him, my anger dissipating. What had I done? There was blood on his lips and his breathing was shallow. For a moment I thought about calling an ambulance, then realised that all he needed was rest. Someone real to take care of him, draw him out of his obsession.

I grabbed his arms and pulled him forward off the chair. I dragged him by the hands to the bedroom, where, after a couple of attempts, I got him up onto the bed. I took off his clothes and pulled the sheet over him. Goddamn you, I thought. For letting me down. For being so weak. I couldn't go through that pain again. I had promised myself. In the morning, I would leave. Walk out the door and not come back.

I went through to the kitchen and stuck a pasta dish in the microwave. Forced myself to eat half of it. Nothing seemed right anymore. Everything was crumbling. This was not how it was supposed to be. I wondered if I'd said the same thing when Nick was killed. Thinking about him I began to cry. Hot, angry tears, full of self-loathing. How little pain I had allowed myself to feel for him. How afraid to accept that such hurt was part of the deal. Was I really such a coward? Could I abandon Ray the way I had Nick?

I returned to the bedroom. Ray lay on his back, his head turned to one side. His chest rose and fell, almost imperceptibly. I undressed and got in beside him. He felt hot and clammy, and the undersheet was damp with his sweat. "Ray," I whispered, holding him. "I'll make it right, I promise."

Ray didn't stir. I tossed and turned for more than an hour before getting out of bed, sticky with his perspiration. I showered, pulled on a clean t-shirt and knickers and went through to the living room. I stood in front of the television, hesitating. Maybe the answer lay in the film. Could I bring myself to watch it again? Would I learn something new? All I was sure of was that something would have changed.

This time at the end it wasn't Evelyn trapped in the final frame, but Ray. He had found her in the motel. She'd looked out the window, her eyes drawing him in. Like a fool he'd gone to her. The final shot was of the detective standing in the doorway, hands writhing, mouthing silent oaths. Caught in an impossible desire.

In the morning I left Ray sleeping and went in to work as usual. I kept telling myself I was not going through the motions, that I would do whatever it took to cure Ray of the past. He was mine now, not some dead woman's.

At midday I found some time to myself and logged on to a movie website Josh had told me about. I typed in Ray's name and after a second a small picture appeared on screen next to a brief biog. He didn't look much different to the way he looked now. His hair was shorter and he had a goatee in the photograph, which suited him. Including his British films, there were twenty movies listed in which he had appeared, dating back to 1986. His TV credits were also listed but there was nothing at all for *The Last Time*. I scrolled back up through the list and typed in the name of the movie. Three titles came up, two recent shorts and a Michael Keaton movie which was in post-production. I must have got something wrong, I thought. I tried different permutations of the film's title, Last Time, The; Last Time; Time Last. None of them gave me anything.

I leaned back in my chair, trying to figure out another approach. I started to enter Evelyn's name before realising I didn't know her surname. I typed it in anyway but when I hit search, the database came back with over six hundred matches. I tried to cast my mind back to the opening credits. I could remember Ray's name being listed, but no Evelyn. I wondered if that was her real name or if she had used another name professionally.

I hurried home from work that evening, half-expecting to find Ray still in bed, or watching his damn movie again. He wasn't there. He'd left no message to say where he'd gone or what time he'd be back. I felt angry with him, finding it hard to believe he could treat me this way.

The windows were still boarded up, small cracks of evening light bleeding through the gaps. I turned on the television and pressed play. I watched the opening credits, knowing I wouldn't see her name. I skipped forward to her first appearance then slowed the disc to normal play. It was there, what I was too stupid to hear all along. Evelyn wasn't the name of the actress, but the character. I was about to skip ahead to the end credits when something familiar caught my attention. It was a view of the Golden Gate Bridge from the cliffs above China Beach. Sweat trickled down my back. Evelyn was there, searching for someone. She wore a black jacket and skirt. I recognised other places in the movie, places I had been to, alone or with Ray. At Ocean Beach. In the bar on Geary, my brother's forlorn voice singing about a woman he'd lost. As the story unfurled I realised that Ray wasn't trying to find

Evelyn. He was trying to get away from her. I could see how it would end, the whole twisted plot curling in on itself. I didn't want to watch any more of it but I didn't have the strength to turn away. Even before they appeared I knew what the end credits would reveal. The woman who played Evelyn Elms was Grace James.

Appalled, I backed away from the TV screen. It was impossible. I would not accept it. I turned towards the door and saw Ray standing there, frail and dark-eyed, a desperate smile on his face. "It's okay, Evelyn," he said. "We found each other."

AMBER RAIN

Neil Williamson

When Colin raised the window to replenish the living room's baked air, he noticed the first specks of water on the pane. It was a fine rain, the kind that effervesces, prickles your skin. He watched the tiny droplets coalesce, gain enough mass to overcome the surface tension and stream down the glass. Each little river scintillated, distinctly pale amber in colour. An unnatural shade – even for Glasgow. Even in a time like now.

Of course, it was only a trick of the light. The city's atmosphere was never *that* toxic. Inevitably, after so many days of unrelenting heat, a foundry of cloud had massed over the city, compressing the evening's remaining sunlight to the weak radiance of cooling ingots. Soon those foundry walls would break open, flash-firing the city with summer lightning, and cooling its inhabitants with such a deluge that the pavements would steam.

Down in the street a woman was crossing the road. Colin only saw her for a moment before she darted between two vans, but there was something about her. Her hair was different, the style of her clothing – a strappy blue summer dress – unfamiliar, and it had been, what, eight months? He almost didn't recognise her, but he was sure that it was Paddy.

When the door entry rasped he almost ran to let her in.

Paddy was soaked through, and immediately headed to the bathroom to dry off. To give himself something to do, Colin slipped a few slices of cheese on toast under the grill. He remembered to be liberal with the Tabasco.

"Smells good," Paddy said, sitting at the table. She had found his old black jumper. It had always suited her, the way it framed the old Goth-chic cosmetic pallor she had favoured back then. She looked good in it now too – but in a different way. She'd allowed her hair to grow, washed out the wacky colours. Now it coiled loose around her face, strands clumped with some residual dampness she'd failed to towel out. Her face too – minus the habitual heavy application of eyeliner and the glittering encrustations of those once beloved piercings, she looked somehow both older and childish. At any rate, life appeared to be treating her well. The pallor gone, her skin radiated health. A sheen of perspiration anointed her brow, nose, cheeks.

"What?" she said.

Caught staring, Colin switched off the grill, and slipped the contents of the pan on to a plate which he placed in the centre of the table. "It's just a surprise to see you." He sat opposite her. "A nice one," he added, nudging the plate towards her.

She took a slice, chewed off a corner, trailing filaments of melted cheese. "Thanks, Col," she said at length, watching him pour two mugs of treacle-coloured tea.

"Thanks for what?" he said.

"I dunno –" she stalled, brow creasing as she searched for the right words. Steam from her mug rose into her face.

"I think I expected you to tell me where to go. But I should have known you wouldn't. You always were too nice by half." Paddy closed her eyes, inhaled the vapour. "It's so difficult now – to know about people," she said, opened her eyes, offered a tiny smile. "Thanks for still being you."

Colin shrugged, returned the smile. As if still being himself was nothing, had required no effort to reconstitute his personality from the mess she'd left behind. As if *still being himself* could possibly have any kind of meaning. After five years with her, as a single entity – sharing a life, a home, a tight band of friends. Then four months of slick, almost invisible unravelling. One splintered evening of mutual abuse, the subject of which: an itemised mobile phone bill and one particular friend. Alan. Half an hour walking the streets to cool off, mentally drafting plans of conciliation. Then coming home to Life Without Paddy.

Colin was surprised to find that the anger he thought he had been saving up had somehow leaked away. He wasn't even interested any more in how the Paddy and Alan thing had panned out. There was no longer any resonance of the fury and frustration. In recent months, his flat had become a place he came back to only to sleep, or more often *not sleep*. It had been too long since anyone but himself had as much as spoken aloud in these rooms. He was just glad she was here.

"So, can I stay?" Her voice cracked.

"Reading my mind again?" An old shared joke.

"Yeah, and it's about as entertaining as that paper you work for," she rejoined. A spark of the Paddy he used to know. Funny how suddenly the flat felt a little like a home again.

The way it had felt when they were together.

Before the aliens came.

Colin watched television while Paddy took a bath. A political discussion show murmured away on turned-down volume. He was tired of hearing the protracted post-mortems caused by the Prime Minister's resignation the previous month. On one side it had become a blustering defence from the loyal elements within his own party – John MacDougall, they claimed, was ill, his unexpected resignation made under severe stress. At the same time, the opposition parties had launched into a feeding frenzy at the political opportunity, clamouring for a general election. Both sides continued to make nervous denials that, despite the recent claims of the country's erstwhile leader, the UK was *not* currently, nor indeed ever had been, host to agencies of extra terrestrial origin.

Colin flipped channels. Question Time was replaced by recent footage of the man himself. MacDougall looked haggard, spoke with uncharacteristic hesitancy, but Colin could see neither duplicity nor delusion in the man's face as he mouthed the words that had become his last sound bite.

"I'm sorry."

And, "No, I can't explain."

And, "There's nothing we can do."

Colin muted the television entirely, but the screen continued to sheet blue lightning around the room.

Eventually, back along the hall, the bathroom door opened. Colin waited a few minutes, switched off the set and followed Paddy through to the bedroom. She was lying on her side, facing away from the window, into darkness.

He lay down behind her. Not too close, but close enough to smell apple-scented bath-soak, and the dampness of her hair. He couldn't tell if she was asleep, but then she reached round and pulled his arm around her. He drifted off trying to listen to her breathing, but could hear only the rattle of rain against the window.

The only difference between Holyrood and Westminster was in the accents of the squabbling. The paper had sent Colin over to Edinburgh to photograph Hibernian's new French striker down at Easter Road. Afterwards, he'd taken the opportunity to drop in at the Scottish Parliament where the Education Minster was unveiling a new pay deal for teachers.

Colin watched from the gallery as the minister tried stoically to deliver her speech over the heckles of the Scottish Nationalists. He sighted her through the viewfinder of his SLR, focused the telephoto lens on the tension in her neck, around her eyes. A wayward strand of hair slipped across her face. He snapped her flicking it away.

"Does any of this *matter* any more?" A skinny, middle-aged man in denims farther along in the public gallery. He looked like he'd neither slept nor washed for days. The minister stammered to a halt, looking up at him, able to continue only when he had been removed by security. Colin framed a quick shot of the two uniforms huckling the guy away. That would fit nicely into the paper's *Out The Aliens* campaign – the most public face of a pressure group aimed at getting the government to back the ex-Prime Minister's story, and come clean about what was happening. A typically tabloid effort, but it was having an effect.

It didn't matter if MacDougall was lying, or mad, or, against all odds, actually telling the truth. Half the country believed him – half the world, it seemed, and many had also had, if not similar, then analogous experiences. Reports came in daily, everyone had a story, knew someone, who knew someone, whose husband, mother, next door neighbour had had an experience of some sort. *Aliens in My Watering Can, Aliens in The Television, Aliens in the Little Chef off the M74, My Grandfather is a Grey, My Teacher is a Pod Person, I was Seduced on Rohypnol by TV's Lieutenant Worf – and I was saving myself for Mr Spock.* The stories flooded in from Glasgow and Edinburgh, the remote reaches of the Highlands, all throughout Britain, Europe, the planet. From Finland to Portugal, Argentina to Canada, and oh, by God, yes, all over the States. Only, there was no evidence. No pictures. No recordings. Just stories. Few of the details were wholly consistent.

The media were loving it. Even if the world wasn't being visited, it was gripped by the *idea* of such an invasion. A quiet, nervous paralysis. Markets were down, investments delayed, everyone waiting. The politicians tried to keep things ticking along, but since they could neither officially prove nor disprove the stories it could only look like they were covering something up. The editors played the uncertainty like expert anglers.

When he returned to the flat it was so still that Colin assumed immediately that Paddy was gone. He had spent all day mulling over their strange, edgy encounter the previous evening, and had half convinced himself he'd dreamt the whole thing. He stooped to retrieve the mail from behind the door, placing the envelopes unopened on top of the pile of bills and circulars and invitations to take out new credit cards, and wondered what it took to upset things enough to bring society finally to a halt. If it was true that aliens were among them, how could it be that he could still buy fresh pesto in Safeway? How could any credit card company seriously offer him a free couple of grand and trust that he'd pay it back, plus interest? How did the buses run, and new movies open at the cinema? If the world was so overrun with extra terrestrials, surely it would all stop. And everyone would *know*. For sure. There would be photographs in the papers, amateur video footage, pictures of grey humanoids, shadowy space ships, *something*; interviews with astronomers, global summits, vigilantes, public unrest, martial law.

And because people would know, they'd recognise that they needed one another.

And Paddy would still be there.

For the second time in two days she surprised him. On the kitchen table Colin found two supermarket bags. Their contents: one bottle of Merlot, one packet of fresh cappelletti, one jar of pesto, mushrooms, capsicums, and a bag of salad leaves, with a bottle of Caesar dressing. Snap. His own bags contained the same – minus the dressing. Paddy had been a selective food lover. She knew what she liked, and if she liked it, she loved it. She'd hated Caesar dressing.

He found her in the bathroom. Colin hovered at the door, despite having seen her naked countless times before. From there he could see one leg arched above the rim of the bath. The leg glistened pale and pink under the stark bathroom light, and he could just make out part of what looked like a tattoo – a recent one, raw and scabbed – as the leg oscillated gently from side to side. The rhythmic lapping of water counterpointed their conversation.

"Thanks for getting the food in," Colin said. "And for remembering that I like that Caesar dressing. But you should have got something we both like."

"It's only food, Col. It doesn't matter to me. I don't have much of an appetite these days." Her voice sounded strange. Perhaps it was the acoustics that made it sound so distant. For a moment Colin wondered if she were on something. The thought was as absurd as the idea of Paddy having no appetite – she didn't even smoke. But then people changed, didn't they?

True to her word, when they had prepared the food, Paddy did little more than push it around her plate. Colin fared little better, the kitchen's humidity whittling his hunger to a vague discomfort. They made up for it, though, with the wine. They drank so they wouldn't have to talk, then took the second bottle into the bedroom to watch the now spectacularly torrential rain. It hissed onto the pavement outside, streamed down the drains, flared amber on the window glass as the streetlights stuttered to life.

Paddy turned away from the window, moved her palm from the pane to his face. Her hand was cool and clammy. There was something in her expression. Some kind of need. Colin remembered that she didn't articulate her feelings well, often needing help in finding the words.

"Paddy, what's this all about?" he began.

"Shh." She stopped his words with her fingers, and then as if they might leak through between them, with her lips, ensuring whatever he said was swallowed down inside her.

When they made love, skin to skin on white sheets rucked beneath them like time-frozen waves, Colin noticed that her skin was damp with sweat from the outset, and for the first time he wondered if she might be ill. Perhaps a flu virus of which she was unaware; maybe something more serious. The need he had sensed in her was obvious now in the hunger of her mouth, the clutch of her hands on his back, the strength and urgency of her legs, pulling him deep into her, where she boiled around him with a scalding liquidity. It was as if her entire body were deliquescing from the inside out. And yet, even locked in her embrace, Colin felt external to the process. There had always been an element of this with Paddy. She was so contained. It was her way, when she allowed herself to be fucked, to keep her pleasures to herself, internalised. Eyes closed, focussing on whatever was going on inside her, acknowledging nothing else. When she came, her breath sounded like steam.

While Paddy slept immediately, twisted around with ropes of sheet, Colin found rest harder to come by. He was staring at the wedge of light fanning across her thigh, illuminating the tattoo. He could see now that it was a swallow – so unoriginal that it could have been picked at random from a tattoo parlour wall. The mundanity of it disappointed him. Outside he heard the occasional surf of cars passing along the rain-slicked street.

He was still awake when Paddy's sleeping body coiled itself tight and foetal and, shaking with tension, she uttered a sequence of throaty moans of such sexual intensity that he became immediately aroused, although he knew that her pleasure had nothing to do with him. Whatever caused Paddy such passion in her dreaming had more effect on her than he ever had. In a few minutes the shaking had subsided, her body relaxed, and the moans faded into the regular breathing of sleep.

It surprised Colin that Paddy persisted in hanging around. It was what he wanted, of course, but that he might get what he wanted did not seem right. She was waiting for him the next evening when he returned from a brass-monkey shift outside the Glasgow Sheriff Court where a prominent local mobster had been been convicted of several major drugs offences. Two frozen hours for a blanket-over-the-head shot at best.

Paddy was dressed for an evening out. Obviously she remembered that his Tuesday nights were habitually spent at the Carnarvon. This Tuesday Colin wasn't sure if he wanted to go, but Paddy persuaded him.

"It's good to keep these routines going, isn't it?" she said.

Colin didn't know what routines Paddy kept going. As far as he could tell she hadn't left his flat in two days.

The Carnarvon, A fair trek up to St Georges Road at the periphery of the West End, was all cigarette-burned leatherette and chipped Formica. They'd settled on it because the beer was cheap, there was no karaoke or covers band like the ear-splitting Young Neils, who 'rocked the free world' at the nearby Wintersgills at unpredictable intervals, and most of all because it had no more than a dozen other regulars. On Tuesdays they practically had the place to themselves.

That night, however, the pub was packed. They found Colin's friends crushed around a single table. Longer standing acquaintances raised eyebrows when they recognised Paddy. Colin looked around the assembly. Here were virtually all the people he might count as friends. A few: Dave, Archie, Ewan and Shell, were core Tuesday-nighters. Others were occasional attendees, partners or friends of friends. One or two faces he hadn't seen in years.

"The gang's all here," he said.

"Aye, and they're thirsty," replied Deepak, waving a half-full pint glass in his direction.

Glasses were filled and drained often during the evening, resulting in an unsteady megalith of towering glass on the table. Colin made the effort to keep the conversation varied, but inevitably it found its way back to the subject they were all trying to avoid. Ewan was forced to expend a deal of energy defending the numerous television science fiction series of which he was a fan. Their anthro-centric, American aliens, he argued, could not be expected to prepare the world for the *real thing*. It was only entertainment after all. Nevertheless, Dave said, the images these shows presented, along with certain block buster movies, formed the basis of public expectation when it came to the extra terrestrial, and *this* – whatever *this* was that was currently being experienced – was just too strange to comprehend. It was so subtle, so tangential. "It's almost as if nothing is happening at all," he said.

"Maybe that's it," said Ewan. "And *this* is all some kind of mass delusion."

"A delusion so convincing that it fills the churches, and the B&Bs in Bonnybridge, and the morgue slabs with the ones who can't cope with it?" Shell replied quietly.

"Isn't that one definition of a religion?" someone else said. Colin couldn't see who. "Just what we need on this planet is a new religion." Two or three people laughed darkly.

"Religions usually require a measure of blind faith," Dave mused. "This is different. People are reacting to personal experiences here. Private raptures."

"Well, not me," said Ewan. "I've not seen a thing. And neither has my family, or to my knowledge anyone I know."

"Same here," said Dave, and a number of others chorused their agreement. Shell and Deepak looked into their drinks and said nothing. There was a dangerous moment then, that Colin saw with uncomfortable clarity. During that moment any one of them could have pursued the experiences of the group's tacit dissenters, but that would have turned the theoretical into the practical, and, in doing so, crowbarred open the carefully maintained consensus normality that persisted around the table. No-one did. The moment passed and the talk reverted to teasing Ewan about his choices of entertainment.

Shortly after, Paddy touched Colin's arm and asked to go home. He handed her the keys, not wishing to leave this island of camaraderie just yet. In the event, the talkers strove to keep going a little longer but the spirit of the gathering had been undermined, and people started to drift off into the night. Besides, he found himself worrying about Paddy.

When he got home he went straight to the bathroom. By the flaccid way she lay in the cooling water, only her nostrils and mouth breaking the surface, he thought that she had drowned. The way her hair floated like weed. The way her white skin, apart from the dark blot of the tattoo, goose-fleshed. The way her eyes stared, oblivious. Only the rapid puffs of breath steaming the air told him she was alive. That, and the mottled rashes chasing each other across her skin like the shadows of clouds. At first he hoped this effect was a trick of the water and light, but saw that it was too regular. The shifting shapes began at her sternum, and radiated outwards across her breasts and belly, sweeping down her arms and legs to her extremities, and then smoothly back again to the centre. Her face was a confusion of overlapping flushes. Colin burned with questions about this illness – it couldn't be anything else – but he could not talk to her like this.

Twenty minutes later Paddy came into the back room where he was leafing through some binders of old work. The blue towelling robe she wore was damp at the collar.

"Can I shoot you?" he asked. "Please."

She was crying, but nodded. "Over here?"

"Yes, the chair's good." He handed her the binder to look at while he set up his gear. "You've changed," he said, noticing that she had slipped a contact sheet out of its plastic pocket.

"I look so young in these," Paddy said with a small laugh. "Look at my hair. And all that make up. What was I like?"

"You were beautiful," Colin said, tightening the locks on his tripod. "But that's not what I'm talking about. You're like a completely different person to the Paddy that – " He hadn't meant to bring it up, but she already knew what was coming. "That left," he finished.

"Well, that's how it happens," he heard her say, as he reached behind the reflectors to flick the lights on. There was a defensive edge to her voice. "Sometimes people appear unrecognisable after a relationship has ended. Like you never knew the real person all that time, or they shed the personality you knew like an unwanted skin." She sounded like she meant it. If it hadn't been for her illness he might even have been convinced.

"That's not what I'm talking about either," he said, sighting through the viewfinder. "It's more subtle than that." He hadn't intended for her to take the robe off, but now it lay on the floor beside the chair he knew that he needed her to be as open to him as possible. The indirect lighting made the sheen on her skin luminescent. The tattoo glistened as if freshly inked. He focussed tight on the tattoo, squeezed off a shot. Tracked up the s-curve of her hip and waist to the well of her navel, took a second.

Paddy sighed. "You always did pay too much attention to the details," she said.

"What do you mean?" A curve of breast obscured by an arm. The hairs at the crook of the elbow sleek with moisture.

"Nothing," she said. "It's just you. The way you look at the world, noticing the tiny things, but never quite aware of the whole picture."

Was that how he came across? Myopic and obsessed with minutiae? He didn't think that was true, it was just that he knew the world at large would roll on whether he noticed it or not – so why bother? But this was straying from the point. This wasn't about him.

"I want to know what it's like," he said. The corner of her mouth twitched with conflicting emotions. He photographed that too.

"I can't tell you," she said. "You wouldn't –"

"I wouldn't understand?" he interrupted.

"I can't explain it. It's like a new kind of weather, or a new note squeezed into the scale, or like a colour no-one's ever seen before. How can you explain something like that?" A bright eye, hazel iris on pure white. Pupil wide and depthless. If he could focus tight enough, Colin thought he might be able to see *it* inside her, looking out. Whatever this thing was that caused her illness.

"Please try," he said. "What do they look like?"

"I don't know," she said. "I never saw anything. One minute I was talking on the phone to my mum, and then –"

"I need to know," he persisted.

"Col," she said. "It's no use. I think it's different for everybody. Maybe some people *do* see little green men, and maybe some see God, and some Yogi-fucking-Bear. But not me. I think whatever it is – whatever *they* are – looks into people and finds something that no-one else has, perhaps the single element that makes them an individual, and then they tweak it to see what happens." There was a weariness in her voice now. He wondered if this illness was killing her.

"I don't know if they are aliens or not," she said, "but I do know they weren't here a month ago – none of this weird shit was happening a month ago – so it's likely isn't it? Whoever they are, I think they are simply curious about humans. They're just giving us a prod and a poke."

He put the camera down. "I envy you," he said.

"Do you? I'm scared. I don't think I'm even human any more."

In the night, when they held each other, the warmth of skin, the strength of muscle and bone, the vitality of two pulses, Colin thought he was convinced that Paddy was still human. What else could she be?

Later when she slept he got out of bed and took a long bath. Eventually the water cooled and his skin wrinkled. When he started to shiver he climbed out, dried off and returned to bed.

In the morning Paddy was gone. Really gone this time. He knew it from the moment he woke in an empty bed, but he checked the back room, the living room, the kitchen. In the bathroom the towels were lying in the bath where he had left them the previous night.

Even knowing she was gone he went out to look. His street deserted, he instinctively headed towards Great Western Road, despite the fact that at rush hour on a Thursday morning it would be so busy that anyone could vanish instantly amid the traffic and crowd. Except it too was deserted. No cars in motion, no trucks rumbling, no people bustling, shouting, chatting. It was as if the world had been emptied in the night, save for himself. This was what an alien invasion was supposed to be like. Of course, it was just an impression caused by arriving at exactly the wrong moment, and it only lasted an instant or two. Then, as if a hidden switch were thrown, or all the world's traffic lights turned green, a butcher's shop door opened and a young mother emerged with a push chair, quickly followed by others from other shops, doorways and side streets, and two surges of traffic filled the empty road. In seconds the moment had passed, and the world, as far as Colin could tell, was as it always had been.

There was no doubt now that Paddy was gone.

When the first drops of rain arced out of the sky, Colin leaned against the frontage of the newsagent and watched. There was something odd. He looked more closely. These drops, disobeying the usual dynamics of falling liquids, were perfect spheres. In fact they reminded him of nothing less than miniature versions of the glass marbles he had owned as a kid.

He held out a palm. The globes of rain landed in his hand, intact for an instant before bursting and seeping away. Cementing the likeness to marbles in his mind, was the writhing twist of life colouring the centre of each.

Colin wondered if anyone else in the world had noticed that the rain was amber, or if he were the only one touched by the invisible aliens to be allowed to see them.

351073

Jeff Gardiner

The day my daughter was born was both the worst and best day of my life, although at the time I only felt the devastation. My wife, Fran, had been ill for some years and we had assumed that we were not to be blessed with children. So when she gleefully told me one night after parish council that she thought she might be pregnant I whispered a prayer as she stepped into the bathroom to try the home test. She had been good enough to wait patiently for me, wondering when my parishioners would finally release me for the night. They did frequently forget that I also had a home and a wife who deserved my time and attention.

The good Lord answered our prayer and we made an appointment with our doctor who did very little except congratulate us and tell Fran what she couldn't eat. We saw the midwife, had the scans and did all the classes as a couple. I was determined to be a dedicated father and share all things equally. Fran also worked full-time and her salary was worth more than twice mine.

On the fateful day it was clear that things were wrong from the beginning. I was hustled out of the way and nobody would answer my frantic questions, including God, as it seemed at the time. So I didn't see the birth as it all happened behind closed doors. They sent two smartly dressed manager-types to tell me the shocking news. Fran had not survived, but I had a baby girl. My brother and sister-in-law were with me at the time, hugging and holding me as I shook and sobbed; but it seemed like I was alone in a void. Only my faith kept me sane.

It was many hours before I could bring myself to look at the baby. Our baby. My baby. The hospital decided to keep her in for a few days under observation and I was advised to go home and rest. I did as I was told. My team Rector came round to pray with me and told me he would look after things at my church for the next few weeks whilst I sorted things out. I was extremely grateful to him and to the overwhelming support I received from the many friends in my wonderful congregation. Food was brought round as well as flowers and cards with loving messages of support and kindness.

My neighbour took me back to hospital the next day to meet my daughter. When I saw her I broke down, crying with more passion than I had felt for over twenty years. The tears were for the loss of Fran and the wasted dreams; but also for the joy of seeing such a delicate and vulnerable creature squirming and holding out her hands in need of warmth and security. She had to be my priority now.

Of course, Fran and I had discussed names, but for some reason they didn't seem appropriate any more. One part of me thought I should choose Fran's favourite, which was Leanne, but a voice in me told me it wasn't right. When I looked at her little face and blinking eyes they weren't the eyes of a Leanne. I wondered if I should call her Fran, but it's important for a child to be an individual and not a copy of her parents.

The first night that I took my precious baby home, I refused all offers of help and company, except for the midwife visitors, and lay with her on my bed, gazing lovingly at her minute perfection. She screamed and made a mess, but who cares? She was mine: a gift from God to prove that all is not bad in the world. I had expected myself to hate God for not saving my wife. But instead I thanked Him for this little miracle.

As I lay on the bed next to the strangely gurgling creature beside me, I wondered again about a name. We had bought books that listed thousands, but none sounded completely suitable. It was as I lay there, my head twisted towards her leg that stretched up awkwardly and hovered before my eyes, that I saw she still wore the hospital identity tag on her little ankle. I stared at it and was stunned to see the word 'ELOISE'. And it was so perfect. My little Eloise. It was pretty and elegant. But why on earth was it already written on her band? Who had named her? I gently took hold of it and stared hard for a few minutes. The name Eloise stood out but then the letters following it were meaningless symbols. And then I chuckled at my stupidity, having to stop myself from choking. What an idiot. I carefully sat up and read it the other way up. It was just a list of numbers printed out in computerised digits and the last six numbers were 351073, which upside down looked exactly like ELOISE.

I kissed Eloise and put her into her crib, ready to sleep for a few hours until her next feed.

As she grew up Eloise took great delight in the story of her naming and was already telling people how it was fate: a message from above. When she looked it up she found that Eloise meant 'noble one', which was very appropriate, for she grew into a very beautiful and confident young lady. She took to signing herself as 351073, which confused people, but was always a good conversation starter. When she found she could program her name into a calculator, it was the beginning of a whole language created by her and her best friends. In her teens she acquired a mobile and started sending and receiving rude and silly messages by text, turning the phone upside down to read them. I didn't think to stop her. With the tragedy at the beginning of her life the least I could do was allow my Eloise to have some fun.

Whilst my faith is of great importance to me I had resolved from the very beginning never to force my beliefs on Eloise. I consider myself a liberal preacher, who teaches tolerance and compassion, rather than fire and brimstone. Being shaky on eschatological theology, I preferred to base sermons on the beatitudes of Christ that encouraged love and peace amongst our fellow men. Of course I wanted Eloise to continue coming to church and build up her own independent Christian faith, but alas, like so many modern young people she soon became bored and disillusioned and couldn't wait to explore more exciting and fulfilling experiences. The silly thing is I understood how she felt and had been expecting it when she finally came to me and asked if she could go round to her friend's one Sunday morning. I smiled and nodded and she never stepped foot inside a church again.

I guessed that she was meeting boys and probably sleeping with them. But I preferred not to know. One time she came home drunk and I tried to act casual when she came down the next morning with a hangover, but my laughter was hollow.

I blame myself for her active and continuing interest in numerology. It stemmed from my discovery of her name and she convinced herself that her name was pre-ordained; somehow given to her by providence.

She discovered the arcane writings of Pythagoras who proclaimed that you could discover the essence of any person by working out their root number. From these mysterious figures, secrets of great spiritual significance could be identified concerning one's future and personality.

Eloise would try to explain things to me with immense patience.

"The basic principles of the cosmos can be expressed through numbers…"

"That's where you're losing me, darling. What do you mean by 'basic principles of the cosmos'?"

"I mean that mathematics can help us gain a greater knowledge of the metaphysical world."

"Oh, really? Blimey and I hated maths when I was younger."

"Don't take the mick, Dad. I don't laugh at your beliefs." She didn't like it when I was flippant about the things she took seriously. I didn't want her to give up or get defensive.

"No you're right, I'm sorry. I think I'm just being a bit thick. Do go on."

Then Eloise would blind me with complex aphorisms that were either meaningless mumbo-jumbo or mind-bending paradoxes. Some of her proverbs made good sense though.

"There is no absolute truth: only the truth of the Absolute," she enigmatically confided to me one day. As I thought about it I realised that we might have common ground.

"I think I can happily say I agree with you on that one," I responded triumphantly. Obviously our definitions of who or what the 'Absolute' might be would probably differ greatly. So I left it there. She would still hug me and cuddle up with me on the sofa even at the age of eighteen. Eloise was a very affectionate and thoughtful daughter.

Then she would leave me little notes in unexpected places: the fridge, my underwear drawer, or even clipped to my latest sermon. 'The secrets of nature will guide humanity to a harmonious destiny,' it would say. Or 'Man is not body. The heart, the spirit is man – Paracelsus.' Now I had no quibble with these little soundbites. I wasn't too sure what was meant by 'secrets of nature' – as long as she wasn't dabbling in witchcraft. And Paracelsus may not be my hero, but I was glad that Eloise appreciated that life is also spiritual. I certainly believe it – being a vicar.

The part I had a problem understanding was when she seemed

obsessed with numbers. She frequently quoted Pythagoras: 'Every man has been made by God in order to acquire knowledge and contemplate'. This sounded wrong to me – far too Gnostic for my liking. Surely love and peace are more important than knowledge.

Above her bed Eloise had made a huge colourful poster with a collage of pictures of herself with family and friends, including two with me. These photographs framed a carefully lettered quotation from her favourite Greek that said, 'All things can be expressed in numerical terms because all things are ultimately reducible to numbers'. Then beneath it in a kaleidoscope of colours was her own numerical name: 351073. That one left me cold. I tried to explain to her that she was so much more than just that number, but she just laughed and said with a twinkle, "Well, you can always shorten my name to 31773." It took me a while to work that one out.

Her interest in occult writing didn't stop there, though. Eloise found a fascination in Kabbalism, alchemy, druidry and any mystical system that delighted in number, calendars, cycles or secret alphabets. Her conversation quickly turned to concepts of 'astral projection' or 'transpersonal consciousness', whatever the heck that is. When she tried to explain to me the Tree of Life from the Kabbalah, supposedly a logical map with many levels that guide the adept into a so-called 'Divine Union', I stared at its eleven circles and twenty-two connecting pillars and could make little sense of its context or meaning.

Eloise saw me shaking my head and squinting.

"You see, men have wisdom, but women have understanding." She smiled as if this explained all my doubts and frustrations.

It was from then that things started getting really strange.

Eventually, she left home and travelled. I got e-mails from New Zealand, Israel, Thailand and Greece all from username 351073. She apologised for leaving me and hoped I didn't miss her too much. But I missed her terribly. I had moved to a new parish and even become Rector but life without Eloise was empty and too quiet for my liking. I missed the cut and thrust of debate and harmless conflict that always occurred between us. It's fair to say that Eloise challenged me to think for myself, rather than just rely on what I had been socialised into believing. I don't mean I lost my faith or felt any great desire to become a druid or join the Freemasons or anything, I was just aware that she helped me to think for myself – which has got to be a good thing. Even Christianity, which has a strict doctrine, scripture and creed, allows the individual to think out of the box on occasions. Or at least, in the Church of England it does.

Some of her messages became encoded and unreadable as she began to develop her own system of employing numbers and symbols to represent objects and people. I don't just mean like this lazy way of writing text messages by missing out vowels and using '4' instead of 'for' or where your friend is your 'best m8'. She had contrived a complex system of numbers that became letters when written slightly differently then turned upside down. But I refused to decipher these daft cryptographs. Sending them back to her I demanded that she communicated using proper Standard English. I didn't hear from her again for several months.

When I did eventually receive a message from her she was in Egypt and she sent me a reading of my 'Life Path Number', which I'd never heard of before, but is apparently 6. According to this my inner being is characterised by feelings of responsibility, protection and balance, whilst I am ostensibly community-oriented. Well, it seemed accurate enough although I had no idea how much she had just made up from her knowledge of me. I took it as a sign that I was forgiven. But then she said she was concerned about my 'Existential Emanation Integer' that pointed to some kind of tragedy, but would also lead to personal awareness and self-knowledge, helping me ultimately to contribute to the universal order. Of course I scoffed, as I do when I read in my stars that I will meet somebody. When don't you?

Her next e-mail announced that she was coming home at the end of the month and I wept with joy. I hadn't seen her for four years.

The changes were obvious. She had cut her hair short and was unnecessarily using dark eye make-up. And then I saw Eloise's tattoo. It was a sunny day and we were in the garden playing cricket – something we had done together since she was about three. She turned and bent down to pick up the ball when I saw a flash of something blue printed on the small of her back. My first reaction was to wonder how painful it had been as that part is so close to the pelvic bone. Her smile disappeared when I asked her about it.

"Is it a skull and crossbones? Or maybe 'I love Dad'?" I smiled pointing to the side of her hip.

"Neither, although it's true that I love you."

Little moments like that warm parents' hearts.

After some convincing she showed me the design. It was a number – what else. 5151.

"Another cryptic message?" I asked narrowing my eyes profoundly. "Let's see. Five thousand one hundred and fifty-one... hmmm... five one five one. Nope. It's not a boy's phone number is it, or the name of a band?" We giggled together but she still wouldn't tell me. "You see, what confuses me is that it can be reduced down to, um, two fives are ten plus two is twelve, which is further reduced to three. A magic number?"

"Well, I'm impressed with your knowledge of simple numerology, Dad. Perhaps you're not a completely lost soul just yet." She stabbed me with her forefinger. "I may well love you, but it doesn't stop you being extremely dim. Watch, Mr. Thicky." She turned around, walked up to our apple tree and cartwheeled into a very neat handstand. 'ISIS' was emblazoned clearly upon her bare midriff. It was on her front and back, like she was a stick of seaside rock with the name running through her.

I did extensive research on Isis as Eloise wouldn't tell me the significance. I knew Isis was from Egyptian mythology, but I discovered that she was a supreme goddess with unlimited power; an Earth Mother who became associated with burial and resurrection. Most interestingly, she was considered the goddess of wisdom who initiates people into occult mysteries. I was led to the writings of Madame Blavatsky, but found them vacuous and artificial.

I had been wondering about the strange symbols on Eloise's bag: horns clasped round a circle. These were symbols of Isis – the circle was a solar disc. Eloise also had a bracelet with an ankh dangling as a charm. She did explain to me that the ankh was a symbol of the unity of body and soul.

Family and friends were glad to see her return, but some spoke to me behind her back and warned me of her 'satanic' tendencies. This made me angry. Okay, so she had gone a bit hippy and new age, but she believed in love and spirituality, albeit in a slightly unorthodox form.

Some of my parishioners even dared to suggest that I should kick her out of the house, and it's likely that they thought I was a bad father and a worse clergyman – one who couldn't even convert his own daughter. Nobody said it, but I knew that some doubted my faith and integrity.

We spent a wonderful few months together going on picnics and walks; to theme parks and cricket matches. Eloise spoilt me, and her company made me so happy and content. She didn't like to talk about herself much and when I mentioned anything mystical or numerical she went silent and rapidly changed the subject. The only time she responded was when I thanked her for the Life Path reading.

"It certainly described me."

"You've always been generous and you put others first." She hugged me and skipped off a little way before stopping to let me catch her up.

"Not in any way detrimental to you, I hope," I asked anxiously.

"Don't be silly, Dad. I always felt loved and cherished. You have no need to worry." She looked me in the eye as she spoke. "I've always felt needed and secure. That's the gift you gave me. You've allowed me to be independent – to think for myself. You have no idea what that means."

Eloise took my hand and we walked a long way in silence. My heart was on fire.

"It's because of you that I can do what I have done."

"What do you mean?"

At first she was silent, gathering her thoughts. "You must promise not to interrupt. Let me finish before you say anything."

I nodded assent.

"My name was the first sign…"

I was about to speak but remembered my promise.

"… but then my first real awareness of my metaphysical destiny came when I calculated and read my own life numbers. I kept checking them and had them verified independently and I knew then that I couldn't escape my fate."

I was still fighting the urge to ask a million questions, but I kept it to a dumb, quizzical look.

"You see, whatever way it was done, I came out as 22."

My blank face revealed my ignorance as to the significance of this.

"22 is the master number. It denotes a visionary – a leader on this plane of existence. It endows the individual with an inner power. The number 22 is a sign of enlightenment and individuation."

"So what does that make you? Some sort of chosen one?" I was shocked by such an heretical idea. What would my dear congregation think of me now with my daughter claiming to be some kind of prophet or messiah?

"Do you believe in the concept of Immanence?"

"I believe that God's spirit is in all things, because he created everything."

"God is one way of understanding the divine. I believe that the divine is manifest in all things and that man is a microcosm of our spiritual universe. The purpose of life is to seek inner knowledge, contemplate its mysteries and follow the paths to the World of Emanation. Some people are put on this world with a higher knowledge and awareness of their Divine-Self. These leaders are ordained to guide others towards that same blissful and harmonious destiny."

"And that leader is you?" I said it calmly and casually.

"It began with my name and it was you who found my name. I have that to thank you for."

But that was not what I wanted to hear. I should have got angry with her and told her to see sense. I didn't. Instead I stood there dumbstruck, watching my daughter lose all sense of reason.

She stepped forward with a serene look on her beautiful face and embraced me.

"I love you, Dad. I'll always love you. Please don't ever be angry with me."

It felt like goodbye. Why would she be saying goodbye? But stupidly I ignored the warnings in my head. And the next day she had gone.

I mourned her then. I raged and smashed up the things around me. I swore at people. Belongings were trashed and broken. People were too frightened to see me. Feeling my life was over I sank into a deep depression and could not continue with my ministry. Where was my so-called loving God now? I swore at him and cursed his name.

The bishop sensibly told my church that I was on long-term sick leave whilst he took responsibility for the everyday running, along with the parish wardens. They found a curate who agreed to take Sunday services for the next few months. Encouraged to seek counselling and help, I tried to pull myself out of my morose stupor. Where the hell was Eloise? How could I find her? She didn't answer her e-mails and she didn't carry a phone.

From that moment I was tortured by numbers cascading in my dreams, devouring all my thoughts. I saw significance in all figures and digits. My heart leapt when I got a new visa card and there in the middle of the long number on the front were six letters in exactly the right order: 351073. My first thought was that she was somehow contacting me, but then I wondered if it was, as she said, a mark of destiny. What if we were all subject to some cosmic fate – a pattern that had been set for eternity?

Other weird things began to happen. Or did they? Perhaps my mind was deluding me. Or maybe I was just seeing things for the first time that have always been around me. When I finally struggled out on my own, unshaved and watched warily by many familiar passers-by, my weekly shopping came to £51.51. What was the likelihood of that? Was Eloise, or someone else, playing a game with me?

I tried e-mailing and phoning anybody who might know her. When I called the police they asked on what grounds I considered her 'missing' and even though I tried my best to explain, they concluded that she was just a religious nut and advised me to contact some specialist service and counsellor. I had images of myself kidnapping and deprogramming her, but it was just wish fulfilment.

Eventually via search engines and a lot of good luck I discovered a website entitled '5151:ISIS'. Clicking on the hyperlink 'Isis Within' I found a long explanation of how numerology had been used to identify a master adept, called a 'human-divine'. This certain individual had discovered that she was an incarnation of Isis and that the Universal Spirit had chosen her to lead humanity into their rightful harmonious destiny, known as Bliss. I wondered at first if 'Bliss' was a drug reference and that Eloise had just got caught up with some kind of hippy, psychedelic malarkey.

I tried to contact Eloise through the website, but the only reply I got told me that I must visit Bliss. Nobody would give me any more information. After hours of surfing the web I was ready to give up for the night, when it struck me that I must think cryptically. How would Eloise refer to Bliss? Eventually, I found a new website called 55178.com and imagined in my head her voice calling me Mr. Thicky. I was shaking as I read the introductory page and I recognised her words and the familiar imagery of ankh, horns and disc. The references to the work of the 'human-divine', the reincarnation of Isis, amazed and stunned me. My own daughter was the leader of a cult. She had supposedly cured people and performed miracles, giving accurate readings of people's futures and was considered a spiritual leader. The secrets were communicated through the arcane numbering that she had developed, connected with various ancient alphabets and Kabbalistic diagrams.

As Isis, Eloise seemed to believe that universal order would come about when she re-entered the underworld to be reunited with Osiris. She described herself as the most perfect microcosm: the key to the Macrocosm.

"My destiny," she wrote, and I could hear her voice saying the words, "is to leave this material world and find the next plane of existence from where I shall be able to help and guide those who have reached the sphere of spirituality and who desire a guide into the Blissful Realm of the Divine. I await you there."

My hand was shaking as if I knew what to expect next. I managed to move the cursor, using the mouse, onto another link on a sidebar called 'Logging In'. Up came a small box that said 'Please Enter Existential Number'. Without thinking I typed in 351073, pressed return and waited.

At first the screen turned to static and I thought there was a fault. But then a dim image became apparent – some kind of video clip. There before my eyes was my baby – my daughter, Eloise. When she spoke to me I felt my heart leap within my ribcage.

"Hello, Dad."

I responded as if she was in the room with me.

"Hello, my darling. How are you?"

But, of course, she didn't respond. She just kept speaking. It was a recording – but from when?

"Dad, I know you won't understand what I'm doing, but I don't want you to be angry or upset. I've found my true purpose in life – and how many people can say that much, huh? Just as you believe you

91

followed your vocation into the church, I know that this is my harmonious destiny. Just as you believe your Jesus died for the salvation of mankind, so I believe that fate has created a path for me, which will benefit humanity. I couldn't tell you about it before because I knew you would try to talk me out of it. You understand about rituals – you have plenty in the church. Well, these universal rituals exist in cycles and it is time once more for Isis to return to the underworld."

To my initial horror the camera panned out to show her standing on a cliff edge. I didn't recognise the location. It was some kind of gorge or canyon. Then I was aware of my own faltering breath as I watched through tearful eyes.

"Death is not the end, Dad. I know you believe it. Let it strike no fear in you. Death can only bring peace and is a new step on a never-ending journey. Always look beyond and believe in the union of spirits."

I was weeping silently as I watched her signal to someone off camera. She turned back to the camera, which zoomed in on her face. Then mouthed the words, "I love you, Dad," and her face was blissful and serene. The picture faded back to a screen of static white-noise and she was gone from me.

I expected to be horrified and shocked, but I wasn't. Strangely, I felt that I understood her sense of peace and that somehow her action was part of something much larger than my own reality. I couldn't begin to comprehend the enormity of universal truth because it stretched into an infinity that my mind could not cope with. But I knew I should be happy for her. It sounds mad, but she had done what she believed to be right and I must think beyond my own selfish loss. And wasn't her ultimate aim intrinsically the same as that of Christianity? Perhaps because of this I was beginning to grasp an even deeper meaning of spirituality. After all, what if she is right? What if she really is now at peace and part of some universal spirit, helping others in some supernatural way that we mortals cannot really comprehend? Perhaps there is more than one pathway to God? Who am I to say?

It would be with me forever, that image of my Eloise smiling to the camera, saying, 'I love you, Dad.' That held me together and even helped me to strengthen my own faith in God. I believe that the essence of Christianity is spiritual love, and accepting God's love is too distant and abstract. However, love through people, who are God's creation, makes complete and utter sense to me. Because of my daughter I have truly loved and been loved, and this has helped me to love God and others more; even making me realise that maybe I never wholly did before. Love is experienced through people and she taught me more about love than any scriptural passage. Somehow, mysteriously, I have been blessed. I always thought love could never be represented by a number. But love is a number for me. Love is 351073.

FOUR A.M.

Gary Couzens

A woman is sitting in the corner of the cafeteria, smoking. From time to time I glance across at her as I serve what few customers there are at this time of night. She's late thirties at a guess, lines under her eyes and framing her mouth, crow's feet. She's wearing a dark blue jumper with a hole worn into its elbow that reveals an off-white shirt. A pair of jeans fits tightly over thin boyish hips. She has an old pair of trainers on her feet. Her collar-length mouse-coloured hair is straggly, dull with grease. Homeless, is my first thought, but when I glance at her there's something about her that suggests otherwise. Something in the way she sits, the way she stares ahead of herself, indicates a spirit that hasn't been blasted by alcohol nor hardened by years on the streets. At times she seems to be falling asleep where she sits, then she jolts herself awake again.

Over in the other corner are three men, long-distance night drivers, seated round a table, their elbows spread so they cover most of the surface and no-one can intrude on their space. Men, none older than thirty, tattooed arms bulging out of T-shirt sleeves, jeans ridden down to display the top of the crack between their buttocks. Normally one of them might walk across to the woman, try to chat her up, even – if their luck's in – entice her to go with them to the back of their lorry. The youngest – he must be no more than twenty-one, with a skinhead crop – tried it on with me. But they spend most of their time drinking coffee, talking loudly and profanely, playing cards. Eventually they get up and leave.

Shortly afterwards, the woman comes across to me and asks: "Excuse me – can you tell me where the Ladies is?"

"Through that door, across the corridor to the right."

"Thanks." She smiles. "Thanks..." squinting at the namebadge pinned just above my left breast "... Louise."

I took the job at the motorway services the summer before the final year of my English degree. When I applied, the interviewer told me how the place was run: "We're open twenty-four hours a day, three hundred and sixty-five days a year. We never close." I was given the option of working nights and immediately took it. There was extra money in it and somehow the thought appealed to me. Quiet. Peaceful. A space all my own. They were worried at first about a woman being on her own in the cafeteria all night, but there's Mick most nights by the petrol pumps in case anything happens. Sometimes when it's slow I'll dial his extension and we'll chat. There's nothing to read into that: Mick's forty-six, married with two teenage children. It's simply friendliness. In any case, I've just broken up with my boyfriend and certainly don't want to involve myself with anyone else for a while. At least not before the new term.

When I'm alone, it's as if I'm travelling in a bubble, lit with a greenish-white fluorescent glare, floating in the darkness, captain and crew and sole passenger of my own ship. Sometimes there's the nightclub crowd, coming in for coffee until three or four in the morning. They know my name and, boys and girls both, chat to me. I hear all the gossip from the evening: who's scored with whom, who's fallen out with whom, whether so-and-so is pregnant. There are the long-distance lorry drivers. And occasionally lonely souls like the woman who's just gone to the Ladies.

She's gone five or ten minutes. The radio is on low. Before now, I've often wondered what's played during the night. If daytime is mainstream, and the evening is more offbeat, then maybe the night-time features sounds that are truly strange and exotic. Now I know the truth: languid ballads to soothe shiftworkers and lull any insomniacs who may be listening to sleep.

I rub my eyes. There are times when I wish I could be tucked up warm in bed. *Think of the money.* Using the glass front of the sandwich counter as a mirror, I renew my lipstick.

The woman comes back into the cafeteria. She has a cigarette in her hand, lit. She sits down where she was before; the ashtray in front of her is smeared grey with ash and full of stubbed-out ends. She must be chain-smoking: I haven't seen her use matches or a lighter or ask anyone else for one.

I'm wiping the tables clean, emptying the ashtrays into a rubbish sack, collecting the dirty plates. As I see her, I straighten, instinctively wiping my hands on my skirt. I go back behind the counter.

"Have you got the time please, Louise?"

"Just gone four."

She sighs. "Four A.M. When only the sad and lonely are awake. I couldn't have another coffee, please?"

"Sure." I set the percolator going. This'll be at least her third, and our filter coffee you can stand a spoon in. No wonder she needed the Ladies.

"How long have you worked here, Louise?" she says. Her voice is firm, glassy-grave, with the sort of standard English accent that could have come from anywhere.

"A couple of weeks. It's a summer job."

"Uh-huh." She nods, and takes another drag at her cigarette. "They pay you well?"

"It's okay."

"Any job's better than none, eh? In this day and age."

"I suppose." I draw the line at cleaning toilets. And as for stories of female students reduced to stripping or escorting or even prostitution to make ends meet... I shudder.

She turns to face me directly. Her eyes are pure deep blue.

"You don't get lonely, all alone in here?" she says.

I shrug. "No, not really. It's nice and calm. I'm alone with my thoughts."

"Your thoughts?" She sits back in her chair. "What do you think about, Louise?"

"Oh... things." The conversation has gone far enough; I can feel my cheeks burn. *Mind your own business*, I want to say, but don't. I don't want to be reported to the management for rudeness.

She sits back and glances at the side wall opposite her.

"I'm making you uncomfortable, I see."

"No, no."

"I am. Don't try to lie to me, Louise. I can spot a liar."

A pause. It's up to me to restart the conversation. "I'm sorry, I don't know your name...?"

"I haven't got a name."

"I'm sorry...?"

"I don't have a name. It's irrelevant. I left it behind with everything else. I'm nobody's daughter, nobody's wife, nobody's mother."

"I told you my name."

"No you didn't. It's on that badge, part of that uniform you wear. You wouldn't have told me otherwise, now would you?"

I bite my lip.

"How about you, then? It just says LOUISE. You have got a surname, haven't you? You're somebody's daughter."

"Jackson," I mutter.

She leans across to me, takes hold of my left hand. I tense, ready at the slightest signal to snatch it away. "No ring. You're not married. You don't have a child either, not that that necessarily follows these days." She smiles and takes another drag.

I shake my head.

"You see? That was a good guess. Do you have a boyfriend?"

"No..."

"No? You're full of surprises, Louise Jackson. I would have thought a pretty girl like you – you could have your pick..."

"If you must know, I've just split up with my boyfriend."

She sits back. "I'm sorry to hear that, Louise," she says, her voice taking a more conciliatory tone. "It's really sad when that happens. You'll still be friends...?"

"I – I hope so."

"He didn't hurt you or anything? Didn't beat you?"

At that, something flares inside me. "Of course he bloody didn't! It's none of your business!"

"Of course? There's no *of course* about it, Louise." She half-stands and lifts her jumper and shirt at the side. About her waist is a bruise, six inches wide, its colour changing from pink to yellowy-puce, to purplish-black at the centre.

I grimace.

"Makes you wince, doesn't it? Makes you sorry for me. My husband did that."

She lets her jumper fall back into place and sits down.

"How could you let him do that to you?" I say after a pause.

"I didn't *let him*, Louise. I could have got help. But I did nothing about it for years and years."

I guess what she's done: she's escaped, disappeared, somewhere where her husband can't find her. You can do that – just not turn up for work one day, simply vanish. A new life somewhere else. She's only recently escaped, too: that bruise is fresh.

"You just hope that he'll change, that he won't drink so much. That he'll improve. You say, do what you like with me but leave the child alone. Sometime you think it's *you*, your fault, you've somehow brought it upon yourself. And then you wake up and you say to yourself, listen you stupid bitch, he's like this, he's always been like this, he always will be like this and there isn't a single fucking thing you can do about it." She grinds out her cigarette in the ashtray and almost immediately there's another one, lit, in her hand. "And all the time that hate, that resentment, just grows and grows inside you like a knot in your stomach, it just grows and grows until you want to *burst*."

She holds up her hand, palm outwards, and at that instant five small blue flames shoot up, one from each of her fingers.

"How did you do that?"

She smiles and blows out the flames one by one, sucking on her fingers to douse the smoke. Her fingers are clean, freshly washed pink, unscorched and unblistered.

"That's a trick," I say. Something must be protecting her fingers – some jelly, the kind that film stuntmen use.

She shakes her head. "It's no trick. I was five when I learned I could do that. I used to show it to the girls at school until a teacher caught me and sent me to the headmistress. She didn't understand how I'd done it. She just gave me a lecture on the dangers of playing with matches." She chuckles. "She never understood anything, the silly bitch."

I say nothing.

She reaches inside her jumper and takes a flat square out of her handbag. She holds it out to me. A Polaroid, taken on a sunny day. It's of her – younger, hair permed, but recognisably her – kneeling down on some grass, towelling a naked boy who must be about three years old.

"That's you," I say.

"And my son."

"How old is he? He's ever so sweet."

She snatches the photo back from me. "He's dead."

I stare at her.

"Yes, that's what I said. Dead. Do I have to spell it out for you?"

"I'm so sorry. What – what happened?"

"It was an accident. He – he got burned."

"*Burned?*" As the implications of that sink in, something clenches inside me. Behind the counter, my hands begin to tremble.

"You see," she goes on. Her voice is calm, but I sense from her body language that she's holding herself in very tightly. "I thought I could control it, you see. But there was too much smoke, it was too hot. My husband was asleep but I'd meant to get him. But I couldn't fetch my son. I had to press a wet handkerchief to my nose. I couldn't breathe. I barely got myself out before the roof collapsed."

She stands up, stubbing her cigarette out violently into the ashtray.

"You're mad," I say.

"Mad? I'm not mad." She stares back at me. "Or if I am, I was made that way." She pauses, then says: "I'm sorry if I've disturbed you, Louise. I thank you for the company. For the chat. It was nice to have met you. But I really must go now."

She turns on her heel out of the door. From behind the counter I can see her walk across the half-empty carpark.

I sit down heavily and put my head in my hands. I shudder. *Jesus Christ*, I think. I should have called Mick on his extension. But this woman made no indication of wanting to hurt me.

As I sit there, watching her small figure walk away, I think: *You really blew it, Louise. The woman was crying out for help. And you turned her away. You're no Good Samaritan.*

And I get up from my chair. I hurry across the cafeteria, my heels clicking on the tiled floor, and out into the cold night air.

The woman is at the far end of the carpark, by the fence leading down to the motorway.

I don't think about the consequences of leaving the cafeteria unlocked and unattended. I run as fast as I can towards her.

"Come back!" I shout. "Come back! I'm sorry! Come back!"

She turns for a moment, then climbs over the fence.

By the time I reach the fence, she's scrambled down the grass verge and is standing on the hard shoulder. She glances to her right, then steps out onto the motorway.

"Don't be bloody stupid!" I yell.

To my right there's a bright light in the distance. It resolves into two, close together. A lorry. Travelling very fast.

The woman stands directly in its path. She holds up her hands, palms facing the oncoming vehicle.

Its horn blares.

Ten small flames shoot up from the woman's fingers. They are stronger this time, and the flames quickly spread down her arms.

I scream –

When the lorry hits her, her hair is ablaze.

WHEN WE WERE FIVE

Marion Arnott

I never have my photograph taken: I know the power of film. The other thing I never do is look at Valentina's photos, because there's no knowing what I'll see. For example, there should be five people in the photo of the garden, but there aren't always. The other pictures are full of her people, but they feel like mine and I don't want to be drawn into their lives again. Thirty years ago, when I returned from Russia, I slid the pictures face down into an envelope and sealed the flap. I put it right at the back of the cabinet, in the file marked 'Z', thinking that would be enough to contain her.

I go into the file from time to time, to add articles about Russia which might amuse her. For example, there's one about Serafim of Sarov, a holy man who died in disgrace in 1833. Years later, he was reconsidered, disinterred, and canonised. Later still, during the religious purges, he was dug up and confiscated by the Bolsheviks. She'd have laughed at that – who but a Bolshevik would confiscate a pile of bones? But that's Russia – the dead are as guilty or innocent as the living, and every state is temporary.

Serafim's certainly was. In the 1990s, he was discovered, crated up and neatly labelled, in the basement of the Museum of Atheism. He was well preserved, cowled in a monk's hood, and holding a bronze crucifix which glowed with new authority. When they lifted the gauze from his face, he was seen to be gently smiling. A miracle, people exclaimed, now that it was legal to believe in them again, and reburied him with honours.

In Russia, Valentina said, no one ever dies, although that does not mean that they live, only that they turn up when you least expect them.

103

I should have listened harder, but I was young and afraid I was going mad, and so she took me by surprise when she appeared in the Sunday colour supplement in a double page spread of photos of victims of Stalin's Terror. There were dozens of them, passport sized in black and white, each one a grimace of fear, shocking in its hopelessness.

Valentina's leapt out at me at once. Even in monotones, her eyes – one blue, one green – were startling: the blue eye pale and bewildered, the green one dark and afraid. She was about to disappear into Nonpersonhood, and she knew it. Whitefaced, she confronted the camera flash, nothingness, and me.

Valentina Vlasikova, age 30
Crime: unknown
Sentenced 1937: 20 years deportation
Rehabilitated 1953

Her vivid face is white skinned and oval, with delicately arched brows, a shapely mouth and a proud little chin. I have seen her face like that before, in the old photos I keep in the 'Z' file, although in them her hair is sleeked down like a South American film star's, and her eyes sparkle with mischief. But even tousled and frightened, she is still beautiful.

This is death in Russia: corpses rise up, sometimes in smiling triumph, sometimes in a white flash of terror.

By the time I knew her, Valentina was not beautiful. We met in 1969, long after she had been rehabilitated. I was a student then and had gone to the Soviet Union on a cultural exchange because I was fascinated by Sophie Masterton-Clark, Young Communist Party member, who used to stand on the steps outside the student union distributing leaflets.

Snapshot of Sophie: eyes like Julie Christie's and long red hair like Samantha Eggar's. She wore a Zhivago greatcoat over a tiny miniskirt, and when she walked, her long legs flashed in and out of the coat flap and hypnotised me.

Snapshot of me: leaning on the wall near Sophie, earnest and bespectacled, with a floppy Beatles haircut – amazed at her cut glass accent, her feeling for the working class, her contempt for her own, and grateful that someone like her talked to someone like me.

I thought the way to win her was to engage her mind. I thought that my factotum status (she let me distribute the leaflets on rainy days) was progress. I thought that the Young Communist meetings round the smoky beery table in the corner of the SU bar was Heaven.

I was only 19.

She had organised a trip to the Soviet Union, but at the last minute, someone discovered spirituality and went to India in a mini-bus instead. I filled the space.

I wasn't impressed by the Workers' Paradise. Just one example. It was raining old iron the day we visited the Young Pioneer camp. We were ushered inside the gates to see the children at work and play, while their drenched parents waited outside. I had difficulty meeting any sodden parent's eye as we left, but Sophie strode by oblivious, simultaneously amused by my bourgeois embarrassment, and delighted by Soviet political education.

It was the same story wherever we went. Privilege. Sophie laughed at my bourgeois obsession with orderly queues, and told me to learn to be a rebel.

Valentina presided over the final breach, although I didn't know who she was then. We had to be up early to visit Lenin's tomb. Sophie knocked on my room door at five in the morning. Pink with excitement, she twirled down the corridor and crashed into a cleaner's trolley. Down went the soapy water, the brushes and mops, the plastic bucket full of litter. Dirty water splattered Sophie's white PVC knee high boots and crocheted tights.

An old woman shuffled forward and started picking things up, her eyes dull with patience.

"Sorry, love," I muttered and bent to help.

"Oh, for Christ's sake, look at my boots! Leave her to it. We'll be late."

I turned the trolley upright. Sophie was waiting in the lift, but I felt like being a rebel and picked up a dustpan and brush. The lift doors snapped shut, and the cleaner touched my arm. Her witch's eyes – one blue, one green –were like a physical jolt. Suddenly my vision was blurred by red and gold sparkles like dust motes.

"Here you are, love," I said, and gathered up tins of scouring powder. She grinned and flashed a row of appalling metal teeth at me. Teeth like that are everywhere in Russia. I managed not to look away, a matter of bourgeois honour: my old Gran was a cleaner at the railway station. I never liked how people looked through her.

Sophie ignored me at the breakfast table. That was OK. I was lightheaded with anger and there was plenty to look at in the Tsarist dining room. It had ceilings like wedding cake icing, crystal chandeliers, and green carpets wide as meadows. Sophie was in scratchy mood.

"Why is it," she said to Ludmilla, "that we get porridge every breakfast but the Americans get eggs?" She lifted her cup and banged it down in front of Ludmilla. "And why is my cup cracked?"

"The cup is very old. The rim and Tsar Nicholas's monogram are solid gold..."

"It's bloody CRACKED!"

Call me bourgeois, but I hated the hush that fell in that cavernous room, and the sight of heads turning our way. My face was hot enough to fry eggs on, which annoyed Sophie.

"Don't they MIND filthy cracked crockery where you come from?"

"If it was good enough for a Tsar then..."

She huffed and puffed enough to blow the hotel down. Finally the manager came. He stood at our table, breathed wetly on the rim of the cup, then polished it with the end of his tie.

"Clean now!" He beamed round the circle of faces at our table. "Who makes request of hygiene cup?"

The air burned red and gold with laughter and it shimmered round Sophie as she stalked out of the dining room.

Lenin's tomb is an out-of-focus snapshot in my mind. We walked by queues of Soviet peasants carrying armfuls of bright wild flowers to lay at the bier. In their headscarves and saggy boots, they could have stepped straight out of photos of Old Russia. Their weathered faces sagged with a familiar weary patience.

Suddenly, I was afraid. The silent Russians seemed to glare balefully; petals from their flowers dripped like blood to the ground. I shivered and shouted a warning: "The Revolution is coming..." The air sparkled red and gold. "Workers of the world unite! You have nothing to lose but your queues!"

Sophie tugged my arm, laughing. "Your face is swelling up!"

I don't remember anything else. I woke up in the hotel three days later, the delirium of fever gone and my ears and neck stabbing with pain. Mumps. I was quarantined in a room on the rarely used top floor. I had a marble washstand without a plug, my own personal chandelier (with two candle globes burnt out), and heavy patched sheets monogrammed with a coronet. Sophie and the others had gone on to Leningrad, promising to return for the May Day parades.

That first night, I walked the floor, chewing painkillers and cradling my puffy hamster face in my hands. From my window I looked across the rooftops at the spires and domes huddled above the Kremlin's crenellated walls. They were eerily lit by a pale mist of lights. A darkness like thick black fur pressed down on the misty halos and on me. I nearly jumped out of my skin when someone knocked at the door.

Snapshot of Valentina: tiny, tired, battered looking. Her skin was like dried up leather, her cheekbones were oddly shaped promontories, her brow lumpy and dented. A big embroidered headscarf covered lank grey hair. She looked up at me, the blue eye enquiring, the green one insisting. I followed her up the hallway along a blood red runner carpet woven with gold laurel wreaths. Under the window at the far end, beside an antique radiator, were an armchair and a concierge's desk with a shaded lamp.

I don't know why I went, except that she was kindly and the light from her lamp was yellow and warm compared to the darkness clogging my bedroom. She had a samovar bubbling on a metal tray. It seemed homely.

Valentina settled me in the big plush chair and reached for the teapot on top of the samovar. I noticed that the backs of her hands were scarred with red puckered gouges which snaked across her knuckles and wrist bones. When she caught me looking, I studied the samovar. It was black enamel, painted with summer fruits and flowers. A dormouse peeped out from behind a bunch of painted grasses.

"This is pretty," I croaked. I didn't expect her to understand, a woman of her age and class, but that seemed no reason not to be polite.

She flashed her dreadful teeth at me, and poured some tea concentrate, black as liquid soot, into a cup, then diluted it with boiling water from the samovar. There was honey to sweeten it. I stirred it in with a long-handled spoon, trying to remember the Russian for thank you.

"Chin-chin, old thing," she said.

It was a moment before what she'd said sunk in.

Sly humour flickered in her peculiar eyes. "You like better 'Down the hatch'?"

Her accent was clipped RP, like Ceila Johnson's in a British wartime film.

"It is a long time since I try English," she said. "Do you care for tea? Is very soothing."

That was the beginning. Valentina talked a lot. I didn't pay much attention at first – lonely old ladies like to talk and it doesn't always matter if anyone is listening – but she was company in the warm circle of light which held back the shadows massed around us.

She mistook my silence for disappointment over missing the trip to Leningrad, which she called St. Petersburg. She was surprised that I didn't know they were the same place. For my benefit, she conjured up its images.

Her memories still squat like lodgers in my mind, as at home as my own: the 150 bridges spanning the Neva and the roiling sea; in winter, the restless waves frozen in silent glistening peaks; in spring, the ice cracking with a roar; in summer, the white nights when the sun never sets and the city drowns in the scent of lilacs.

I had half an hour of these glimpses of a city before I went back to bed and slept. I dreamed of a girl, a little mischief, strolling along a paved embankment with her parents, admiring the steel blue roll of the river. She was munching sunflower seeds, and her tall father wouldn't let her spit the husks on the pavement like a peasant; later, she ran under lime trees in the park, rattling a stick along the wrought iron railings. Her mother turned, her face shadow-patterned by the lace of her parasol: "You're too far behind, Valechka!" and the child called back through the lilac air, "No, Mummy, you're too far ahead. Wait for me at the corner!"

I woke up with the cry of 'Wait for me' ringing in my ears and the darkness shining with red and gold specks. The clean scent of lilacs was on my pillow. I took an analgesic against fever.

Next night there were two chairs by the radiator. She'd brought a jar of preserved sour cherries, which is what they put in the tea in St.

Petersburg, and a box crammed with photographs.

The tea was vile. The photos were something else: gentle grey shadows of another place, another time. I recognised my dream family at once. The little mischief was there, luminously pretty in a white flounced smock with big sleeves. She was standing beside a seated woman, who was luminously beautiful in gauzy summer flounces, with masses of soft dark hair swept up around her head. The details were clearer than in the dream. Her parasol had a swan's neck handle and the tall sternly handsome man standing behind her chair wore a Russian officer's uniform and a peaked cap at a jaunty angle.

"My parents," she said, lightly drawing her finger down the sides of their faces. "And this my good self, seven years old in 1914, the year the world changes."

I looked from the smiling fairy child to Valentina's lumpy face. Last night's silvery giggles bubbled up in my mind, my breath came in the quick pant of a running child calling 'Wait!' I shivered and my hand trembled. Valentina noticed and patted my arm.

"Do not distress your good heart, old chap. I am changed much. But it is only life. It leaves its mark."

We went through all her photos. There were many of her parents, her mother in astonishing hats with ribbons and flowers, always on the verge of laughter, her father in and out of uniform, always half smiling.

As Valentina talked about them, her small scarred hands fluttered in the air and her weariness fell away.

Her mother was a seamstress. She met Valentina's father, Alexander Ivanovich, when she came from the country to work in his father's tailor's workshop. He fell in love with her instantly, although she was very shy and proper in the way of country girls and would not talk to him. But he got round her as he got round everyone who opposed the match and they married. It was a good match. Even grandfather came round in the end because she brought wealthy ladies flocking to the shop to buy the styles she wore herself. Valentina laughed, a rare thing with her.

"This wide," she snorted and threw out her arms, "and they thought to look like her!"

The night sped by as she introduced me to her family. Face after face was lightly caressed as she told of picnics and sailing parties, marriages and funerals, Christmas and Easter Masses. A little girl in white ran everywhere, laughing in the lilac air.

By dawn Valentina had grown wistful.

"There is no place like St. Petersburg then. Moscow is darkness and midnight. The people have no laughter – they were afraid too long."

"Why don't you go back there?" I said.

"Because I must wait here," she replied and fetched her cleaning trolley from the cupboard at the other end of the hall.

I fell into crowded dreams as the sun rose:

Ekaterina sits drenched in dusty sunlight at the end bench in the workshop. From first sight, Alexander sees no one but her. Her grave dignity makes him feel clownish, like a gauche boy. His guts churn painfully when he looks at her because he knows it's her or no one. Every day, he makes paper darts and writes notes on them – 'Come to tea. I don't bite', 'Come and stroll in the Summer Gardens' – and flies them on to her bench. She throws them on the floor among the cloth trimmings, but one day she smiles behind her hand. With a great surge of hope, he flies one more dart: 'Ekaterina, beloved soul, it is you or no one, ever, no one but you, ever.' Finally, she smiles at him.

Grandfather is not pleased. A peasant girl! His ruddy face grows ruddier and his white moustache bristles. But he remembers his own uncle who shot himself for unrequited love in the St. Petersburg way. He sighs and agrees to the marriage.

I woke around lunchtime, bursting with happy anticipation, relieved that the old man had come round so easily. It was an hour before I realised that I had nothing to be happy or relieved about. I laughed at myself and settled down to mumps and boredom again, sorry that my glimpse of someone else's life was over.

That night, Valentina kept glancing over her shoulder. I peered round too, but the shadows were hushed and empty.

"Something special," she said and reached into an old tapestry bag under the desk. "No one else sees this."

Something special was a photograph. It had been taken through an archway cut in a deep stone wall. Beyond the dim arch, in an explosion of light, a group of people stood smiling in a sunny garden. There were five of them. Definitely five. I recognised Ekaterina and Alexander, who was in his army tunic. His face was drawn and he was leaning heavily on a cane. The other three men, Valentina said, were Bolshevik commissars who lodged with them. Was it my imagination, or did Ekaterina seem nervous? I certainly felt a tremor of fear at sight of them.

It was 1917 and Alexander had been shrapnel wounded in the knee during the terrible Galicia campaign. He returned on leave to find a Revolution in progress and everything changed. The city was starving. The tailor's shop had been closed because no one had any money. The wooden fences round the back garden had been pulled up for firewood months before. Ekaterina had taken in lodgers to survive.

Alexander was resentful of the three lodgers in his apartment. They were strange men who called him comrade and bored him with incessant political talk. They were permanently drunk on vodka and political rhetoric. One night they harangued him about the necessity for blood and violence to heal mankind. "Blood and violence?" Alexander was furious. "You are brave sitting cosy in my house with your vodka in your hand and your feet on the fender. We could have used fire-eaters like you in Galicia. There was plenty of blood and violence to go round there."

Ekaterina, who had been sweeping crumbs off the tablecloth, became alarmed. She often did around her lodgers.

"Alexander Ivanovitch, is your knee paining you? You seem a little cross tonight."

He thrust her hand away.

"No, it is my head. It aches from listening to armchair warriors lusting for death, while the real men of Russia die in their thousands."

Valentina stabbed a finger on the face of one of the men in the photo.

"Sorokin," she whispered. "The worst of them. He had a voice like honey, but his soul was mean. And this is Kovalenko. And this Malenkov. They were a troika – judge, jury, and executioner. This is a Bolshevik joke. In old Petersburg, a troika was a three horse carriage, decked with bells and flowers."

The shadows around me crowded closer.

Sorokin was a slightly built man with wire-rimmed spectacles. In the summer's heat, in his long leather overcoat with the collar turned up, he squinted into the light, smiling thinly at big curly haired Kovalenko.

"He wore high heeled boots to give him height." She pointed at the coat. "The uniform of a Bolshevik," she said. "They liked to look tough like gangsters. When my father spoke of the real men of Russia, Sorokin let his coat fall open. He had a Mauser strapped to his waist. He moved his hand towards the gun and my father lashed his cane across his knuckles. Sorokin yelped like a puppy as the blood gushed. My father ordered him and his friends out of the house. They took rooms in the widow's apartment upstairs."

Valentina poured us both more tea. "For weeks my father mocked him whenever they met on the stairs. 'Good day, Comrade Mauser'." She sipped at her tea. "Maybe that greeting condemned him. Maybe his life was already forfeit."

She would say no more.

I slept fitfully because of a throbbing in my knee and a woman weeping quietly in the empty darkness around me. "Alexander, don't provoke them."

The Bolsheviks soon toppled the Provisional Government. St. Petersburg drowned in a sea of scarlet calico banners while the streets rang with the sound of gunfire and cheering drunken mobs. Sailors from the battle cruisers roamed wild and helped themselves to whatever or whomever they fancied. Decent people stayed off the streets. "We were the freest people in the freest city in the world," Valentina said. "It was terrifying."

Snapshot of the first night: the Church of Our Saviour was set alight. The bronze saints and apostles on the roof ridges writhed in the leaping flames in mute agony. Melting bronze tears ran down the face of the Christ at the door. Valentina's mother watched from her window and wept.

"They have taken away the saints and left us in Hell with devils," she said.

Valentina could not continue for a while. I was left thinking of devils and writhing saints. When it came, her story was grotesque. Alexander went with his brother Dmitri to check up on Grandfather. Hours went by and he did not return. Valentina could not bear her mother's tearful agitation and slipped out of the apartment. She waited with her doll under the stairs of the common entranceway where she fell asleep. She woke in darkness. Sorokin was stumbling along the hallway, muttering to himself, making the sign of the Cross, and mumbling, "Death, death, death" at each point.

He slipped on the first step and swore. Valentina peeped out and shrank from the sight of the heels of his boots. They were clotted with blood, great LUMPS of blood. The skirt of his long coat was slick with it. His hands too. He grinned and raised his hand to make the sign of the cross over her. "The blessings of Death be upon you, little Valechka," he crooned in his honey voice.

She jumped over him and scampered upstairs. Her father never returned.

I could not look at Valentina. Her eyes had filled with tears and her nose was running. I poured her some tea and stirred in the sour cherry jam. She drank a whole cup before she was able to go on.

Grandfather came calling the next afternoon, with his hunting rifle and some of Alexander's Army friends. He had been visited the night before, at three in the morning, by Dmitri, who trembled like a leaf as he told his story. He and Alexander had been snatched off the street by Sorokin, Kovalenko, and Malenkov and were being driven round St.Petersburg in a big black car. They would be allowed to live if Dmitri could collect enough ransom. Grandfather gave all the money he had in the house, plus his wife's jewellery, but neither Dmitri nor Alexander returned. Grandfather had come hunting commissars, but the widow's apartment upstairs was empty, and though he scoured the city, all he found were family friends who had donated to the ransom fund – the commissars had called at many houses.

Years passed before Valentina heard the rest of what Dmitri told Grandfather that night. Alexander had been bundled into the back of the car and made to lie on the floor. Sorokin swilled vodka and chanted "Death! Death! Death!" When Alexander complained, Sorokin drummed his heels in his face. And when he screamed, Sorokin drummed harder.

Valentina mopped her eyes with a cleaning rag. "The old boy never recovered from it," she said. "He died before the spring, of too heavy sorrow. His sons had disappeared as if they had never been. All Russia was full of holes where people should be. The Bolsheviks called it healing the world with revolvers." She leaned back in her chair behind the desk. "They are buried under some bushes, somewhere on the road to Tsarskoe Seloe, although I did not find that out for a long time."

"How did you find out?"

But she was staring sightlessly into the distance. She flapped a hand in my direction. "Tomorrow. *Spakonya Noche, Malcheek.*"

Sleep well, dear boy.

I knew I wouldn't.

A country road, white with moon and frost, lined with a dark mass of rustling trees. A car bucks along frozen ruts, and halts in front of a pair of iron gates hung between white stone pillars. A man lurches from the back of the car, swilling vodka.

Dreaming, I sweat with fear of the man, of the place, of the terror that it's not a dream although I know it is, of not being sure whether I'm watching what's happening or whether I'm part of it, in a dream or in reality, but horribly afraid...

The man burps and smashes the bottle against a pillar. "Bring out the real men!" he cries. Two men are dragged from the car, one shaking from head to foot, but supporting the other who is unable to stand. They cling together, swaying like lovers, while Sorokin makes the sign of the cross over them. "Death bless Thee and Keep Thee! Death make his light to shine upon Thee..."

The man with the shattered face, sagging in his brother's arms, spits blood and broken teeth. The drunk seizes him by the collar and presses a Mauser to his temple.

"Show us how to die like a real man," he sniggers.

But curly-haired Kovalenko steps forward. "Not like that, Sorokin! You'll get brains all over you!" He walks behind Alexander and Dmitri – "Like this!" he shouts – and presses a pistol to the back of Dmitri's neck. He kicks him, and just as Dmitri tumbles forward, he pulls the trigger. He holds out clean hands to Sorokin. "See? Not a splash!"

Sorokin hauls Alexander, who fell with Dmitri, to his feet. "Turn round!" Alexander sways and groans. Blood gushes from his mouth and nose and one of his eyes. He holds his hands out before him like a blind man groping his way. The three men converge on Alexander. Two support him while Sorokin kicks and fires.

I moan… It's cold…

I woke up and could not see for a thick stickiness which filled my eyes. I was lying in a hollow in the ground. A spade crunched and earth thumped on to my face in big icy clods. Ekaterina's name slipped through my lips in a gush of blood.

"Fuck! He's still alive!" a honey voice complained.

A searing flame, red and gold and sparkling, exploded in my head. Darkness.

It was terrifyingly long before I realised I was not dead, but safe in my Moscow bedroom. I lay there, unable to move, remembering what it felt like to die. No one alive should know what that's like. It isn't right.

I wondered if Valentina knew that her father's last word had been her mother's name. But how could I tell her without exposing my night journeys? I was mad or possessed and didn't want to know which. So I said nothing and listened while she told me how she had found out about the road to Tsarskoe Seloe.

In 1935, Valentina, now grown and married, cut out an article from the newspaper. She showed me the clipping. It was a photograph of four people which had been taken through an archway cut deep in a stone wall. On the left a man in a long leather coat squinted into the sun. On the right, a man leaned heavily on a cane, his wife beside him. Sorokin in his heeled boots and leather coat was there, and curly-haired Kovalenko, but where Malenkov had been, there was only a rose bush slightly darker in tone than the rest of the picture. Malenkov had vanished. The caption read: 'Comrades Sorokin and Kovalenko. Relaxing with friends in a Leningrad garden, 1917.' There was another picture of the two of them, attending some sort of reunion dinner. I recognised the dining room downstairs.

Valentina's strange eyes dazzled with green and blue light. "I never found out what happened to Malenkov. He might have been a rightist

Trotskyite, or a Jewish intellectual, or a Pole – any of those was enough to get him smacked in the Purges. A photo in his company would be embarrassing for an important official. Therefore they erased him from all records."

She placed the original photograph beside the other on the desk and pressed one thumb on Malenkov's face, and the other on Kovalenko's. Gently, she moved her thumbs up and down. "They rubbed people away. Death was never enough. But people leave traces. They turn up. Everyone comes back. Everyone. Sometimes they cannot keep their mouths shut."

She rubbed harder on the face of Kovalenko. He had turned up, she told me, in this very hotel, in 1960. The old Bolsheviks came every year, for the anniversary of the revolution. They filled the dining rooms with the clanking of their medals and their loud talk. One man boasted of executing the Tsar and wore the Tsar's old peaked cap to prove it. They drank their tea from long glasses, and between sips and the crunching of sugar cubes between their teeth, they conjured up old secret graves for their comrades' entertainment.

Valentina was emptying ashtrays when someone mentioned St. Petersburg. They shouted with laughter at a curly haired man's tale of a Tsarist officer on the floor of a car getting his face battered in, while his brother pleaded for mercy. Kovalenko exclaimed, "We took them out to the estate near Tsarskoe Seloe. Sorokin nearly shot me by mistake. I tell you I felt the draught of the bullet on my cheek."

Valentina was still rubbing at the original photograph with her thumb. Was I surprised that Malenkov's figure was thinning out and paling? That the rose bush was beginning to take shape under her hand? I don't think I was. I was mad or she was a witch. Anything was possible.

Her metal teeth flashed when she told me that Kovalenko fell down the lift shaft that night, so drunk that when the doors opened, he failed to notice that the lift wasn't there and plunged to the basement.

I left her rubbing away. I knew Kovalenko would have disappeared from the photo by the next night. Would he also have vanished from the newspaper photo? What were the logistics of that when the Party had not vanished him? I remember giving a cracked laugh as I shut my bedroom door behind me.

I could not sleep. Several times I had seen her wedge the door of the lift open, so that when she was cleaning the lift, it stayed on the top floor. Russians have never heard of Health and Safety. The lift doors are the old pullback ones, and there are no inner safety doors. On a floor below, a man might pull the door open, or someone might open it for him, and he might step out, or be pushed...

I glimpsed it happening, fleetingly. I wasn't asleep and therefore not dreaming. I did not 'see' it or feel it. She never hinted at any such thing. But I knew what had happened. And I wasn't surprised.

I didn't join her the next night. She listened at my door for a long time – yes, you can hear someone listening – and then went away when she heard my snoring. When I was sure she was settled at her desk, I let myself sleep, but there was no escape. She was there in my dreams before me. There was a long road with many turnings and a pale mist scented with lilac. A little girl in white skipped along behind me but couldn't catch up. "Wait for me!" she cried. When I turned, she held out her arms and smiled piteously.

"Valechka!" I cried in the voice of Alexander, and swung her up on to my shoulder.

Valentina's eyes moistened when she saw me emerge from my room, yawning and bleary-eyed. Her metal teeth shone with pleasure. I was touched, and a little guilty.

"*Malcheek*, I had given you up."

"I was tired earlier. Now I can't sleep."

"Take tea with me." She reached for the teapot. The samovar hissed comfortably. "You must hear my life," she said calmly as she poured and mixed, "otherwise when I die, I will be forgotten. "She raised an eyebrow, and was suddenly stern, with a look of her father about her.

"You see how things were, old boy? Don't condemn."

That was all that passed between us on the subject of Kovalenko.

She produced her wedding picture. She was a stunning bride. Her dark hair was sleek and glossy, covered with a lace square. She wore a long narrow suit with lilacs pinned to the lapel. The groom was good looking in a light-hearted characterless way; but her face, underneath the sparkling mischief, had strength.

"My Pavel," she said, with such longing and affection that I felt ashamed of my negative assessment. "That was a happy day. 1934."

They met when she was a translator in Moscow, in a building with endless corridors, many floors, and countless government offices which performed functions it was wiser not to ask about. Her speciality was English and she translated foreign newspapers, books, and magazines for the censors. Pavel was an assistant cinema projectionist and one day he came to her with a film script. It was in English, a romantic musical, and she was to translate it into Russian. There were many scripts after that. He never said what they were for and she never asked. In Moscow, ignorance was safety.

Why did she fall in love with Pavel? He slipped her a note inviting her to come for a stroll that evening. This reminded her of her mother's courtship, although the note was not in fact a romantic gesture, but a precautionary one. Walls had ears in that place. Maintaining privacy was a game.

Pavel made her laugh at his stories. He worked in the Kremlin's private cinema, and saw Father Stalin often. Stalin was a movie fan, but would never have foreign films dubbed or subtitled. He had their scripts translated, and then the cinema manager had to read all the parts out, yelling at the top of his voice. When Stalin was in boisterous mood, he would have the poor man show Tarzan films, and then collapse with laughter at his efforts to jungle yodel. So funny… So much laughter with Pavel. It was good to laugh again. Pavel was kind and gentle, with the gift of looking on the bright side. So she married him. I asked if her mother liked him, and she fell silent. Then she began to rock slightly in her chair, her little scarred hands clenched, her eyes wet with tears.

"She never met him. We were estranged."

From her bag, she pulled out another photo. Her mother, unsmiling in a black dress, looked past the camera, her face stamped with an ancient pain. She was shrunken, her laughter gone, her radiance dimmed.

"She never got over my father," Valentina said. "She clung to the old comforts, to religion and icons, although it was punishable. We quarrelled often."

Valentina received a Soviet education, at school, at the Young

Pioneers'. She could never take religion seriously after exposure to rationalism. She embraced the Party, industrialisation, and modernisation, and had no patience with her mother's ignorant country piety, or with her refusal to forgive Alexander's death. Not that Valentina forgave it, but she saw no connection between it and the achievements of the Soviet Union. Her mother said so often that what began in blood would end bloodily, that Valentina lost patience entirely. Finally, Ekaterina returned to her parents' village in the country and exchanged dutiful letters with Valentina two or three times a year.

Valentina halted there, breathing heavily. Silvery tears flooded the web of lines under her eyes.

"She wrote to me," she sobbed, "so formally. 'Valentina Alexandrovna', she greeted me, never 'my darling Valechka'."

She pulled her apron over her head and wept. I was struck dumb with embarrassment, but I poured more tea and patted her arm clumsily. She emerged from under her apron, red eyed and snuffling. There was a depth of misery in her eyes that I have never since seen replicated.

"I paid no attention when my mother said things were bad in the country. The country folk were enemies of the people, undermining the state, trying to starve the cities out by destroying the crops. Pavel heard all this in the Kremlin. The peasant farmers were traitors."

Ekaterina's second last letter came. 'Valentina Alexandrovna, I am ill. Come to me that I may see your face once more.' Valentina got permission to go, but postponed the visit until after Pavel's sister's birthday party.

"But it was not for the party that I delayed," she said. "It was irritation that she was cold to me. And guilt. And having to tell her I had married."

She leaned forward suddenly and took my hands in hers.

"If only you could see what I saw on the journey there…"

Outside the city, the train sped along shining rails into a land empty and remote. Frost hung from trees like silver hair; it furred the fences and the rails; it entered the chest like tiny cold claws. The villages were empty of people, the chimneys of smoke, the fields of crops. Once a group of children, gaunt and barefoot, walked alongside the train at a country halt. Tears froze on their cheeks like diamonds. They held up empty hands to the windows.

"What do they want?" a man snarled and pulled down the blind.

There was a terrible silence inside the compartment. And then a sweet clinging stench thickened the air. Someone opened the blind again. The doors of the cattle trucks on a parallel track were open, revealing stacks of corpses inside. Long hair trailed out of the trucks, a muscular purplish arm hung stiff and useless, a grey dead face with staring eyes glared right across at the living. In a moment, all the blinds were drawn again.

On the long journey, it was the same everywhere.

Valentina pressed my hands. "You saw, old chap?"

I nodded.

"They starved them, you know, and filled Russia full of holes, while Stalin watched Tarzan and sang along to romantic musicals."

She ran her fingers up and down my hands, warming them, for I was very cold. I wanted to get up and go, but her strange eyes compelled my attention.

"My mother," she said. "My poor mother."

I saw the village – one street lined with houses built of logs, a mud road, a wooden pavement. Ekaterina's house was cold and dark, choking on the hush of a place where the dead lie. I smelled the sweet putrescence before I entered the house. She was on the floor by the stove, curled close to it. Perhaps there had been some little heat left at the end. She was a pile of bones and skin; her eyes were half closed, their luminous light quenched. In her clawed hand was a scrawled note, the last she would write.

"Daughter, I could not wait for you."

My heart broke.

There was nothing to be said. Valentina and I sipped tea, silently sharing the memory. For better or worse, her guilt and pain and misery were mine too, as she had intended all along.

That isn't an excuse for what happened later.

By the next night, Kovalenko had disappeared from the newspaper photos of the St. Petersburg garden and the reunion dinner. In the original photo, where there had been five, now there were only three, Alexander and Ekaterina together, and Sorokin beside a rose bush, smiling thinly at a tree trunk which hadn't been there before.

Valentina poured our tea and added a slosh of herbed vodka. It was pleasantly aniseedy, and while I drank, she sat clenching and unclenching her hands in her lap. I could not take my eyes off the red scars, which seemed to writhe with the movement. She did not speak as the corridor darkened and I felt myself slip away...

It was dark and cold and the air was foetid. At the edge of my vision, I could see the distant yellow halo of light from Valentina's lamp, but where I was, the only light came from outside the room, though a gap under the door.

The door burst open with such force that it banged off the inner wall. I cried out and jumped to my feet. The two men didn't say anything. They seized me by the hair and dragged me to the table. They forced my hands palm down on the surface and held me there. I hadn't the strength to struggle – my jaw was on fire and pain flashed like lightning in my head. The light from the open door was blocked by a man's shape.

"How are you, my dear Valechka?" a voice said, smooth and golden as honey.

The shadow in the doorway moved forward. He had a cane in his hand. The pain as he slashed it across the back of my hands was white hot; blood gushed like acid. I fainted many times, but there was no escape that way. I gibbered and pleaded, cried and screamed, but he had no mercy...

Valentina was beside me, hushing and soothing, when I came back. "All right, old chap. What a little silly you are! It was a long time ago, in the Lubianka, not here."

I was cold with fear and my hands were on fire. When I looked at them they twitched and flexed in visible agony, but there was no damage – not a scar, not a single broken bone.

She sat down opposite me. "Sorokin. He had a scar across his knuckles where my father struck with his cane. He said I must have ten for his one."

She shook her head sorrowfully. "Not quite cricket, was it?"

It was 1937, the year of the Great Terror. Valentina and her colleagues dreaded coming into work in the morning. The doorman, nicknamed Comrade Charon after the ferryman to the dead, used to greet them every day with the names of those who had been arrested overnight for reasons no one ever heard. The nickname was a joke, bitter and fearful as all jokes were then; grim humour made the empty desks and offices bearable.

Sometimes they encountered strangers in the building, men in long coats who never met anyone's eye or smiled. Everyone knew they worked for the 'serious institutions' – one of the lethal security organisations. They darkened the building with the shadow of death.

Once, when it rained heavily, the girls stayed inside the building at lunchtime. They had a wireless tuned to a station which played dance music. Valentina taught her friends the Kremlin Waltz, an invention of Pavel's. When men of serious political standing in the Kremlin wished to discuss business with other men of serious standing, they went outside and walked round and round the walls, where they could not be picked up by hidden microphones. In summer heat and winter blizzard, they walked round and round, varying their routes and stopping now and then to emphasise a point with a wave of the hand. Pavel's dance was delightfully silly, round and round and up and down with many sudden halts and turns.

Valentina waltzed to a halt at the side of a staircase. A man in a long coat descended, his hand trailing down the marble banister. She saw a long red scar across the knuckles, but she didn't know him until she heard his honey voice.

"Ah, it is good to see the ladies enjoying themselves."

Their eyes met for an instant, and both looked away immediately, but she knew him.

Pavel, when she told him of the encounter, was certain he wouldn't recognise a grown woman whom he hadn't seen since she was ten years old. But Valentina, studying herself in the mirror, seeing startling eyes very like her mother's, knew that he had. She thought of Malenkov, removed from a photo because his association with two comrades was inconvenient, and wondered how much of an embarrassment she herself was.

When they collected her she was on the way to the dentist to see about an abscessed tooth. She had a scarf at her mouth to keep out the cold, and was worrying about the extraction, when a black car drew up beside her. She was thrown on the floor in the back of the car. Remembering what had happened to her father, she lay very, very still.

There had been so many arrests that the system was overloaded and she was left undisturbed in a cell at the Lubianka for several days. The pain of her tooth was excruciating and she begged for a dentist. Three men in leather coats came with pliers. They promised to cease extracting if she would name her confederates in an unspecified crime. Just saying someone's name would guarantee mercy and someone else's arrest. Valentina denounced very quickly.

"Sorokin!" she screamed. "Sorokin!"

For hours, for days, she denounced him, over and over. No one else. Just Sorokin. But her case was different from everyone else's. There was no mercy, only the arrival of Sorokin one cold night.

She thought at first that she was to die. They always fetched the condemned at night. By this time, she was glad to be going. It would be over quickly. They would remove her shoes (they always took the shoes of the doomed – no one ever knew why) and hustle her across the yard to the execution shed with its log walls and the sloping floor which kept the blood from spreading. Death would have been merciful – but it was Sorokin with his cane who came.

Valentina narrated all this. I was spared dreaming or seeing or experiencing it. Perhaps she could not bear to think of it herself. Perhaps her fondness for me prevented her from sharing the very worst. At any rate, there was only one glimpse granted me. Sorokin, when he had finished with her, told her that her Pavel had been arrested and executed, but that before he died, he had denounced her.

I saw the scene: the bloody whimpering creature on the floor with its damaged hands hanging uselessly. I felt her surge of rage as she tottered to her feet. I saw her spit blood full in Sorokin's face and scream "Liar!" They beat her about the head with coshes until she fell to the floor again, her cheek and brow bones splintered. "Liar!" she mumbled. But in her heart she knew it was true. Her strong spirit gathered itself up and flowed out to his: Pavel, I forgive…

She was not executed. Incomprehensibly, she was deported.

She shared that with me: a long train journey; a march across a windswept plain. In the twilight, they trudged along a track glimmering with white dust. It was rutted so deeply by cartwheels that people stumbled and cried out in the gloom, but the shrieking wind tossed their voices up among the evening stars and no one heard. One woman was clad only in the tatters of a satin evening dress with a corsage of ragged artificial violets still clinging to the bosom. She stumbled frequently as she had only one shoe. "You must tell my husband," she cried out often. "I am the wife of…"

But the wind snatched her husband's name away and no one heard who she was. Then night rushed down from the distant mountains and blotted out all trace of the struggling people and the white road ahead. By morning, the lady in the evening dress was gone. Someone claimed to have heard a sound like a shot in the night; others insisted it was only the wind snapping the dry stalks of the sunflowers which thronged the plain. It was cold, they argued, Comrade Lady had only frozen to death.

"It was the height of summer," Valentina said, "but in 1937, people tried to hope for the best."

Deportation: a process where hope was a quiet death by freezing among whispering summer flowers.

She lived in the labour camps until 1953, when suddenly, hundreds of thousands of people were discovered to have been mistakenly imprisoned. Those who survived were freed; those who did not were pardoned. Valentina was finally fitted with metal teeth, although there was nothing to be done about her misshapen brow and cheekbones. She was bent and aged before her time, but she returned to Moscow and claimed her belongings from Pavel's sister – her mother's black enamel samovar, and her photographs, carefully treasured in case she returned.

She was some time in finding employment because she would work in only one place – this hotel.

"But why?" I asked.

"Use your head, old boy," she said and pointed at the newspaper photo of the reunion dinner. "They come here every year, those old Bolsheviks and Stalinists. They must relive the finest days of their lives.

Where else would I wait for Sorokin? Kovalenko came, and so will Sorokin. I will meet him again."

And so she did – in a way. As May Day approached, the hotel filled up. Every room, every corner, was crammed with Soviet luminaries from the past. Even on my floor, they crammed them in three and four to a room. I was lucky – no one wanted to share a room with a man whose face was swollen with mumps. I was left undisturbed except for nightly drunken sentimental renditions of the *International* and *Kalinka*.

Valentina was tense, watching people come and go, studying faces. She still managed to miss him though. But I didn't.

One morning I saw a man in the hall. He was impatient, repeatedly pressing the button to summon the lift. Across his knuckles was a long red scar. Sorokin. I knew his heeled boots, and wire rimmed glasses, and that upright walk he cultivated to make himself look taller, but I wanted to be sure.

"Good morning," I said.

He turned and smiled thinly as he returned my greeting. He had a remarkably pleasant voice, warm as honey.

I was excited all day, longing for Valentina to come on night duty, but gradually I thought better of telling her the news. What if she did something about him? What then? The rest of her life in prison? Was Sorokin worth that? Could I live with it if I triggered a chain of events? I didn't think so. We had tea that night, and chatted. I persuaded her to tell me more Petersburg family tales from the time when a troika was a horse drawn carriage.

It was my last night in Russia – I was flying home first thing in the morning and I had already packed my suitcase. She and I said our farewells, oddly formally when I think about it, and I kept silent about Sorokin.

I slept deeply and dreamed of the cousins she had told me about. They were sledging with Alexander. Little Ilya fell off the sled and broke his arm. I saw him tumble in a spray of frozen snow. Alexander ran forward to scoop him up in his arms, but the child was Valentina, not Ilya. Alexander clutched her to him, weeping. "Valechka, where's your mother?"

Before my eyes, his handsome face dissolved into a bloody broken mess. They searched for Ekaterina, but did not see her lying under the bushes, deep in the snow, like a heap of old clothes thrown carelessly away. Her eyes were half closed, their lovely light gone; her shrunken outstretched hand was a claw which clutched a note: *Daughter, I could not wait…*

Valechka began to scream. She showed her father the gashes on her hands. Blood dripped like petals and turned the snow pink. Alexander wept.

I awoke with tears in my eyes, desperate to see Valentina, but when I went out into the corridor she wasn't at her desk. The lamp was off and the samovar gone. The emptiness of our corner terrified me. I stood trembling in the shadows, willing her to come. I wanted to take her in my arms and shelter her, to protect her from Sorokin and keep all that world away from her as a father should, to take her back to Petersburg where she was happy. Then a door further down the hall opened.

I could scarcely believe my eyes. That murderous Bolshevik, still staggering under the influence of vodka after all these years! He wasn't so brave with his Mauser when I struck him with the cane – he yelped like the mongrel he was.

My face hurt. My eye hurt. I was half blinded by blood and seeping liquid, but I heard him pad down the hall to the toilet in his slippers. He left his room door open. I was waiting for him in a patch of moonlight when he came back.

He spoke pleasantly. "Comrade, you are in the wrong room."

"Don't you know me, Sorokin?"

He peered uncertainly at me – he didn't have his glasses on.

He stepped back when I moved towards him, but I was quicker and slammed his door shut.

"Don't you know me, Sorokin?"

I came a little closer and he gasped. "Comrade, you are injured," he said.

"It isn't real," I said. "It all happened a long time ago."

He backed away. I walked towards him, taller and stronger and younger, smelling his fear. Oh, his fear was good – it was right that he should feel fear before he died. He stumbled backwards, towards the window with the wrought iron balcony. The window was open because of the summer heat and soon his back was pressed against the balcony and he could go no further.

"Take off your slippers," I said.

And he did. That was good too – it was right that he should die barefoot like all the others.

I took him by the shoulders and spun him round to face the starry sky. I delivered the kick in time-honoured fashion and shoved hard as he toppled forward. He screamed once as he went over but the rowdy choruses of the *International* ringing round the dining room stifled the sound. I closed the door quietly behind me as I left.

I didn't bother going to bed. The bus to the airport was picking us up at 4am. I dressed and sat waiting, my suitcase at my feet. What was I thinking? I don't know. I'm not sure if I was there. But I know what Alexander felt. He was satisfied and at peace. I hoped Valentina would be pleased.

I hardly spoke to Sophie on the flight back home. I was in no mood for the achievements of the Soviet Union or her tales of Leningrad, which was a different place from the Petersburg I knew.

At home, when I opened my suitcase, there was a samovar wrapped up in a couple of my shirts, and a pile of photographs. That brought me up short. When had she done that? And why? I never guessed the answer until years later when she turned up in the Sunday supplement.

I cut out her photo to put it in the 'Z' file. I was going to drop it in beside the envelope, but when I opened the drawer, I caught a dizzying whiff of lilac. I hadn't opened that envelope in thirty years, but I had to that day. Valentina insisted. I took the photos out – Sorokin had vanished from both the newspaper photo and the original. Through the dim archway, in the broad sunlight, I saw Alexander and Ekaterina. By the tree was Dmitri. I recognised him although I never knew him so well as Alexander. He was grinning, and looked very like his brother. In the foreground of the picture stood Valentina, her hair slicked down like a South American film star's, one arm linked through Pavel's. Her eyes sparkled with mischievous humour. There were five in the garden again.

I put them all back in the drawer. So far as I know, there are still five. I hope so.

SHOPPING

Antony Mann

June 5
Milk
Newspaper
Sandwich
Chewing Gum
Banana
Cat Food

June 6
Milk
Newspaper
Sandwich
Chewing Gum
Banana
Cat Food

June 7
Milk
Newspaper
Sandwich
Chewing Gum
Banana
Cat Food

June 12
Milk
Newspaper
Sandwich
Chewing Gum

Banana
Cat Food
Razors
Shaving Foam
Soap

June 14

Milk
Newspaper
Sandwich
Chewing Gum
Banana
Cat Food
Aftershave
Shampoo/Conditioner
Hair Tonic
Shoelaces
Nail Scissors
Clothes Brush

June 15

Milk
Newspaper
Sandwich
Chewing Gum
Banana
Cat Food
Breath Freshener

June 16

Milk
Newspaper
Sandwich
Chewing Gum
Banana
Cat Food
Theatre tickets
Men's health magazine

Shoe polish/new shoes?
New tie
Haircut

June 18

Milk
Newspaper
Sandwich
Chewing Gum
Banana
Cat Food
Fresh coffee
Wine
Cheese and bikkies
Toilet deodorant
Kitchen/bathroom cleanser
Bucket
Scourers
Fresh Flowers

June 20

Milk
Newspaper
Cat Food
Petrol
Drinks cooler
Picnic cutlery
Napkins
Cold meats
Cheeses
Bread
Wine
Fruit
Salads
Chocolate torte

June 24

Milk

Newspaper
Sandwich
Chewing Gum
Banana
Cat Food
Condoms

July 6
Milk
Newspaper
Sandwich
Chewing Gum
Banana
Cat Food
Condoms (ribbed)
Squirty cream
Strawberries
Honey

July 10
Milk
Newspaper
Sandwich
Chewing Gum
Banana
Cat Food
Condoms (novelty)
Ronald Reagan mask
Baby Oil
Handcuffs
Blindfold
Masking Tape

July 11
Milk
Chewing Gum
Banana
Cat Food

Card (To Say I'm Sorry?/Let's Be Friends?)

July 12

Milk
Newspaper
Sandwich
Chewing Gum
Banana
Cat Food
Flowers
Chocolates

July 13

Milk
Newspaper
Sandwich
Chewing Gum
Banana
Cat Food
Flowers (3 bunches)
Chocolates
Stamp
Envelope
Writing Paper (scented?)
Cigarettes
Matches

July 18

Milk
Chewing Gum
Cat Food
Cigarettes
Disposable lighter
Vodka
Stamps
Envelopes
Writing Pad

July 24
Cat Food
Cigarettes
Vodka
Flowers (5 bunches)

July 30
Cigarettes
Vodka
Flowers (12 bunches)

August 7
Cigarettes
Vodka
Razor blades

September 11
Milk
Catfood
Cigarettes
Vodka
Petrol
Rubber gloves
Heavy plastic sheeting (8sq.m)
Garbage Bags (strong) + ties
Shovel
Quicklime
Hammer
Saw

September 12
Milk
Newspaper
Sandwich
Chewing Gum
Banana
Cat Food
Nicotine Patches

SOMME-NAMBULA

Allen Ashley

My father first took me to the theatre when I was eight. It was a respectable end of the pier venue with only the occasional bawdy song up from town to suggest there might be a repertoire beyond the hymn book. *Double entendres*, however, went right over my callow head. What really interested me was the headline act – Casper Fallow, a white-haired, silk-suited hypnotist and magician. Commencing with card tricks and coin manipulation, he swiftly moved onto false-bottomed wardrobes, a sawn in half female assistant and a claim that he could put anyone into a deep trance and control their mind for as long as he chose. At this particular performance a raucous young fisherman suggested Casper "put a spell on all me creditors so's I never "ave to pay me bills again." When the amused hubbub died down, the fisherman – Henry, I think he was called – was invited onto the stage and with hardly twenty words and only the subtlest change of tone, Casper had him sleep-walking and impersonating all the creatures of the deep for everyone's amusement during the succeeding five minutes. I was both impressed and annoyed. Impressed for the obvious reasons; annoyed because even at a tender, barely schooled age *I'd* wanted to be the one chosen to go under and experience that slightly distanced state. I thought I was the obvious choice for it because I was already a noted somnambulist.

Not that I said anything of the sort to the recruiting officer as he placed light pencil ticks on my enlistment papers.

I could imagine his likely reactions. At best: "I'll have to speak to my superiors." More probably: "I'm afraid we can't have you wandering out of your trench at night, sonny. Not under orders, you see."

So I waffled on about King and country and how I was School Dash champion two years running and did a bit of boxing in my time there, as well. They let me in, of course. Too desperate for saps to do otherwise. With my father's business acumen and my well-read pretensions propping me up like the fingers of a ventriloquist, I even managed to scrape my way onto an officer training course. I'd landed in clover, I thought.

Clover in the path of a scythe.

"A show," the Captain called it. But it wasn't the sort of show I used to frequent back home far, far from Ypres. It's how we deal with things, how we've always dealt with things – by using silly little euphemisms:

"Poor old Charlie bought one last night."

"Chap who lent me a fag is pushing up the poppies now."

"We'll be safe from the bloody Boche in this trench, old son."

I used to go to the music halls whenever I had the cash about me. The reek of cheap gin and stale cigarette smoke was all part of the experience and just occasionally there was a petticoated lovely of dubious reputation to help while away the after hours with my half crowns or shillings. Indeed, I harboured thoughts of a stage career in either mesmerism or sleight of hand until maybe a year ago when I finally had to admit I was neither dextrous nor fast enough to make a go of stage magic. Now I was crouched, freezing and hungry, in a French foxhole worrying that I might not be swift enough to dodge the enemy bullets.

But I might try again when – if – this lousy war is over and we serving soldiers are taken with the urge to live more hedonistically than ever.

Snapper caught me sleep-walking last night. He's a good chap and will keep it from the other fellows. I don't want to lose my authority over them, for what it's worth. And what is authority worth, anyway? *Trust* is the all-important commodity.

Snapper, Ginger and Haddock talk about "calculated risks" when shuffling the francs and the playing cards in the mess tent of an evening. We have lost any residual faith we might have had in the blind orders issued by Headquarters, which leaves all their lives in my probably incapable hands.

I dreamed that I was a boy again, but a boy in a uniform like my own and not the popular sailor suit of yesteryear. I was watching

Casper Fallow on stage again, all white hair, neatly trimmed beard and piercing blue eyes. This time he had responded to my wishes and hypnotised *me*. The distance from stage to stalls must have been over twenty yards but my dream state accepted his long-distance ability without question. He held an oddly shaped bell and when he rang it the first time I was to rise to my feet. I did so. The attention of the audience was upon me but I could not respond to them in any way as Fallow almost immediately rang the bell a second time to usher me forward into his presence. It was a theatre of the common sort because I could smell and almost taste the rancid odours of cigarettes, spilled tea, old vomit and booze-assisted urine. But it was dark, too, dark like the trenches on a quiet night, lit for brief snatches by the bright flare from a Swan Vestas. I stumbled once or twice and even in my mesmerised state remembered to mutter apologies. There was now a short flight of steps ahead of me and I could clearly see that in his left hand the magician held not a gong or a bell but the square-topped grey helmet of the Rhine Army. He raised a thin stick in his right hand, ready to strike again with a resounding clang. And on the third stroke I would –

I felt Snapper's strong arms around my somnambulant shoulders preventing me from raising my bare head above the parapet. His onion and tobacco breath was pungent in my nostrils as he pleaded with me to return to the land of the conscious.

We shared a tot of rum later and I pressed a half crown into his sweaty palm but he returned it with a shake of the head as if taking it upon himself to clear away the last remnants of my troubled dreams. A flare went up to the east and the silence of the night was temporarily punctuated by the stuttering of a German machine gun. I returned to my bunk, wondering when my night wanderings would eventually lead me into its murderous path.

To the Boche, with their guns ever trained on us, we were all identical, just a bunch of Tommy targets. Worse still, our own top brass perceived each of us as merely another expendable pawn in the sacrificial chorus line of the latest bungled show.

"Several gaps in the front row, old chap? Never mind, there's a bunch of willing young recruits on the next boat from Dover. Soon have them marching like ants again, what ho!"

Whereas, of course, a couple of cold trench nights spent talking and gambling with the chaps proved to any doubters that we were all finely honed individuals and certainly not the round pegs the army and the government required us to be. Perhaps it was this right to selfhood that we were ultimately fighting to uphold. When the war was over – if it was *ever* over – the survivors must needs return and build a society broad enough to encompass our valuable differences.

It was at one and the same time both an indispensable and a dangerous commodity, this comradeship of battle. Snapper, Invisible, Rapunzel, Chalky, Haddock and the others – they were all my mates and I would gladly risk my life to protect my mates which is the very essence of soldiership. And yet these friendships were so fragile and tenuous, liable to be irreparably broken at any moment by a sniper's bullet or a stray piece of shrapnel. What was the point of all this fellow feeling when at the next pointless charge across No Man's Land or even simply patrolling this six foot deep, sandbagged ditch of death our best friend in the muddy universe could be snuffed out quicker than a candle on the altar?

Forgive me for rambling on and raising so many questions, rhetorical or insoluble. I had an onerous duty to perform tonight. One of our number – Private Mark Jones, better known as Sniffer – had volunteered to venture out beyond the barbed wire in order to retrieve some of the guns and ammunition from yesterday's fallen. In a war of attrition it might come down to who had the last magazine or mortar bomb left up their sleeve, or so we were reliably informed by HQ. Jones was a wiry but immensely strong chap, an ex-farmhand; technically too young to enlist but that hadn't held him or thousands of others back from the front line. He'd ploughed fields, milked cows, shorn sheep and sustained a slight rash from visiting a brothel in Bethune, the one time he'd known the pleasures of a woman. We called him Sniffer because he was desperately trying to grow a moustache even though the black hairs on his top lip were a constant irritant to his nostrils. We'd arm-wrestled for a wager that very afternoon, best of three, and he'd beaten me two-nil.

Crossing the mud and the debris in a low crouch he'd accidentally stepped on an unexploded shell. And yet even as his boot came down he must have withdrawn it slightly because instead of being blown to pieces he'd lost a leg and suffered serious chest and facial injuries; but was alive enough to spend the next two hours emitting tortured screams for merciful relief. Even with our hands over our ears or the gramophone turned up to full volume we could not blot out his agonised cries.

After about an hour of this aural torture, the local CO called a party of us together and demanded something be done.

"Come on, you chaps," he chided, "it's a mercy mission. I need a volunteer."

Silence as we studied the mud on our boots or scratched surreptitiously at the lice lining the seams of our trousers.

"Are we not English?" he demanded. "Where's your mile-wide brave streak? Where's your fellow feeling for a comrade in trouble?"

Eventually, we tired of his ranting and raving. Snapper scanned the horizon with the Captain's field glasses. The blokes had a whip-round for cigarettes and chocolate rations but, really, *I* was more interested in shutting up the CO as I clambered over the parapet in the semi-darkness armed only with a revolver and a grubby handkerchief which would show up as white in the beam of a searchlight. I hoped. If the German sentries decided I was leading an advance party I could have no real complaints at their obvious response.

Oh God, let me die instantaneously when my time comes!

I found Sniffer sprawled amid an array of helmets, spent bullets, half-buried skulls and glutinous mud.

"Come on, son," I said cheerily, "let's drag you back over our side of the fence and let the medical boys sort you out."

We both knew this for a kindly meant falsehood. The stretcher parties had been drafted over to the fighting on our left flank and news reached us regularly that those with more than a simple case of trench foot were left groaning in a crowded corner of the clearing station for days on end without attention.

"I'm done for, sir," he whispered.

"Nonsense," I countered. "You might not play football for England but in the country of the lame the one-legged man will be king."

He smiled, holding back a grimace with courage beyond his years. "My leg's not the worst of it, sir. I can't breathe much longer. It's like I got a whole Hun battalion on me chest, sir. Make it easy on me, sir, I can't fight no longer."

I bent down to put my hands under his shoulders. Blood erupted from the side of his ribs and he began coughing and choking without the physical capacity to make his position any more comfortable. One eye was already hollow and he'd lost half the caterpillar moustache along with the skin covering jaw and cheekbone. Put a mirror down his middle and he might have passed as presentable in the moonlight. He screamed suddenly like a soul in torment and I laid him back down on the squelchy ground. Momentarily fearful for my own safety, I glanced across at the dim shadows of the German entrenchment. Maybe they were busy cooking and consoling and would not jump up at every squeal unless the sounds became too proximate.

"Make it easy, sir," he gasped again. "Please."

I unholstered my pistol. A bullet to the brain would be quickest, I judged. I held my gloved hands steady as I rested the barrel against Sniffer's skull but I averted my eyes. It was just another pointless death among so many but was no easier to bear for all that.

The sound of the shot echoed off the barbed wire entanglements and the low-lying clouds which promised further rain within the hour. I did not hang around to witness my handiwork but scuttled back to our position like a rat to its lair.

Chalky broke the outmoded rules of etiquette by clapping me on the shoulder and stating, "You did the right thing, sir. You had no choice."

I spent the rest of the night awake in my cold, damp dugout wondering how one could ever know what was "the right thing" and when exactly any of us had last had a real choice.

I was given a few days recuperation back at HQ. The chance to sip fine liqueurs, scoff palatable three course meals and spend all day perusing jingoistic newspapers was a welcome relief to my shattered nerves. There was even talk of me being shipped home with an honourable discharge. Mother would have been thrilled and the chance to track down my beloved Mary – the lost Eurydice of my youthful fumblings – was a prospect I savoured.

Perhaps too obviously, for it was snatched away from me just as I'd dared to believe in its probability. My hands had ceased shaking and in all other respects I was as normal and average a citizen as any chap within the uniformed ranks. Perfect cannon fodder, in fact.

This was the moment to mention the re-occurrence of my somnambulating and thus at least achieve a stay of sacrifice. But I kept a typical British stiff upper lip, accepted my lot and was back at the front line before you could say General Kitchener.

Dimwit. Dunderhead.

Patriotic simpleton.

When I saw Casper Fallow's magic act again he had added a new trick to his repertoire: he claimed to be able to catch a live bullet fired through a pane of glass. It had to be enormous sleight of hand, I assumed, and yet I went again to see his demonstration on the following evening and was lucky enough to be the Johnny Public invited up into the spotlights to check his hands and various pockets for hidden props and replacements. His assistant squeezed the trigger and there was the cone headed cylinder caught perfectly between thumb and forefinger like a metallic cigarette butt. Still warm to the touch and grooved from its rapid expulsion. The man's reactions, I had to believe, were faster than the eye could see and no doubt faster than the photographic processes of Mr Eastman or Mr Kodak would be able to capture.

He would have made a great comrade in arms. He had the necessary trait of trench humour, also. With a thin-lipped smile, he turned to his applauding audience and said, "Promise me that you won't try this trick at home."

For King and Country

           Against Kaiser Bill

A gentle breeze across the downs,
The thwack of willow upon leather,
Cucumber sandwiches and evensong.

           Another broken night
           Wet feet and mud-stained clothes,
           Blood seeps through the gaps in
             the sandbags.

The pealing church bells.

Victory will be ours with God on our side.
Men of Britain – Enlist!
Save our schools and our Empire.
Save our stately homes.

141

The stench of gas and urine.
Rations not fit for a pig – when there are
any.
Give us a light, boy, but quench the
match before the Boche sees us.
Dead horses and gun carriages sinking
in mud like quicksand.
Reminds me of when I –

Buckets and spades and
bathing machines,
End of the pier shows and
"What The Butler Saw".
Throw another shilling in the pot:
we'll have a right good old knees-up.

Endless, senseless killing.
Face down in Flanders.
Certain death on the Somme.
Lights out and don't listen
to the wounded wailing.
Hush, here comes a whizz-bang.

Rumours sweep along the front line like the early morning mist off the stinky Somme. The casualties from the last show are put well into the hundreds. By afternoon the figure will have been exaggerated into thousands. Still, we reputedly gained twenty square yards, so that's all right then, isn't it? Twenty stinking yards of stinking, cloying, grey French mud that might once have nurtured a vineyard but is now ruined for agriculture and building alike for at least the next decade. I'm no mathematician but it seems to me that if we lose men and gain ground at this stupendous rate we'll need the population of China and Mongolia on our side as well as the current allies in order to make headway into the Fatherland. That's if we did actually move our barbed wire emplacements forward at all yesterday.

No doubt the top brass are ensconced safely back at Divisional HQ – General Haig and all his bloody cronies getting saddle sore in their comfy armchairs – and *our* positions and *their* positions are carefully plotted and pinned upon a large-scale map and it maybe makes some kind of sense but to me out here it's just the usual mess and confusion of all infantry based wars through the ages.

My battalion has gained no ground. My nerves are shot to pieces and I can hardly hold this pen or grip my tin mug of lukewarm tea. My colleagues have suffered serious injuries and are even now being carted back through the communications trenches to the Field Hospital where their chances of surviving are slight at best. For the honour of England? Fighting to save our green and pleasant land? Showing a firm hand to a hated aggressor? I don't think so.

General Haig, don't be vague,
How many yards did you gain today?
Douglas Haig, king of slaves,
How many men need a fresh-dug grave?

I've been here less than six weeks but already I am completely disillusioned with my life, my lot and the team I'm ballistically representing. So why do I not simply throw down my arms and surrender? Or desert?

Like any soldier at almost any other stage of such a protracted engagement, I fight because I fight. Nothing more. I'm a soldier; it's what soldiers do.

Another grey dawn somewhere in the Autumn of 1916. The sun rose behind the enemy lines, shining onto the barbed wire enclosing their fortifications as if illuminating the thorny hedgerows of the mechanical age. I was partway through my first cold water shave of the week when I was summoned to Captain Featherstone's dugout. I hastily wiped off what little lather remained, checked the straightness of my shirt and issue tie and made my way through the two closest communications trenches – Harrow Road and Rayners Lane – to his palatial abode. The sound horn of the gramophone was showing signs of damp-induced rust; the wooden supports by the rear wall looked ready to give way at any moment. Still, the metal pot was gurgling on the hob and I gratefully accepted his offer of a hot drink.

"Is there something bothering you, sir?" I inquired. "Over and above the usual," I added.

"Yes, Lieutenant Dove, there is something more than the usual. I'm concerned about Private Fairclough and Corporal Boatman. Rapunzel and Haddock, I believe the chaps call them."

"That's correct, sir. Fairclough has unruly ginger curls somewhat longer than regulation length, hence the fairy tale reference. Boatman is from a fishing family, sir."

"Yes, thank you, a very fine lesson in etymology, I'm sure. What concerns me is that I discovered these two in intimate contact last night and I'd like your advice on what action I should take."

"Uh, how intimate, sir?"

"Let's just say their contact was of the Oscar Wilde variety. Bloody nancy boys! My school was full of them, you know. They ought to be rounded up and shot at dawn as a moral example."

I smiled. "Well, Captain, it sounds like you've already made your mind up."

He banged the folding table, spilling the remnants of both our teas. "That's my heart speaking, Lieutenant!" he roared. "My *gut* feeling, if you will. I remain, however, a professional soldier and will be guided by the head in matters such as these."

"Well," I began, "one or two snide comments were passed along the line about Rapunzel simply because of his physical appearance. Haddock, however, has never once given us cause to question his masculinity. The point is, sir, that these are men under fire and we all require a comforting arm from time to time in the face of such stress. With no wives and girlfriends on the front line, some blokes can't help seeking, uh, physical solace with each other. I believe similar instances have occurred in His Majesty's prisons and on board ships long out at sea."

"Hmm, Dove, very eloquently expressed, I'm sure, and, frankly, the sort of justification I half-expected from you. So, what disciplinary measures do you suggest I take?"

"Uh, none, sir."

"None!"

"Who has been harmed by it and who even knows about it?"

"It's illegal and immoral and downright depraved! And you suggest I do nothing!"

"Let it go, sir, as a temporary aberration. They're both good fighting men and, in any case, we might all be mown down in another over the top charge in a few days' time."

He wrinkled his nose as if I'd emitted an unpleasant eructation. Not that the trenches could have smelt any worse than they already did.

Eventually, he answered, "Have it your way, Dove. Typical *laissez faire* attitude. The sort of outlook that got us in this mess in the first place, if you ask me, but an expedient one in this instance."

"Think of their families, sir," I suggested.

He required a moment to glean my meaning, then nodded silently.

"Get back to your duties, soldier," he ordered.

"Yes, sir."

Notions of home comforts and hearth fires burning took my thoughts scurrying back to Mary, my lovely Donegal lass with the shiny chestnut hair and rounded hips. My father had worked his way up the slippery Adam Smith ladder and by my teen years we were quite a well-to-do family with a respectably addressed property in central London. Ours was new money, so polite society was less than welcoming. It was money, nonetheless.

Mary's mother, Mrs O'Keane, had prospered in service after arriving penniless and with a babe in arms almost two decades previously. She worked for one of my father's business associates and when we were able to afford a housekeeper her daughter came with the highest recommendation. She was a couple of years older than I, her face already a little care-worn by burdensome domestic duties but bright and smiling during our shared moments. Yes, I know, I know, the old master and servant set-up but I really felt passionately about my warm Irish miss, even to the extent of professing love and a desire to legally cement our union. Besides, I was not so much a master as a penny-pinching student struggling to compete with the lush lifestyles of my college peers. I told none of them that Mary was of the servant class; nor did I speak of the affair to my parents. When we met for chaste woodland walks we were as any other two love-struck young people. Our intimate contact occurred mostly in her own chilly quarters. Such fecund treasures lurked beneath her starched linen uniform, such Grecian alabaster thighs were uncovered by her ridden-up lacy petticoats!

She left our employ suddenly.

I neglected my classes for a full two weeks as I attempted to track her down. Eventually I received a tip-off that she was hiding in a sorry and penniless state in the back room of a laundry near Whitechapel.

She'd had "some business I had to take care of, John, sir." That she was no longer with child left me with sorely mixed feelings. At that time I was not in a sound enough financial position to adequately care for her and any offspring. I emptied my pockets, implored her to stay in touch, swore fidelity that I held onto for more than a year. Inexorably, it seemed, she slipped out of my life.

If I'm fighting for anything, it's perhaps for the chance to re-create my life with Mary within a juster, fairer, less class-restricted society where I would not be frowned upon or disowned and she would not be viewed as an opportunist or gold-digger.

She was my comfort. Socially right or wrong. An earthly paradise... lost.

Then suddenly I was up and over the barbed wire again. Usually, it was never anywhere *near* quiet at night, what with the stray shells, the creaking wheels of the corpse collecting wagons and the anguished cries of wounded men in muddy trenches. And yet a certain calm seemed to descend over me and my surroundings also as I stepped light-footedly through the patchily lit quagmire of No Man's Land. Half-awake or half-asleep, I wasn't sure which mental state was dominant. In theory, I was in more danger at this moment than at any other during this so-called Great War and yet I felt almost divinely protected as if surrounded by an invisible shell rather like the Martians in Mr Wells' fine novel.

Nothing could touch me. I could undertake the glorious one-man death or glory mission so beloved of our top brass, our sat at the rear "we sustained a few hundred casualties today but gained two and a quarter yards of Somme River border bog land so that's all right to print in the papers" blundering generals and majors.

I moved beyond bitterness. Light as Ariel, errant as Puck. The incessant rain was back to its mere drizzle stage and a hint of moonlight teased and tantalised way on high like a whore to a sailor. Or an angel like the one so many claimed to have seen at Mons.

I must have walked a good mile and a half along the disputed hinterland. It was as if I was outside time. I watched a horsefly cross my path about ten feet in front of my nose, its progress slow and laboured as if swimming in glue. I walked to *their* barbed wire unseen and unhindered and was about to vault across and wreak bloody havoc when something – caution? fear? morality? – got the better of me and I opted instead for a casual stroll back to my starting point. The ditches and the foxholes were uncannily quiet, as if everyone had suddenly seen the pointlessness of this attrition and gone back to grooming horses or driving trains. Only the irritable lice in the lining of my trousers kept up their busy night's work.

"Are you all right, sir?"

It was Snapper, a good old East End boy on sentry duty, breaking my reverie as I stumbled back into the firing trench.

"Just stretching my legs, private. Too much weak tea – made me restless, what?"

"Yes, sir. I thought for a moment you'd – no, that's ridiculous. Well, good night, sir. Hope you settle to sleep soon."

"Thank you, private. Good night."

For a time I harboured youthful ambitions of becoming a stage magician. I nagged at my father to take me to as many performances as he could. The nature of the theatre was changing, however, and some of the shows we ended up frequenting were of the less salubrious variety, to say the least. Bawdy songs with sing-along choruses delivered by over-painted ladies in frilly French petticoats seemed to be the order of the day. On closer inspection, some of these songstresses proved to have dark stubble to match their husky voices.

I returned to my books but found I could not properly manage the swift sleight of hand necessary to pull off even the simplest card tricks, let alone produce rabbits from hats or apparently saw some buxom lovely into two pieces.

I managed to see Casper Fallow again, however. Some ten years on from the first occasion, he seemed to have aged at an alarming rate, rather like Dorian Gray's hidden portrait. From my seat at the edge of a side aisle, I espied a stagehand up in the rafters responding to the performer's nods and winks by pulling levers and ropes to keep the illusions coming fast and fleeting. Casper caught the bullet again and I was struck by the way a silver-haired, somewhat shabby old man could still command dominance over our state of the art killing technology. It was a matinee performance and afterwards a couple of shillings placed in the caretaker's grubby mitts enabled me to nose around the empty theatre for half an hour or so on the pretext of having lost a sentimental fob watch.

A cursory examination of discarded props and partition boards yielded nothing of the mesmerist's secrets. I began my search anew and just before the doors opened for the later audience I found what I was looking for: a pointy-nosed, still slightly warm, brass shell along with two, unused live bullets. The trick was surely in their composition. I broke both open with a pocket-knife. They seemed to be of the regular sort and contained a substance which looked and smelled like gunpowder, so I was none the wiser. Maybe Casper Fallow really could stop the bullets in their flight. Maybe it was genuinely *speed* rather than *sleight* of hand.

Short of confronting him in a dark alley with the advantage of a sharp dagger in my hand, I might never know the truth. I wasn't sure the knowledge would in any way justify such ungentlemanly unpleasantness.

Enlist now!

Die later.

Your country needs you.

Your country considers you expendable.

We must stop the advance of the Kaiser's war machine.

We must continue with the advance of our own.

Are you a man or a mouse?

Only rats have a realistic survival
rate in the bogs around the Somme.

With your education and background we could get you a commission as an officer

You can watch your subordinates die five minutes before the bullet comes for you.

All the nice girls love a serviceman.

Catch a dose of the clap from some French whore old enough
to be your grandmother

Daddy, what did you do in the
Great War?

You'll never be a daddy with
your bollocks shot off.

I think I have been sleepwalking again, although it's so hard to differentiate dreams from reality.

The blood in my body, perennially frozen by the ceaseless rain and deprivations of trench life, must have risen to the surface because the sensation I was most aware of was warmth. Not the so-called heat of battle but the blazing of a summer sun bringing rivulets of sweat coursing down my forehead like tiny tributaries of the stinking Somme.

Yes, it was daylight. Yes, therefore, I was almost certainly dreaming. That doesn't negate my experience any.

The tanks had arrived to save the day for the brave English. I saw huge, futuristic machines and gigantic guns out of the imaginings of Jules Verne. Instead of the inconsistently issued – and often ineffective – regulation gas masks, many of the combatants around me wore whole suits to protect themselves against the chlorine and mustard potions from our Mephistophelian enemy. Manoeuvres were underway, if not an actual conflict, and occasionally the air was rent by the banshee scream of aeroplanes unrecognisable from the buzzing hornets barely able to stay up more than five minutes I'd seen demonstrated down at Farnborough in 1914. Either our government has followed the conjuror's example and kept a huge arsenal of technological marvels concealed up its collective sleeve awaiting the opportune moment to smash the Kaiser's minions or else... or else, I had, like a shell-shocked Nostradamus, fallen into prophetic mode and been transported like the traveller in H. G. Wells' *Time Machine* to a yet more violent future. This latter improbability was given possible credence by the way in which I seemed to be both present and absent at one and the same time.

Careless of my own personal wellbeing, I reached out to grab several of the uniformed personnel as they scurried busily past me. Most would not meet my eye or simply shrugged away my gossamer touch. When one finally did acknowledge my existence he proved to be one of our Yankee cousins. I was not aware that they had yet sided with us *militarily* in this current conflict. He had remarkably good teeth for a front line soldier. He gave a crisp salute at my stripes and said, "Have a nice day, sir." Who said Americans can't understand irony?

The sky to my right was hellish red and I became aware of the pungent and almost overwhelming smell of burning oil. This olfactory impression must have jogged some safety mechanism in my brain as the next thing I recall is jerking awake to the sight and smell of Snapper greasing his gun and dragging hard on a weedy little hand-rolled cigarette.

"The first one of a new day and the most important, eh, sir?" he grinned.

I muttered something haughtily incomprehensible in reply.

My recollections are *so* mixed up. I may have wandered or I may merely have writhed in my slumber. Only time will tell.

I was shaking and crying but Mother's loving arms were around me.

"Poor Johnny," she whispered like a religious ritual, "there, there, it's all right."

"Was I dreaming again, Mummy?"

"Yes, darling. And walking about the house. We were worried you might have an accident."

"I saw Billy again, Mummy. He was calling me towards him. I... I was so happy to see him again."

"I'm sure you were, darling, but... your brother's with the angels now. He's peaceful and happy there. He wouldn't want you to join him just yet. Not till you've lived a long life just like Grandpa did."

"I'm not going to die yet, Mummy, am I? Not like Billy did?"

"No, darling, you're going to be with us for... ooh, ages and ages! Just as long as you keep taking your tonic."

She pulled me in to the warmth of her bosom. Although I was five I was still reminded of milk and sugar by her tender proximity.

"Mummy," I mumbled, "I don't mean to walk in the night. I was just thinking about Billy, that was all."

"I know, darling. I never suggested there was any mischief about it. I'm sure you'll grow out of it but I'll speak to Dr Cranleigh again in the morning."

"Who was that strange looking guy I saw you talking with?"

"Dunno, didn't get his name. Some Brit. Cuckoos in the nest, if you ask me."

"Waddya mean?"

"Kept going on about fighting the Germans and digging trenches and stuff. Weird shit from, like, donkey's years ago, you know what I mean?"

"Jesus. Reckon Saddam's gases have really got to that one?"

"Yeah, I guess. Unless he's that famous unknown soldier the sarge told us about back at base camp."

"Aw, come on, that's kids' stuff! You're having me on!"

"Yeah, course I am. Just some poor saddo lost his gas mask. What're you drinking?"

"Pepsi. I'll pretend it's got some Bacardi in it."

"Yeah, fucking A-rabs and their alcohol ban. Should let 'em fight their own war, if you ask me."

"Can't. All wars are American wars from now on. And don't forget you heard it here first."

"Meathead!"

"Cornball!"

Looking for a nice little two up two down or a country manor with a bit of an estate, sir? Maybe I can interest you in *Five Trench Chateau*, an extensive property on the banks of the picturesque River Somme that's been on our books for several months now without anyone taking firm possession? Ah, the delicious smells of the countryside! The stench of mud and urine. Somebody crapped themselves by the mobile canteen but nobody really noticed. Wonderful indigenous wildlife! Rats the size of cats that nip at your exposed features and run off with the bulk of your meagre rations. Lice in whole colonies down the lining of your trousers. That comforting, itchy feeling day and night; who would be without it?

The place comes with a whole coterie of youthful and manly domestic servants. Admittedly, some have been crippled during the course of their duties. That there's Mister Haddock, the world's first arm-less butler. Young Master Snapper would be pleased to look after your dogs and horses once he's picked up his spilled guts and sewn them back into his bullet-riddled torso.

We believe in the class system, of course, sir. It's the natural order, ain't it? It's what made this country great. So do your new neighbours, in their own way. Yes, I admit they're a little lively but that's to be applauded, surely? They're German and they do like their beer gardens and patriotic songs. But we exchanged presents with them at Christmas and reputedly some of the lower orders engaged them in an association football match. I'm a rugby man, myself. And they have such heavenly voices when you can hear them above the mortars and whiz-bangs. *Stille Nacht...*

The area has many claims to be an important historical site. The major landmarks are indicated on this rather quaint hand-drawn map: that's where Ginger lost his left leg; over there Jenkins stepped on a live shell; and a yard to the east a dozen men lost their lives on a forgotten charge over the top. Some suggest the plot is haunted – like the Angel of Mons and all that rot. Not a superstitious man myself, as it goes.

It's a property that comes highly recommended, sir. As the Great War poets would surely say, "There is some shit hole in a foreign bog that is forever England."

I grew up essentially as an only child. My brother Billy was two years older than I but died of pneumonia when I was only three. I, too, was afflicted and temporarily weakened by the disease. *Why* I should have recovered whilst my seemingly stronger sibling succumbed remains a painful mystery to this day. Though I knew him for just a few formative years he left a huge impression on me and his loss is something I've struggled to come to terms with every day of my life.

My mother did give birth again much later in life, a girl and a boy twelve and ten years my junior. They are more like a niece and a nephew to me. I've had little contact with either of them what with boarding school, college and work commitments.

I know Billy would see through the iniquities and blunders of our commanders and yet he'd still be proud of me for signing up to fight the Hun. I said nothing at my interview or medical about my childhood somnambulation. Why should I? Until I set foot in the trenches I'd been cured of it for over a decade.

Maybe we're never really cured of anything; perhaps all we can ever hope for is an extended period of remission.

It had rained all day. We had fired the occasional useless volley through the barbed wire at our invisible foe but mostly we had spent the time crouching in whatever makeshift shelter we could find with our scrofulous socks and wet cigarettes. Even Jerry seemed to have called a temporary halt to the ceaseless chatter of his machine guns so that today's danger was falling props and sudden mudslides caused by the deluge. One such avalanche revealed a stray right arm from some hapless Tommy who'd have difficulty performing juggling tricks or shaking hands with Saint Peter.

Tonight, however, the clouds had moved away to allow a sliver of moon to illuminate the ghostly desolation that had been home to us survivors for the past few months. The last home we all might ever know.

And there I was, *again*, upright in No Man's Land, a stupefied, somnambulant target careless of my personal safety and hardly in control of my actions.

"Come and get me, you bastards!" I wanted to call out but in truth my voice was little more than a phantasmal whisper in the semi-darkness. "Do your worst, see if I care."

No volley of metal-death was forthcoming. Not a peep. It was as if the German platoons were all fast asleep with not a single sentry minding the shop. Maybe they weren't even there at all any more, if they ever had been. The enemy we fought was some sort of grotesque supernatural projection of ourselves: the devils within us, made substantial.

"All right, Fritz and Hans," I offered in a stage whisper, "ready or not, I'm coming to get you."

I maintained a lightness of step despite the quagmire beneath my booted feet. *This time*, I promised myself, this time I would exact sweet ice cream cold revenge for all my late or maimed comrades. If it meant laying down my own life as a glorious sacrifice, so be it. What are we here for, anyway?

Oh Mary, I want to come home a hero and sweep you up into my arms and say, "Hang the class system, we were destined to be together!"

– But she's probably found a companion of her own station in life by now. And after all I put her through, who would blame her? If only... if only I can survive this endless battle of attrition and return to London, I *will* seek her out and we will be married. Oh, to rest my hands on those warm, firm thighs again!

As I crossed over into enemy lines, I amended my earlier dancing acrobatics to the more considered progress of the tightrope walker. At the very edge of their barbed wire I became aware of a slight buzzing in my ears. I paused. Midnight was usually a quiet time for flies and mosquitoes, or so I had always assumed.

To my left, at the periphery of my vision, I spotted something *burrowing* through the air like a whisk churning through a vat of butter. I reached out with a curious, rapid, grabbing motion worthy of a creature in the London Zoological Gardens and grasped the airborne object.

It was a bullet.

But travelling *so* slowly? Had that been how Casper Fallow performed his act? And yet, in that case, most of the audience would have perceived the deception. Besides which, this was a combat zone in the war to end wars – what use would a *slow bullet* be here?

With a nut-cracking pincer movement, I broke open its casing. Like birds and rabbits from a conjuror's hat or an endless string of flags from an illusionist's sleeve, the contents seemed to be too bulky and too *many* to be contained within such a small vessel. To my astonished eyes, I withdrew: a twist of silk, its heady perfume still detectable above the mephitic odour of mud and carnage; a gold wedding ring, inscribed microscopically with four initials; a valentine's card quoting a Shakespearean sonnet; and a miniature baby's crib which fell out of my tired hands and seemed to inflate into full size as I watched open-mouthed! I ran my fingers over its wicker-work, feeling a little like the Egyptian maid who discovered the infant Moses in the River Nile. What strange sorcery was this – a bullet containing all these icons from a man's life?

Then I did something you should never do on a battlefield at *any* time unless you have an over-riding desire to join your ancestors: I closed my eyes.

I held the bullet like a precious jewel. My vision cleared to reveal a spring day in leafy England and two young people absenting themselves somewhat from a mixed age group exploring the edge of a coniferous forest. She lifted the train of her white skirts as she set a dainty foot on the forest floor and his gentlemanly hand supported her and stayed clasped even when conditions underfoot improved. I guessed them to both be on the cusp of twenty. The woman giggled as the man's pencil moustache tickled her lips when they kissed for the first time. But she invited him back for a second and third helping. Then they both became a tad embarrassed as if scared of detection.

They made their way back to the main party and the vision faded.

The crib, I noticed, had almost sunk into the welcoming mire. I continued walking.

I could see the German soldiers now, sleeping and immobile like the lions in Trafalgar Square. All except for one private who moved in a painfully snail-like manner as he attempted to turn his machine gun and spray a further barrage of bullets into the chill November air. *Slow bullets...*

Was he crippled in some way? Were they *that* desperate for fighting men?

Or was it that, in some inexplicable manner, I was able to move with greater speed and grace than those around me and thus possessed an insuperable advantage? *This* was my chance to achieve the glorious retribution that not only would avenge my dead companions but might even gain me deserved promotion *away* from the Eastern Front.

Oh Mother, look at your little studious boy now with his guns and his uniform... and his heart full of hatred!

I moved slightly to the side of the Jerry's firing line – it was an easy task, believe me. I casually picked more of the flying cylinders out of the air. I broke a couple open. More mementoes and memories: a fading photograph, a school certificate, a gold cross and chain and entwined locks of blonde and brown hair. Their purpose seemed clear to me now; their easy avoidance, too.

The square head finally managed to get his weapon trained upon me. I let the lead bullet crawl towards me and caught it more casually than Casper Fallow could ever have dreamed of doing. This one I didn't open. Instead, I placed it safely within my jacket pocket and stepped towards the sluggish aggressor.

I thought of using my pistol but decided that an unsheathed bayonet was probably a better bet. The fear on the man's face was brighter than a hundred Pole Stars. I thrust, wounded him in the side of his chest. The blood trickled out red and torpid. He required one more blow to finish him off, what our French allies call the *coup de grace*. But I didn't want to deliver it.

The bullets I was collecting all had their set targets, identified by the significant contents they contained. I was beyond their range; no bullet had my name on it or my identifying icons within. I was the soldier who could not be killed. I had my time, so why not extend his for a little longer? Oh, nowhere near as long as mine will last, but measurable in minutes, maybe hours. Let him try to slither away.

And let me wander. There was no rush. There *is* no rush. No rush at all.

VISITS TO THE FLEA CIRCUS

Nick Jackson

Sensational and harrowing news.

An attractive young woman, elegantly dressed, climbed to the top of the southern tower of the cathedral accompanied by the clock winder, Bonifacio Martinez and two other persons, one by the name of Eagle and the other Sotano. It is not known exactly how the young woman, Rosa Sofia Gutzman Lopez, managed to become separated from her party but, having reached the second floor of this prodigious edifice, some two hundred feet above ground level, she determinedly threw herself from the parapet.

The fall immediately attracted a large group of people who clustered around the young woman as she lay on the ground. The crowd quickly grew very dense as more and more people gathered, attracted by the noise and emotion. The police were alerted and Sen☐ or Inspector Mun☐ oz was the first to arrive on the scene, accompanied by an assistant. It was then that the first practical steps were taken to move the corpse on a stretcher to the police station nearby.

When Rosa's fingers touched the smooth cold marble of the staircase she trembled and felt her knees quiver. The steps were quite shallow, less than the length of her hand, so that her feet fitted only just onto the step, edgeways. They had been smoothed by generations of clock winders and masons so that the front edge of each was slightly concave and gently rounded. The stairs rose in a tight spiral and the ceiling was so low that the men had to remove their hats and lean forwards to avoid colliding with the underside of the stairs above. She was following Mr Eagle and was the last of the party to ascend.

The echo of those above, their shuffling steps in the gloom, came down to her together with the murmur of the clock-winder who was explaining the history of the bell tower. She heard how one of the bells had cracked and had to be replaced, not once, but three times. She imagined the dark fissure in the bell, creeping across the smooth surface, like the cracking plaster in her bedroom wall.

The effort of lifting her skirts drained all her energy. She was vaguely aware of her hands on the cold marble, her long dragging skirts, her parasol hanging lifeless from a finger. Her mother had been so insistent on the parasol: "You have to think about your skin, dear."

The corpse was in a pitiable condition: one of the eyeballs had been dislodged from the socket. The skull had been fractured and a part of the cerebellum remained on the cornice of the first floor of the tower, where the skull had struck it during the fall. The lower jaw was broken in three places. There was extensive bruising to the torso and the lower limbs were dislocated and had severe fracturing.

[This was noted down by the coroner's assistant in a book kept for that specific purpose]

The victim was wearing a linen skirt and short jacket trimmed with lace. There was a matching hat and parasol. The victim's handbag contained a purse with seventeen pesos, a half pencil, a tram ticket (used), a glove button and three loose rosary beads.

The silence of the crowd was the silence of those who contemplate not misfortune but sensation. They were grateful to her for making their mortality palpable. Her demise was an act of generosity, a gloriously public event in which they could all share and an opportunity for endless speculation and comment. Slowly the silence became a furtive murmur.

"Is she dead?" asked a child.

"Her shoes are off," said a little girl, her voice shockingly loud.

"Shh!"

"Why would she kill herself?"

"Who knows?"

"Maybe her fiancée was knocking her about."

"It could have been a debt."

"Or drugs."

"So young and already an addict!"

Those at the back of the crowd, who had no view, began asking others at the front what they could see and those at the front, or who were tall enough to see, were relaying fragments of information.

"Is she young?"

"More or less."

"Is she dark?"

"She has brown hair."

"Is she American?"

"She could be."

Gradually the strange halting dialogue petered out. It was as if the crowd silently admired the moment of grandeur, the moment of absolute power which the dead one exerted over them. No-one dared touch the corpse.

There was a collective exhalation. Perhaps it was no more than anxiety, the anxiety that overpowers people when they are faced with tangible proof of the destructibility of the human body. But as well as anxiety there was relief. It was the fulfilment of a desire for something to happen, for there to be a closure, a termination. And it was 1899, a fitting year for final happenings.

Emelita was fascinated. She had never before witnessed death. The body looked like a doll she had once broken by twisting the limbs out of the sockets. The legs of the corpse appeared to be at a strange angle to the torso, as if they did not belong. She noticed a little red shoe with an iron buckle in the shape of a butterfly lying a little distance away. She wondered whether the shoe would fit the broken foot and wanted to reach out to try the experiment. But the pavement was glistening with a thick russet liquid, like red pepper sauce, and a powerful odour around the body mingled with the sweat of the crowd, so that she felt her head begin to swim.

On his first morning in the city, Nathan Eagle opened the shutters of the hotel room and looked out. He looked down into the stark street where the sun threw its hard light, baking the broken pavement and bleaching the clumps of grass that grew against the walls of the buildings. There was a man in a dirty white shirt kicking a yellow dog that was trying to mount another dog. He saw a ragged leafless tree and a lazy black and ochre butterfly floating above the traffic. Following the idle flight of the insect he raised his eyes to take in the fringe of the distant mountains and beyond, like a paper cut-out against the violet sky, the form of the volcano, in the flat blue far-away haze. This great triangle of silver-tipped rock seemed to impress its sense of mystery and absolute permanence on him, so that, closing his eyes against the glare, he could still see its form clearly etched on his retina.

Usually he recovered quickly from his love affairs but this time it was proving less easy. He had got involved with a widow, not beautiful but wealthy, and she had seemed to be more than willing to become attached to him so it was a matter of surprise when the subject of marriage had finally been broached and she had rejected him out of hand.

He thought of her now: in her black mourning dress with the necklace of jet, telling him that she could not, would not, marry him.

"It's not that I don't love you. It's just that I have too much respect for the memory of my husband..." She had felt his eyes on her. He was too handsome, too powerful and controlling. And she found herself afraid of him. But she reminded herself that she had a rich woman's fancies and did not have to explain herself.

"You've led me along," he claimed in that final embarrassing encounter, quivering on the brink of allowing himself to become angry. They had been interrupted by the unexpected arrival of some friends. Some time later he learned that she had become engaged to a wealthy ship owner.

He left the window and went into the tiny bathroom. As he sat on the toilet he watched a cockroach making its way with deliberation across the expanse of tiles towards him.

He crushed it with the heel of his boot. "Damn this city to Hell!"

Rosa Lopez was born in 1880 at the commencement of a period of great social unrest. The dark clouds of political turmoil rolled around the city like the summer storms that raged. Sometimes coteries of men and women would gather spontaneously on street corners. Their outraged voices were an anguished reminder of a different world. But inside the house, within the high castellated walls of pink stucco, she was cosseted by her environment.

In the patio grew plants with huge leaves like the spread palms of hands. Her first memory was of grubbing in the soil of the flower beds, engrossed by the squirming life she found there. When her mother came looking for her daughter, Rosa greeted her with handfuls of soil.

"Put down those filthy things!" Sra. Lopez had screamed, slapping the dirt away.

"I never want to see you in such a state again. Look at the filth on your clothes!"

Rosa looked down at her white skirt seeing the dark spots on the bleached linen for the first time. She had been too busy to notice them but now she rubbed at them ineffectually. Her mother made her sit in a chair in her underwear whilst the skirt was taken to be washed.

Lupita Lopez had to rescue her daughter from death by scorpion bite at the age of two and a half. She had walked to the window to see if it would be a cloudy afternoon and whether it would be worth the effort of asking Mercedes to peg out the washing on the roof, and happened to glance down into the courtyard where she saw Rosa with the fascinating creature glittering dangerously at her feet and holding out one small fat little hand to gently stroke it. The scorpion rattled its claws at Rosa and jerked its cunning tail, but the little girl laughed and crouched down closer.

"Rosa, come here dear," called Sra. Lopez.

She drew her daughter's attention just long enough for Mercedes to crush the body with the flat side of the broom and sweep up the corpse leaving only the exquisite pincers which looked as though they had been worked in filigree.

In the park the old man showed his collection of *pulgaditos* for a peso, tiny figures carved from slivers of wood, almost invisible unless viewed through a magnifying glass, then the detail with which they were painted became apparent. *El viejito* as everyone affectionately called the old man, wore an oversized coat in dark cloth which served as the backdrop to his tiny menagerie. He took the shiny silver pesos with a hand sprinkled with liver spots, a leathery hand, yet soft as kid.

He handed Rosa the magnifying glass so that she could see the tiny lady with a parasol dressed in a frock of paper lace – how he could make her spin. There was a man on a horse jogging along through a landscape of cacti and a drunkard waltzing with a red-painted devil with horns. The devil waltzed with the lady and Rosa laughed as the drunkard tried to stand but was knocked down time and again by the horseman, the old man made funny voices for his flea-sized characters. There was another figure, who bobbed and weaved behind the others.

One never quite managed to see him properly, but there was something odd about him. Was it a stick he carried before him? Red, engorged, sticky with varnish.

"Oh!" The lady in the paper frock screamed faintly. Rosa was not sure what she had seen. "What is it Rosa?" Her mother peered at the little circus. The old man shuffled his cast of characters, his eyes as blank as boiled sweets. They were gone, the *pulgaditos*, back in their matchbox. The tiny theatre closed its curtains.

In this place Nathan's money brought him a new status he could enjoy. He ate in the best restaurants and strolled in the affluent districts, showing himself off to the wealthy patriarchs and, more importantly, matriarchs of the city. Those with daughters to dispose of looked with interest at a wealthy American.

Lupita Lopez was out with her daughter in the Alameda Gardens and had been introduced to him as a journalist writing a feature about the Day of the Dead for an American magazine.

Was it true, he asked her, that Mexicans liked to decorate the graves of their dead with flowers and sugared skulls?

"Oh yes, Mexicans laugh at death. For them it's a game. A time for celebration. But my daughter could tell you more. Her English is better than mine."

Rosa told him about the customs for the Day of the Dead: how families revered the memory of dead relatives by taking a feast to the cemetery at midnight, garlanding the gravestones, celebrating and singing songs to the departed.

"Death is joyful. We don't grieve for the dead. They're lucky not to endure any longer the humiliations of life."

"You seem too young to be talking about the humiliations of life."

"Life is full of endurances, small tests of strength."

"You are perhaps older than you seem."

"How old do I look?"

"Sixteen, or younger."

"I'm nineteen. But how do I seem to you? I'd like to hear the opinion of an American."

"A young woman, well-spoken, well-dressed. You seem sophisticated for a Mexican girl."

He thought she couldn't fail to be flattered by his speech. She would surely aspire to an image of bourgeois confidence. But she fell silent after that and he cursed the depths of women. It was so hard to know how to please them.

She was pretty. He could not deny it to himself. She had a long neck and carried her head high, revealing her pale throat. He looked at her sideways, trying to decide whether she were beautiful or merely pretty. He weighed the words in his head.

"Sophisticated," she demanded, "What does that mean? It doesn't sound very attractive."

For sixteen years she sat dreaming in the courtyard. The fussy silks and lace ruffles she was forced to wear made it impossible to run. She was moulded by the tedium of the afternoons, hot enough to fry tortillas in the sun, the buzzing insects and the dry rustling of the trees. In the shade she imagined places that she would escape to. Yes, one day, when she was old enough, the world would open its possibilities to her.

"One day," announced her mother, "you will marry a handsome man."

"Why must I marry?"

"That's the way the world is made. You'll give yourself to a man. You'll belong to him."

She began to envy the creatures that inhabited the courtyard. There was an emerald green lizard that lived in a crack in the wall by her window. It clung to the brickwork, its claws grasping the minute faults in the surface, its throat slowly pulsating in the heat. It put its head on one side and looked at her. She felt it had been there for a thousand years and that she was a fleeting shadow like the clouds that obscured the sun. The insects had no desires – only insatiable appetites: she witnessed a caterpillar's relentless consumption of a leaf and watched the birds pecking for crumbs. Their desperation and single-mindedness made her own existence seem pointless. She didn't understand what it was she had been created for, since she felt no such urges herself.

When she was fourteen she began to bleed. It frightened and disgusted her. She dreamed of men. She had no idea why, since she loathed the smell of them, but they populated her dreams all the same. She was trapped in idleness, having no ways of occupying her time other than cutting patterns from folded paper and embroidering the edges of linen. She could neither cook nor clean. The boys her mother brought to the house were limp beardless youths who shook with embarrassment whenever she looked at them. She wondered how she would ever bring herself to accept one of them as her husband.

But Mr Eagle, the American, was different. He had amber eyes like a wild dog. She did not understand his conversation. He seemed to wilfully misunderstand what she said and to twist the conversation to mean more than it did.

"Do you like the heat?" he had said to her when he came to their house.

"No, I like the coolness."

"You like to be distant then? You like to play at being difficult to get to know?"

His topics of conversation were too intimate for her: He asked her whether she bathed in the morning or the evening and which was more sensual. She thought perhaps it was because she did not understand the significance of the words he used.

He came every day, wearing a green silk jacket with a velvet collar. The birds fell silent when he came into the patio, perhaps it was the smell of his tobacco. The little hummingbird she kept in a tiny cage sat shuddering on its perch and did not feed again until he'd left.

One day he surprised her with a sudden kiss. He chose a moment when her mother was helping Mercedes to tidy away after lunch and her father had gone out to smoke. She stood by the window watching the blue smoke of his cigarette rising from behind the foliage. She had her back to the room but half turned, hearing a rustle of clothing behind her. He caught her and pressed her back against the wall feeling her small body moving against his. She caught the odour of his armpit that mingled with the cold scent of the lilies that stood in a jar on the table. Her nose was crushed into the velvet collar. He breathed into her hair and found the bony cartilage of one of her ears against his lips under her silky tresses. He drew back a little and found her mouth. It was a reluctant mouth that refused to open against his probing tongue. He cautiously moved his hips against her torso but his clothes felt tight. All he could feel of her waist was the bony rib of her corset.

Mr Eagle had a small brass microscope which he brought one afternoon to demonstrate to the family. First of all he showed them a feather, a small green parrot's feather in the palm of his hand. Beneath the lens he showed them how it became a forest, each fibre branching and dividing. Within the fibres he showed them one of the bird's ticks, how it clung to the feather as a bird clings to the branch of a tree.

Within a drop of water he showed them cyclops and daphnia, delicate pulsating organisms that jerked and trembled into focus.

"Of such minute particles is life composed," he told them as they took it in turns to peer into the microscope. "They are moments of existence; not individuals as such. They do not think, as we do. They have no higher capacity for thought and yet without them we could not exist." Rosa felt that she understood these moments of relapse into nothingness, into white space, as the mere state of being of the animals; no consciousness, just being.

Her father squinted into the lens. He saw nothing, only a monstrous grey shape that seemed to suck in on itself. It did not seem a miracle to him. He went back to his gilded colonial miniatures.

Rosa saw how, within the smallest droplet of water, a myriad of creatures fought with each other, swallowed and divided. She watched the eggs of a brine shrimp burst out of the body of their mother. This world, within the compass of a lens the size of a pigeon's eye, squirming with life as if it were a great urban metropolis. Then she felt very small, surrounded by the white space that she could not fill.

The wedding day drew near. Sra. Lopez fretted over arrangements for the feast. She slaved in the kitchen over dishes of pepper sauce, haggled in the market for the best turkeys and decided that she would have to have one sent from the country. She spent hours at the house of the dress-maker arranging for the sewing of the wedding gown and the trousseau. She was too preoccupied to observe the subtle changes in her daughter. The wedding cake, she decided, would have four tiers with a frieze of feathered icing and a trio of cupids at each corner.

Rosa had nothing to occupy her mind except the thought of her husband. She found herself looking for his approval.

"Very pretty," he said when she showed him a piece of embroidery or a sketch she'd done. "What a clever wife I'll have." He took her chin in his hand or laid a hand on her hip slowly caressing, ascertaining the shape and feel of flesh.

Meanwhile he went to meetings and wrote his political articles.

165

Rosa's father had introduced him to the young Flores Magon, a burgeoning orator, and he interviewed him for his magazine.

His talk of politics irritated her. She tried to focus on what he was telling her but found a buzzing fly at the window distracted her attention and she slipped into that sense of white emptiness which had become a daily retreat from the pressures of the impending marriage. Yet she sensed it did not matter to him that she did not argue with him or comment on his work.

One afternoon she was helping her mother to prepare the guavas for the dessert. She scraped out the soft pale pulp and it lay in a glistening heap on the wooden chopping board. She stood, mesmerised by the flesh swimming in its viscous juice like the entrails of some slaughtered animal.

"What are you doing Rosa?" Her mother was irritated by her daughter's limp and placid stare.

"I don't know."

"What use will you be to your husband if you stand about in that vacant way?"

"No use at all." She wandered out of the kitchen, absently wiping her hands on her dress.

He will have nothing to say to me, she thought, as she worked on a piece of embroidery.

She remembered him explaining to her: "You are no more than a collection of organs. You think there is a higher purpose to your existence but there is not. You've heard of the medusa, the great jellyfish that lives in the warm waters of the Gulf? It's not one creature but many: a complex community of interdependent organisms. You believe you are an individual with control over your life, but you are no more than the jellyfish that floats at the whim of the tides."

Now she began to think that he was right; that she was no more than a collection of organs and substances: the fluids that coursed through her veins and the acids swirling in her stomach.

As she stitched the bright red thread into the white cloth, tiny scarlet flowers like none she had ever seen, she had the curious sensation that the thread was all that held her life together, that without it the fabric would begin to unravel and she would be nothing more than a floating raggedness like a vapour.

One day, she did not realise it was a Saturday, only that it was close and hot, she took the parasol that her mother handed to her and put her hand on the velvet sleeve of Mr Eagle. It was a very soft sleeve. People passed them in the street and their mouths opened but no sound came out.

They walked and walked until they came to the Zocalo, the great square that stood before the cathedral of shining stone.

All along the shaded side of the square, the peasants had laid out their wares. Little piles of fruit symmetrically arranged, cashew nuts in twists of blue paper, finches hopping in tiny cages. Nathan stopped to buy some nuts but had no small change. As she stooped to hand over the coins to the child who was selling them, she had to put out a hand to steady herself. Her fingers brushed the pavement which was littered with crushed nut shells and cigarette ends. She noticed that the lines in the girl's face were ingrained with a fine layer of dirt making her seem like a very tiny old lady.

"It's too much," said the girl who had never seen a note for twenty pesos before and was worried at the prospect of finding change for so large a sum.

"It doesn't matter."

They arrived at the massive door of the cathedral. Nathan insisted on arranging a visit to the tower. She climbed up and up and found her skirts grew heavier and heavier. Finally, when she thought it was possible to go no further and was ready to fall, she stretched out her hands in the blinding light and was delivered into it.

The image of the lady lying on the flagstones, one perfect eye regarding the crowd with animal calm, sank deep into the mind of Emelita. She looked around at the puzzled faces of the crowd. She could not understand what made them gasp and beat the tears from their eyes.

With her mother she walked to the zoological gardens although it seemed strange to occupy their time so frivolously after what they had seen. But life had to go on, as her mother said. Emelita wandered around the enclosures and, distracted by the animals, she forgot about the crowd and the prone body. She watched the quicksilver fishes in their green-furred tanks and the cross blue-faced baboons with their sneering mouths. And the animals observed her. Some, like the birds and fishes, would not meet her eye, simply staring past her with cold indifference, but the monkeys gawped and clustered by the bars of their cages and held out their pink loose-jointed hands for pine-nuts. A herd of deer turned to watch her as she walked past their field. Their limpid eyes followed her as she in turn watched them.

One of the deer stood awkwardly. It opened its great brown eyes and in the black centre of the pupil she saw a distant image of herself in her yellow dress. The deer seemed to shudder, half-crouching, arching its slender neck. The hind legs buckled and then, as it turned away from her, she saw a great blue-black bag that slid from the dappled haunches with one quick convulsion. There it lay, crumpled, a bag of knotted bones and flesh.

The mother nosed it, the black glossy bag of slime, and it stirred. The bag split and a tiny head was raised. The mother licked away the sheets of mucus to reveal an eye, a clouded milky orb, slowly peering round and seeming to fix Emelita with its bleary gaze. When she thought later of the lady who had lain bruised on the pavement she could not quite picture her eye, instead the misty eye of the fawn came into her mind.

Emelita Reyes had seven children herself and countless grandchildren. Many years later she thought of the day when, on a trip to the city, she had seen a lady flying from a tower and then the birth of a fawn in the zoological gardens. Whether the eye of the one was contained in the eye of the other, whether the death and the life were separate or joined, she could not recall.

ALSISO

Justina Robson

The seeds of life fell on Teriapt as on a thousand other worlds, scattered by the Hand of Gaia Obasi Nsi, The Tortoise-Shelled. She was the first, the last and the only daughter of Earth gifted with the grain of DNA, nanoreplicators and the capacity to leap to any known space in the hopes of bringing forth other worlds fit for humans.

As Earth failed – her core too cool now, her magnetosphere waning, her atmosphere fatally struck by a coronal mass ejection which stripped a third of it away in a single night – Teriapt quickened. In a mere snap of evolutionary time Obasi Nsi's orbiting Fingers detected that the time was propitious and sent word back for explorers. The message arrived on the morning of Tuesday June 10th, eighty years after Obasi Nsi first set out, twenty three since her last known whereabouts.

Earth was a rock by then, and of all the excited adventurers in Teriapt's first Expeditionary Team Captain Delicia Conté was the only one ever to have been there. Her final report arrived back home a year later. It said…

'Teriapt not suitable for colonisation. Please send evacuation assistance.'

Her message was followed within the second by one from Timehorse Orynko, the mission second, who had ferried the expedition out there.

'Due to the compromising nature of circumstances on Teriapt I have assumed command of this mission and hereby declare the planet and its solar system beyond reclamation. I recommend that it be struck from all maps and records and that beacons be set up to warn any incidental travellers of its unsuitability.' She appended a few terabytes of additional information on the back of which Solargov and the Jovian Desolates decided they had to know what had happened in more detail, in case other planets went the same way. Teriapt was one of the first to show fruit.

They sent a second expedition; better scientists, harder gear.

(It was another two years or so until Orynko got back herself and the situation which greeted her was the defining moment in the fragmentation of her political naïvete: she discovered that the dictates of her perfectly valid scientific reasoning had not been followed.)

The second expedition fared no better. Their recorded journals, somewhat corrupted by a radiation leak, were returned to Solargov aboard the dead hulk of the Timehorse Expediency Chastaine who was towed in from deadspace where he'd failed to emerge safely from transit through Origin. An enquiry was set up into his death. Much later the government would collapse as a result of this investigation and what it uncovered about the relationship between the human worlds and the Unity alien entity which had given them the Stuff technology enabling this project, but that's far in the future. Today the journals arrived and today they seem to contain facts which bear only on Teriapt and its particular problems.

Recording #23, Day 2, Distance from Expedition Base 5.4km SW

<< Alsi-so <beat> Alsiso Alsiso Alsiso <beat> Alsi-so >>

Birdcall. Repeated at intervals throughout daylight hours with varying frequency. Bird in question is pigeon sized, mostly black with a few iridescent feathers upon back and wings and a yellow beak. Its notes, as you can hear, quite sweet and melodic. Males repeat the calls. The females are silent, but when approving of the rendition they appear quickly from the forest foliage and are a more lively selection of browns. Not quite the spectacular plumage of the Teriapt Oriole, I'm afraid. (See photos 1 through 38).

This recording was taken during our search for the primary expedition base, which must be very close according to Orynko's coordinates. Although we hadn't intended to take any nature notes the proliferation of birdlife is so startling that none of us could resist – particularly since we had expected to come to the base straight away and have been searching for it without success since we arrived.

[endjournal Roderigo Med1]

Recording #41, Day 3, 5.6km SSW

The pictures you're looking at are from very close to the site of the first expedition's huts, fragments of which you can see if I zoom in on the structure... There... and there... Those are actual splinters of the solardome shining among the... Oh for the love of Christ... I didn't realise... Oh god... << retches. Picture pans down to forest floor: bare earth. Later pans up again and backs off. Within a small clearing, perfectly circular and open to the sky, upon bare ground, there is a stunning small cathedral which looks made of basketwork. Instead of withies the basketry is made of tendons, flesh, skin, bone, metal, twigs, magnahyde, leaves and pieces of the base solardome. Visible for a second, on playback, is a nametag hanging in the leaves as part of a glittering decoration of shiny surgical and engineering implements. It reads: Captain DF Conté. After a break recording continues. Inside the woven architecture are some arrangements of other body parts among flowers and the ordinary plant life of the area. A pattern of beads reveals itself to be a collection of buttons, beetles and unfinished miniature lenses.>

>>11.08am

The death of Captain Conté is confirmed by DNA sample. God. We're all so exhausted emotionally. First we thought we'd found some kind of house, some kind of life signs, intelligent life, like the early expedition reports mentioned. Further digging around there reveals that this location is just outside the first base perimeter. Um. All of Captain Conté has not been accounted for. Most of the organs and major muscles are missing, we guess eaten by... whatever. No signs of life around now. Nothing. Not a thing.

>>18.17pm

It's dark now so we've given up on that site and come back. Here's another recording we took on the way – it's kind of like Roderigo's from earlier on, but... Well, you'll see.

<< Yassur Aye. <indistinct loud blast of white sound> Yassuraye.>>

(repeats twice)

I'm attaching all the other hoots and calls we can get from round here. There's a hell of a lot. It's so loud at night when the insects start too.

<<sample sound, mixed animals, wind, insects, frogs, bats>>

We left recording devices at the Conté site.

We can't agree as to whether we should recover and bury what we can of Captain Conté, or if we should leave the site undisturbed in the hopes of understanding what happened. Kuba thinks that whatever, whoever did this is bound to return because the structure has a ritual purpose. Everyone is talking about the murder.

[endjournal Elaine Sci2]

Five other bowers have been located. Their sites are all within a twenty-kilometre radius of the first base. They defy description. I append visuals.

<<image access denied>>

As you can see, each is its own unique masterpiece, but analysis of the local geography seems to confirm that they are the work of a single animal/person. The way that all of the written materials surrounding the skeleton of J Finney Caracayne, Science Officer, have been meticulously placed the correct way up between his femurs, although out of order, is most baffling.

Meanwhile the wreckage analysis of Base One reveals the use of the team's own energy weapons plus explosives and fire damage. There are major scavengings within the base, which all took place after it was breached. Many articles are unaccounted for, including the spare ammunition battery, eight autorepeater rifles and two cobra missiles. Some of these have turned up in the bowers (see Bower, Kwame Abufeira, Biological Analyst). Here the gun in question was found to be jammed with mud, a good job since the Achilles' tendons woven to hold it fast have such pressure on the trigger that a single step into the basketry of the bower itself would otherwise have killed its discoverer – myself.

There is still no sign of any large game, although we have found some kinds of deerlike animals and small elephantines in the forest glades. Predators do make ordinary kills – see plates 13321-13432. We haven't so far seen one, but believe them to be the animal which hoots very softly all night. Other calls can all be attributed to the vast wealth of avian species and a few froglikes. There are even butterfly size birds which live within single tree colonies, feeding only a single species of flower.

We log this merely as a distraction from the main task, which is now to locate the last four bodies. Morale is very low. Everyone is edgy. The more the bowers themselves reveal in terms of their pattern sophistication the more that Elaine and Roderigo interpret this as intelligent and meaningful display on the part of a larger and much smarter predator, perhaps a planetary guardian.

Needless to say I fear this is adding two and two to make eight.

[endjournal Marco, Statistician]

<<Object: Personal Abacand and stylus. Found 15 metres from bower of Andie MacEllroyd. Perfect in every detail save for solid interior. Constructed of local wood and bark.>>

<<Object: Camera, V61Polarflash, personal headcam. Found 28 metres from bower of Captain Conté, bearing Captain Conté's initials. Constructed of leaves, woven greensticks, remains of dome, other scavenged materials from Base One.>>

Another perfect day in paradise. It is now generally accepted that the bowers are the work of the birds, the Greater and Lesser Teriapt Bower Birds, as they are now named. Farther afield, away from all our technology, we have sent a team to collect information and preliminary findings reveal bower structures of varying sizes and complexity widely spread throughout the Southern River Basin.

Despite the apparent horror, we were hugely relieved to realise that what we and the first expedition had mistaken for a malicious intelligence was an indifferent exercise in the perennial struggle to attract suitable mates. Other bowers also include pieces of local animal carcase, frequently used for their engineering properties and perhaps also for the startling smells they produce on rotting, which contrast vividly with the smells of other collected objects, including fungi, fruit and certain insects and amphibians. The objects catalogued above are amazing replicas, created by an astonishing talent, but one without a sophisticated mind behind them. They are simply copies.

[endjournal Roderigo, Med1]

Roderigo Vansanta was officially reported missing at 16.35 hours local time. He had gone on a solo mission to continue his research at Captain Conté's bower site. A team has been out and back. They report following a trail into the forests for two kilometres – apparently he was walking normally – but this then was lost. Full dark has now been reached, making further exploration impossible. His communication equipment remains inactive.

[endjournal Elaine]

Roderigo returned at 17.03. With him was Captain Delicia Conté.

Although appearing in good health she was wearing only rags, was in possession of no technological help and was unable to speak coherently. When approached by others she became extremely violent and is presently unconscious under sedation for her own safety.

<<23.00 hrs>>

DNA analysis of Delicia Conté has revealed a small discrepancy. The dismembered body found in the bower is already identified as Captain Conté. The woman in medical is also without a doubt Captain Conté, but the radiation signatures of some of the elements in her body plus the fact that she has significantly shortened telomeres suggest that this Captain Conté is not the original, but a locally made variant.

[endjournal Elaine]

<<Recording of conversation between Roderigo and Delicia Conté:

Roderigo: Do you know where you are, Captain?
Conté: Alsiso. Alsi. So. Al. Al. Al. <appears puzzled, stressed>
Roderigo: Captain, what is your name?
Conté: <confidently> Alsiso.
Roderigo: Do you know what happened?
Conté: <attentively> Dyunoh. Wotapund. Dyoonohwhat. Appund. Do you? Do you know. What. Happened. Do you know what happened? <finally repeats phrase in perfect imitation of Roderigo's intonation and even tone and timbre> Captain Conté Do You Know What Happened? <looks questioning> >>

During the time of Captain Conté's return and rehabilitation I have continued to collect and analyse the songs of the birds. I am confident that these are a kind of recording of what happened to the original party and the fact that one particular area contains very similar patterns to those that Captain Conté has also been repeating seem to confirm my theory. I also have an explanation for how such a thing might occur.

At last we have managed to revive the medical centre AI from the original base, although it was badly damaged by fire. It was able to reveal that experiments conducted there had revealed errors in some of the genetic tweak nanoreplicators, the same ones used to originally seed the planet with life and accelerate its development. This has given rise to a general trend in many Teriapt life-forms to copy other structures. There is a particular bacterium which has had its DNA altered to invade and develop foreign cells – part of the life acceleration technology which is now causing the spontaneous creation of copies… Although, now I think more about it, perhaps this must be wrong since I cannot see that DNA alone could bring about an adult form, less still one with any knowledge whatsoever that may have belonged to the original. My speculations fall far short. Nonetheless, this mimetic plague has become most apparent in the avians, although it exists elsewhere.

I believe that Captain Conté, as we have her now, is a copy, perhaps even a copy of a copy of the original. By gathering what we may from her, and from the Lyre and Bower birds of the area, we may discover the fate of the original expedition.

[endjournal Marco]

Today Roderigo and I went out to search for other recordings in the local wildlife. Our efforts to communicate with Captain Conté have been unmercifully successful, revealing her to be a paranoid, dangerous delusional with only a tenuous grasp of reality. She recalls being shot to death by her science officer. Analysis of the recordings in the Lyre birds around her bower (we have not exposed her to it) have revealed that her last words to him were, 'I'll see. So…' We also believe from some of her statements that she may have encountered a copy of herself somewhere, but where is not clear.

I preferred it when we thought of all of this activity as the workings of a terrible beast. Morale has reached a second trough. Everybody wants to leave and privately I suspect that the stress is affecting Roderigo – he seems peculiarly lacking in affect today.

[endjournal Elaine]

Today Roderigo and Elaine returned from their recording expedition. Then Roderigo returned again. One of them is a copy, and both have agreed to be tested, although much shocked to see the other, as you may expect.

[endjournal Marco]

By ranging much further afield, up to 200km from our base, we have discovered entire populations of copied team members from the original expedition living ferally in the forest. When they caught sight of us they rushed to attack, trying to gain control of our weapons and our communications equipment. We had to shoot several before they left us.

They are fearful and weakened by inadequate protein breakdown – the local food is of poor value and causes many allergic responses – and we fought them off successfully but now we face the problem of what we are to do about all these people.

[endjournal Marco1]

I returned to our Base today and said a hello to Alsiso. She was happy, playing with some pencils and paper which Elaine2 had given her. She keeps on asking when we will go back to the Solar. She is confident that we will go and that she is now saved.

I have tested my own DNA. I am not the original Roderigo. It is the other one, which is a peculiar thought. How many more of us are out there now I cannot bear to think of, but I realise that we must decide to leave very quickly, for the urgent terror which drives the copy-people is their fear of being left behind, and now they know we are here.

They are not in good condition although it isn't the landscape. Not being native they do not fare well. The most sentient fear the most degraded copies of themselves who haunt them as ghosts and night terrors. The most distant copies are unable to speak at all, unable to remember a single human thing, only able to copy what they see and hear from others, as emptily as the idiot birds. They fear their own madnesses. I too.

I can see in Roderigo's face that he would rather leave all the copies behind, including me. I know that's what he's thinking because that's what I think when I look at him. If I were to leave him or kill him it wouldn't be the same as an ordinary murder, because I'm still alive either way. Besides, I have a wife and kids to think of. We can't both have the same life. We can't live here forever either.

I know that he would kill me, if he had the chance, if he wasn't seen, because he thinks of himself as the original, the father, and that he has the right. Somewhere in the jungle he'd have his chance if I let him but I make every effort to be accompanied by others. So does he. So do they all. So do we all.

Today Elaine1 suggested that we must wear numbers on our foreheads so that it is clear who is an original and who a copy, and what kind of copy.

I wonder if the first Roderigo knows what the terrible noises are which the birds repeat outside the windows all night. I know. He must know. Hell, they all know.

It's the soundtrack of the survival of the fittest.

[endjournal Roderigo2]

JASMINE

Andrew Tisbert

I cannot lose the memory of the first Jasmine, no matter how I try. She had creamy dark skin, but for the thick scars on her thumb and left breast. Her eyes were big and expressive, though she could stare so intently at nothing for minutes on end, troubled or perplexed or maybe just blank. When her eyes brightened and connected with the world – my world – I felt as if she had given me a precious gift. I remember how she would tug playfully at my beard and hair, and wrinkle up her eyes and thick lips into a smile, then shriek. And she liked to pat her puckered lips or swat her own ears when she was feeling pleased with herself. She had this way of jerking her head from side to side while flailing out with her good arm, then watching her hand return to her like a dedicated bird. She was completely and utterly herself; whatever thought, whatever impulse she had was freely and openly displayed and acted upon, without any guilt or awareness of social expectations. That made her the most real, the most complete person I have ever known. She weighed about ninety-five pounds and in spite of the clubfoot, and the contractures twisting up her left limbs, she was beautiful. She got around in a wheelchair using one arm and one leg. She couldn't speak. She was what they call 'severely retarded.' She lived in a cage they called Willowbrook, on Staten Island.

I started working there after my divorce. I was in a kind of shock. I'd decided to leave the Bronx and take a new job on the other side of the city in an attempt to crawl from under the bitter weight of my regrets. I had even considered signing myself off to the Research Institute for Accessible Possibilities – RIAP. It was a friend of mine from the married years who persuaded me from that notion. I can barely recall what Stan looked like now – destiny finds short memory convenient, doesn't it?

"Not one volunteer from RIAP has ever returned, you know," he'd said to me, glaring.

"Of course not," I replied, or something like that. Either by chance or design there was nothing like RIAP in any known alternate reality. At least that's what the Pentagon said. Besides, volunteers had to sign a contract binding them to remain in the targeted reality even if they could find a way home. In the science of possibility there are laws of conservation, reciprocation and balance. Realities also drift naturally; possibilities constantly spin, converge, shift. The Pentagon wanted to cause such a drift by exploiting these known laws of flow. By flushing people from one reality to another, they hoped to tilt the balance. By creating an imbalance between nexuses, conservation principles could be manipulated to alter a given variable in our world – or what they call reality prime. Among other projects, RIAP and the Pentagon were working on altering the fact that the Soviet Union had been the first nation to develop nuclear weapons. "No one is supposed to return, that would defeat the whole purpose," I continued. "Besides, what are the odds that I would be the one guy lucky enough to discover RIAP in another universe?"

"Sure, sure. Look, what good would it do? You think you're going to find another Laura? You're only hurting her more, you know."

I could have made a scathing remark about how she'd had me arrested when I tried to visit our daughter. Instead I stared off at some pigeons. We were in the park. The sun glared unrelentingly on the greasy sidewalk, the dusty bushes, the garbage, my shoulders. I don't think people should cry in public.

"Look. I don't give a shit about you," said my friend Stan. "Things would be a lot easier if you weren't around. Laura is worried about you and I promised I'd say something."

It was with this revelation – that things would be easier for Stanley – that I decided not to sign the RIAP contract I'd had drafted. Instead, I moved across the city and presumed to make a new life in this world. Did I mention Stan was the reason for my divorce?

The first day at the Willowbrook Institution overwhelmed me. Nothing could have prepared me for the stench alone. It was a mixture of sweet shit, stale saliva, dried urine and sweat. It was a seething summer day and there were no fans anywhere. The smell hung with the heat like a great stifling weight. It was all I could do to breathe. Nor could I have been prepared for the deformed people who lived there, or the crowded, wailing halls, or the meager staff – they looked beaten and angry; most of them had stopped caring a long time ago. There just wasn't enough room or staff or clothes or time inside these dark, crumbling buildings. And nothing could have prepared me for the feelings that consumed me when Jasmine had her seizure. But that was later.

I try not to remember walking into my 'classroom' for the first time. They called it a classroom and me an instructor. I was there to teach 'adaptive living skills.' I taught no such thing. There was a blind man in a wheelchair with its lapboard locked in place. He'd been restrained in it that way for years to keep him from masturbating. Now he'd forgotten how to walk. There was another blind man squatting on the floor, trying to dig his eyes out with his thumbs. An autistic girl rhythmically banged her head on the barred windowsill, yanking out her thin hair. A boy in one corner sat on the dirty floor tiles and tried to swallow his own hand. The wailing echoed through the whole building. I was sick with the smell of piss and smeared shit. And there was Jasmine against the wall, withdrawn, chewing on her shirt. This was my classroom. I was the only staff. I looked around me and only wanted to turn and find my way out of there, back to the innocence of never having been there. Then I heard Jasmine squeal as she awkwardly wheeled toward the boy in the corner trying to eat himself. She stopped behind him and grabbed his hat, an orange toque, the only thing he seemed to care about. Grinning, she wheeled away as the boy came out of himself – literally and figuratively – and started hollering. Jasmine dropped the hat and her good arm swung up. She patted her lips and twitched her head from side to side, still grinning. The boy crawled to the hat and clumsily pulled it over his head. For a moment there was life in the room. I smiled. And stayed.

I lasted about six months. I changed diapers, helped people onto the toilet, I taped a white sock on the boy with the toque's hand to keep him from stuffing it into his mouth. I tried to teach the blind man, Bill, to walk again. I held the autistic girl down when she tried to beat her head through the bars, and I moved furniture out of the way when they had seizures. I was lonely during this time, for my attempt to make a new life was failing. Laura had forced me to abandon my daughter just as my father had abandoned me. I was ashamed of my whole life, my inadequacy. The deformed in my classroom were the only new friends I succeeded in making – especially Jasmine. I felt trapped in this reality by my bitterness and my shame.

I think the feeling of being trapped gave me something in common with Jasmine and drew me closer to her. For even while she played with herself and chewed on rubber toys, dripping puddles of saliva on the tiles, I saw another woman; who quietly gazed at the wall wondering why she'd been caged in a deformed body, a dull, malfunctioning brain. In my dreams I saw her free. I believed in God back then. I saw Him as an inconsistent glass blower. Our spirits were blown into the hot liquid glass of our flesh, we were born, we cooled and hardened. But some of the vessels were hopelessly flawed. They were created broken, trapped by poor craftsmanship. I did not want to think of God in that way. I concentrated on my dreams.

I remember those dreams now more vividly than I can see the 'real' world around me. Yet images of the first Jasmine continue to obsess me. I remember how her eyes blinked when I touched the tip of her nose, how she would crawl across the room to see me, her bad arm banded across her chest, her useless leg dragging behind her. I would be at my desk doing paperwork and as she crawled she would shriek to get my attention. I'd drop my pen, grinning, slide from my chair and sit on the floor. She would smile and make a soft noise that was warm and smooth like her skin and came partly through her nose. I remember once taking her hand, and she resting against my legs as I hugged her. My pen rolled to the floor and she grabbed it and started chewing on it furiously. Then, still chewing and drooling, she looked up at me. There was something in those eyes, something I didn't really understand then. I only wanted to see the Jasmine I dreamed – who was hidden in this body cage. This woman, I thought, is my own age and she squats here with saliva running down her arm. She'll spend her life learning to get to the toilet on time and how to use a fork. My mind kept returning to RIAP. Somewhere, in another universe, another variable nexus (as they called it at RIAP), the real Jasmine lived and was whole – and she could walk and speak and dance and do a cartwheel. She could drive a car and she didn't chew on her shirt or her underwear, though maybe she chewed gum or fingernails or her lower lip. And there were other things not denied her: adolescent excitements, first dates and kisses, all giddy and clumsy and ridiculous. Her life had mystery and euphoria. It was not a dull room full of rejects and an overwhelmed trainer with simply too many clients to handle or even care about.

I would lie in bed at night wondering how it was possible for me to see such beauty and spirit in Jasmine's eyes. Again and again I thought of RIAP and reality and 'variable nexuses.' I thought about the poor craftsman, the God of the flawed and broken. And I thought about cheating Him.

The day she had the seizure was the day I quit. Jasmine was in her wheelchair when it started; I was sitting at my desk. Her head jerked to one side and her eyes rolled backward as if drawn taut by cables in her skull. Her body went rigid and jerked and she stopped breathing. I got around the desk and reached her as the thrashing started. Her chair rocked precariously and I grabbed it by an arm to steady her. Then, as abruptly as the contortions had begun, she began to flow back into shape. Gasping, her head went forward and she regained control of her eyes. For a second those eyes met mine. Make it stop, they said, please make it stop and save me and don't ever let it happen again. I stroked her shoulder and told her things were all right now. I put off calling the nurse to check her blood pressure and started unbuckling her from her chair so she could lie down for a while on the exercise mat.

I was about to lift her out when it started again, but this time differently. She bit her left hand, the bad one, right where all the scar tissue was. Her other arm flew out and caught me in the mouth. She started spinning wildly in her chair. She cried out once. The chair tipped and she lurched over the side. When I tried to catch her, her arm swung out again, hooking my shirt and ripping it down the front. I went down with her to break the fall. My elbow slammed into the tile, sending something like glass splinters up through my arm. Even on the floor she thrashed, trying to spin and spin. I tried to shield her from the floor, the wheelchair, the wall near us, with my body. She was stronger than she should have been. Her eyes were big black nails of fear. I got it in the mouth again – a knee this time. When she finally stopped, she lay on her back, trembling.

I tried to hug her. She pushed me away. All right, I told her, it's all right, things are okay, over and over as if I thought it were true. She finally let me take her hand. I didn't want to leave her to call the nurse. I gently pulled her arm and she rolled closer to me. She dropped her head on my lap, suddenly weak, and I stroked the back of her neck. My lip was numb and when I looked down to locate the burning on my chest I saw the deep scratches. I ran my fingers through the tight curls over her forehead and didn't care. I watched her cling to my knees and knew then that I loved her, this retarded woman, who couldn't speak or go to the bathroom alone or walk, who had grand mal and psychomotor seizures. I loved her. And as long as I worked at the institution I was her jail keeper. My ultimate superior, my boss, was the poor craftsman, the god of this reality. I looked around me at the other 'clients,' in their prisons of flesh and bone and neuron. The institution, too, was a prison, like a great fist of God, and I wanted nothing to do with it. I lived in my own cage, too, but I knew where to find the door.

After work I took the subway deeper into the city, then walked five blocks to the RIAP tower, breathing deeply, my hands trembling. I went inside through the revolving doors and someone dredged up my file from the computer and a bald, fat man with liver spots on his face in one of the offices told me if I was prepared to actually sign the papers this time, processing would only take about twenty four hours. I had already been through all their counseling, which was valid for a year, and all we needed to do was discuss the details of the specific variable adjustments I hoped to attain. They had to orchestrate the alternate variables of their current project with mine. They would apply their possibility theory and send me off and I could only return in my dreams. That was fine. I wanted this world to be the dream, and my dreams to be the reality.

And it would be no more than a dream to me, this world, for no matter what changes in reality RIAP took credit for whenever Congress reviewed the project – winning the Panama War, perfecting plastic hearts, democratizing Iran – they still worked blind. They simply didn't have the ability to pull anyone back from the alternate realities even if they wanted to.

I walked back to the subway station as the shadows and lights gradually turned on around me. As I rode home, I picked a new name. RIAP had suggested I do that. And I thought it fitting to begin my new life with a different name. I was their good little soldier now, just another one of their social misfits snared into the program to disappear forever for the Greater Good, even though no one ever seemed to prove unequivocally what exactly it was they were doing.

RIAP tells us that variables are naturally cohesive, so the ripple effect from one change in a nexus is limited. Natural groupings of variables hold together tenaciously – which is why though the second Jasmine had not been committed to Willowbrook, she was still somehow associated with it, or what passed for it in this reality, and did not live on the other side of the world. Finding her again was simple. The only complicating factors were the conservation and reciprocity laws which, though they were opaque and unpredictable to me, seemed not to concern RIAP at all.

The Willowbrook Institution had been shut down, but I found a school and some residential facilities not far from the old site. The buildings were ensconced in the residential community with the intention of attracting as little attention to themselves as possible. I met the second Jasmine for the first time in the parking lot of the two-story school (the Staten Island Center for Habilitation Services) after applying for a job there. Not that I needed the money – RIAP had taken care of that. But I knew she would be there – she had to be there, RIAP had shown me. She had finished work and was walking toward her car as I left the brick walled school behind her. Her limp was slight, but she had learned to use it to her advantage – creating a unique gait that I found attractive. I hurried to catch up to her and match her stride. "Hello," I said, and because I didn't have anything else to say, "How is it, working here?"

"I don't think I know you," she said, but the words were not hostile. Her voice was smooth and soft, a creamy dark like her skin. And the sun was shining on that skin, on her face, on the small but wide nose and the striking lines of her brow, the deep mahogany of her eyes. I forgot to reply to her because we were close, because the same sun shining on her beauty heated my own ugly, pallid skin. She was about to open the driver's side door of her Sentra when I realized I'd been walking with this woman – who could only respond to me as a stranger – in total silence. Embarrassed, I cleared my throat.

"I've just applied to work here."

"Really." She opened the door, sat with her feet out on the pavement, and slid a cigarette from the pack in her purse. "Have you ever done this kind of work before?" She lit up and inhaled an enormous amount of smoke.

"Well, yes. In the institution. Willowbrook –"

"No kidding." She blew out curling clouds. "Over half of my consumers come from Willowbrook. You must have been there before the court order, huh?"

I looked blankly at her.

"You know. Deinstitutionalization. Community based services. The Seventies; Cuomo, Geraldo Rivera."

"Right, right." I nodded. I didn't have any idea what she was talking about.

"I bet you could really tell me some stories, huh? Maybe you'll tell me about it sometime." Tucking in her legs, she reached out to shut the door, then hesitated. "I hope you get the job," she said. Her door slammed and her window slid down. "Be seeing you."

"Sure." I smiled, still embarrassed. But she winked and returned my smile.

Two days later I was called back to the school – the 'day habilitation center' – for an interview and the administrative director gave me a tour of the building. She was a wiry old woman with a creaky, rusted sounding voice. I tried to pay at least a little attention to her as she explained what was happening in each classroom, but all I could think about was finding Jasmine. We had visited three classrooms before I finally heard Jasmine's voice. I looked down the hall to see her pushing a wheelchair into the room ahead of me.

"We call this room Adaptive Daily Living Skills," said the director, stepping back to let me through the door.

The room was busy, with clients (they were called 'consumers' here) at tables filling boards with plastic pegs, stacking building blocks, and scribbling with crayons. But there was a man in a wheelchair who had thrown a box of lego to the floor and was swatting clumsily at the young instructor who tried to grasp his hand. She was a fat woman with thick glasses and a high, wavering voice. You need to calm down Bernie, she was saying; it's all right, Bernie, please, now stop this Bernie. His pants were not properly buttoned and a worm of drool hung from the edge of his mouth. There was a stupid, flabby look about him. Even in rage his eyes weren't focused. He bellowed a tormented, barely articulate, "Noooo!" His wheelchair teetered as he lurched and tried to hit the woman. He caught her temple once, sending her glasses across the room. "Noooo!" he bellowed again. He had thick pads of scar tissue over his eyebrows. The sight of him set me to shaking. I remember the director leading me out of the room, apologizing and explaining about some of the consumers with 'behavioral problems' who attended the facility. I was suddenly sick to my stomach, but I managed to get out into the hall. She excused herself for a moment and went back inside the classroom to help the instructor. I wanted to go outside for some air, but my legs had gone weak. I leaned a shoulder against the painted cinder block wall and looked at my hands. They trembled. I studied the palms, the fingers, the blue ropes under the skin of my forearms. I was thin, not like Bernie, who still screamed from the room behind me. And I was at least a little tanned. He was so pale. Almost all his hair was gone – from pulling it out in tantrums, I imagined. I pushed myself up from the wall. This was still my body, those were still my arms, my hands. Laws of conservation, reciprocity, be damned. I wanted to get away from Bernie's screams. I moved down the hall toward the next doorway. For a moment I felt I was dreaming and the first Jasmine would be in there, spinning her wheelchair around, shrieking, and I started to feel relief. But it was the second Jasmine, a Jasmine who walked, who almost collided with me as I turned into the room.

She looked up and immediately recognized me. "Oh, hey. Hello again."

I tried to smile. There was an awkward silence and she started making a face and looking down the hall.

I had come across a universe for this chance to meet her. I wasn't about to turn shy and passively let my opportunity slide by. I swallowed and took a deep breath, and this time I did smile. "It's you."

"It's me," she said.

"Don't I owe you a conversation?"

She frowned for second, then remembered what I was talking about. "Willowbrook. That's right. Sure, any time."

"How about tonight?" I said. When she began to frown again I said, "I know we've hardly just met, but I'm kind of new in town, and well –"

"No, that would be all right." She smiled and rested a palm briefly on my bicep.

The director returned from behind me. "Do you two know each other?" she said.

"We've met," said Jasmine, still looking at me. I couldn't turn away from her. It was like a wakeful vision into my dreams. I was still shaking, but for that moment the past did not matter, Bernie did not matter, nothing mattered but this woman. Touching her. Holding her. Being a part of her. In the cleansing flow of these feelings I could almost convince myself, if I didn't really scrutinize the thought, that it was only a chance resemblance that had so shaken me in the other room. Nothing mattered. Jasmine was here, she was whole, she was real.

I will not say that getting together was inevitable, but after traveling over the moiling sea of alternate realities to find her, my perspective on courtship had definitely changed. I made our time matter aggressively. I wasted none of it waiting for Jasmine to make a move. What did I care of the unspoken rules? This wasn't even my world. Perhaps this made me too forward, but she was always receptive to my advances. I took her to the movies that first night. And to dinner the second night. It was Jasmine who suggested dinner at her house for our third date.

"I'm not exactly a great cook," she said, "but I can manage to order a pizza."

We sat together on her sofa; an ugly, oversized blue thing with ripped arms that dominated her crowded little apartment like a hulking carcass. We smiled at each other. "You never did tell me," I said, "about your name. Your mother must have been interesting to give you a name like Jasmine. My mother wasn't so imaginative. She couldn't decide what to call me, although she wanted it to start with a B so my initials would be the same as my old man's. That was real important for some reason. For the first day I was just 'Baby,' then for a week I was 'Bobbit,' or something – "

"My mother was a slut and a drunk and it's a wonder I was born without fetal alcohol syndrome. I don't really like to talk much about her."

I looked away and studied the ugly flowers on her wallpaper. "I'm sorry."

"Look. No, I'm sorry. I don't know why I blurted that out." She touched my hand. "I didn't mean to snap at you. Let's just talk about something else."

We did. I told her more about the institution – the stench, the strait jackets, the drugs. "You know," she said, scratching her chin. "You seem young to have worked at Willowbrook. I mean – " she looked at my uncomfortable expression. "Well, never mind." At some point she touched my knee as if by accident. When the pizza arrived we began to talk about other things. I found that America had indeed developed the Bomb before any other country in this world. Jasmine laughed at me when I called it 'the Bomb.' Apparently people had stopped calling it 'the Bomb' decades ago. There were other differences in this reality: RIAP had targeted their desired variables well. The United States was the only true 'superpower' here, and dominated the world with its military and huge amounts of corporate power.

I can't remember everything we talked about. It doesn't matter. Somehow Jasmine and I were very close, touching. When I kissed her, her soft thick lips responded immediately and enthusiastically. Once our lips had parted, she brushed my cheek with the tip of her nose. Her hand rubbed my thigh.

"After what I said about my mother you're going to think I'm some kind of whore or something." She smiled and stroked my neck. "It's just that I feel as if we've known each other for such a long time."

I said it. What I had wanted to say for so long. "I love you, Jasmine."

We kissed again, then she hooked my arm and led me to her bedroom. I sank into the small bed as she lit a candle on her dresser then unbuttoned her blouse. There was no scar on her small left breast. She slipped out of her jeans and gently pushed me backward on the bed. Her skin was smooth, moist; my hands slid around her back and she licked my nose. I realized I was weeping.

"Shhh," she breathed, "Shhh," and parted her legs over me. I pulled her undergarment down and she moved her legs again to help me. Then she had rolled to her back and I was over her pushing, and she arching against me. I could feel her left ankle rubbing my lower thigh and there was nothing – nothing – wrong with that limb. Her body was a fine, perfect machine lubricating and pressing up beneath me and I was suddenly strung up in the darkness over her, connected to her world only by the rising tension in my loins. I was alone. I saw images of the first Jasmine as the woman under me sighed, pushing against me. Her useless arm curled against her breast between us, her useless leg a kinked cable lying on the bed. And drooling, she mouthed her shoe, pushing futilely against my chest. Pushing, convulsing, thrashing under me, she arched upward, and I tried to shield her from the floor, the wheelchair, the wall near us, with my body, my body over her. And her eyes, the big black nails of her eyes. I became flaccid as Jasmine cried out, writhing. Waves of nausea built from deep in my belly and rose, and rose, and I fought them down. Jasmine still arched against me, but I kept doubling out of her. Shaking, I slid to the side of her and buried my face into a pillow. I felt her sit up beside me, touch my shoulder; I heard her whisper my name. But I couldn't move. Finally she stopped trying to stir me. She lied down and eventually fell asleep. I crawled out of the bed. The candle on the dresser was all but burned out. Good. I did not want to see myself in the mirror. I left the room.

I have searched this thing they call the 'Internet,' and traveled through various cities. It is true, there is no RIAP in this world. But science has changed here, filled itself with fantasies beyond what men can see. Coiled dimensions, strings, invisible matter, quantum superposition. There are rumors that the ability to reach into other worlds already exists. I don't know if they're true. It would seem unlikely I would be lucky enough to find a way back to reality prime.

I remember the things that moved me about the first Jasmine. That complete freedom to be herself. How she would grab me by the hair and give me a one armed hug, just because she felt like it, then shove me away. And I realize that the charm of her personality was entailed in her deformities. The dream of another Jasmine, a whole Jasmine, was never really what aroused me.

I see her now, slapping her ear; I hear her shrieking. I can feel her rest her head on my lap. I want to hold her twisted hand. But I am the craftsman's most faithful apprentice.

I am going to go back. I will find a way. I want to teach her to walk, to brush her teeth. I want to see her smile up at me as I brush the tip of her nose with a finger. I will go back. Somehow, I will.

But first I'm going to kill Bernie.

TELEVISIONISM

Maurice Suckling

1

I once had a girlfriend who was famous. I suppose she still is in a way, but I can't really say she's my girlfriend anymore. At least we don't go out and we don't see each other, and people tend to see that as significant. Maybe she's not even actually famous anymore either. I doubt anyone much under 15 has heard of her, and there're still some people much older who'd have no idea who you were talking about, not that I ever mention it. If anyone ever brings up the subject it's never me. That would be like giving a little piece of her away each time, and where she is now I can't get any more of her so I have to look after what I have left. Not that she's dead, or anything like that. Not exactly.

But the people who do know about her, who do remember, all saw the same TV programme. It's been shown on repeats plenty of times, but it's never had the same impact on people as it did the first time, the time it went out live. It was one of those in-the-moment things; one of those this-was-the-year-that… kind of things. It's six years since it happened, and there's still people, who saw it live, who talk about it like they permanently carry the experience of watching it around with them.

My girlfriend was called Ciara. (Say *was*? Say *is*?) We met in a bar early evening, when I'd just popped in with some people from work. It was a Wednesday, and I usually only drank with them for one or two on a Friday. I was at the bar getting drinks when I was tapped on the shoulder. I turned round and there was Ciara. She was standing in front of a lamp by the wall, so her whole head had this strange glow of light all around it. With the bar being low lit and her face being the wrong side of that light, I suppose it should have been harder to make out her features than it was, though I didn't think about that at the time. Her sharp blue almost luminous eyes seemed to go right through my own eyes and play ping pong all around the inside of my head. She looked like the kind of person who could be famous. People that good looking can always get famous. I suppose her hair should have been in shadow and not been so bright and blonde nor emitting the kind of hazy radiant gold-tinged glow either.

I realised that not only was I staring, but that also she was trying to hand me something; a mobile phone.

My mobile phone. I hadn't even got halfway through my confused expression before she spoke.

"That's right, it's your phone. You're going to need it if I'm going to call you."

I thanked her and asked if I'd dropped it.

"Oh no," she said, "I just magic'd it out of your pocket."

I thanked her again and picked up my previous expression from where I'd left off and kept it going for just under a week.

She did call. It was just under a week later. We arranged to meet at the same pub. We got our drinks and got the last free seats in the place at a table, just as it was starting to fill up.

I had an older brother and a younger sister. She had an older sister and a younger brother. We both worked as junior producers in advertising firms. We'd both been there coming up to three years each. Our favourite band was the same, our favourite film was the same, our favourite place in the whole city to watch the world go by was the same.

It was my turn to go to the bar. The pub was heaving right then and it must have been three ranks deep, maybe four in places. Ciara must've seen the look in my eyes.

"I'll get them," she said.

"No, no, it's my round," I insisted. I didn't want her to think I wasn't a drinks buyer.

"No really – look at it," she said. "Close your eyes."

"What?"

"Close your eyes."

I shot a few looks to the side, not sure what she was up to.

"Close your eyes," she said, in a voice that made me want to.

So I closed my eyes and before I'd barely had time to smile at the thought of how I must look, she told me to open them.

There, in front of us were two fresh and pint-full glasses of beer.

"Howdyou do that?" I said.

"Magic," she said.

2

We met up next at a restaurant. I had the task of choosing so it was important to get the balance right between effort and over-fancy. I went for a low lit bistro friends had told me about but I'd never tried. Ciara and I both chose the same starter and main course, and we shared a bottle of wine. She picked it, but it was the one I was just about to mention.

The second bottle of wine came.

"Jim, what do you actually believe in?"

"Err, the same as you?" I tried.

"And what is that, then, do you think?"

I overfilled both glasses slightly, as the young so-Italian waiter cleared the table next to us.

"You know, the usual: don't do stuff to people you wouldn't want done to you... don't litter... and don't drink milk past it's sell by date."

The waiter backed into us by accident, spun round and lost control of his arm-balanced plates as they crashed onto our table, sending my wine glass over my clean and specially ironed white shirt. The waiter began apologising. It takes me twenty-five minutes to do a shirt.

"No, no, it's fine," I said.

The stain looked the size of two hands splayed out, one on top of the other. He started setting things right on our table and picking the glass up.

"I sorry, I sorry, I sort it for you."

"No, really, it's fine," said Ciara, standing up and helping to brush me down. She seemed to pick up a cloth that the waiter had dropped, though it was hard to tell in that light and it was so fast. I saw her wipe at my shirt a couple of times as I was sitting back down.

"No, it's fine, Ciara, it's fine. Don't worry about that."

I sat back down and the waiter continued picking things up and apologising and offering to pay for the shirt to be cleaned.

"No, don't worry about that," I said, and looked down and saw that the stain wasn't there at all. Then I looked back at Ciara.

Whenever she touched me it felt like my sense of touch, which must have been usually set at somewhere between 1 and 2 on the dial, had been spun right round as far as it would go. I could feel everything much more, like every cell in my skin had grown tiny microscopic hands of their own. Like all my nerve endings were much closer the surface than ever before. If she put her hand on my skin it almost felt like it hurt and it made my whole body shudder. I used to ask her to do it as often as possible. Sometimes she'd wait till I stopped shaking till she did it again.

We kissed for the first time that night. I thought maybe my head was on fire, but in a way that I liked. I tried to stop it shaking by putting both my hands round it. It made my hands hot.

A month after that we went to the theatre together for the first time. At the door they were taking tickets and tearing them. I put my hand in my jacket pocket and had one of those busy hands, empty head moments. Before my hands had given up I'd already come to picture the two tickets left in my flat in the kitchen in the special *Do Not Forget These* place by the kettle I'd put them in. I was about to explain to Ciara, but she could already tell from my face.

"Doesn't matter," she said, and walked me towards the door. From her pocket she pulled out two tickets, looking just like the ones I'd left behind, handed them over to the ticket woman, who put a rip in them and handed them back to Ciara. Ciara put them back in her pocket then we went in to see the play. Bits of it were pretty good, but I couldn't really concentrate on it.

Ciara had to go back to her place after coz she had to be up extra early for work in the morning – we'd got the tickets a while before and the original plan was to stay someplace near the theatre, but we'd had to shelve that plan. The taxi took her back to her place first. She apologised again as she got out and I told her it didn't matter as it wasn't her fault. Then the taxi dropped me off at my flat. As soon as I got in I walked straight through to the kitchen and found the tickets just where I'd left them. They both had rips in them.

I didn't want to phone her because she'd be trying to get to sleep for her early morning, so I sent Ciara a text telling her I thought she should be on television.

3

I'd warned Ciara about my mum's cooking, but she was sporting enough to come for dinner anyway. My mum and dad were delighted to see her, and they did these little approval looks to each other when they thought no one else could see. Living together for such a long time must somehow dull your awareness of other people being around.

"So you do the same work as James, is that right?" said my dad, helping himself to the rice. My mother, thinking Ciara sounded foreign, had cooked an Indian meal, at least she called it Indian. Once when my mum had tried cooking a Chinese meal for Chinese New Year I didn't eat another one for nearly two months. It used to be my favourite food.

"Sort of," said Ciara, "but I'm thinking of doing something else."

"Mum! What have you done? This tastes absolutely amazing!" I'd just had my first tentative helping of korai lamb. Usually the names of my mum's dishes were loose clues more than direct answers.

"Thank you James," she said. "It did work out rather better than I was expecting, didn't it."

"Mum, this could be in a restaurant!" I said. And then I remembered seeing Ciara disappear into the kitchen a little earlier when my mum had come into the lounge with drinks.

"Like what?" said my dad, who didn't seem to notice anything unusual in the food. I think his taste buds had been systematically eradicated over the years so that he could now only differentiate foods by size and colour.

"Like what? What are you going to do instead?" pressed my dad, interested.

"Oh, well I'm hoping Jim's going to be able to come along with me to find out," she said.

And I did.

We both had to take the Friday afternoon off work. I'd tried getting clues from her about what we were doing but she refused to tell me anything. Maybe I could've guessed from the tube stop we met at.

At the security gate she said we had an appointment and they let us through.

"We?"

"Well, no, just me, really, but I wanted you to come along too."

We walked through to reception and I waited while Ciara spoke to the people there. We took a lift to the fourth floor and followed the red signs along the cream coloured corridors. We were told to wait on a brown leather sofa in a secretary's office. There were awards and photos of famous people all around the walls.

When it was our turn to go in Ciara led the way. She shook hands with Mr Jeremies and introduced me as her manager, which was the first I'd heard of it. Mr Jeremies, curly black hair, dark features and exec-shaped body, stepped back into the room and perched on the front edge of his large desk, looking towards us.

"So…" he said, and held his palms up, like he was waiting for something. "Show me something. A trick. A card trick or something."

Ciara stepped forwards and held out both hands, as if she wanted him to count how many fingers. She then turned and showed them to me, so I could see. The same number as usual.

"Mr Jeremies, would you please take a card from the deck," and she gestured to the deck that neither I, nor Mr Jeremies from his expression, had noticed on his desk before. Then he recovered himself and pulled a wry face. He picked up the cards and seemed to spend a while looking through them, turning them upside down and glancing at some of the backs.

"If you could choose a card, show it to my manager, but not let me see it, please."

Again, Mr Jeremies had this wry look, and again he seemed to take a while to look through the cards.

"It's a full deck, Mr Jeremies, not doctored in any way."

He smiled back at her; wry, once again. Then as he chose a card Ciara closed her eyes put her hands over them and turned her head away. It was a Queen of Diamonds. Then he put it back in the deck.

"You want the deck back now?" he said.

Ciara turned round and opened her eyes.

"No thank you. You can keep them."

There was a moment's pause in the room and I couldn't hear anything right then, no sounds of traffic on the nearby roads, no sounds of people in corridors, no office sounds at all.

"So are you going to tell me my card then?" he said.

"This is your card," said Ciara, and held up her left hand to show him her palm.

He folded his arms and rocked back slightly where he was, then looked at her more closely. Ciara spun round to show me the Queen of Diamonds perfectly drawn on the palm of her hand.

"The card itself, Mr Jeremies, is in the CD-tray of your computer."

He blinked at her, then walked round to the back of his desk, pressed a button on his desktop pc. I heard the whine of it opening. He didn't move for a moment or so. Then he picked out the card and held it up. The Queen of Diamonds. He looked past me in the doorway, out to his secretary, flashing suspicious look.

"Card tricks..." said Mr Jeremies dismissively.

"It's not really card tricks I want to do," said Ciara.

"So what would you do if I gave you a show?" said Mr Jeremies, for the first time sounding like he was warming to her, opening up and becoming interested.

"Why don't you call my agent and we can discuss it," she said, then threw all the cards into the air and the whole deck stuck face to the ceiling, so all the patterned red backs of the cards were showing and arranged into shapes giving out a string of numbers. She didn't even stay long enough to see the effect, she walked past me on her way out as I was still staring upwards.

"I didn't know you had an agent," I said as we got back into the lift.

"Oh... well... There's lots you don't know about me, Jim."

Then she kissed me until the lift came to a stop and we both opened our eyes and she was laughing and holding my pants in her hand. My vision was a little blurred by the quivering but I reached down and could feel my trousers were still on, fully buttoned, and zipped up.

4

Things were still going well between us as Ciara started filming for her show. It was going to come out in six half hour episodes to be shown late at night. When Ciara worked late we used to get cabs back from the studio. Every time we got lucky as soon as we left the building and a taxi had either just dropped someone off at the front doors, or was just driving by on the main road with its light on. We would go for something to eat in restaurants that were still open even though it was so late, or so early, and we would frequently be the only people eating there. Sometimes she would reach across and put her hand near mine. Sometimes she would make her hand touch. This was messy if I was eating soup.

One particular night we got back to her flat late and she had a line of twelve tea lights on the windowsill. She clicked her fingers and all twelve lit at once. It was very romantic and I was about to take her clothes off when I realised she didn't have any on. I was about to take my own off when I realised I didn't have any on either. We couldn't have slept more than four hours that night. I woke up with a bruise on the back of my head. Ciara said I'd been shaking and my head had knocked against the metal headboard for a couple of hours but I looked so peaceful she didn't want to move me.

Now I think about it, I never once had an orgasm when she didn't have one at the same time. That ought to have made it absolutely clear to me what was going on. But it didn't. I am a bit slow that way, and probably a bit quick the other.

The Ciara Wilson Show was enjoyed by students, insomniacs, shift workers and people who were tired and had already decided to go to bed, but didn't turn the TV off in time and so got caught.

She and the producers had decided to go for a reality TV, this is really real, type of approach. In the first episode she took her ever-present camera crew into a shopping centre. She stopped a couple in their 20s, all dressed up in high street designer wear, weighed down with shopping bags and asked them if she could show them some magic. When they said she could, she took out a £20 note from her pocket and asked the woman, called Jenny, to write her name on it in lipstick. She wore an *Estee Lauder Hot Copper*. Ciara then asked if Jenny had recently bought anything that they'd wrapped up in front of her in a shop. Stacey told her there were a couple of things. Some *Clinique* perfume for a friend and some *Body Shop* soaps for her mum. Ciara asked Jenny to make a choice between them. She chose the soap. Ciara asked her to open it, and Jenny went into her bag, took the package out, moved the green ribbon to one side and carefully unwrapped it. There was the soap, still in its tight cellophane wrapper. Jenny looked up puzzled.

"Turn it over," said Ciara.

And inside the heat-sealed cellophane, in contact with the soap, tightly folded, was a £20 note. When Jenny opened it she found the note had her lipstick signature on it. Jenny and her boyfriend, who remained known as Boyfriend, looked stunned. Ciara handed a package to Jenny that looked like the one just opened.

"One with its wrapper still on," said Ciara.

There was a lot of this kind of stuff across the whole six episodes.

She took her camera crew into a pub. She made a pint of beer travel the length of a bar to a gawping group of lads. It hovered head height through the air and she didn't spill a drop.

She took her crew into a park at night. She said there was a rain cloud just above her head, just out of reach if she tried to jump up to it. You couldn't really see anything because it was so dark. She explained it was a cumulus cloud, though much lower than usual. She then clicked her fingers and the rain started pouring over her, soaking her, but nothing around her – just her. She proceeded to walk around in the otherwise dry park and it seemed as if the cloud followed her wherever she went, until she was utterly drenched.

In her last show she went into a restaurant and appeared to change someone's leftover desert into a birthday cake. When the birthday person said she couldn't eat the cake because she was too full, Ciara suggested she at least cut into it because the birthday person's house keys were inside. On cutting into the cake the birthday person discovered not only was this true, but that there was also a specific Cretan earring to replace the one she'd been upset about losing earlier in the evening. In the shock she knocked her glass onto the floor. Ciara reached down onto the ground, gathered all the pieces together, seemed to throw them into the air and caught a fully formed wine glass. Almost fully formed, there was a tiny chip in the lip of the glass. Ciara reached down again, found a piece of glass no bigger than the stud of the replacement earring. She seemed to do no more than touch it to the glass, and the glass was fully repaired, you couldn't see any cracks or repair lines in it anywhere.

TV programmes and internet sites were rife with speculation as to how she made the tricks work and the complex research and preparation that must have to go into each one. I surprised Ciara with a cup of tea and caught her scrolling through a website one afternoon, looking scowly.

"They think they can work out how it's done." She sounded hurt.

"Well..." I said. "That's a good thing, isn't it. It creates a buzz."

"You're right," she said and put her hand on mine and looked musing out of the window at the road below, then noticed I was spilling hot tea over my leg and whimpering.

As a result of the success of the show Ciara was invited on to a talk show program. She looked unbelievable in a black dress with a low V down her cleavage, showing off her naturally dark and inviting skin. As her manager I naturally wanted the interview to go well. As her boyfriend I wanted her to turn around before she got to the bottom of the stairs and get straight into a cab with me.

When the talk show host asked, without really expecting an answer, how she managed to do the tricks she did, she looked him straight in the eyes and said 'because I am magic.' Even if you'd never seen her show you'd agree just by seeing her in that dress.

The host pressed her some more about the ways she did things. She agreed to show him a trick then and there. He suggested a card trick.

"You people always want card tricks," she mused, good naturedly.

"You say that like you're not one of us," said the host, chuckling.

"Oh, I'm not," she said. "Not exactly. I am, but I'm also something else." She was looking at him seriously now. She looked amazing in that dress.

"And what would that be... magic? I suppose." He chuckled, bringing the studio audience with him.

"Sort of." She smiled and nodded sincerely. The audience laughed. She looked amazing in that dress.

She asked the host to take the pack of cards from his top pocket. A pack he didn't know he had there. She asked him to pick a card and show the audience and the camera. The Three of Clubs.

She asked him to put the card back in the pack, and then hand the pack to her. Once he did, she took them and then threw them into the air. All the cards disappeared, as if they'd been sucked in to a specific invisible point. The audience applauded.

Ciara then asked the host to pick up the egg he was sitting on. He didn't know he was sitting on one. The audience applauded. As he held it in his hands it began to crack and a tiny hairless, slightly alien looking chick emerged. There was something in its beak. Ciara took hold of the bird and extracted the thing from its beak. She unrolled it. It was the Three of Clubs. The audience applauded. From out of the space where the deck of cards had disappeared, out of nothing but the air, there suddenly appeared a small red-brown kestrel with something in its mouth. It came and rested on Ciara's free hand and fed the chick. The audience went quiet, too stunned to know what they were seeing. She looked amazing in that dress. A patter of applause broke out into a run.

That night's lovemaking was the most intense so far. I asked her to keep the dress on. She wanted me to pull her hair and call her magic.

By the digital clock at the side of her bed it was 4.32am when we finished making love. I was lying in bed in the same position we'd stopped in, with my eyes still open staring blankly at the clock at 11.08am, when I finally stopped shaking.

After the talk show the TV company asked Ciara back for another series. We went to their offices and she explained that she might consider it. But before that she wanted to do something else. She wanted a *Ciara Wilson Special*.

"And what are you going to do with that?" asked Mr Jeremies.

"Something special," said Ciara, plainly.

"Like what?"

"Explain to people who I am," she said.

5

I never liked the idea for this show and I told her. I didn't like anything to do with guns. But she insisted this was the right trick to do on the show and, what was more, it had to be done live if there was any point doing it at all. The TV channel weren't sure, but Ciara managed to persuade them she could make it work. In the end, they agreed and paid for us to shoot the show overseas, to get over the legal problems with filming the show in this country.

The large posters went up in city centres, the papers talked it up, the TV stings appeared and the date got closer and closer. On the plane over to the studio specially prepared for us I told Ciara she really didn't have to go through with this. I told her there was still time to change the trick she was going to do. Part of the appeal in the media had been that she hadn't said what the trick was actually going to be. She said it involved her and a gun, and that the outcome would be magic, but that was all.

She touched my hand, made me spill my in-flight white wine all over my lap, and told me she really did have to go through with it, because it was time that people knew.

"Knew what?" I said, feeling just how cold the wine was in my lap.

"Knew about me," she said, and turned to look out of the window. There was a thick snowscape of clouds just underneath our plane and the sun was high and bright. When we'd left the ground it had been a horrible dark, rain-dreary day. Now we were above the weather, like we lived in paradise, or were at least visiting until we had to land.

The Ciara Wilson Special went out live at 8pm GMT. In it Ciara wore a stunning, plummeting neckline white dress which went as far as her belly button, in which she wore a simple single fake diamond stud. I had bought it for her – I couldn't afford real diamonds, but she said she liked it more than real ones because they were common.

Ciara was on stage for just under an hour. There were two 28 minute sections broken by adverts for *Audis, Clios, IBM, Oil of Olay, L'Oreal*, and a psycho thriller released on DVD in between.

In the first half she explained that she was going to show that she was, in fact, actually magic. She was going to stand opposite the large revolver on the stand at the opposite end of the stage. The gun somehow resembled an angry parrot. Other than that the stage was almost bare. The only other thing on it was a backdrop of a large projector screen, which showed no image at all.

The first half involved lots of checking of the gun, of its sights and the lethal quality of the bullets it fired, how it wasn't connected to any remote apparatus and all that. It also involved finding a volunteer from the audience, a man in a blue shirt called Gary, who was given a sealed white envelope by Ciara. She explained that no matter what happened in the second half of the show Gary was to read out this envelope and it would all make some kind of sense.

She looked amazing in that dress.

In the adverts Ciara was backstage, alone in her room in the dark, sitting cross-legged on the floor. The door was slightly open and I watched her breathing slowly in and out in the slice of light from the corridor. I left her as long as I could. One of the stand-by medics walked past the door and the sound seemed to disrupt her. She opened her eyes and looked at me. I shuffled a couple of steps closer and was about to speak.

"I know," she said, in a voice that made me feel like I didn't need to say anything anymore. She jumped up and her eyes looked exhilarated, somehow bluer and brighter even in the dark room. She snapped a quick kiss on my lips and it stung my mouth like static.

Like the professional she had now become, Ciara built up the tension in the second half whilst doing little more than recapping what she'd said before. Finally she stood in position with the angry parrot pointing straight at her beautiful face on the other side of the stage.

"The real beauty of this is the simplicity of it," she said.

"In a moment, at my command, a bullet will shoot out of the gun straight towards me. As we have already seen, I have no wires and no wireless connections to the gun. As we already know, the gun has been checked, its sights tested, the bullets tested, and there is no one else controlling the gun, or able to control the gun from off-stage. There is also no one else able to control the bullet once it has left the gun."

The lights dimmed. The sound dropped out of the studio, apart from my heart, which sounded as loud as a drill. This all happening live, being beamed out to millions of people watching back at home, was generating a strange, intense buzz inside the studio.

I saw her lips move. "Fire."

The bullet seemed to take so long to reach her. I had time to think, will she catch it in her teeth? Will the bullet turn into a butterfly halfway? Will she say 'stop' and make it hang in mid-air? Why wouldn't she tell me what the trick was?

Then the bullet struck her and she collapsed. Blood seeped from her head before anyone could take in what had happened. A woman in the audience shrieked. The lights went on. Panic and uncertainty, and the show was still live on air.

Ciara's body was rushed off stage. I was kept away by the medics as they put her on the stretcher in the ambulance. Because I was back stage I didn't see this at the time, but the floor manager came on stage, calmed people as best he could and asked for the guy in the audience, Gary, to bring his envelope on stage. Gary, visibly shaking as he tried to open the envelope, took out a piece of paper, and in a deep, faintly stuttering, estuary English accent, read out:

"Sorry if I've shocked anyone but really there's not the slightest need to worry, because I should be appearing via the pre-arranged CCTV connection beaming live from the ambulance."

The screen at the back of the stage suddenly blinked on displaying images, hard to make out in the studio lights. The lights were cut. Grainy black and white, slightly jerky images appeared to show Ciara's inert body, medics attending to her.

Gary read on:

"I am actually dead right at this moment. The bullet entered my brain causing devastating, instant damage. Then passed right through my head to the other side. Medics attending to me now will be able to verify that I am technically, medically, actually dead.

I will however, leave the ambulance in the next 10 seconds and magic myself back into the studio, alive."

Gary stepped away from the stage as he looked over his shoulder and the audience noticed the timer in the top right of the screen, picking up the count down from 5.

4.

3.

2.

1.

Ciara ripped through the projector screen and stood there, arms out wide, beaming a wide, toothy smile, a small red mark on her forehead in the close up.

The audience were silent. I have never known a room so stunned. The recording shows it took twenty-four seconds for the applause to start. It felt like that in minutes.

6

Ciara said she had a headache that night. Sometimes she said it was at the front of her head, sometimes the back, never consistent. I suspected she was using it as an excuse. I could tell something wasn't right. We spoke little right after the show and slept in separate bedrooms.

The next morning Ciara came into my room with a coat on, newspapers under her arms and a suitcase in each of her thick gloved hands.

"Morning," I said croakily, in what I hoped was a forgiving voice.

"Jim, I have to go," she said.

"Sure, give me ten minutes and we're gone." I said it, but my body hadn't moved.

"No, Jim. I mean me, not us."

"What are you talking about?" Now my body moved and I was half dressed by the time I'd got over to her at the door.

"They didn't get it," she said, dropping her suitcases to the floor either side of her.

She flung the papers on the bed.

"You're on the front page!" I picked through the papers, not able to take everything in.

"They think the medics were in on it. They think the footage of me in the ambulance was someone else."

"You're on the front page!"

"Jim, I have to go." The tone in her voice made me stop.

"What's this got to do with us?"

"Do you think I'm magic?" she said.

I looked in her eyes as hard as I could, even though it seemed to hurt to look. I thought carefully, and answered as definitively as I could.

"Yes."

She grabbed a hug and kissed me on the lips, stopped my head from shaking by holding it still with her thick gloved hands and stepped away.

"Then you understand what I have to do then," she said.

"Do I?"

"Yes," she said, "another way, or another time," and she picked up her suitcases and stepped away.

I felt something in my hand, looked down, opened it up and saw a blunted silver bullet with its head smashed, rolling in my palm.

Ciara left. I still have the bullet.

THE MARRIAGE
OF SEA AND SKY

Chris Beckett

"They say," mused Clancy, looking down on a planet whose entire surface glittered with artificial light, "that Metropolis is the city on which the sun never sets. It's true in a literal sense because the city covers the whole planet. But it's true in another sense too. Sunset never happens in Metropolis because there is *no-one watching*. The city's inhabitants live inside absorbing worlds of their own construction. They have no attention to spare for that rather bare space under the sky which they call, dismissively, the *surface*."

Here he paused.

"Have we finished dictation for now?" enquired Com.

"Wait," said Clancy.

Com waited. Having no limbs, Com had no choice. Its smooth yellow egg-shape fitted comfortably into Clancy's hand.

"I am a writer and a traveller," continued Clancy, reclining on cushions in a small dome-shaped room, its ceiling a hemisphere of stars. "I am a typical Metropolitan soul in many ways, restless, unable to settle, hungry for experience, hungry to feed the gap where love and meaning should be."

He considered.

"No. Delete that last sentence. And I've had a change of heart about our destination. Instruct Sphere to head for the Aristotle Complex. There are several worlds out there which I've been meaning to check out."

Com gave Sphere its instructions in a three-microsecond burst of ultrasound.

"Message received and implemented," said Sphere to Com, in the same high-speed code. "Shall I send standard notification?"

"Did you wish to notify anyone in the city about your new destination?" Com asked Clancy.

"Hmm," said Clancy, with an odd smile, "that's an interesting question. And the answer, interestingly, is no. Take another note, Com, for the book."

He leant back with his hands behind his head.

"Ten thousand kilometres out," he dictated, "I changed my destination so that no one could find me if anything went wrong. I wanted to disappear. I wanted to dispense with the safety net, to get a sense of what it must have been like for those early settlers in the fourth millennium, setting out on their one-way journey into the unknown."

He considered, then shrugged.

"Right Com. At this point add a chapter about the Aristotle Complex. What we know of the early settlers, their motives, their desire to escape from decadence... and so on. Themes: finality, no turning back, taking risks, a complete break with the past."

"Neo romantic style?"

"Neo romantic with a small twist of hard-boiled. Oh and include three poetic sharp edge sentences. Just three. Low adjective count."

"Okay. Shall I read it through to you?" said Com, having composed a chapter of two thousand words without causing a gap in the conversation.

"Not now," said Clancy. "I'm not in the mood. Get me a dinner fixed will you, and something to watch on screen. How long will it be till we reach the Complex?"

"The distance is about five parsecs. It'll take three days."

It was not the first voyage of this kind that Clancy had made. This was his career. He travelled alone to the 'lost worlds', he got to know them – their way of life, their myths, their beliefs – and then he returned with a book.

Returning with the book was his particular trademark. The completed book went on sale, in electronic form, at the *exact* same moment that he stepped out of his sphere. It had become a publishing event. He sold a million within an hour and became for a while the city's most talked-about celebrity: the literary spaceman: brave, elegant, utterly alone. He attended all the most fashionable parties. He invariably embarked on a love affair with at least one beautiful and brilliant woman.

And when the love affair grew cold – as it always did, for there was a certain emptiness where his heart should be – and when he sensed that he had reached the end of the city's fickle concentration span, he would go off once more into space.

He had a fear of being trapped, of being tied down, of becoming ordinary.

"The first approach to a settled planet," said Clancy, "is a uniquely humbling experience. Here are human beings whose ancestors have gone about their lives without any reference to the universe outside for thirty generations. Invariably, in the absence of the vast pyramid of infrastructure on which modern society rests, their technology has become very basic. Invariably the story of their origins has been compacted into some legend. They have had more practical things to worry about for the last thousand years. My arrival, however it is managed, is inevitably a cultural bombshell. Their lives will never be the same again."

He considered. They had reached the Aristotle Complex an hour ago. Sphere was now using the shortcut of non-Euclidean space to leap from star to star and planet to planet, looking for inhabited worlds, very quickly but mechanically, like Com searching the Metropolitan Encyclopaedia for a single word.

"Some say that for this reason I should not disturb them. This is surely poppycock. On that argument no human being would ever visit another's home, no one would talk to another, let alone take the risk of love. Not that I ever *do* take that risk of course."

He frowned. "Delete that last sentence."

"Deleted. Sphere has found an inhabited planet."

A fisher king was fishing in his watery world when the sphere came through the sky. Standing in the prow of his fine longboat, the tall, bearded upright king watched a silver ball, like a tiny, immaculate moon, descending towards his island home. And his household warriors, sitting at their oars, groaned and muttered, watching the sphere and then turning to look at him to see what he would do.

Aware of their gaze and never once faltering as he played his hereditary role, he ordered them in a calm and confident voice to cut away the nets and row at once for the shore.

When Clancy emerged, his sphere perched on its tripod legs on the top of a tall headland, it was mainly women and children who were standing round him. Most of the men were out at sea.

He smiled.

"I won't harm you," he said, "I want to be your friend."

The words didn't matter much of course. After all this time these fisher-people had evolved a completely new language. It was salty as seaweed, full of the sound of water.

"Iglop!" they said. "Waarsha sleesh!"

Clancy smiled again. They were pleasant looking people, healthy-looking and well fed. Men and women alike went bare from the waist up, and wore kilts made of some seal-like skin.

"Sky!" said Clancy pointing upwards.

"Sea!" (he pointed) "Man!"

It took them a while to grasp the game, but then they did so with gusto, drawing closer to the strange man in his rainbow clothes, and to his strange silvery globe.

"Eyes," said Clancy. "Nose. Mouth."

"Erlash," they called out. "Memaarsha. Vroom."

Hidden in Clancy's pocket, Com took all this in, comparing every utterance with its database of the language of the settlers before they set out a thousand years ago.

Com knew that there are regularities in the way that languages change. Sounds migrate together across the palate like flocks of birds. Meanings shift over the spectrum from particular to general, concrete to abstract, in orderly and measurable ways. Com formed fifty thousand hypotheses a second, tested each one, discarded most, elaborated a few. By the time the fisher king arrived with his warriors and his long robe, Com was already able to have a go at translating.

It was as the king approached that Clancy first became really aware of the massive presence of the moon.

"I was on a rocky promontory of the island. Beyond the excited faces, beyond the approaching king, was a glittering blue sea dotted with dozens of other islands. But all this was dwarfed by the immense pink cratered sphere above, filling up a tenth part of the entire sky.

"What is our moon in Metropolis? A faint smudge in the orange gloom above a ventilation shaft? A pale blotch behind the rooftop holograms? We glance up and notice it for a moment, briefly entertained perhaps by the thought that there is a world of sorts outside our own, and then turn our attention back to our more engrossing surroundings.

"But this was truly a celestial sphere, a gigantic ball of rock, hanging above us, dominating the sky. I had known of its size before I landed, of course, but nothing could have prepared me for the sight of it.

"I had yet to experience the titanic ocean tides, the palpable gravity shifts, the daily solar eclipses, but I knew this was a world ruled over by its moon."

Clancy paused and took a sip of red wine, seated comfortably in his impregnable sphere where he had retired, as was his custom, for the night. He had declined an invitation to dine with the King, saying that he would do the feast more justice the following evening. The truth was the first encounter was always extremely tiring and he needed rest. And alien food always played havoc with his digestion the first time round, guaranteeing a sleepless night.

"Com," he said, "prepare me a database of lunar myths."

He considered.

"And one on lunar poetry, and one on references to unusual moons round other inhabited worlds."

"Done. Do you want me to...?"

"No, carry on with dictation."

"The King is a genuinely impressive individual. His voice, his posture, his sharp grey eyes, everything about him speaks of his supreme self-assurance. He has absolutely no doubt at all about either his right or his ability to rule. And why should he? As he himself calmly told us, he is the descendant of an ancient union between sky and sea. He greeted me as a long-lost cousin..."

Clancy hesitated. A shadow crossed his mind.

"I pin them out like fucking butterflies!" he exclaimed. "I dissect them and pin them out! Why can't I let anything just *live*?"

Com was sensitive to emotional fluctuations and recognised this one, not from the *inside* of course but from the outside, as a pattern it had observed before.

"The first day is always extremely tiring," Com suggested gently. "In the past we've found that a cortical relaxant, a warm drink and sleep..."

"Yes, whatever we do, let's not face the emptiness," growled Clancy, but he seemed to acquiesce at first, collecting the pill and the drink dispensed by Sphere, and preparing to settle into the bed that unfolded from the floor...

Then "No!" he exclaimed, tossing the pill aside. "If I can't feel anything at least I can fucking think. Come on Com, let's do some work on the theme. Listen, I have an idea..."

Lying with two of his concubines in his bed of animal skins, the fisher king was also kept awake by a hectic stream of thoughts. His mind was no less quick than Clancy's but it worked in a very different way. Clancy thought like an acrobat, a tightrope walker, nimbly balancing above the void. But the king moved between large solid chunks of certainty. Annihilation was an external threat to be fought off, not an existential hole inside.

He thought of the power of the strange prince in his sphere. He thought about his own sacred bloodline and the kingdom which sustained it. All his life he had deftly managed threats from other island powers, defeating some in war, making allies of others through exchanges of gifts or slaves, or bonds of marriage. But how to play a visitor who came not from across the sea in the longboat but down from the sky in a kind of silver moon?

He woke one of the concubines. (He was a widower and had never remarried).

"Fetch me my chamberlain. I want to take his advice!"

"There are three kinds of knowledge," Clancy said, "let's call them Deep Knowledge, Slow Knowledge and Quick Knowledge. Deep Knowledge is the stuff which has been hardwired into our brains by evolution itself; the stuff we are born with, the stuff that animals have. It changes in the light of experience, like other knowledge, but only over millions of years. Slow Knowledge is the accumulation of traditions and traditional techniques passed down from generation to generation. It too changes, evolving gradually as some traditions fade and others are slowly elaborated. But, at the conscious level, those who transmit Slow Knowledge see themselves not as innovators but as preservers of wisdom from the past. Quick knowledge is the short cut we have latterly acquired in the form of science, a way of speeding up the trial and error process by making it systematic and self-conscious. It is a thousand, a million times quicker than Slow Knowledge, and a billion, billion times speedier than Deep Knowledge. But unlike them it works by objectivity, by stepping *outside* a thing.

"Deep, Slow and Quick: we could equate them to rock and sea and air. Rock doesn't move perceptibly at all. Sea moves but stays within its bounds…"

He laughed, "More wine, Com, this is *good*. Get this: Metropolitans are creatures of air, analytical, empirical, technological; lost worlders are typically creatures of the sea. They all are, but these guys here are literally so. So here's the book title: *The Meeting of Sky and Sea*. See? It ties in with the king's origin myth!"

"That was a *marriage* of sky and sea," observed Com.

Clancy had retired for the night on a headland overlooking a wide bay, with a coastal village of wattle huts squatted near the water's edge. But when he woke in the morning there was no sea in sight. A plain of mud and rocks and pools stretched as far as the horizon and groups of tiny figures could be seen wandering all over it with baskets on their backs.

The moon was on the far side of the planet, taking the ocean with it. The sky was open and blue. And when he climbed down the steps of Sphere (watched by a small crowd which had been waiting there since dawn) Clancy found that he was appreciably heavier than he had been the previous day.

Followed closely by the fascinated crowd – made up mainly of children and old people – Clancy went down from the headland to what had been the bay. A group of women were just coming off the mud flats with their baskets laden with shellfish. He smiled at them and started to walk out himself onto the mud.

Behind him came gasps and stifled incredulous laughs.

Clancy stopped.

"Is there a problem?" Clancy had Com ask. (Everyone was diverted for a while by the wondrous talking egg). "Is there some danger that I should be aware of?"

"No, no danger," they answered.

But why then the amazement? Why the laughter? They stared, incredulous.

"Because you are a *man*!" someone burst out at length.

Clancy was momentarily nonplussed, then he gave a little laugh of recognition.

"I've got it Com. Their reaction is *exactly* the one I would get if I headed into the women's toilets in some shopping mall and didn't seem to realise I was doing anything wrong."

He addressed the crowd.

"So men don't go on the mud when the tide is out?"

People laughed more easily now, certain that he was merely teasing them.

"These things are different where I come from," said Clancy. "You're telling me that only women here go out on the mud?"

A very old woman came forward.

"Only women of course. That is a woman's realm. Surely that is obvious?"

"And a man's realm is where?"

The woman was irritated, feeling he was making a fool of her.

"To men belongs the sea under the moon," she snapped, withdrawing back into the crowd.

"Sky and sea, sky and sea," muttered Clancy to Com, "it's coming together nicely."

The book was the thing for him. Reality was simply the raw material.

That night the king piled the choicest pieces of meat on Clancy's plate and filled his mug again and again with a thick brew of fermented seaweed. Clancy's stomach groaned in anticipation of a night struggling to unlock the unfamiliar proteins of an alien biological line, but he acted the appreciative guest, telling tales of Metropolis and other worlds, and listening politely as the king's poets sang in praise of their mighty lord, the 'moon-tall whale-slayer, gatherer of islands, favoured son of sky and sea.'

As he lay inside Sphere in the early hours, trying to get rest if not actual sleep, Clancy became aware of a new sound coming from outside – a creaking, snapping sound – and he got up to investigate.

He emerged to an astonishing sight. Over at the eastern horizon, the enormous moon was rising over a returning sea. Brilliant turbulent water, luminous with pink moonlight, was sweeping towards him across the vast dark space where the women had yesterday hunted for crabs.

But the creaking, snapping sound was much nearer to hand.

"What *is* that?" Clancy asked.

The king had posted a warrior as guard-of-honour to Clancy's sphere and the man was now sleepily scrambling to his feet.

"What is that sound?" Clancy asked him, holding out Com, his yellow egg.

The sound was so ordinary to the man that he could not immediately understand what it was that Clancy meant. Then he shrugged.

"It's the moon tugging at the rocks."

"Of *course*," exclaimed Clancy, "of course. With a moon that size, even the rocks have tides that can be felt."

He walked to the edge of the headland. He heard another creaking below him and a little stone dislodged itself and rattled down the precipice.

"Lunar erosion," he observed with a smile.

The warrior had come up beside him.

"It tugs at your soul too," he volunteered. "Makes you long for things which you don't even know what they are. No wonder the women stay indoors under the moon. It tugs and tugs at you and if you're not careful, it'll pull your soul right out of you and you'll be another ghost up there in that dead dry place and never again know the sea and the solid land."

Having made this speech, the young man nodded firmly and wandered back to his post at the foot of Clancy's steps.

"Wow," breathed Clancy, "good stuff! Did you record all that?"

Of course Com had.

The moon had nearly cleared the horizon now. It towered above the world. The wattle huts below were bathed in its soft pink light and the water once more filled up the bay.

"Take a note, Com. I said we in Metropolis had forgotten our moon, but actually I think our moon has gobbled us up. After so many centuries of asking for the moon, we have…"

"… we have…?"

"Forget it. I think I'm going to be sick."

"I visited a quarry," Clancy dictated, a week into his stay, "a little dry dusty hollow at the island's heart, where half a dozen men were facing and stacking stone. It was the middle of the day but quite dark, due to one of the innumerable eclipses, so they were working by the light of whale-oil flares. The chief quarryman was a short, leathery fellow in a leather apron, his hands white with rock dust. I asked him why he worked there rather than on the sea like most of the other men. He had some difficulty understanding what I was asking him at first, then shrugged and said his father had worked there, and his grandfather and great-grandfather. It was his family's allotted role. (A *slow knowledge* approach to life, you see, a *sea knowledge* approach. Any Metropolitan would want to demonstrate that his job was chosen by himself.)

"But I realised that my question had left the man with some anxiety about how he was perceived. He stood there, this funny, leathery human mole, and stared intently at my face for a full minute as if there was writing there which he was trying to read.

"'It isn't on the sea,' he said at length, 'but it's real moon work! No women are ever allowed here.' And he told me that there were some rocks they only attempted to shift when the moon was overhead. The strain of the tide going through the rock made the strata more brittle. Hit the rock in the right place under the moon and it would suddenly snap. Hit it any other time and it remained stubbornly hard. With some rocks, he said, it was enough to heat the rocks with fire when the moon was up, and they flew apart into blocks. It was real moon work all right.

"So I told him that I had no doubts whatever about his manhood."

Clancy paused.

"You know Com, I think we've got nearly enough material already. We just need one more episode, one more *event* to somehow bring the themes alive. Whatever 'alive' is."

He got up, paced around the tiny space of Sphere's leisure room.

"What is the point of all this? Back and forth across empty space, belonging nowhere, an outsider in the lost worlds, an outsider in Metropolis, no one for company but a plastic egg. What are my books anyway but mental wall-paper?"

Com conferred with Sphere by ultrasound, then suggested a glass of wine.

Clancy snorted. "You and Sphere always want to pour chemicals down me, don't you? Come on, back to work. Resume dictation."

Next day when the tide was out, Clancy got into conversation with a harpooneer, a sly, sinuous, thin-faced man, with two fingers missing from an encounter with one of the big whale-like creatures which he hunted under every moon.

As with the quarryman, Clancy asked the man why he did the work he did, and received exactly the same answer: his father, grandfather and great-grandfather had done the same. Then Clancy asked him would he not like to have a choice of profession?

When Com translated, the man did not seem to understand.

"I know the word for choice in the context, say, of selecting a fish from a pile," Com explained to Clancy, "But it does not seem to be meaningful to use this word in the context of a person's occupation."

"Okay," said Clancy, "ask him like this. Ask him does he prefer his ale salty or sweet? Ask him whether he prefers whale meat fresh or dried? Ask him does he prefer to fish when the sun is hot or when it is cloudy? Then ask him, how would it be if someone had said to him when he was a child, would he rather be a quarryman, a harpooneer or a fisherman with nets?"

Com tried this. The old man replied to each question until the last. Then he burst out laughing.

"They simply have no concept of choosing their own way in life," Clancy recorded later. "They follow the role allotted to them by birth and don't resent it because it has not occurred to any of them that anything else could be a possibility. How would they react if they could come to the city, and see people who have chosen even their own gender, changed their size, their skin, the colour of their eyes?"

He considered.

"There is something idyllic about their position. In some respects they are spared the burden of Free Will. Even marriage partners, I gather, are allocated according to complicated rules to do with clan and status, with no reference whatever to individual choice. I see no evidence that people here are less happy than in our city. In fact a

217

certain kind of *fretfulness*, found everywhere in the city, is totally missing here, even though life is certainly not easy for those allocated the roles of slave, say, or concubine or witch…"

He considered this. Com waited.

"It is this idyll of an ordered, simple life (isn't it?) which the city pays me so well to seek out. Not that anyone wants it for themself. This life would bore any Metropolitan to death in a week. But they like to know it is there, like childhood…

"By the way, one new thing the harpooneer told me. He asked me when I would meet the king's daughters. I told him I didn't know the king *had* daughters and he laughed and said there were three, and no-one could agree which was the most beautiful."

Clancy dined that evening on the high table in the hall of the king, with all the king's warriors ranged on benches below. In the middle of the room the carcass of an entire whale was being turned on a spit by household slaves. The whole space was full of the great beast's meaty, fatty heat.

"*Wahita wahiteh zloosh,*" chanted the king's poets on and on, "*wamineh weyopla droosh!…*"

Clancy leant towards the king.

"Your majesty, I am told that you have three very beautiful daughters. I hope I will have the pleasure of meeting them."

The effect of this on the king was unexpectedly electrifying. He jolted instantaneously into his most formal mode – and, seeing this, the entire hall full of warriors fell suddenly silent.

"Prince from the sky, I am most honoured that you should ask. They will be made ready at once."

He called to a servant, gave urgent orders and dismissed him with an imperious wave. The warriors began their talking and their shouting once again.

"An hour passed," Clancy dictated later, "and then a second. The warriors grew restless, wriggling on their benches like naughty children. The whale carcass, what was left of it, grew cold. The king and I, whose relationship consisted entirely of exchanging information, ran out of things to say to each other, and he eventually gave up all attempt at conversation, sinking into his thoughts, turning a gold ring round and round on his finger, and from time to time jolting himself awake and pressing more sea-weed ale on me.

"I began to wonder whether there had been some mistake. Surely it could not take that long for the princesses to be made ready? Had they been summoned from some other island? Had I perhaps completely misunderstood what was going on? But Com assured me that, yes, the king had said his daughters were being got ready.

"Another hour passed. I endured the king's poets repeating their repertoire for the third time. (*'Wahita wahiteh zloosh / wamineh weyopla droosh!...'* repeated after every one of twenty-three verses!)

"And then a door opened at the end of the dais, all the warriors lumbered to their feet, and the king's three daughters were led in."

At this point in his narration, Clancy asked for wine.

Sphere poured it for him.

"The harpooneer had not lied to me, all three princesses were indeed beautiful and it wasn't hard now to see why they had taken so long. Their hair was plaited, ribboned and piled in elaborate structures on their heads, their bodies, bare to the waist, had been freshly painted in the most intricate designs of entwined sea plants and sea creatures.

"They came round the table and knelt behind my seat, the youngest first, her sisters behind. Then, at a word from the king, the youngest daughter stood up, offered her hand to me briefly and went to stand behind him. The second daughter did the same. And then the third, the oldest..."

Clancy gulped down his wine and went across to the dispenser for more. He was agitated, scared.

"What the hell *is* that feeling?" he demanded. "It's not like lust at all, but you can't call it love, not when you don't know the person. It's like a buried longing for some kind of *sweetness*, which we try to stifle beneath worldliness and weariness and all the busy pointless tasks we lay upon ourselves. And suddenly a person touches it for some reason and it erupts, all focused on that one person, her lovely sad intelligent eyes, her unconscious grace..."

He checked himself.

"What a load of crap! What do I know about her except her face? What is it I want from that face? What can a face give me? What is a face except muscle and skin? Damn it, it means nothing, nothing! It's all just a trick played on us by biology!"

"Are we still doing dictation?" Com politely enquired.

"No of course we aren't, you plastic prat!"

Clancy swallowed the wine in one gulp and shoved the empty cup straight back into the dispenser for more.

"Okay, let's admit it. The oldest daughter, Wayeesha. When I met her eyes it felt as if something passed between us, some recognition, some hope that it might not always be necessary to be so... so terribly alone. It's all crap, of course: she's not much more than half my age, she's been brought up to marry some iron age warlord on some bleak little island. We don't even speak the same language."

He downed the third cup of wine in one, with a little shudder.

"All that we might possibly have in common is some kind of longing to *escape*..."

"Sometimes it helps to talk about what happened," said Com, after a ten-microsecond conference with Sphere. "Perhaps if you finished the story..."

"Oh for God's sake spare me your second-hand wisdom you sanctimonious *rattle*!" exclaimed Clancy.

But in spite of that he sat down again and carried on.

"So then when all three women were standing behind the king's chair, he smiled proudly at me and asked me whether or not they were indeed as beautiful as people had told me. Of course I said yes.

"'That's good,' he said, 'and now the choice is entirely yours.'

"I suppose I had been rather naïve, but until that point I hadn't understood that when I asked to see his daughters he had assumed that I wanted one of them for a wife."

Again Clancy jumped to his feet.

"Damn it Com, this is intolerable. One minute I was falling for a woman in a way that seemed scary and new to me, the very next minute I was being offered her hand in marriage. How could *anyone* deal with that? I played for time, of course. I said that in my own world a man sleeps on a decision like that... Delete that whole paragraph. You rewrite it. Leave out the nonsense about my personal feelings. Just describe her as very attractive and tempting. Generic rather than personal. Worldly rather than sentimental. Low adjective count."

"Done. Shall I read it back to you?"

"Later... It's maddening. This is *precisely* the event I needed to bring the book together. The marriage of sky and sea! The space traveller falls in love with the daughter of a fisher king. What could be better! *Damn! Damn!* Why has reality always got to be so awkward."

"Go on." said Com, who was a good listener.

"I mean it might make a good book, but if I marry her I can't just go back to the city with the book, can I? I have to go back with *her.* How would it look if I bring back some kid half my age who doesn't even know how to read or write? I'll look like a dirty old man."

"Don't forget," said Com, who had filed and indexed everything they'd learnt about the local culture, "that here it is the man who moves to live with the woman. Woman are not allowed to cross the sea."

"So I couldn't take her back with me? Yes, that's true. And if a marriage fails here a man returns to his own island doesn't he?"

Clancy sat down, picked up the yellow egg and turned it over in his hands.

"You may look like a kid's rattle, Com, but you have your uses. I could marry her here, and if things didn't work out, which of course they won't after a while, I can take off home. No harm done, a lovely honeymoon, and a nice sad end for the story. Sky and sea try to marry, but in the end they just don't mix. Spaceman has to be free, even at the price of loneliness and alienation. Ocean princess has to be with her people..."

Then he frowned. He was very cold and empty inside, but not wholly without scruples. He was concerned, at any rate, with how his actions might be *seen.*

"But that is just using her, isn't it? I can't do that. My readers wouldn't like it. They don't expect me to be an angel, but they do expect a certain... integrity. Damn."

He thought for a while.

"And anyway she is so beautiful, and so sad. I don't want to..."

A thought occurred to him.

"By the way, I meant to ask you. When she shook my hand she said something, very quietly, so no one else could hear. What was it?"

"*Eesha zhu moosha* – you have my heart. Do you want me to play it back as she said it?"

"*No!*"

Clancy jumped up as if he had been stung. He was shaking with fear.

"Oh alright," he whispered, shrinking back down, as if in anticipation of a blow, "go on, play it back."

When he had heard it, he wept: just two tears, but tears all the same, such as he hadn't shed for years.

"Damn it, Com, I'll do it. In this culture marriage is all *about* using people. It won't do her any harm to have been married to the sky man! I'm going to bloody do it. Do it and be damned for once."

He glared at the yellow egg as if it had questioned his action.

"Don't worry," he said, "I'll make the book come out right somehow."

Down in the wattle and daub settlement the fisher king had a lookout post beside his hall. It consisted of two tree-trunks fixed cleverly end to end, with a small crowsnest at the top. He invited Clancy up there on the night before the wedding to watch as the other grooms arrived from across the sea.

Weddings in the sea-world were communal affairs, taking place on a single day just once a year. Bonfires burned all along the beach. Under a huge half-moon that dwarfed the island and made the sea itself seem small, canoes appeared in the distance among the glittering waves, first of all as faint dark smudges and then gradually growing more distinct as they approached the land and the firelight. Each one was cheered as it approached and, as they drew close to the beach, the king's warriors waded out into the sea to greet the new arrivals and help to drag the boats ashore.

Clancy turned to the king and smiled. It was a magnificent spectacle.

The king laughed.

"And now," he said, "the burning of the boats."

He raised his arms and gave a signal to his followers on the beach, who at once set to, dragging the canoes one after another onto the fires. The grooms objected ritually and had to be ritually restrained, but there was a lot of laughter. It was clearly all in fun.

Clancy frowned.

"Why do you do that?"

"When a man marries, his wandering days should end, isn't that so?"

The king winked.

"That moon-boat of yours, it won't burn quite so easily!"

"What do you mean?"

Clancy looked over to the headland where Sphere was perched on its tripod legs. A fire was burning beneath it.

"Hey! What are they doing! Stop them!" he cried out, and then laughed at himself. How could mere fire harm a vessel designed to cope with space?

The king laughed good-naturedly with him, putting a friendly arm round the shoulders of his son-in-law to be.

"Those rocks are easily shattered under the moon," he observed, "and we have fires in the caves below as well."

When he heard Com translate this, it took Clancy a few seconds before he grasped the implications – and in that short time the first boulder had broken loose and crashed down into the sea.

"No!" Clancy shouted. "Make them stop! It's my only way back!"

The king roared with laughter.

"I'm not joking!" cried Clancy, looking around for the rope ladder to get down. "Have the fires put out at once!"

Over on the headland a second boulder crashed down, then a third. And then the sphere itself tipped over, its surfaces glinting in the pink moonlight as it rolled onto its back, its tripod legs sticking up in the air as if it was a stranded sheep. Some more rocks exploded. In agonising slow-motion, or so it seemed, Sphere went over the edge, crashing against the cliff – once... twice... – hitting the sea with a mighty splash, then slowly sinking beneath the waves.

With one foot on the rope ladder, Clancy watched, appalled. And the king, still laughing, his face wet with tears, reached down, helped him kindly back onto the platform and gave him a warm, fishy hug.

"The boats are burnt! So now you can go to Wayeesha."

Clancy walked over to the rough wooden rail at the edge of the platform, looked out at the bonfires, the glittering sea, the giant moon, and remembered Wayeesha waiting for him in the hall below.

As he had trained himself to do in even the most extreme situations, he examined his thoughts. What he found surprised him. He turned to the king with a smile.

"I'm going to regret this. And I fear that you, my friend, are going to be *seriously* disappointed. But right now, it's strange, I feel as if I've put down a burden. I don't think I've ever felt so *free!*"

"A good ending for the book!" Com observed.

"What book you idiot?" said Clancy. "Are we going to write it on seaweed, or carve it into the stones?"

Then he proffered the yellow egg to the king.

"Here," he said, "it's yours. I don't need it, and I feel you ought to get *something* from your alliance with the sky. No need to translate that last sentence, Com."

"Is this wise?" asked Com, as the king turned it over reverently in his large hands.

"No," said Clancy. "In a few months your battery will run out and you really *will* just be a plastic egg. Then what will the king think of my gift?"

He went to the rope ladder and began to lower himself, carefully avoiding looking down.

fIGHT MUSIC

Tim Nickels

I

After the air raid, I go to a grey and green room that smells of pencil shavings. An anglepoise throws a yellow miniature moon onto the linoleum. Long shelves of manuscript; a little platform on wheels. Wall clocks created from viola carcasses. Photographs, signed scores; the frames and glass repaired with buttery adhesive tape.

Far away a piano stops and starts; stops. A second piano answers. Forlorn, too late.

Professor Gnessin pares an acorn husk into a small glass of sugary hot water. Her starched shirt cuff wipes the excess from my résumé as she surveys me, lips thin and disappearing into their arrow-shaped chin. Is Professor Gnessin willowy? Or as thin and shrill as a clarinet reed? The lips sip with distaste before they open into a lopsided smile. She leans her bony elbows on the desk and nods me to a broken chair. A finger hovers over the Dictaphone and she motions me to begin.

»

Yes? Am I speaking loud enough? Well, my father didn't die in the war like the other dads. He drove trucks out of Agapova where the salt Green Sea gives way to fresh water and the crawfish have their home. A troop carrier drove out of the darkness as Dad thundered down a steep incline through fir trees. He was carrying ten tonnes of water and crawfish and couldn't stop. Didn't stand a chance. The water became a living thing, rocketing onwards as the truck tried to brake. The soldiers were hooking crawfish fragments out of the telephone wires with bayonets. My mother told friends that her husband had soared a little higher.

And so my life in music began.

225

| |

A train rattles into a tunnel within the foundations of the building. It sounds even closer than the remaining piano in its determined decrescendo.

Until today, I have never seen a train.

"*Your life in music*, Victorvna Yudelvna? You mean you had a life before?" The professor is good natured, her small eyes merry. Her questioning of my vocation is light but I sense there are more than two of us participating in this interview. I glance at the green walls, as thin as the professor's chuckle.

I lean forward – and very much aware of her thumb on the | | button – I hiss: "My secret history, professor. You will be aware of how I have arrived at this juncture."

She is even more amused. "Good lord. And how fifteen year-old girls speak these days. This *juncture*? At your age it's all arrival and departure, isn't it. And most of them desperately dramatic. Every week's a new doorway. Each year an eternity."

"Why? How old are you, Professor Gnessin?"

"Precisely three times your age. Forty-five last birthday."

"Old."

"Older than the national average, granted. And you're well nosy for a co-op girl."

"Farm girl. We had our own farm ten kilometres from the village."

"Living in your own shit and not the state's?"

"No shit at all. Me, my mother and my sisters saw to that. We worked sixteen hours a day to keep the chicken sheds clean."

"Mutation rate?" She has her pencil out.

"Between fifteen and twenty per cent. Far better than those city farms."

"And your sisters. Not musical in any way?"

"You know they weren't."

"Nor mathematical."

"No. And nor was I until Dad died."

The piano painfully works through some scales. A touch of melody. Something in C Minor.

"So your secret history. I'm waiting." The professor's finger settles on the Dictaphone. "I'll re-wind. Let's start at the beginning."

«« »

I was delivered to my family on my third day on earth, muslined and shivering. The midwife was silent, the ambulance driver a bundle of talkative nerves. The money would arrive soon, she said. Go out and plan what you're going to do with it. A new shed for the chickens with a sprinkler system for antibiotics. Or perhaps a down payment on a mini-tractor from the new factory. And it went without saying that the family's land would go unseeded by land mines. Families like ours, she said, needn't be put on the ten year list. We were eligible already. Cinema news reels mentioned our names in hushed tones. Newspapers manipulated our images amongst those of the Governing Committee. Family members were already heroes of the state.

My mother was pale after they drove away; her irises the colour of lemons as she looked down at me.

She tried to smile but the war had been going on too long.

| |

"Tell me about your non-musical, non-mathematical sisters. They're both dead now, aren't they."

"Rimma's dead. She died in the Hasmal anthrax attack. Elice is still alive. She works in a barracks canteen somewhere in the south. I haven't seen her for years."

"You write to Elice?"

"No, she can't read."

"Nor count either, I'd be bound."

"Hardly unusual these days."

"Continue."

»

My two elder sisters were four and six then. They smiled gleefully into the little tin crib that Mum had set up in the kitchen. The eldest – Elice – had dark hair and walked like one of the chickens with stiff movements and nodding head. She was Daddy's favourite, sitting up in the cab and humming as he played the bazouki –

| |

"You said they weren't musical."

"They weren't. Do you teach bazouki at the Conservatoire?"

"Point taken."

»

Her sister Rimma never stopped talking. Or writing. She was bright. That's why the Committee sent her to the Codes Department.

||

"You said they weren't mathematical."

"They weren't. However, Rimma's position in the Department was reactive: a foil to the code breaker alphas using inverted logic. Essentially non-logic. That's why she was transferred to the Hasmal listening post. Have you ever played chess against someone who merely knows the moves as opposed to the classic strategies?"

"Yes. It's hellish."

"Exactly. Rimma's non-logic has probably shortened this war by as much as thirty years."

"I'm suitably sobered." A swift bleak smile. "Schooling?"

»

Rimma and me used to walk out to Madame Stok's house near the village twice a week. She liked Rimma but I know I was her favourite. She would set Rimma exercises with the other girls – spelling and graphs – while she let me sit on the back step and drink pop –

||

"You're a quaint one. You mean lemonade?"

»

Yes. My mother had eyes the colour of lemons and I drank lemonade with Madame Stok during lessons and my favourite sister died horrifically. Are you joining some dots with that pencil and paper? Anyway. Madame was more of a conversationalist than a teacher. She would lay out concepts. We'd be staring out across the great plain almost as far as the Green Sea and she would ask me if I thought there was such a thing as solid light. And did I know that the ancient Greeks believed our ability to see was because our eyeballs emitted light beams? And she talked to me about – about –

||

The old coldness pours back into my head. My tongue shrivels and numbs. Professor Gnessin looks at me with an expression of utter non-surprise before deftly flourishing the steel wastebasket for me to vomit in.

"I know, Victorvna. The suppressants are still kicking in. Don't worry. You'll soon learn to think freely here. Madame Stok talked to you about music."

A heavy curtain seems to have been pulled back. I almost laugh, take the tissue she hands me. "Yes. She talked to me. About music."

»

She talked to me about music. About the place where mind and soul collide. Where numbers take on the soft cloaks of angels. Sequence, rhythm. Charles Ives, Benny Goodman, Alice Faye, Mamma Cass. Madame had no instruments though. Her little schoolhouse held a blackboard and five chairs. She had a funny hairless cat and her voice was odd. Very deep. But somehow she managed to conjure melodies in my head. Was she a witch? I used to stand in the farmyard at night looking for her broomstick as I watched the satellites strafe each other with laser fire. I counted the stars and started to consider each one a musical note. Is this madness?

||

"Yes. But I understand. Madame Stok was one of my finest Academicians. I'd like to tell you that she's here. But I won't lie." The professor refills the little glass from her kettle. "A little more of your family?"

»

Dad was away a lot, of course. Sometimes he would bring us a crawfish, one of the damaged or handicapped ones. He used to make a fire in the farmyard and we'd pretend we were pioneers. Elice would rake the charcoal until it was white hot. Dad played that bloody bazouki while my mother shuffled and danced, one arm above her head, the other gathering up her skirts, bare feet sliding back and forth in the mud. Dad would carry her off into the engine shed and we'd rush to listen and peer through chinks in the door. They knew we were listening. Dad's penis was huge and when they'd finished Mum used to piss on him.

| |

The piano has fallen silent.

"Good lord. And how fifteen year-old girls speak these days. And did anyone come to see you?"

"See me?"

"See you. Not them. You."

»

A couple of times before I was ten perhaps. They came in a minibus, an Opel maybe. I had a feeling they were touring around and just happened upon me. Usually two – a woman and a girl not much older than me. They took skin and nail scrapings and poked about under my tongue and seemed to already know that I could identify my mother's eye colour aged three days. Infantile prescience, you know.

| |

"I know."

The first piano begins again.

»

They gave me pills for the constipation but seemed disappointed that I wasn't ambidextrous –

| |

"You are now."

»

– I wasn't then – and made known their satisfaction that I'd passed through puberty at the age of eight. Some of us never get pubescent out on the farms. And then they'd drive off. Mum was just in the room next door but they never even attempted to speak to her.

| |

"Did the Committee send any money in the end?"

»

No. Dad said he'd got a bit of a promotion at the haulage co-op. But I reckon he was making it up. But Mum loved me. I know that. She never differentiated between the other two girls and her little Victorvy. She loved me –

||

"I'm stopping the tape but the interview isn't over."

I won't cry. "Where is she, professor?" She thinks I'll cry but I won't.

"In the city. She's safe. You'll be seeing her soon."

"I don't believe you."

The professor begins to chuckle, her coathanger shoulders heaving, tiny acorn fragments in her bent teeth.

"Actually – you're right not to believe me. I'm telling you a lie. Your mother has been informed that her daughter Victorvna Yudelvna has been returned to the Fostering Institute on account of her blabbing about you and your talents to the neighbours. She's allowed to write you letters. But I don't suppose you'll be reading them."

"You look stupid with a grin." I can feel the hot tears now.

"I look stupider without one. My chin is weak. Bad teeth distract the viewer."

"More stupid, professor. Your grammar is appalling."

"I am a musician. Proceed, little Victorvy. How did you learn of your father's death?"

»

It was funny. I walked alone to school as usual on the Thursday. Rimma was already dead by now. Madame Stok sat by herself in the schoolroom with a pot of tea and the cat. It was called Munsk, I remember. The cat. She took me out to the back step but didn't offer me lemonade. My tummy really ached for it but she wouldn't pour any. Instead, she hauled me into an outhouse and locked the door. I thought about Mum and Dad in the engine shed. Madame had occasionally commented in her curiously deep voice on my changing body in terms of gestation dynamics. However, I was no less disturbed when she pulled a tarpaulin off something I'd never seen before. But I can hear one now.

||

"A piano?"

»

An upright piano. She led me gently, making a thing of dusting the stool and opening the lid. The keyboard was covered in crawling June bugs – there must have been a way in through the back. I remember looking at the keys and wondering if they were black and white pupae. The bugs were in my hair but I ignored them. "Play, Victorvna," she said. Well, I tried. I'd never seen or heard anything like it. She took my hands and showed me how to make sounds. I enjoyed the way my fingers were able to splay across the keys, from sharp to sharp. I suppose I did some rudimentary scales. Madame then instructed me to stop and look out of the window. She told me that my father had been killed very suddenly and very painfully and that I would never see him again.

||

"Proceed."

»

The notes fell into place. I was crying, of course – but more through this mad rush of – of creation. This something out of nothing. I didn't know it was music. Madame Stok left the recorder running and walked out across the grasslands and left me. I never saw her again either. Munsk sat in the sun and watched me through the doorway. She rolled and chased her stringy tail in the dust and provided me with my rhythm.

||

Professor Gnessin holds up the disk. "It has a lot of coiled drama. Rah rah rah raah. You crash right in, don't you."

"My impetus was sudden. I'd had a shock. But the motif just uncoiled from my body. As if, as if – "

"As if it had always been there?"
"As if it had always been there."

»

| |

"Could you say that again? I need it on tape." The professor offers a cough of embarrassment. "It's, er, relevant to a minor funding issue."

»

As if it had always been there. Well, I walked home carrying that disk – even though I had no means of playing it when I got there. And it's sat on the mantelpiece next to Dad's picture ever since. Three and a bit years? And last Saturday, true to form, the minibus pulls up when there's no one in the house but me. I'm dumped at a railway station and spend half a week in a wagon full of beets and bison manure. And now I find myself sitting at your desk next to a bin of sick watching you make that mad little glass of acorn tea while I haven't eaten since God knows when.

• «««

"And how fifteen year-old girls speak these days. Arrivals and departures, departures and arrivals. Bisons and beets? Life's so unfair. Dear me. My tea's gone quite cold listening to you." The professor has stopped the machine, rewinds and raises her voice ever so slightly. "Clarabella Veronni?"

A tall girl – at least a metre and a half – opens the door and steps into the room.

"Clarabella. Please take our new Academician to the dormitories. She's had a long journey – beets and bison, don't y'know – and the day tomorrow may seem longer."

They can probably hear my stomach in that basement tunnel. "Food?"

"Take heart, Victorvna Yudelvna. We breakfast early."

Clarabella Veronni might be smiling as she goes ahead with my knapsack.

I wearily rise and pause in the doorway. "Professor Gnessin. My

233

father's death was an accident. Tell me it wasn't meant to happen."
The anglepoise is switched off and the room plunges into darkness
behind me.

II

Dawn stares in, the colour of my mother's lemon eyes.

There are no curtains. The glazing is uni-polarised so that light can
enter but not depart: a directive from the Aerial Bombardment Sub-
Committee. How do I know this? I don't. I'm making it up. Madame
Stok and her cat sucked something out of my head and three years of
rubbish has piled in to fill the gap. And not just my own. I've pushed
the sensors off my brow while I slept. A gentle putter inside my head
tells me the earbuds are still secure: Professor Gnessin and her thin
walls would have made sure of it.

I slide up the mattress and rest my head against the wall; feel the
frozen limb of the metal bedstead against my neck. Flecks of pinkish-
beige paint lie on the pillow. I find my spectacles in their case beneath it
and put them on. The fuzz shapes resolve into sleepers: thirty? Forty?
The big light from the single window halos their breath; starkly
highlights freckles and the occasional melanoma.

"Quick! Put them back on!"

It's the tall girl Clarabella hissing in the bed next to me, whacking
her own sensored brow like a mad baby bird. "Shitsop will make you
sleep on a plank, Victorvna Yudelvna."

I fumble and find the little suckers. They adhere eagerly, undeterred
by my swiftly raised eyebrows.

"Shitsop?"

"Mrs Shiltsoff. Eugenia Larissa's sister says she actually has balls.
Shitsop hauled Eugenia Larissa off to Sick Bay and showed her once."

Eugenia's sister – a girl of ten with a naked scalp – nods her head
vigorously several beds away.

"Eugenia is obviously highly observant." The paint flecks begin to
annoy me.

"Too observant. They transferred her to the Surveillance Section
but the Yankees caught her en route and now she has no eyes."

"You're joking."

"Or legs. Ssh!"

The other girls have begun to stir at our exchange but Clarabella's warning is enough to shut them up.

In the silence, I listen to the city's morning: the train in its tunnel, the croak of a helicopter. Water pipes, quiet weeping from the beds. A sort of purring cry from the corridor: not urgent, repetitious; a set of wheels. The door opens and – through half-closed lids – I see a small figure in a wheelchair float in. The chair deftly weaves its way among the untidy array of bedsteads and comes to rest beside me. My eyes are tight closed now.

"So, Victorvna Yudelvna." The voice is thin, immature; the mind behind seeming to hold an infinite age. "What do farm girls dream of? Something pretty good if they have to wear their glasses in bed."

A dry chaffing hand is on my cheek and my spectacles are gone. My eyes are so tightly shut I'll have crow's feet for a week.

"Wire rims. A little bit in the old style, eh girls?" Silence. "Eh, girls?"

"Yes, Mrs Shiltsoff." A single voice. Poor girl. I bet it's Eugenia's bald sister.

"Well, a voice. And not such a good one. I hear your sister's had a bad time with the Yankees, Georgievna Larissa." God, it is Eugenia's sister. "Lost some limbs and her eyeballs. Dear oh dear, how careless. Come, come."

My lids crack open to let in a little lemon light. I see Shitsop in profile, her face almost level with mine as I sit upon my high hospital bed. It is a child's face, finely featured; the hair full, coarse, complexly dressed perhaps in the style of the 1900s; earlobes holding pearl drop earrings. Yet she has the voice of a woman. The eyes of a woman as she swivels them suddenly on me, shows her teeth in the briefest of smiles and turns back to Georgievna.

"When I say come come I really do mean... come." She holds up a hand to Georgievna and the girl mutely slips down onto the freezing floor and works her way towards Mrs Shiltsoff.

Startling child-in-woman Mrs Shiltsoff.

Georgievna is before the wheelchair now and – bully for her – she looks Mrs Shiltsoff straight in the face. Mrs Shiltsoff turns my spectacles in her hands. I only have the one pair. They used to belong to Rimma.

"Give me your voice, Georgievna Larissa."

Georgievna is silent and now begins to bow her head.

"Your voice, girl. You know I can take it if I want to. Here, farmer. Give her your chamber pot."

Chamber pot? I didn't know I had one. I wish someone had bloody told me. I look under the bed. There it is. I haul it out and hand it to the girl. Her hand is steadier than mine. Her eyes are smiling. Her eyes tell me not to worry as she puts the pot on Shitsop's lap and kneels.

Georgievna has a couple of goes, coughs and nearly kills herself. In the end she gets it with two fingers stuffed down her throat. She wretches, wretches again and suddenly it's there. I smell the acridness of bile for the second time in twelve hours.

Shitsop shows me the chamber pot with that quick grin before she wheels away to oversee breakfast. She takes my spectacles with her.

I'll never forget peering in: there it was in its little soup of sick.

The voice of Georgievna Larissa.

There is practice before breakfast.

I expect to be lead into the bowels of the building where I heard last night's pianos. But a blue-overalled woman with a scarf around her neck conducts me up the bare stairs. She carries a music case. The walls are covered with further photographs of the musically gifted and probably dead. She pauses on a landing with a window that looks out over a bombed shoe factory; leans on the sill and points back to a curled monochrome picture pinned to the plaster. The photo's emulsion is cracked. It features a boy and girl; he with guitar, she with dulcimer. They sit in an orchard surrounded by fallen apples.

"Couldn't you just eat them?" My guide is enthusiastic. Her voice is slow and precise.

"Apples or children?" I wonder if she can hear my stomach rumbling.

I look out and down on the scattered shoes: hundreds or thousands of mismatched pairs clouding the wasteland as far as the shrunken river. All of them waiting for feet that will never be born.

The practice room is windowless, the ceiling covered in egg boxes. The room contains an upright Klemt & Sons piano, a stool, metronome and a family of spiders low down in one corner. I find this out when I examine the floor. The floor and wall are painted the same colour but even close inspection fails to tell me what that colour is.

I wonder if I'll get my glasses back.

The woman – I suppose she's middle-aged – hands me a single sheet from the music case and departs.

I study the music. I peer closer, have to screw my eyes up. It looks normal enough. Simple even. Just a few notes. Something in C Minor. It's quite similar to my audition piece. But as I begin to play, I become confused. The notes could almost be the spider's relatives: they vibrate when I look too hard at them; fade into the white paper as I try to casually interpret with a sly sideways glance.

The metronome is broken. I play nothing.

The woman returns. She tightens her scarf in an unconscious gesture; takes the manuscript back and locks the door behind us. "How did you get on, miss? I could hear some very pretty music in the corridor."

We climb a further flight towards breakfast. I might just live another day.

"Fine. Very good. I can't believe how easily I took to it."

Georgievna Larissa sits in the corner of the canteen at a small table by herself. The voice – still in its chamber pot womb – sits between her spoon and fork. The tabletop is scattered with her fingernails: now that's what you call rotten luck. She sucks lemonade through a straw that connects to a hole in her throat. Following voice loss, Georgievna's mouth swallowed its own tongue and the nurses had to carry out a tracheotomy. Georgievna Larissa sucks steadily in spite of hiccoughs.

"Poor Georgievna. Quietest girl in the Conservatoire," says Clarabella as she tries to make a meal of her oats and water. Her observation is without slant or judgment.

The girls around me keep their heads down, intent on the round ceramic universes before them. The oatmeal is surprisingly good, in spite of a metallic undertaste. We are almost queens at breakfast: women in blue overalls run around with trays and tea towels. My guide fills the urn in the corner. I catch her eye and realise she's a good deal older than I thought.

The same age as my father might have been.

While much of my mind wanders, a smaller part understands that Clarabella is a focus of attention. She sits beside me, a light bulb in the dim morning, not always speaking but the first to be turned to if there's any listening to be done. She listens now as a dark girl called Dulcie reads an official trawler report from the Finnish Ocean. The girl's family live on a ship that circles the eternal day of higher latitudes. They are pirates plundering the lochs of fish farmers; releasing and stealing the domesticated cod; allowing them to spread their viral contagions amidst the deep seas.

"I'd like to be a fisherman," says Clarabella suddenly. "Not just fish. Anything from the water. Oysters, crawfish. How about you, Victorvna Yudelvna?" Her turn to me is even more sudden.

"I don't know." The cereal fibres catch in my throat. "We're so far from the sea here. Seafood has to be fresh."

"But you can use transports. Even now." This from Yergeniya, a girl with permanent earbuds.

"But the trains are so slow." Lizan, a long-limbed redhead from the south somewhere.

"You mean the roads aren't?" Aja: black staring eyes.

"Well, the rivers aren't much good anymore. My mother fought river fever all her life. Her guts glow like a lantern." Kara: skinny limbs, large hands. I notice her fingernails hinge away from their cuticles.

"People will find a way if they want to dine on crawfish. Am I right, little Victorvy?" Clarabella dwells at the centre of her halo in the canteen, the others just watchers looking in.

"You're right." I don't mean to cry. "You're really really right."

There's a light pressure on the bridge of my nose, the hooks of my ears.

I open my eyes to find I can see.

Clarabella leans closer to ensure the new glasses fit snugly. I am fascinated by her face: the tight skin stretched on finely-furred cheeks. Freckles, nostrils wide like a pony. Legs longer than she knows what to do with. Is she pretty?

Clarabella smiles at me. Blue-grey eyes.

Yes, she's pretty.

"What's the time, Victorvna Yudelvna?"

I glance at the canteen clock through my spectacles.

"07.25, Clarabella Veronni."

"Five minutes to go, girls. Might as well make a start for the shelter."

The air raid is early.

We barely reach the bomb shelter before it's over.

On the way down Georgievna Larissa trips over a body. She can't scream. I gather her voice into my hanky and we carry on just as the big landing window implodes. It's one of the old-fashioned sonic weapons and its hum carries through the steel superstructure of the building long after the munition has discharged. I have Georgievna in my arms and we fall down the stairwell. Her body is full of glass. I am aware that Clarabella observes this even as we all run and trip and scream. Little Aja actually stops for a proper wee in the janitor's doorway. Heroic or foolish, Clarabella holds the iron door open for us wearing the world's biggest grin.

There could be a hundred in here: pupils, staff, the blue overalls. A piano sits in one corner below a row of steel helmets. Yergeniya has her earbuds plugged into the News Service and screams a running commentary.

"Our forces are triumphant! The slack-jawed Yankees are running across the sky faster than they have come, driven by our heroic pilots as a shepherdess drives her sheep. But not to any green field go the Yankees, but into a burning place of kerosene and cordite and irradiated munitions. Damn their tiny cocks! We are victorious! Victory! Victory!"

A beaming Professor Gnessin squats on a rations box at the piano. "Well done, Yergeniya. An excellent précis of the broadcast. And I hear the All Clear sounding so it's time to start our lessons. But not without a stirring rendition of the Imperial Anthem. Come on girls. Let's show Victorvna Yudelvna how we conduct ourselves in the war zone!"

As the professor strikes up, all the faces turn towards me and the body of Georgievna Larissa still cradled in my arms.

"Look," calls Clarabella above the singing. She toes a loose flex on the floor. "Bloody radio's not even plugged in."

The lemon dawn has given way to grey mid-morning. Smoke hangs over the city.

I lay Georgievna's cold body out in the deserted Sick Bay. The room's as empty as its large dispensing cabinet. Where can everyone be? I look through an archway into what seems to be the nurses' station. That chamber there might be an operating theatre. From behind a large set of double doors I hear echoing shouts and splashes. A sharp smell of disinfectant.

I leave Georgievna's voice on the night stand: pinkishly organic, moistly mechanical.

As we sit and wait for class in the boarded-up lecture theatre, I ask Clarabella about the double doors.

She brushes her forearms, arranges her notation manuals. "Water polo." She almost looks at me. "The nurses can't get enough of it."

Water polo? What the hell's that?

Doctor Kaulay arrives in a cloud of spilt manuscripts and we have an hour of ensemble theory before break time. The girls have explained that ensemble means playing with others: I consider the lonely practice room with its egg box ceiling – presumably a deterrent to prevent those mysterious others from hearing your music.

Doctor Kaulay is a brightly plaintive graduate of the Conservatoire. The Conservatoire is her existence. That year twixt graduation and a return to doctoral residency was the worst of her life. A wasteland. In fact the theory lesson is pretty much taken up entirely by that nest of horrors that was Life Beyond The Conservatoire.

Doctor Kaulay continues to chunter on as she oversees our break. A side door is unlocked and we find ourselves on a shattered netball court beneath exhausted lime trees. Needless to say, the doctor is able to recall a time when the lime trees were over-burdened with sap and the court possessed more lines than a geometry lesson.

We are placed on salvage duty. It is explained that the metal rain that drops from the sky during aerial bombardment is valuable and can be turned against the enemy.

The girls have a system. Aja and red-headed Lizan work the Geiger counters while Kara scrabbles on her knees, those great hands spread out on the tarmac like the rippling whiskers of catfish. By break's end, they have quite a haul of ball bearings. Yergeniya and a small girl called Calli follow Clarabella as she douses the ejected aviation fuel with sand before sweeping the result into great leather satchels for recycling. I laugh as I discover the satchels have been home to clutches of yellow frogs. They jerk away across the broken ground, doubtless smelling the river. Most seem to be copulating on the run – but Yergeniya removes her earbuds to explain that they are actually Siamese twins, cursed to drag a comatose sibling through their stunted tiny lives.

The bell sounds and Doctor Kaulay goes inside. I am about to turn in too when a movement catches my eye beyond the high fence. Mrs Shiltsoff weaves between piles of steaming debris on a course roughly parallel with that of the amphibians. She makes good progress: some of the concrete must be red hot.

Professor Gnessin lingers at the side door: her face colour matches that of her starched cuffs. The professor calls us inside, her manner vague: she watches Mrs Shiltsoff go, and presently slinks down to the fence and scratches around until she finds a badger hole. She crouches in and catches a thread of her dark gown on the razor wire; disentangles, straightens and jogs after the wheelchair.

Clarabella and I are the only ones left in the playground. She holds a frog in her left palm and gently strokes it and its twin in the half-light of morning. In the dull brightness, her irises are almost transparent. More blue than grey in the out-of-doors. "Just another unexploded bomb, I expect. They can't get the fuses right lately."

I can't stop looking at Clarabella. She smiles slowly and says: "Can you run, farm girl?"

"Chicken girl. We kept chickens."

Before we slip under the wire, she lets her frog go. It darts across the netball court; pauses to drink from a puddle of aviation fuel.

Shitsop and the professor have made good progress. Their silhouettes are barely discernible through the oily smoke. The sun is a disc that slips in and out of visibility.

Clarabella yells back that the area we're running across is the collapsed metro entrance – part of the tunnel system that I heard below the professor's study last night. The dust is heavy yet still hangs; phosphorus sticks smoulder and steal oxygen from the air. Tram ponies limp and whimper on the superheated black-top.

Clarabella stops, rests hands on knees, tries not to breathe too deeply. "It must have been a ground detonation. Air rounds are much cleaner."

A pair of naked legs hangs from a lamp post; only one limb has a stocking. A moving staircases – I learnt the term on my train journey into the city – is miraculously still moving. It snakes up from below and unravels into a clattering coil. Rationing leaflets and those for special travel privileges are beginning to helix up into the air, buffeted by the heat underground.

"It is a bomb! I can hear it. Come on, Victorvy..."

She uses a pile of travelling trunks to scramble up a wall that used to be a roof, the tiles lacerating her long legs. I make to go around – realise the grizzly reason for her clambering – and hoist myself up after her. I can hear screams, but not from this ruined ticket office; there's no one left here.

They come from the river.

"Wait, Clarabella. You're bigger than me. Just wait..."

She stretches an arm down, dust catching the fine blond hairs. "Mind your hands. The piano needs them for later, cowlick."

"Chickenlick."

She just catches my fingers and hauls me up in such a painful grip that I almost cry again: I'm obviously being punished for my insolence.

From here we can see clearly down to the nearly-dry river. Clarabella quickly points and I listen: the Food Committee factories; a couple of Dulcie's beached pirate trawlers with their riverine camouflage. The abandoned zoo and an old bridge that they've never bothered to bomb, the piles allegedly filled with our own high explosive ready for the Yankee's final push. To the east, we can see the remains of two other music academies that were built too close together. They know better now. The blackened masonry looks like my near-broken fingers feel. Clarabella used to attend the nearest one: she says she can see her dormitory window with its new transparent walls.

Shitsop circles something half-sunk in the river mud about fifty metres off. At every circumlocution, she gives the object a hefty whack with a piece of driftwood she's found. Shitsop's been pretty fearless, obviously gambling that the mud will remain stony enough to prevent her chair from sinking.

Professor Gnessin advises from firmer ground. Her voice whips up to us on a thermal. "Do you think we can save it?"

"I'm not sure. It's still responding." Shitsop circles and gives the bomb an almighty wallop.

The bomb screams again.

We sprint back to the netball court where the blue overalls are assembling equipment: a gurney and tarpaulins. My practise room guide is with them. She carries sandwiches in greaseproof paper and a bottle of lemonade.

The woman's all concern. "Shouldn't you be at lessons, Victorvna Yudelvna? It's time for accompanist vocations. And I'm surprised at you, Clarabella Veronni."

But she passes on through the fence, her concern eclipsed by the riverside discovery.

Clarabella kicks at the molten asphalt. "You've got to keep an eye on Erica."

"Erica?"

"Yeah. She used to be a Yankee. Didn't you clock the paunch?"

"She's stick thin."

"In her brain, silly. Too much flab and wastage."

"How did she end up here?"

"The usual. Wandered over the border. Had the operation. Debriefed and put to work in the service sector. Anything to be a tiny fragment of our glorious revolution." She looks right at me. "It's funny though..."

We tread on frogs, gelatinous and snappy. I'm not exactly laughing.

Clarabella continues: "She hasn't got the glow. The super fanaticism that makes them defect. She's got a sort of lazy look."

As we reach the side door, I turn back one last time. Erica has paused on the ruins of the ticket office to slug back lemonade.

The Vocational Accompanist Module is taken by Professor Gnessin herself. She's a little late to class and her fingernails are filthy. She sends Dulcie off for a bowl of water.

The professor's delivery is flat, the small eyes distracted. "The accompanist often goes ahead of the principle. The accompanist is the scene-setter but not the scene itself. There is a withdrawal, a return, a replication of the principle's motif."

She sits and steeples her fingers over the desk, skin moist as a yellow frog's above her thin top lip. She ponders the blotter. Dulcie returns, but the bowl and towels are ignored.

"A suitable metaphor would be that of a thermobaric air-fuel weapon. Consider the accompanist as the initial discharge of fuel, that mist of ethylene oxide that must be laid down so the principle – acting as the primary charge – can ignite and deflagrate. As we know, a thermobaric impulse can initiate pressure spikes within internal organs of over three-hundred pounds per square inch. The accompanist/principle relationship should have no less an impact. Erica?"

Erica peers through the celluloid window in the classroom door.

Professor Gnessin rises. "Unfortunately I'm needed on other business, girls. Aja, please take over the class."

Aja's black eyes are ready to pop from her head as the professor scurries away.

The talk over luncheon is especially small as we stir our blue soup and fight over paprika. The blueness of the soup has long ceased to be a viable topic for the others. I am curtly told by know-it-all Yergeniya that the Food Committee steals it from the sky and boils it in their factories by the river. I look at Clarabella but she doesn't look at me. She's taken up with Lizan at the far end of the table.

Gnessin and Shitsop hurry through. I hear a snatched dialogue but am unsure which is which, so hissed is the exchange:

... Does this mean our own programmes can be accelerated? ..

... Doubtful. The technologies are so different... ...Surely there must be some concordance...

...Well, you try talking to it. I can't understand a word it's trying to say...

They are gone, a gaggle of blue overalls travelling in their wake.

Blue soup, blue overalls.

I rub my bruised hand and notice that a fine blue sweat has pooled on my fingertips. I try to draw on the plastic table top.

I might write my name but I can't quite remember it.

I'm on the floor in the corridor, my dress covered in sick. My eyes feel like great throbbing nuts. I've been dreaming of Georgievna Larissa, laid out on her bed back in the dormitory. Except her legs are missing and I just know that I'll find them on top of the lamp post in Professor Gnessin's office. The same lamp post where she hangs all the melted mis-matched shoes. I can smell the professor's wastebasket and it smells of me.

Clarabella kneels close by. Lizan is there: she has an elastic bandage around her neck; it leaks a little.

I vomit, blue and acrid. This is more than last night. I'm soaked. The girls pull me up and drag me to the washrooms. Lizan scrubs my dress in a basin while Clarabella looks after my spectacles and keeps my head down the toilet. The sick keeps on coming. I half expect frogs. I stagger out and lean against the cubicle to a round of applause.

Lizan turns back, laughingly works bauxite into my dress. "You'd better stay in the bog. It'll be coming out the other end soon."

She's probably right. I can feel my intestines distending, a worm uncoiling downwards across my stomach. I catch Clarabella looking at me as I stand in front of the mirror. I'll need my spare vest.

"Big old agricultural thing isn't she, Liz? Elevate your mighty arms, Victorvna Yudelvna."

They seem thick and yellow as I raise them under the strip light; old chicken beak scars, a flash of hair in the armpits.

Lizan has stopped scrubbing. They both stare at me as I look at myself in the glass. Suddenly, I can smell the oil from Dad's engine shed. The smell of the animals; my mother squatting over his face...

The tall girl gently touches my elbow, slides her finger down the arm.

"I'm not feeling too well, Clarabella... What are you..."

"Nothing, Victorvy." She delicately holds the sweaty, calcified strands between thumb and forefinger. "Just bloody jealous, that's all."

I absorb the other girls' bodies as if for the first time: flat and unrounded, lithe and destined for some other purpose.

I stumble back into the cubicle and only later realise that Lizan's voice once belonged to Georgievna Larissa.

III

The practise will be even easier this morning.

In my weeks at the Conservatoire, I have discovered a rhythm both to my life and to my music. The air raids and the oatmeal and the theory and the reality.

Erica again leads me to the room of egg boxes. She seems anxious that I might forget the way. The music seems the same – and yet I now notice pencilled annotations that must have been there all the time. Erica sits on a second stool in the corner and watches me as I make the spider notes come together. I activate the metronome but she swiftly leans over to lever it off.

"You won't need that, miss. You'll find the rhythm in your mind."

She seems very sure about that. I run through a couple of cascades then turn to her.

"Erica?"

"Yes, Victorvna Yudelvna."

"Where do you come from?"

I don't need the metronome to count the beats between question and reply.

"One of the outer dependencies. Near the Green Sea. An Asiatic you've never heard of."

Liar.

"You speak our language very well."

"Thank you. I had a very good teacher. Mrs Shiltsoff. She has great patience." The scarf is loose this morning and I watch the Adam's apple as it bobs. "Small c and small m, miss."

"Sorry?"

"You've written C Minor in the margin with a big C and a big M. A small c and a small m are fine for your purpose."

My purpose? I had no recollection of writing C Minor. I had no pencil. "So why's it fine for my purpose, Erica."

"It's quicker." Bob, bob went the neck. "It's quicker, Miss Victorvna."

I crouch beside the dispensing cabinet and hear Shitsop's voice behind the double doors. It's like a buzzy squib amongst the water and echoes. She's been questioning the bomb for weeks in its own language. The bomb chatters and screams. It must be in unimaginable pain now. Professor Gnessin's voice requests thermobaric data. Demands knowledge of their fight music. Will the bomb submit or will they have to kill it? The bomb wails as the professor opens the doors and steps into Sick Bay. Behind her I see the rippled reflections of water against an aquamarine ceiling.

The professor has a high colour. There is a muskiness about her. She falls onto one of the beds; knots her hands into her skirt and pulls it up over the bird-thin thighs.

When she sleeps, I slip away.

"So tell me about your father."

"You know about him. You knew about him that first morning at breakfast."

"I just listen. They tell me to listen." Clarabella and I sit top to toe on my high bed in the early evening. We darn asbestos hoof socks for the tram ponies. Kara's been losing her hair for the past week and is confined to the dormitory. We keep her company as she lies in the bed next to ours, looking at the ceiling. Her big hands are folded across our ball of coarse wool. Her fingernails have all gone and Mrs Shiltsoff has told us her voice is taking well.

Otter meat for supper and no one's feeling good.

"And what about your father, Clarabella?"

"No, that's too easy. You need to try harder. You should say: And I suppose you don't want to talk about your father, Clarabella Veronni."

"I bet he's some neutered arse wipe in a minority groups sub-committee."

"Brilliant! You're good."

"She's good." Kara's new voice has a smile in it.

Clarabella jumps off the bed. "For that, you deserve a special treat. I'll take you to him. He lives in the city –"

"He lives in the city?"

"Yep. Even works at the Conservatoire – but he comes and goes so early you'll never notice him. Officially, he's not on the books. Music's not his real job but it keeps the crusts from crawling off his table. Come on, Kara Reginid. All of us."

She slips some packages from under her mattress into the tubes of Kara's bedstead, kicks away the locking pin and has left the dormitory before I've even had time to put my sandals on.

The goods elevator complains on its cables as we descend through the layers of the building. The stamp issued by the Committee of Public Safety is taped to the control panel and was signed seventeen years ago.

"Faster, Kara? Faster?!" Clarabella's a demon, her teeth bared, her blond hair sticking up like a scarecrow.

We hit the ground floor and the gates groan open. A sudden silence.

"Check for blueys, Vic."

"Where do Gnessin and Shitsop sleep?"

"With each other probably. And they summon Kaulay to tickle their toes on alternate Wednesdays. Now poke your nose out and see if the coast is clear."

I peer into the dank corridor and realise my glasses could do with a good clean. But apart from a fire bucket the corridor's empty and we propel Kara down a ramp and into the rear courtyard. It's full of rubbish. Broken upright pianos are stacked on the cobbles, several piled upon one another. Picture frames and glass tanks and oxygen bottles. Mummified birds in a cardboard box. And something white on a wheeled stretcher. I move closer. The object glows in the dimness. Clarabella has matches and we both jump in the sudden light.

"Gosh, what is it? Some sort of giant salamander? It must be a metre long."

I strike another match as she strokes the flowery external gills, the stubby paws that could almost be hands. The body is quite desiccated and the head has been severely beaten. But I can still smell the river mud. And disinfectant.

Abruptly, Clarabella loses interest and climbs up onto the pianos. She cries with laughter as she thrashes at the strings through their naked broken backs. She plays until the blood must shine on her knuckles. I join her to take the rhythm and follow her lead as she continues to work the melody. Accompanist and principle. Kara goes at the bedstead with a big spoon. We fashion a bleak boogie-woogie out there in the twilight courtyard.

We'd howl at the moon if there was one.

The hole through the fence has been shored up – but we manage to find another. I strain my ears but the whole city is wrapped in nothing. The daytime raids accentuate the nocturnal silence. Something catches in my hair: a moth or June bug drawn by our residual radiation. Perhaps they were living in the pianos.

We're on the other side of the underground station and there's less debris. A few trams venture down the street, headlights slitted for the black-out, their ponies' hooves muffled. The drivers are as nervous as we to be out after dark. The Committee's curfew regulations have been left deliberately vague.

The sidewalks are wide in this part of the city – Clarabella tells me there used to be a street market here – and we've room enough to push

Kara along. One of the bedstead's wheels has seized and our navigation is erratic: several times we career into piles of rubbish or carcasses.

And the bloody frogs are everywhere.

"Here."

I realise I've been mesmerised by the semi-gloom – the blind lamp posts, the fleets of confused insects – and Clarabella's cry makes me start. We stop by a wide shop front: boarded-up plate glass either side of a short passageway that ends in a door. The boards display repeated fly posters advertising Pioneers' Day Special Offers on Bicycles. Clarabella skips up the passage and knocks: a rhythmic tattoo that carries meaning. I look at Kara but she sleeps. I stroke her eyebrows but she doesn't stir.

The door opens a fraction and I realise it's a curious one, the shape of a bullet in profile, pointed at the top. A tatter of paper is pinned to the wood: 962110 Kovarskaya 48. An orange splinter of light streaks out across the sidewalk. Someone holds the ring handle: I can only see an outline against the warm luminescence. The door is wider than it looks and we push the bed in.

Immediately, my senses are engulfed: an overwhelming stink of beeswax and damp tapestries. The light – a single source that depends from a chain in the high roof – is sheathed in a copper and jade cocoon above a table of once-milky linen. Our feet make gentle crunching sounds as we enter and I glance down to see that the stone floor is covered in large skeletal dry leaves. Chickens live in a corner and I find myself kneeling amongst them, stroking their broken beaks as easily as I stroked the sick girl's eyebrows.

Clarabella is unscrewing parts of Kara's bedstead. "Don't worry. Victorvna Yudelvna's a whizz with chickens."

I notice our door-opener is nervously considering me from a distance. He is a man, tall like his daughter; a nail-biter with a long black beard and large forehead; dark robes over a bony body. Down at chicken level as I am, I notice he is shoeless.

"I can see she has a way." The voice is quite high: it has music in it. "That one – the one with the thick neck – what is wrong? She no longer lays. Don't cut your knees on the palm leaves."

Clarabella pulls out compressed bread and dried oatmeal from the metal tubing and goes into a room beyond the lantern.

I carefully crouch and cradle the bird. It has dull eyes and its crop is inflamed. A beak blackened by faeces.

"Do the others hurt it, Master Veronni?"

My knowledge of his identity catches him out. "Yes. Why yes, Victorvna Yudelvna. She never gets any grain, that one."

"The others know. She has distemper. Have you noticed the white eyes. She can see very little and can smell nothing."

I hand him the bird and he takes it as if it were a child. "Thank you. Thank you. I'll just put it with – with the others." He quietly slips into the room beyond the beautiful light and presently returns with tea. He is followed by Clarabella and two other girls – one a miniature version of Clarabella, the other even smaller, staggering under a mess of dark hair above over-sized gumboots. They carry cups and saucers and small plates of bread and cake.

"Allow me to introduce my other children. Dulciana..." – the mini-Clarabella puts down her tray and curtsies – "... and Bourdon." The littlest grins widely and with great kindness and I know her father will be safe in old age. "Pour the tea, Clarabella. See I've put an extra cup for your little friend in the bed. Be careful, her ears seem very dry. Victorvna Yudelvna, you will sit up with me."

I take his proffered hand and he leads me into a dim corner away from the chickens. Apart from my father, I've never been so close to a man. We sit on a long bench together and he lifts the stained lid of a double keyboard. The ivory keys are worn and have tiny chips like old teeth. A candle is lit and dusted with powder: the fragrance is overwhelming. "They don't have myrrh at the Conservatoire, do they. Do you like it?"

Clarabella calls over with a mouth full of cake: "Dad's a piano tuner. He comes in at 4 o'clock every morning. Takes the same route we took to get here."

"Don't eat and talk, Clara. Bourdon, come and pump."

The tiny girl jumps to her work eagerly, almost trips in her big boots. She leans on a sprung stool, see-sawing once she gains her rhythm with the bellows.

"Used to just plug it into the mains once. Right! How many fingers?" Master Veronni has his fisted hand in the air.

The delighted children all answer 'Three!' in a rush, with Clarabella perhaps taking the advantage.

He winks at me as his left hand – which indeed is missing a finger –

slides across to a peg beside the upper keyboard. The peg is marked Clarabella.

"We call them 'stops', Victorvna Yudelvna. Even though, in a manner of speaking, they actually make the organ go..." And as the girl pumps the organ and the thin man begins to play, I notice the other stops: Dulciana, Bourdon. And yet more: Lieblich Gedackt, Open Diapason...

He watches me. "Don't worry. I'm not planning on having any more kids. I have some compassion. Do you like Vidor's toccatas? He's a bit mathematical..." His right hand is at the upper keyboard, ascending and descending in eighths; the bare feet move more slowly over the long pedals. Square wooden pipes the breadth of a torso transmit resonances through the organ stool.

It's marvellous. I've never heard anything like it.

Abruptly, the music stops mid-beat. He raises his feet; puts his hands behind his head. "Or maybe you prefer Miles Davis? I have some records."

"Madame Stok – my teacher back in the country – liked Alice Faye."

"Ah, yes." He strikes up Vidor again, this time more quietly. "Speaking Confidentially... I've Got My Love To Keep Me Warm... She was a very natural contralto. Do you play those songs at the Conservatoire? Dulciana! Bring our guest some tea."

"No. Just our scales. And there's a short practice piece we have to do before breakfast. In C Minor."

"Beethoven's magic key? He was addicted to it. Why don't you play it for me? I'll stop in for you."

He pushes the stops home and slides across the bench.

"It's molto mosso with a sostenuto at the end."

"Good lord. And how fifteen year-old girls speak these days." Master Veronni regards me unblinkingly.

"Um. It has to be very exact. I'm not sure – "

"Try. I'm sure you're better than that crotchet-tangled Clarabella."

A hunk of tea-moistened cake hits Master Veronni on the ear.

So I do try, my hands relaxing in the presence of this comfortable man who seems to want nothing more than to make me feel better about myself. I start to take the notes in on an unconscious level. They no longer register as notes in my brain. No longer are they spiders of physicality. They are deeper, so much deeper than that.

I stretch my hands and play.

Master Veronni's gnawed fingernails slide across his lips as he rocks to and fro, hums and anticipates the melody that he obviously knows so well.

They're all waiting when the elevator reaches dormitory level.

The girls and the blue overalls; Professor Gnessin, Doctor Kaulay and tutors hitherto unseen. Mrs Shiltsoff promenades up and down and says nothing as Erica heaves the lift doors open. We nudge the bedstead into the corridor and Lizan slips forward and seems on the brink of speaking; Yergeniya hovers too, almost there yet still deep within the world of her earbuds.

Shitsop pauses, leans up to rest her hand on Kara's barely moving chest; brushes the skin scales from her forehead.

And the next person she looks at is me.

"You. Farm girl. You will hold vigil over Kara Reginid tonight." Her eyes turn elsewhere. "Clarabella Veronni, you will know how disappointed I am. You are responsible. You are the senior girl here. There will be punishment."

Clarabella grips the bedstead tightly. I thought she would answer. Where is the girl of glory who thrashed those twilight pianos, that food fighter? She seems slighter; seems younger even than her little sisters.

The eyes swivel back. Shitsop's like a demon, her speech bursts like hot poison. "She is responsible isn't she, Victorvna Yudelvna? Isn't she. You're not answering so I know it's her fault. Don't speak. Don't defend her."

My mouth won't open. I know Clarabella's blue-grey eyes are clinging to me but I can only look at the floor. God! I'm still thinking about the colour of her eyes! A nausea plays with my stomach. I fold my arms across my chest, sure that everyone can see.

My throat feels like there's glue in it.

"There will be punishment, Clarabella Veronni. We shall talk tomorrow." Shitsop beckons me closer; her low voice is husky, the ear pearls try to hypnotise. Deep inside, the last and strongest part of me thinks: You won't have me, you ancient bitch baby. I am for another. But Mrs Shiltsoff merely purrs, as if in the presence of proud parents: "You are one of the best here, child. I cannot punish you as I do the others. Watch this poorly girl and do not be afraid. Erica will bring you a stool and some warm milk."

And then she is gone. And soon I am alone in the corridor with Kara and her travelling sick bed.

I wonder what Clarabella's face looked like as her friends dragged her back to the dormitory. I peer into the nighttime window pane and behold the ghostly face of the chicken girl, etched as it is with misery and a sudden knowledge of loneliness.

"Kara play now. Kara ready to deploy."

I have been dozing; the milk has sewn my dreams with a thread of sourness.

"Kara play now. Kara play fight music."

I'm thrown by the spluttering on/off kerosene light at the end of the corridor.

"Kara Reginid?" I am fully awake now and stand over her. Her eyes are wide open. The irises have lost all their pigment. They are not even the colour of lemons. I look directly into them; they've mislaid their sheen, almost as if the fabric of the eyeball has thickened. She spits teeth and I hold her head to prevent choking. She's really agitated now. The nailless fingers are working at her ears. Compared to those of Master Veronni, the fingers are smooth and slightly translucent; nearly fused, almost joined...

I hold her arms down but she's taken on an impossible strength and thrashes like the eel her mother might have landed on the riverbank. She scratches an ear away. She shrieks. She sneezes snot onto my dress; a moment passes and implodes before I realise she's blown her nose off.

I don't cry out. I am not afraid. Shitsop was right.

The other ear sloughs away and I flail like a fool beneath the bed trying to retrieve it.

Somewhere, at a great distance – or so it seems – the passage doors open and Mrs Shiltsoff is here, murmuring to Kara, stroking my hair as I scrabble on the floor.

Erica is behind her and Kara is wheeled away, a white shining vision gasping for breath; something caught between earth and ocean; a pale barking sea lion.

"Kara play now. Kara request ordnance status. Kara play fight music."

Erica makes no mention of the previous night as she hands me the music. I give a reasonable performance. It's in me now. The time at the organ seems to dwell in a long ago somewhere else. I try to hold the memory.

Erica slips me a ticket as we leave the practice room.

"Report to Professor Gnessin's study. She will want to speak to you before you leave. Then walk to the bus depot. It's not far – just beyond the underground station in the same street as Master Veronni's church. The bus driver will understand and will know what to do. Go. Breakfast and go. Remember your purpose."

The girls are bitches in the showers; they taunt me with boot polish painted on their stupid little hairless quims. They use towels like bullwhips. Clarabella's bed has not been slept in and nobody will tell me anything.

And so I sit at a table by myself in the canteen and ponder the ticket. But I feel a curious new strength. The night has been a long one. I'm aware of the watchers but I'm in a different place now. I hoped to journey with another but I think I'll be travelling alone.

I turn the ticket over. My name is there in pencil:

vic

Small letters.

Master Veronni pokes his beard out of the passageway as I hurry past and grabs the strap of my haversack.

"Steady there, Victorvna Yudelvna!"

I wave my ticket. His approach is so playful that I'm mute in his presence.

"I know where you're going. I've been to the Conservatoire. Just pop inside, won't you?"

The interior seems bigger in the dim morning. High windows shaft in the rancid light, turning the palm leaves into shadow ripples across the floor.

He invites me to sit at the organ but makes no move to lift the cover.

"I want you to be kind to Clarabella. She knows so little."

I'm thrown. "But Clarabella's so clever. She's been at the Conservatoire so much longer than I. She's knows everything."

"She's learnt many things during her time there. But how much did you know even before you'd heard of this city?"

I thought about Madame Stok's house and her hairless cat: she talked to me about music. About the place where mind and soul collide...

Master Veronni rises and goes to stand by a hole in the wall above his chickens.

"Clarabella would do anything in the world for you. And one day she'll probably have to." He gestures me to join him. "Look through this and tell me what you see."

I stare into the hole: it's set at shoulder height and is perhaps a half metre tall, a little narrower in width. It has been cut clean through a major structural wall of the building. Through it I can see the soiled linen table; that amber lamp of much magnificence.

"This is silly, Master Veronni. All you need do is step around this buttress. Why burrow a hole?"

"Because it concentrates the mind, my girl. They call it a hagioscope. Literally, a viewer of saints. It forms a frame for God's glory. It's also a blast blind for the building: let off an explosive in the hagioscope and nothing would happen." Now that's a funny fact to tell a fifteen-year old – but he continues urgently: "Again, what do you see?"

I see the lamp, of course. And part of a window that seems to be held together by bits of string. And something that looks like a black carpenter's nail hanging from a hook midway up the wall. It is bent into a right angle; something is wrapped around one half.

Something that gleams.

"I see you've noticed it. That's my priest's ring. They came and broke the door down and hacked my finger off and threw it in the toilet. Ransacked the church's gold to manufacture Committee members' pacemakers and then tried to blow up the building by stuffing nitro-glycerine... guess where?"

I notice the scorch marks inside the hagioscope for the first time and Mr Veronni continues:

"Even then I was better than them. I traced the pipes and the forgotten underground streams of this city. I crawled like an ant over the shit stink of their sewerage farms. And I found it. I bloody found it. I staggered back here more dead than alive and hung it up on the wall. And..." He smiles into the middle distance: Dulciana and Bourdon hover, shy in the daylight. "... And my children were waiting for me. My precious children."

He speaks quietly now and I realise that he must have a knowledge of what has passed between Clarabella and myself. "In future times, you will need to concentrate your mind. This moment is one you must remember, Victorvna Yudelvna."

There's no one on the bus but me and the driver.

At first I think she's too busy snapping cashews and flooring the clutch to save fuel to say much.

I'm drowsily grateful after the long night. The industrial chimneys seem to form prison bars across the eastern sky, their belchings too heavy to drift. Smoke slides down the chimneys like black treacle. Fumes swirl and choke the older buildings into invisibility.

Our route takes us through a triumphant arch to some long-ago battle: words and symbols circle briefly above our heads and are gone. The arch is mid-way through its demolition: massive blocks are being craned down onto pony-drawn palettes.

"And when they run out of ponies they'll just use people. Same as it ever was." The driver has me in her mirror. "The greatest battle this city has ever seen. Makes the Yankees look like insects."

We are in an area of tent towns and low buildings covered in pipes. Memory snapshots: mounds of artificial limbs and battle tanks, split muzzles pointing to the sky; overturned helicopters on off-ramps. An old couple in thick anoraks waltzing in a car park. The sudden beauty of an oak tree in full and green leaf in the middle of a traffic island. Endless allotments sprouting dwarfish ingredients.

A bulldozer filling in an excavation in a field of excavations.

"They're not what you think, Victorvna Yudelvna. Most of the bodies have already been atomised. But people have got to have somewhere to go and mourn. Look. That's my house. The red one." The driver nods to a shack amongst others within the confines of a missile silo. The silo's twin doors have been welded half-open by rust. Lines of washing dangle between them. She snorts: "Laundry's buggered if someone remembers the codes."

And so the country:
My land. My place.

A plain runs for a hundred kilometres before softly colliding with a low range of mountains. The bus follows a river, loses it then finds it again. The bulrushes grow strongly. Plum orchards and plantations of trees for the winter festival. Co-operatives with their heavy horses; tables by the roadside with honey for sale. I want to buy one and the driver stops.

"But I have no money."

"Just show the old girl your ticket."

I do so and the wizened face gazes up with a mixture of terror and joy. I think she blesses me in the old language.

I sit on the big back seat and dip my finger in the jar as we cross an old causeway into an avenue of cypress trees; tall, undiminished. Parkland beckons: a lake, figures picnicking or doing eurythmics. A little beyond, a large villa; nearer, a running track and facilities for field sports. An open-air cinema and swimming pool.

The bus comes to a halt. I can hear girls laughing and splashing. I step down onto the unmade road and call up through sweet sticky lips. "Do I wait here for you to take me back?"

But the driver turns around and is gone, our brief connection severed.

Clever how she knew my name.

The sun plays tricks in the settling dust and I almost giggle to be out of doors. Perhaps they have some chickens here. I must have consumed half a jar of honey: the world glistens and vibrates before me.

A gasping wheeze makes me turn and Mrs Shiltsoff stands before me, her crooked shoulders level with my waist.

"Hello, Victorvna Yudelvna. Take some tea with me, will you?"

The leg-irons are quite modern but she's obviously in pain. The smile she favours me with is a fixed one.

We pass the crowded swimming pool: the girls are muscled and well-tanned and seem so at home in the water. There must be thousands of gallons of it. And it's so clear.

"Do you play water polo, little Victorvy?"

Ah, water polo.

"No, Mrs Shiltsoff. I'm afraid I don't even swim."

"Really? You might surprise yourself."

She moves as if to push me in. The girls wait, upward-turned faces stretched in anticipation. She reaches up and brushes something off my shoulder. "Maybe later, dear."

We manage to avoid a hail of javelins as we cross the cinder track. "Bloody little Junos. They think they're pretty tough." Her complaint is good-natured. "I bet Clarabella Veronni would love it. All the girls are so athletic."

I am unswayed. She'll have to try harder. "Is everyone a musician here?"

"Of course. They come from academies from all over the country. And a couple of the dependencies too. Recreation is important."

We reach the villa's verandah and she offers me a seat while carefully crouching herself into the waiting wheelchair. I put my honey on the table between us. I'm in a sort of gentle joyous stupor, made lazy by the sunshine and cut grass and distant friendly voices.

"Clarabella? Come here will you."

A figure undips out of the shadows, walks in short studied steps.

She stands in her black vest and running shorts; eyes turned towards the swimming pool, lank hair tied back with an elastic band.

Her neck is bandaged.

I surprise myself; my jumbled mouth actually speaks: "Long? Have you been here..?"

"No. Not long at all." Shitsop's tone is light. "Nip and get some tea and pastries, there's a good girl."

Clarabella trots into the house.

Mrs Shiltsoff smiles. "I used to be a clever girl too."

"Is Clarabella clever?" What is this mad game she's playing?

"I'm talking about you. I'm reading your thoughts. You were thinking how clever you are."

And I suppose I was, sitting there and looking out at the beautiful grounds in the less-lemon sunshine.

"But things change, Victorvy. Do you see the lake where they're doing their exercises? A meteorite crashed there a thousand years ago and wiped out all life within five hundred kilometres. The world went through a mini ice age. Growth rings from trees are very close and dense from that period – and consequently the wood from them makes the finest violins. Thank you, Clarabella Veronni."

The tall girl places a tray on our table. I search the beautiful eyes in vain. She comes around behind me and I'm aware of her hand on the back of my seat. It smells of disinfectant.

Mrs Shiltsoff pours tea and chatters while I cut the baklava.

"When I first entered the Conservatoire the tutors tried to change me. They thought they were clever, they thought I would just give in." She smiles with her woman-child lips. The sugar tongs drop from her tiny fingers onto the tablecloth and she leaves them there. "I resisted and look what happened. A seventy year heart in a toddler body. I'm getting polio now because I didn't get it when I was younger. They tell me I could die from meningitis at any moment. You have to do what we say. Don't fight it, girl."

I realise my hand has unconsciously gone to my throat.

"Hah! Your own voice is perfect for your purpose, Victorvna Yudelvna. You've got a real talent! It's only the drones and blind grubs who need help along the way."

The wicker chair groans under Clarabella's grip.

Shitsop peers intently above my head. "Yes. Once upon a time, a girl called Clarabella was my chief principle. A beautiful girl with a precious musical ability. So precious. But now she's just an accompanist. Your accompanist, Victorvy. Sink into change. Change can be beautiful." Shitsop is almost radiant as she gently helps me lay the daft little cake knife back on the table.

Presently, I take a sip from the steaming cup but I already know.

Shitsop smiles. "Oh? Does your tea taste a little odd?"

After the interview, I look for a piano.

I leave them together on the verandah; Clarabella has been permitted to sit and finish off my baklava. I hope my honey helps her throat.

I seem to have regained a little of my mood from the bus journey. There is a wonderful warmth in the air. A golden anticipation. Soon, I discover an empty lodge among several behind the main building. Pyjamas in my size have been laid out on the bed. I can't wait to play.

Maybe tomorrow.

in the centre of the night i unsleep. no. No. in the middle of the night i wake up. come on, vic –

Come on, Victorvy.

The dream was one of tininess, of shrinkage, of tight tree rings. Of efficiency through density. And in the dense darkness, my hair's an oily mess, my pyjamas soaked. I'd made up a bed of blankets on the lodge balcony; had fallen asleep while the summer evening was still light. I slept with swimming pool laughter.

I sleep again. I wake.

i wake. I wake and go inside to the bathroom, run water over my head and unravel my hairs from the plug hole. i sit. I sit on the loo but nothing comes. my My my image seems unclear in the mirror. i stand in a haze. i remove my spectacles and can see better without them. they are left by the basin as i ignite a hurricane lamp and carry it onto the balcony. i extinguish it. the darkness takes on a green brightness far stronger than a flame.

without thinking, i focus on the leaf of a plum tree 8.3 kilometres away. the leaf is one of eighteen million two hundred thousand and seventy-one in the whole orchard. this particular tree is besieged by a cloud of june bugs with an average wing frequency of 23.9 mhz. only one of them is a male, leaping out of my spectrum as a fiery crimson. i can smell clara Clara clarabella's disinfectant as she plays water polo in the steaming pool.

i want to play my music. in c minor.

refocusing, i see i have a new bedmate. a siamese frog is ailing on my balcony pillow. i slip under the blanket and help it onto my palm. the four eyes are wide but i realise it's too late. my senses already trace its failing cardiology and renal systems; can map the flood of carbon dioxide through the tiny bodies. but there's something else. the corpses continue to shiver: and a third frog struggles out from the ruins of its parents.

change. change can be beautiful.

with a mighty hop it is gone.

i gather my fingernails into a little pyramid and try to sleep.

professor gnessin picks me up three days later. I've learnt to swim and can throw a javelin like a young juno. i haven't talked with mrs shiltsoff since our tea. i may have seen clarabella holding her breath in the shallow end.

the professor puts my haversack in the boot and opens the minibus door for me. "cat got your tongue, victorvy?"

"it is a bit swollen, professor."

"does it still hurt?

"no. hurt went on the first day. everything feels condensed."

"good. you must start upon your exercises. erica's got the practice room ready. we've installed a heater. you'll start to feel the cold more now. nothing will get in the way of your Music."

we drive between poplars and plum orchards. i can see sun spots; the solar flares buzz. i soak up my last day in the country.

i won't be coming again.

IV

life is simple now. barely have to think. drink tea and lemonade with erica and practice. bunk has been placed in recital room. never have to leave. notes are in my body now. notes of Music. they are like blinking. sequence is natural to me. "hey, vic, you'll do," erica says. she smiles and is kind. "one more time, vic, one more time." and vic plays the sequence ten more times. c minor. g, g, g – e. f, f, f – d. easy.

feel good. feel better. like tea. warm enough for Music. blue woman-man smiles, says play again. i play twenty times twenty. g g g – e. f f f – d. sleep now. no. sleep now.

100 x 100 i play good i play same for days ggge fffd ggge fffd ggge fffd i play fight Music rah rah rah raah

V

i am in a swimming place.

i float without pain.

there are shadows. others.

my tongue has become detached; a thick slug suddenly huge inside my mouth. i spit it out and watch it spiral to the bottom of the big tank. a movement dashes out and grabs it; consumes my tongue, that most intimate piece of me, in great heaving swallows.

grubtown. ignore them, vic. kara hangs beside me and is beautiful. her head is grey and streamlined; microscopic air bubbles catch in her tiny auricular openings.

grubtown?

the failures. failed their studies and are now no longer fed. they scrap for what they can. you're looking good. do you mind?

kara elongates her fin and scratches at my eye. scales flicker away in the dimness like pinkish-beige paint. i remember that. why do i remember that? i blink and my eyelids slide like curtains.

battle-proof. like armour. you'll need them. come and meet the others.

we cruise over grubtown in a cloud of skin fragments.

do we play Music here?

no. kara smiles. she has no teeth. we've been waiting for you to show us.

they circle just below the surface, glorious in their diversity.

they glitter.

aja has a wonderful set of long semaphore-ready fins while dulcie and calli sport light-sensitive antennae on their mouths: they swim upside down and taste the air with their arrays.

and dear georgievna larissa, round and fat like a brown expressionless balloon; her progress dependent on the eddies of others.

but aren't you dead, georgievna?

dulcie answers, her eye telescoping down to me. don't bother with her. she can't understand you. watch.

she rockets down from the surface to fasten on georgievna like a lamprey. muscles ripple their way along dulcie's body as she sucks in the protein.

she feeds us. that is her purpose. aja furls her fins around georgievna and takes a large bite from the hind-quarters. her nervous system has been dismantled. she feels nothing.

i look into the eyes of georgievna larissa and remember her voice and how light she felt in my arms. and the rest of the class? where are they?

yergeniya's still outside. slow learner. the others are in grubtown. dulcie regurgitates. never made it up here. lizan and whatshername. nor that other girl. you remember. the tall one.

a plastic keyboard suckers to the side of the tank. i don't need to use it.

i know the Music. i swim around it for days. i know they're watching me. kara and the others. and above the surface are the hazy walkways; an ever-moving wheelchair, keening and restless. groans from the double doors carry sharply through the water.

i try not to think of clarabella. i hover over grubtown and blank her out. but i know she must be able to see me. i take bites from georgievna and casually let them fall.

georgievna tastes like honey, her scales sweet and sugary.

unknown days. weeks.

dulcie and calli have left the tank for further training. aja too. kara is still here but keeps to herself; lays dummy mines on the further side of the swimming pool.

my ears drop off – it's taken longer than usual – and i am distraught. kara swims closer. her presence has a harder edge.

but without ears how can i sing my song, kara? how will i know if i sing too loud?

you've still got little holes, vic. they're cute. let me poke you.

we tread water while kara works a flipper into what's left of my ear.

you're tickling.

some sensation then. look. you're growing wings. that's more than i've got.

she clicks her voice box.

i can still hear you, kara.

you only need ears in the air. vibrations carry much further in the water. have you done your practice today?

the waiting keyboard shimmers through refracted light.

unknown weeks. months?

they drop yergeniya in. she resists, tries to clamber out only to sink away to the bottom, unable to inflate her float sac. a steel hoop plunges down and stops her progress just short of grubtown.

... i resisted and look what happened...

yergeniya is dumped on a slipway, half in and out of the water. i peck at her malformed feet but soon lose interest.

clarabella? clarabella?

surely years have passed now.

i am squeezing georgievna's tail till it comes off, leaking viscous bones. i chew and regurgitate georgievna into grubtown.

clarabella. i love you.

decades later, there is nothing left but georgievna's eyes, unblinking pale marbles suspended midway between bottom and surface, slaves to neutral buoyancy.

clarabella.

yes.

georgievna's eyes hang between us. clarabella gently slides them aside. she is still slender, a freckly white salamander all multi-lidded blue-grey eyes and gliding vanes. i let her lick my lips like i wanted her to lick the honey from them. she sucks every milligram of nutrient.

we settle at the keyboard together, select c minor, play the eight letter sequence and are immediately summoned to the surface.

principle and accompanist.

VI

i'm ready for the drop. the blower's belly hatch is open. battlefield fog scuds below us. clarabella is in a cradle beside me, breathes hard through external gills. our co-ordinates are presently unknown, will be fed through sensors when we enter fight Music. the territory below remains classified. clarabella prepares to freeze herself for the drop. from 7000 metres, we will plummet through the crust above the long-drained artesian wells of a secret city, our vanes spinning us into the crystallised soil ten metres below the surface. as night seeps over the war zone, our bodies will reactivate their bloodstreams to dowse us in the chemicals that will warm our brains into wakefulness. we will unscrew ourselves from the soil and continue in hibernation for a further fortnight as our wings – which would not have survived the freezing process – mature inside their chalky membranes. and inside me the bomb will grow.

i wake and clarabella has gone. she has struggled up through the topsoil and i follow her tunnel to the surface. lemon sky, smoke grey. i crouch in a crater, allow my wings to dry too quickly. i snatch a frog and eat it. its still wriggling body nudges the thermobaric weapon inside me. i am ready and beacon gnessin to boot fight Music. she is angry. i have failed to discipline my accompanist. gnessin's system start-up is jagged. my vision whites-out and the Music has me

fight Music | thermal glide + vic glides too | rise 3 km in 2 min | enemy airshot + girders from satellite platforms | swerve beneath barrage line | breathe hard | try to keep larynxes at 97.2 like gnes has told vic | smoke spiral change to fog as firestorm vacuum drags flames 1/2 way round planet | hope clar has bead on enemy fireships | diversion far below | liz + yerg | zip over tank traps | contrails like icicles | yerg resists fight Music | vic concern | vic dip | dip again | wings well-angled | leading edge air flow sparks w/electricity | create radar-absorbing plasma pulse | sing w/joy + run through scales | rah rah rah raah | hot air rises up to meet vic | vic invisible | sensors from below | yerg loses head to pylons | liz flies on | knows voice not hers + probably won't sync | tracer lacerates stabiliser + vic drops 500 m | re-triangulate | comsat off-line | request clar support | static only | smell river | turn w | wsw | w into sunset | lemon sun | vic reaches line | drop to 30 | 20 | 10 m | wings retract | sacrifice front legs to razor wire | shit say vic don't resist | engorge float sacs w/battle gas + slide across mud | flooded slit trench | vic cough cough | sonar bursts into life | fills vic's mind w/1000 echoes | trench bottom | bones + shrapnel | loam + leeches | beyond walls vic senses dugouts | see/sense soldiers as they rush w/stethoscopes to track vic's progress | brightness | clar must have hit main magazine | cordite stings eyes | 2 frogmen wait | wear plastic egg box-suits to confuse vic's sonar | they are stealthy defenders | arm w/yank's last + finest weapon | gnes warn vic | they have devil in a bottle | wave it in front of vic | taunt vic | laugh at vic's nakedness | vic laugh back + sing | laugh + sing fight Music as vic's tail thrashes + turns their bones to rubber | sewer pipe | vic slip through | coil bone structure | stretch spleen | float sacs | fart battle gas | clar is behind | clar has found vic | vic feel clar's bead on vic's back | feel good so good | co-ordinates come through for final assault | feel bead on back red hot | clar sings private transmission uses abort codes | battle won vic | battle over | vic sings back | battle on clar | objective not satisfied | bead is hotter hot hot |

force-quit fight Music. clarabella's weapons have fragmented my left shoulder; i sense a re-phasing of microwaves for a headshot. reaching a sewerage sub-station, i haul myself up; unzip and activate my morphine gland. a glow beneath the water; i duck and fold as a force beam slices out and liquefies the metal cylinders behind me. morphine tickles my throat. i slide back in but clarabella has already gone up the pipe. she leads. the principle. i scrape my shiny hide through the last 200 metres as professor gnessin re-connects, force boots fight Music

confirm vic | confirm | 200 | 150 | 100 | 50 m | switch throat to manual | cough | cough | 15 secs | confirm vic | civil grid ref 962110 k/kaya 48 | through toilet cistern | diphtheria + dead chickens | slip around door + clar is there with rotor weapons | pieces missing from my side | my beautiful tail | clar has man | protects man | kill him clar | kill men | activate fuel atomiser prior to detonation | G | G | G | fail |

clarabella has me on the floor, pins me, pummels my broken body. the little children scream, their father tries to wrench away the blast pack. but i have the fight Music. my purpose. my focus. i stand and flex and they drop from me like the leaves of a plum tree

vic will win | Music's in my head | my throat sings the fight Music pitch perfect | beethoven 5th | rah rah rah raah | G | G | G | E | fuel atomiser activated | ethylene oxide fills church | prepare 2ndry charge in head | ready for deflagration | 300 psi | 300°c | 3 km/s blast | beethoven 5th | morse v for victory | i am victory | i am victorvna yudelvna + i sing fight Music | Music is part of me | F | F | F | D | rah rah rah raah | my focus | chicken girl crawl up into hole | vic die now

ABOUT THE AUTHORS

Marion Arnott is a Scottish writer who has appeared in a variety of publications. She was the winner of the CWA Macmillan Award in 2001. Her Elastic Press short story collection was *Sleepwalkers* (2003).

Allen Ashley is a British Fantasy Award winning editor and prize-winning poet. His story "Somme-Nambula" is taken from the Elastic Press collection *Somnambulists*, which was short-listed for a British Fantasy Award in 2005. Allen works as a creative writing tutor, with six groups currently running across north London, including the advanced science fiction and fantasy group Clockhouse London Writers. His most recent book is an updated, revised version of his novel *The Planet Suite* (Eibonvale Press, 2016). www.allenashley.com

Chris Beckett's Elastic Press collection, *The Turing Test*, was the winner of the Edge Hill Prize in 2009. His second collection, *The Peacock Cloak*, was published by NewCon Press, which also published a new and revised edition of his second novel, *Marcher*, in 2014. His most recent book is *Daughter of Eden*, published by Corvus in 2016, his fifth novel and the third and final instalment of the Eden series. The first Eden novel, *Dark Eden*, won the Arthur C. Clark award in 2012. Chris lives with his wife and dog in Cambridge.

Gary Couzens has had stories published in *F&SF*, *Interzone*, *Black Static*, *Crimewave*, *The Third Alternative*, *Midnight Street* and other magazines and anthologies. He has had two collections published: *Second Contact and Other Stories* (Elastic Press, 2003) and *Out Stack and Other Places* (Midnight Street Press, 2015). For Elastic Press, he edited

Extended Play: The Elastic Book of Music (2006) which won the British Fantasy Award for Best Anthology. He has a complete collection of Elastic Press books.

Jeff Gardiner is the author of five novels: *Pica, Falco, Igboland, Myopia* and *Treading On Dreams*, a collection of short stories, and a work of non-fiction. Many of his short stories have appeared in anthologies, magazines and websites. *Pica* is the first in the Gaia trilogy – a fantasy of transformation and ancient magic, which Michael Moorcock described as: "An engrossing and original story, beautifully told. Wonderful!" "Reading is a form of escapism, and in Gardiner's fiction, we escape to places we'd never imagine journeying to." (A.J. Kirby, 'The New Short Review'). Visit his website: www.jeffgardiner.com and blog: http://jeffgardiner.wordpress.com

Editor **Andrew Hook** has had nine books published since ceasing Elastic Press, including novellas, novels, short story collections, and non-fiction. His next publication will be his sixth short story collection, *Frequencies of Existence*. Unable to stay completely away from publishing, he ably assists his partner, Sophie Essex, with Salò Press.

Brian Howell lives and teaches in Japan. He has been publishing stories since 1990. His first collection, *The Sound of White Ants*, was published in the U.K. by Elastic Press in 2004. His novel based on the life of Jan Vermeer, *The Dance of Geometry*, was published in March 2002 by The Toby Press. His second novel, *The Curious Case of Jan Torrentius*, about the notoriously libertine Dutch painter, will be published this year by Zagava. It was part-published in 2014 under the title *The Curious Case of Jan Torrentius and The Followers of the Rosy Cross: Vol.1* by Zagava/Les Editions de L'Oubli. He likes cycling, Japan, the Low Countries, listening to podcasts, and takes life seriously.

Andrew Humphrey had two collections published by Elastic Press; *Open the Box* and *Other Voices*, the latter of which won the 2008 East Anglian Book Award. His debut novel, *Alison*, was published by TTA Press, also in 2008, and Andrew has had stories published widely in the independent press. He lives and works in Norwich.

N. A. Jackson (**Nick Jackson**) is the author of two collections of short fiction: *Visits to the Flea Circus*, 2006 and *The Secret Life of the Panda*, 2011. His writing flow has dried to a trickle in recent years but every now and again a story seeps out such as *microeroticon*, in the anthology *Milk* forthcoming from Salò Press. If a dripping tap was a metaphor for his literary output, it would take 287 years to fill a bathtub.

Antony Mann's short fiction has appeared in *Crimewave, Interzone, Ellery Queen's Mystery Magazine* and many others. He is a winner of the Crime Writers Association UK Best Short Story Dagger and Best Short Film Award at the Edinburgh International Film Festival. His most recent project is *The Christmas Killer*, a choose-your-own adventure story for English-as-a-second-language students. He is currently working on a feature screenplay called *Friends and Other Enemies*.

Tim Nickels: still here | status inactive | pondering reboot | home unit prioritised | post-life solutions still engaged | alice faye says hi | rah rah rah raah | elastic forever | tim gone now

Mike O'Driscoll lives and works in Swansea. When not writing he works with adults with mental health problems. His fiction has been published *in Black Static, Interzone, Fantasy & Science Fiction, Crimewave* and in numerous anthologies, including *Inferno, The Dark, Gathering the Bones, The Year's Best Fantasy* and *Horror, Mammoth Book of Best New Horror*, and in the recent anthology of Bird related horror, *Black Feathers*. His first collection, *Unbecoming*, was published by Elastic Press in 2006, while TTS Press published his novella, *Eyepennies* in 2012. His new collection, *The Dream Operator*, is forthcoming from Undertow Press in July 2017.

Justina Robson is the author of eleven SF and Fantasy books plus a collection of short stories and the definitive Transformers Prime bible, *The Covenant of Primus*. Her books tell stories of AI, far-future transhumans and near-future human technologies. She also writes fantasy: high and urban. She has been shortlisted for numerous awards. She lives and works in the North of England.

Maurice Suckling has helped develop over forty video games since the late 1990s, writing for a diverse range of titles, including *Borderlands:*

The Pre-Sequel, Killing Floor 2, and *Civilization VI*. His other publications include the collection of short stories *Photocopies of Heaven* (Elastic Press, 2006), the novel *Life With A Porn Queen* (Ink Monkey Books, 2013), and the text book *Video Game Writing from Macro to Micro* (Mercury Learning, 2016, second edition). He has also been BAFTA nominated for co-writing the BBC TV series *Alphablocks*. He is currently Professor of Practice leading the game writing concentration at RPI in Upstate New York. mauricesuckling.com

Andrew Tisbert is. A man who. Was having so much fun the first time he jumped out of a plane he forgot to pull his ripcord; got an awful lot of sympathy the first time he broke his neck, but not so much the second time; was the lead flute player in a metal band and swears no one found that strange, ever; gave his latest book the most improbable title of: *The Hippie Hacker the Happy Hooker and the Great Clone Orgy*, against everyone's better judgement. Find his electronic footprint at andrewtisbert.com.

Since Elastic Press published *The Ephemera*, **Neil Williamson** has published a novel (*The Moon King*), a second collection (*Secret Language*), a novella (*The Memoirist*) and many short stories, and his work has been nominated for BSFA, British Fantasy and World Fantasy awards. Otherwise, not much has changed. He still lives and works in Glasgow and he still sees the alien in everything.

BEST OF
BRITISH
SCIENCE
FICTION
2016

Editor Donna Scott has selected the very best short fiction by British authors published during 2016. Twenty-four stories, from established names and rising stars.

At 340 pages, this is a truly mammoth collection of quality Science Fiction.

Peter F. Hamilton, Gwyneth Jones, Adam Roberts, Jaine Fenn, Ian Watson, Eric Brown, Keith Brooke, E.J. Swift, Tricia Sullivan, Una McCormack, Den Patrick, Ian Whates, Tade Thompson, Nick Wood, Neil Williamson, Joanne Hall and more…

Released July 2017; available as an A5 paperback and a limited edition hardback signed by the editor.

www.newconpress.co.uk

Entropic Angel
Gareth L. Powell
Introduction by
Aliette de Bodard

Award-winning science fiction writer Gareth L. Powell delivers his first collection in nearly a decade. Gathering together twenty stories, including four that are previously unpublished as well as some of the author's best-loved tales, the content provides highlights from across twelve years of his career; a powerful collection that is both entertaining and thought-provoking.

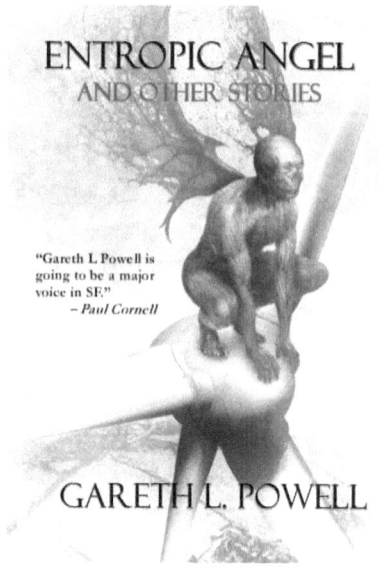

ENTROPIC ANGEL
AND OTHER STORIES

"Gareth L Powell is going to be a major voice in SF."
– *Paul Cornell*

GARETH L. POWELL

Cover art by Ben Baldwin

"Powell is an author to watch. His work is the spyglass of science fiction, the ship just over the horizon." – *The Fix*

"Powell is showing his prowess, and fast becoming a master storyteller." – *The Wry Writer*

"Red Lights, and Rain – This story you guys, this story was just plain, unadulterated fun. – *A Fantastical Librarian*

Forthcoming From
NEWCON PRESS

Visionary Tongue
A Selection of Stories & Poems from the Magazine

Edited by Storm Constantine

In the autumn of 1995, Storm Constantine launched *Visionary Tongue*, a small press magazine, co-edited by Louise Coquio. They aimed to produce a fiction zine with a difference – by recruiting a team of established and successful authors to act as editors and mentors for new writers. Some of the contributors to *Visionary Tongue* went on to have successful writing careers and are now well-known within the genres of Science Fiction, Fantasy and Horror. In this collection, you'll find a selection of the best of *Visionary Tongue*, including tales and poems from the issues when Storm and Louise passed custodianship of the magazine to Jamie Spracklen and Donna Bond.

"You'll glimpse ghastly and gorgeous locations – sometimes both at once. You'll wander through rooms redolent of passionate melancholy. Characters live in or create fever dreams, luring others with treacherous spells of glances, scents and sighs. Water conceals tragedy or propels victims to their inevitable fates. Murderers hide behind smiles or beauty or clever words. Demons dance. The visionary tongue speaks. Now listen to its voice."

From the Introduction by Storm Constantine

Includes, among others, early stories from **Jaine Fenn, Tim Lebbon, Fiona McGavin, Justina Robson, Liz Williams and Ian Whates**.

NEWCON PRESS

Publishing quality Science Fiction, Fantasy, Dark Fantasy and Horror for ten years and counting.

Winner of the 2010 'Best Publisher' Award from the European Science Fiction Society.

Anthologies, novels, short story collections, novellas, paperbacks, hardbacks, signed limited editions, e-books...
Why not take a look at some of our other titles?

Featured authors include:
Neil Gaiman, Brian Aldiss, Kelley Armstrong, Peter F. Hamilton, Alastair Reynolds, Stephen Baxter, Christopher Priest, Tanith Lee, Joe Abercrombie, Dan Abnett, Nina Allan, Sarah Ash, Neal Asher, Tony Ballantyne, James Barclay, Chris Beckett, Lauren Beukes, Aliette de Bodard, Chaz Brenchley, Keith Brooke, Eric Brown, Pat Cadigan, Jay Caselberg, Ramsey Campbell, Anne Charnock, Simon Clark, Michael Cobley, Genevieve Cogman, Storm Constantine, Hal Duncan, Jaine Fenn, Paul di Filippo, Jonathan Green, Jon Courtenay Grimwood, Frances Hardinge, Gwyneth Jones, M. John Harrison, Amanda Hemingway, Paul Kane, Leigh Kennedy, Nancy Kress, Kim Lakin-Smith, David Langford, Alison Littlewood, James Lovegrove, Sarah Lotz, Una McCormack, Ian McDonald, Sophia McDougall, Gary McMahon, Ken MacLeod, Ian R MacLeod, Gail Z. Martin, Juliet E. McKenna, John Meaney, Simon Morden, Mark Morris, Anne Nicholls, Stan Nicholls, Marie O'Regan, Philip Palmer, Stephen Palmer, Sarah Pinborough, Gareth L. Powell, Robert Reed, Rod Rees, Andy Remic, Mike Resnick, Mercurio D. Rivera, Adam Roberts, Justina Robson, Lynda E. Rucker, Stephanie Saulter, Gaie Sebold, Robert Shearman, Sarah Singleton, Martin Sketchley, Michael Marshall Smith, Kari Sperring, Brian Stapleford, Charles Stross, Tricia Sullivan, E.J. Swift, David Tallerman, Adrian Tchaikovsky, Steve Rasnic Tem, Lavie Tidhar, Lisa Tuttle, Simon Kurt Unsworth, Ian Watson, Freda Warrington, Liz Williams, Neil Williamson, and many more.

www.newconpress.co.uk

IMMANION PRESS

Purveyors of Speculative Fiction

The Lightbearer by Alan Richardson

Michael Horsett parachutes into Occupied France before the D-Day Invasion. He is dropped in the wrong place, miles from the action, badly injured, and totally alone. He falls prey to two Thelemist women who have awaited the Hawk God's coming, attracts a group of First World War veterans who rally to what they imagine is his cause, is hunted by a troop of German Field Police who are desperate to find him, and has a climactic encounter with a mutilated priest who believes that Lucifer Incarnate has arrived...

The Lightbearer is a unique gnostic thriller, dealing with the themes of Light and Darkness, Good and Evil, Matter and Spirit.

"The Lightbearer is another shining example of Alan Richardson's talent as a story-teller. He uses his wide esoteric knowledge to produce a story that thrills, chills and startles the reader as it radiates pure magical energy. An unusual and gripping war story with more facets than a star sapphire." – Mélusine Draco, author of "Aubry's Dog" and "Black Horse, White Horse". ISBN: 978-1-907737-63-3 £11.99 $18.99

Dark in the Day, Ed. by Storm Constantine & Paul Houghton

Weirdness lurks beyond the margins of the mundane, emerging to dismantle our assumptions of reality. *Dark in the Day* is an anthology of weird fiction, penned by established writers and also those new to the genre – the latter being authors who are, or were, students of Creative Writing at Staffordshire University, where editor Storm Constantine occasionally delivers guest lectures. Her co-editor, Paul Houghton, is the senior lecturer in Creative Writing at the university.

Contributors include: Martina Bellovičová, J. E. Bryant, Glynis Charlton, Storm Constantine, Louise Coquio, Elizabeth Counihan, Krishan Coupland, Elizabeth Davidson, Siân Davies, Paul Finch, Rosie Garland, Rhys Hughes, Kerry Fender, Andrew Hook, Paul Houghton, Tanith Lee, Tim Pratt, Nicholas Royle, Michael Marshall Smith, Paula Wakefield, Ian Whates and Liz Williams.
ISBN: 978-1-907737-74-9 £11.99, $18.99

Blood, the Phoenix and a Rose by Storm Constantine

 Wraeththu, a race of androgynous beings, have arisen from the ashes of human civilisation. Like the mythical rebis, the divine hermaphrodite, they represent the pinnacle of human evolution. But Wraeththu – or hara – were forged in the crucible of destruction and emerged from a new Dark Age. They have yet to realise their full potential and come to terms with the most blighted aspects of their past. *Blood, the Phoenix and a Rose* begins with an enigma: Gavensel, a har who appears unearthly and has a shrouded history. He has been hidden away in the house of Sallow Gandaloi by Melisander, an alchemist, but is this seclusion to protect Gavensel from the world or the world from him? As his story unfolds, the shadow of the dark fortress Fulminir falls over him, and memories of his past slowly return. The only way to find the truth is to go back through the layers of time, to when the blood was fresh. ISBN: 978-1-907737-75-6 £11.99, $18.99

Animate Objects by Tanith Lee

 There is no such thing as an inanimate object… And how could that be? Because, simply, everything is formed from matter, and basically, at *root*, the matter that makes up everything in the physical world – the Universe – is of the same substance. Which means, on that basic level, we – you, me, and that power station over there – are all the exact riotous, chaotic, amorphous *same*. Here is an assortment of Lee takes on the nature, and perhaps intentions, of so-called non-sentient things. And you're quite safe. This is only a book. An inanimate object.

From the Introduction by Tanith Lee

The original hardback of this collection, of which there were only 35 copies, was published by Immanion Press in 2013, to commemorate Tanith Lee receiving the Lifetime Achievement Award at World Fantasycon. It included 5 previously unpublished pieces. This new release includes a further 2 stories, co-written by Tanith Lee and John Kaiine, and new interior illustrations by Jarod Mills. ISBN: 978-1-907737-73-2, £11.99 $18.99

Immanion Press
http://www.immanion-press.com
info@immanion-press.com